HAVOC

SWiMs

JADeD

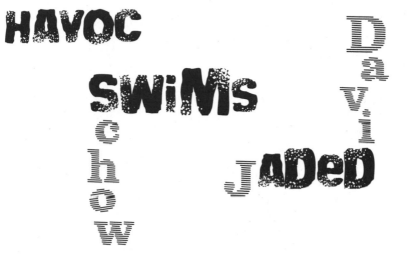

HAVOC

SWiMS

Schow

David

JADeD

FICTION S SCHOW, D.
Schow, David J.
Havoc swims jaded

$25.00
CENTRAL   31994012903560

SUBTERRANEAN PRESS ▨ 2006

Subterranean Press
PO Box 190106
Burton, MI 48519

www.subterraneanpress.com
e-mail: subpress@earthlink.net

In publishing parlance, this page is frequently known as "the legal page," where writers indulge in chapter-and-verse regarding the assertion of certain rights.
Paradoxically, it is also where the same writers often list "original publication" data,
which recounts a licensing of certain rights to certain venues. Or copyright data,
which boils down to two truths: Either the writer holds the copyright, or somebody
else does. The former should be obvious and the latter amounts to an admission that
one does not control one's work, or one was less than attentive when they were in a
big hurry to cash a check. Nobody seems to know how this goofy tradition got started, but insecure writers sure love to whack it unto death because it supplies a page-
load of arcane gobble that sure looks...official. These are all my stories. I don't feel
the need to remind everybody that they're mine, mine, mine, thirteen more times, in
a shopping list of magazines that no longer exist or anthologies that are out of print
as you read this, right now. I just examined the legal page of one well-known writer's
story collection, and came to the conclusion that its purpose was simply to enable
him/her to enter his/her name nearly *fifty* more times in his/her own goddamned
book! Here's another book, different writer, with over *sixty*. Silly! Vain! Pointless!

My question is, Do you, the reader, actually want or need to know this? Isn't this
behind-the-scenes minutiae? What are you, a bibliographer? I *know* both my bibliographers, and you aren't either of them. Nosy? Curious? One of those "it's never
enough" types? What's the matter, too lazy to do your own research? Come on,
what are you going to do, huh? You gonna cry?

Official DJS website: *Black Leather Required*
www.davidjschow.com

CONTENTS

"FRONT MATTER"
by Bertrand Nightenhelser 9

"THE ABSOLUTE LAST OF THE
ULTRA-SPOOKY, SUPER-SCARY
HALLOWE'EN HORROR NIGHTS" 13

"EXPANDING YOUR CAPABILITIES
USING FRAME/SHIFT™ MODE" 33

"THE FIVE SISTERS: A FABLE" 51

"PLOT TWIST" 57

"SIZE NOTHING" 79

"THE THING TOO HIDEOUS TO DESCRIBE" 89

"WAKE-UP CALL" 101

DISMANTLING FORTRESS ARCHITECTURE
      5 6   28 1 34   7
by David J. Schow & Craig Spector 109

"SCOOP VS. LEADMAN" 165

"WHAT HAPPENED WITH MARGARET" 203

"THE PYRE AND OTHERS" 213

"OBSEQUY" 227

"WHAT SCARES YOU" 265

AFTERWORD .281

FRONT MATTER

*NB: The following Introduction was adapted (with permission) from Bertrand Nightenhelser's editorial ephemera for **Necropolitan** Magazine (Vol. III, No. 5 [whole number #25], June, 2005 issue).**

I t is customary, as I am sure established readers of *Necropolitan* have noticed, for the editor(s) to maintain a low profile, singing the praises of contributors old and new. And we've certainly got them in this issue; wordsmiths of the sort who don't need to ask "what sort of stories" we're looking for—they just know. Artists with bleak worldviews, the kind who offer a slap in the face and a double shot of napalm to any tea-cozy reader who thinks vampires and werewolves are still scary. Incisive, invasive, belligerent, provocative names. I could run them down like a grocery list and put you into a narcoleptic coma. You'd feel your brains running out of your ear before you could summon the wits to turn the page.

But it occurs to me as I write these words—this prefatory foma, designed to ease you into what you can already discern from our Contents page—that in a magazine devoted to the cause of scaring the readership, these intimate little

maunderings have less than no meaning. It is egotistical chitchat, really, the editor addressing the audience impatient to get on with the show. Worse, for a magazine of this type, it's not scary. It's not even ominous. No sense of unease or droll dread to be found here.

Read any introduction to any anthology or collection of short stories (even Faithful Readers often fail to distinguish between the two, and if I can do nothing else in this slot, I can enlighten: an *anthology* is a book of stories by different writers; a *collection* is a group of stories by a single writer), and you'll find the tone to be mostly…well, apologetic. Exculpation for horrors temporarily imprisoned between neat off-white pages. Writers attempt to explain why they write fearful fictions with the air of a guilty pleasure, or slumming. It's self-therapy, they say. It's "getting my dark side out"—not that the "dark side" of most of these cringers and cowards would be worth much as fiction. In fullbore excuse mode, most writers will lock and load every bullshit alibi from catharsis to emesis, and open fire on a readership about as interested in motive as you might be in handing away all your pocket change. Worse, I've never read anything genuinely terrifying in an introduction, and for this flavor of enterprise, *that* strikes me as kind of, well, ominous.

Moreover, having edited several complete volumes of *Necropolitan* since its inception—a total of twenty-five issues to date—I begin to sense we've prolapsed into the terminal stage, where format degenerates to formula. *Who reads these things*, I find myself asking. Certainly not our corporate overlords, who require that X amount of space be filled in Y amount of time. That's a reality of commercial, mass-market, newsstand-distribution magazine publishing that we accept begrudgingly, like taxes or smog, while never challenging it.

But it's a funny thing that tempts me to test its limits. I have begun to suspect that were I to go on sick leave with a deadline looming, the printers would raid my computer, find the files marked "INTRO," and cut and paste the text into the appropriate columns without regard to content. You never know.

Probably the man for the job would be Roger DeWitt, my esteemed Associate Editor. Roger came to *Necropolitan* through the good offices of Scimitar Books, where he trolled the slushpiles as assistant editor. Our issues would far exceed deadline were it not for the efforts of Roger, who keeps the wicks trimmed and the lamps burning, from a little side-office adjacent to mine, barely more than a closet—the sort of holeup in which classicists are presumed to write master-pieces in quill pen by candlelight. Yes, if I fell down a man-hole or was abducted by aliens, Roger could keep *Necropolitan* going for several issues more, solely on fumes and scavenged bits of copy.

Actually, Roger thinks he could probably run this maga-zine better than I can. He wants tacky little trophies and the attention of the sort of people who frequent science fiction and horror conventions, which I abhor. He sits in his office and waits with the patience of a spider. He knows he'll get my job if I slip up in the least. He's spoken to our corporate masters and is just waiting for a chance to prove his mettle. He got his gig at Scimitar the same way.

What Roger does not realize is the extent to which I see through his scheme. I know where he lives. I know his water-ing holes. I know how long he takes in the restroom. What he orders for dinner on Thursdays. And the single fact to which Roger has not paid adequate respect, during his tenure at *Necropolitan,* is how simple it would be for me to stroll into his monk's cell during any one of our late-late midnight oil

sessions, and modify the contour of his skull with the claw hammer I keep in my desk drawer, lower right.

You get to know a lot about people when you work with them day-to-day on a common project, and I know Roger's routines like I know my own morning regimen. What exercise and how much. Whether to wash my hair (and expose it, still damp, to the Manhattan morning chill) or let it go for a day. Coffee and yogurt or tea and toast. How long my downtown stroll to the office will take, versus the fact that he has to come in on the train. It might be days before anyone noticed that one of us was gone. Or both.

Editors rarely *edit,* these days. Very strange. We buy names and spend too much time on spin control and placating bigwigs. At the publishing houses, the last of the editorial adepts was ruthlessly hunted down and eliminated nearly a decade ago. The assistants took their places.

None of that, of course, should keep you from enjoying the offerings in this latest issue of *Necropolitan* to the max, and what I should really be saying here is *what are you waiting for?! The stories start right on the next page!*

It's time we both got on with what's really important.

> — Bertrand Nightenhelser
> Editor-in-Chief

—ooo—ooo—ooo—

---

* *(**Necropolitan** # 25 was the final issue of the magazine. To date, neither the whereabouts of editor Bertrand Nightenhelser, nor his assistant, Roger DeWitt, have been accounted for.)*

THE ABSOLUTE LAST OF THE ULTRA-SPOOKY, SUPER-SCARY HALLOWE'EN HORROR NIGHTS

"**M**ummies, take the tram to the prep trailer in Area Two. Ghouls and zombies, anybody who's not a straight rubberhead—trailer four, right behind me. I want the Frankensteins to line up according to height in the parking space over by Ops, which is right next to Security on your map. Draculas, your dressing room is the big space near the cafeteria. Rubberheads, you've got a thing looks like a sorta circus tent not too far from the restrooms, 'cos you don't need so much prep. Everybody else—if you're a Wolf Man or a Pinhead or a Freddy or Leatherface; all the Aliens and Jasons and Beetlejuices—report directly to Ops to see the script grid and get an assignment from Tracy or Kimberly; pick up your chainsaws, whatever gear your character needs. Everybody tracking? Can you all hear me, monsters?"

That's the problem with monsters, thought Oscar. *They never pay attention.*

He looked around at his fellow players. They were probably all like him, wondering how the performance life had brought them to this low ebb—playing monsters for some movie studio's amusement-park exploitation of Hallowe'en. Oscar had six years of formal dance training and tutelage with top choreographers under his Spandex belt. He had been in *Cats* and *The Lion King,* for christsake.

He was still waiting for the first review that actually *named* him.

Hallowe'en SpookyNight had come via the usual cattle-call, and for Oscar, making the cast cuts, was a breeze. The ads for the annual horror-themed in-park "adventures" promised a *hair-raising, bone-chilling smorgasbord of monsters.* Basically, it was your standard All Hallow's haunted house gauntlet, but super-sized into a combination of live theatre, wax museum and modular walk-through chamber of horrors, diverse and just time-consuming enough to justify the pricey admission fee—due north of over thirty bucks per head. The adjacent multiplex was screening a Spook-a-Thon of cheap rentals (nothing not already available in better shape on DVD), and patrons could avail their bone-chilled psyches of genuine alcohol at several clearly-labeled watering holes. Needless to say, the Spook-a-Thon cost extra, as did the cocktails. No specials or mark-downs, especially during a buying season where retailers were already caterwauling about making their nut.

The show runner with the megaphone was named Randy…something. He was slumming, too, having lost an assistant director slot on some sitcom. From beneath his studio-logoed baseball cap, which might as well have been embroidered with the word ASSHOLE, he deployed attitude as though he was Patton whipping the Third Army into a killing frenzy.

"A-Number One priority, people," announced Randy. He had one of those bullhorns that strapped to his shoulder and permitted him to speak through a mike. "We can't stress this enough. You are reminded not to grab or physically interface with the guests." Everyone nodded or murmured; they had all been told dozens of times, and this item came first on the hot sheet that had been distributed on the first day.

Following the Disneyland rule, visitors to the park were called "guests," though that term was freighted with none of the obligatory courtesy. The unspoken understanding was that the "guests" were really the Enemy, and for the entire crew staffing the studio's annual scare show, the objective was to survive long enough to get paid the going flat rate for "ambient atmosphere," that is, monsters.

The juice of genuine danger had amplified the touchy proposition of having live monsters on the lurk. Last year, one of the Draculas had gotten dragged to death when he got hung up in the tailgate of a tour tram. A teenager had gotten hit in the shoulder by a bullet fired into the air outside the park. And more and more non-preferred social element was showing up just to raise hell and start shit. Park security was lumbered beyond their capacity just breaking up gang fights, so a visible police presence had been attenuated. The show had to go on, basically, because the gate was irresistible to the studio suits, who thus deterred blame when their movies flopped.

Executives needed to promote the illusion of a "safe and sane" consumer entertainment experience, and in response had assigned pagers with panic buttons to park employees. This year they were tied into a satellite tracker that could pinpoint trouble spots instantly.

Oscar reconsidered the park property surrounding him. It was a mile and a quarter in circumference, this bubble of

make-believe pretend Hollywood hoo-hah. The rock scarps were spurious, unreal. Much of the strategic vegetation was plastic. Theme areas were boldly delineated and convenient restrooms, benchmarked. All visitors had to do while inside was spend money. The whole place was like a compound in a zoo—low maintenance, entirely fabricated, patently fake; an exemplar of the illusion of security.

The park was split up into mazes, theme tunnels or rooms, stage-bound presentations like the Vampire Magician or the Séance Tent, and tarted up backlot areas such as the Haunted Bayou, the Phantom's Sewer, and the Stairway to Hell. Some of the rides had been converted to night-time operation; you could strap yourself into the Chunkblower and ride it backward, in the dark. For one week only, Western Street had turned into Satan's Gulch. Rubberheads, or park extras wearing simple over-the-head masks, hung around mostly to provide guests with monsters to pose against, for snapshots. Ambient monsters in more complex makeups and gear populated the scare zones. Oscar's assignment was an area inside the Ghostly Graveyard known as Lycanthrope Trail.

"Your basic movement grids are on the maps handed out to you," announced Randy. "Stick to your grid. Jump-and-scares are okay so long as you don't scare little kids or catch guests *too* off-guard."

It was okay to be scary, thought Oscar…as long as nobody actually got scared, experienced fear, of suffered genuine dread. When had horror become so hypocritical?

Oscar thought that Hallowe'en should really fall on Friday the 13th, but he bowed to tradition, since few were left amid the mercantile consumerism packaged to the buying public as "holidays." Hallowe'en had never been an official holiday within his lifetime. No red numeral on the calendar; everybody worked. Seasonal employees were usually

treated like the worst sort of chattel—temps, forever bludg-
eoned with reminders that they should be thankful for the
gig and could be shitcanned for the slightest infraction.

His combo brow-and-snout piece was a featherweight
appliance of breathable latex, affixed with non-allergenic
spirit gum. He paid special attention to the hairlines and
blends. Details mattered. He had suited up out of his own
pocket in order to duplicate Lon Chaney, Jr's venerable wolf-
ing garb, not that anybody still paid attention to the classic
chestnuts. Most civilians found *remembering* those old movies
preferable to actually *watching* them, and indeed, most
guests could not be expected to have done the basic course-
work. They knew Frankenstein, Dracula, the Creature as
words, not names; they existed into the new century only as
forms of iconographic product placement. They were supposed to be scary, but only on Hallowe'en, then they were
mothballed until the next SpookyNight. They no longer
scared anybody, not really.

—ooo—

Gordito, Flaco, Chispa and Tiny came strictly to raise
hell. Gordito's homegirl was a spidery white chick named
Ashleigh. The rest were partnered with buoyant hoodrats
proudly displaying the spackled foundation makeup and sky-
high, needle-thin eyebrows that trademarked them as expa-
triates from Ramparts, which most Los Angeles-area
newswatchers routinely shortformed as Gang Central.
Flaco's girl was Chiqui, bratwurst-encased by skin-tight silk
which amplified the size of her butt into a wonderland of
possibilities. She still bore the gothic O.C. tat on her neck
from her dalliance with some cholo in Costa Mesa; much
internal ragging and discourse was devoted to how the ink
could be modified, embellished or obliterated. Her pasted-on

acrylic nails were three inches long, and each fingertip bore the image of one of the Homies cartoon characters.

Only Chispa had kept his beautiful hair. "See, white guys are all jealous of Mexicano hair," he'd say. "So they promote the image that bald is super-bad, so all the cholos shave their heads. You guys are humiliating your heritage, man." Gordito and Flaco and Tiny, all shaved and goateed, teased Chispa about cultivating a pachuco pomp and therefore not being worth shit in a fight. Like snaps or the dozens, the ranks went round and round, everybody insulting everybody else to show their love.

Park security and the on-site feel-up was a joke. Gordito's crowd entered SpookyNight strapped with pins, razors and short, stubby combat blades. Flaco, not wanting to dress down from his customary six-inch stiletto, had concealed it in the crack of his ass, and taken a lot of ragging for it. "What if you cough and it opens, dude?" said Tiny, sniggering. Flaco stoically endured the usual barrage of crap about stinky blades and "cutting" farts; what mattered was, he'd kept his weapon of choice.

Chispa's girl, Connie—short for Concepción—had stripped the micro-blades from safety razors and hot-glued them beneath her scarlet fingernails. Most of the guys had copied Tiny's trick of dropping their lock-backs into a shoe or boot and walking it through the pat-down, standing on it and trying not to limp. If the scanners tripped, steel toes and soles were blamed and no one ever forced you to take off your shoes. Once in the park, the footwear came off in the bathroom, and the blades were nestled back where they belonged, in a pocket or waistband. Nobody ever searched you when you were *exiting* the park.

"Check it out," Flaco said, cocking a thumb.

He directed their discreet attention to what Security and the cops could not see: A wall of shadows near the entryway where the dimmed floods of two intersecting theme zones of

the park joined. There was an unsightly swath of concrete barricade visible from Flaco's angle; normally bogus foliage would have concealed it. A couple of trespassers clambered over the wall from the parking garage. They were visible for all of a half a second, but Flaco had spotted the hidden activity with the surety of a concentration camp guard. "Go, dudes," he muttered. "Gonna be some shit *tonight.*"

They had been attending SpookyNight for four years running. It was too much fun to fuck with the monsters that were supposed to frighten you. "Couldn't scare nobody," Gordito always said, triumphant over some disposable menace. "Couldn't scare *shit.*"

—ooo—

"What's the record?" said Archie, crouching in the bushes like a Green Beret, his face streaked with black and green camo paint.

"Guy supposedly snuck into Disneyland and spent the whole night on one of the Jungle Cruise islands," said Mace. "But the one I heard about the guy who dressed up as a buccaneer and spent nearly forty hours inside Pirates of the Caribbean—that's gotta be the gold."

"What about the kid who lived on Tom Sawyer Island, for, like, days?"

"Doesn't count. I think he drowned."

"What, in four feet of water?" Archie gave him a curdled expression.

Nobody ever got the damned stories straight.

"That's what I heard. It doesn't count if you die."

"The Pirates dude kept it up for nearly two days?"

"So they say. You know how many friggin security cameras are inside that ride? He foxed them by pretending to be a robot. That redefines cool. I am in awe."

"Any proof?"

"Proof was on the news," said Mace. "They arrested him when the cameras caught him taking a leak, but he never said how long he was actually inside." He fiddled with his digital rig and flipped the viewscreen around so he could tape himself. "This is zero hour, eight P.M., and we've just penetrated the park."

Archie stuck his face into the shot, too, for posterity. This was the ultimate in clandestine, behind-the-scenes spy-camming. "Let's find the women's prep tent," he said. "Some of those chicks dressing out as the Bride of Frankenstein are ripped beyond belief. We might get to capture some flesh."

"I read ya," said Mace.

Their personal monster hunt had begun.

—ooo—

"Crowd Control expects three to five thousand guests through here tonight," said Randy into his bullhorn. "Everybody stay alert and do your job. If it gets hairy, let Security do theirs. *Do not* intercede."

All Oscar could smell was adhesive and latex, his head painted and glued into Wolf Man appliances, his hands already sweating in their fur gloves. All around him, ghouls, zombies and classic monsters were trying to dope out their assigned grids by penlight. Groups of otherworldly horrors grabbed their last chance for hydration at the snack bar.

Already, his inner voice was chanting: *In six hours this will be over.*

Oscar assumed his post and commenced to startle giggling nitwits and the dates of bigger nitwits, getting a photo-flash in the face too damned many times. Even in the land of the supernatural, they acted like the tourists they were. One guy had shoved him, all huffed up because Oscar had actually caught him unawares, but the guy turned his back and strolled away laughing. No harm, no foul.

There was some vigorous activity going on in the bushes about twenty yards to the rear, off the beaten track of Lycanthrope Trail. Either humping minors, Oscar knew, or, occasionally, a pair of fornicating show monsters, which was a weird enough possibility to distract his notice from his job. Last year, he'd seen one of the rubberheads, a Frankenstein Monster, with his pants down and his Bride with her legs in the air; now *that* was a photo op. He decided to take five to check it out, but by the time he fixed a direction, the commotion ceased. All he'd find was a wet Kleenex, or maybe a spent condom hanging on a branch, glistening like a glow-worm.

It took him an extra heartbeat to identify what he found as a person—a man, lying on his back, his eyes wide and fixed, his throat completely excavated to visible bone. He glistened, all right, mostly due to the ebbing glurts of carotid blood. His hands were frozen into claws and he was the deadest thing Oscar had ever seen.

Oscar's first thought was: *Maybe this is a really good prop.*

His second thought was: *Okay, it's just more urban violence, this is the 21st Century, don't panic.*

He fumbled out his pager and instantly dropped it. He groped around for it. Hopeless. When he rose again, he banged into something living and breathing, and rebounded onto one knee. Even in the bad light, he could make out that this was one of his fellow Wolf Men. He started to ask if this was for real when his voice died out in his throat, drying up to desert.

The creature regarding him had chatoyant eyes and smelled like a wet bloodhound fresh from a wallow in offal. It cocked its head, considering what it saw versus what it could scent—conflicting information. It ran an ebony talon along one side of Oscar's face and flicked one of his rubber ears. Its breath stank of carrion. Its teeth looked too practical to be a sham. Then it blew out breath in a hot snort of dismissal, released Oscar, and bounded away into the underbrush on backward-jointed canine hind legs.

If it was a werewolf costume, it was the best Oscar had ever seen.

—ooo—

Several jello shots later, Gordito fingered the edge of his blade, grinning like a demon and never letting his now-bloodshot eyes stray too far from the park fountain. "If I cut him from behind, right along that fin on his back, dude'll fall right out of his suit," he said to Ashleigh, who snickered and popped her gum.

The attention of the green amphibian monster in the fountain was focused away from them, toward the park. Not a lot of traffic right now, with the Chunkblower at full capacity and showtime for the Vampire Magician just commencing. He splashed about desultorily, awaiting an audience, pondering aquatic scare tactics.

"I'm gonna go for it," Gordito said, always anxious to be first. The deal with his homies was that each of them would target a different monster, and each had to score a trophy—a plastic appendage, a slice of monster suit, an artifact of the hunt. A simple bloodstain would suffice, too, but Gordito had his eye on that backfin. Ashleigh did not like the part about the blood.

"Gordo, don't *hurt* the fuckin guy, okay? That's not funny."

"*Callaté.*" It was a command, a warning, and the end of the argument. Inwardly, Gordito was relieved that none of his boys were around to hear his bitch mouthing off. Sometimes, listening to Ashleigh whine was worth it, just so Gordo could be proud of his trophy blonde; other times, well, what was it about white chicks that made them so whiny?

He edged up behind the fountain like a commando. Nobody was strolling by. If he had to step into the two-foot depth of water, Ashleigh's instructions were to yank him back so he did not fall.

When the Creature meandered back to Gordito's side of the pool, Gordito arm-barred him from behind and made a clean cut straight down the length of the dorsal double-fin. "What-up, fishie!" he growled, making a monster voice. The fin did not peel back easily. Fat droplets of dark purple blood hit the clear water like ink. That was the last thing Gordito saw.

His victim turned with a bullrush roar, snapping both bones in Gordito's forearm. The knife dropped into the water. The scaled thing revolved in his limp grasp, slick as motor oil, and razor-keen talons husked Gordito's face off his skull. When Ashleigh screamed and pulled back on her boyfriend's free hand, she fell on her rump because the arm was no longer attached.

Her screaming attracted no notice in the park as the water turned vague pink and Gordito's corpse splashed face-down. She was borne into the air, light as a broomstick, and body-slammed into the bushes behind the fountain. All she could see was blurry movement and shifting light; the world turning upside-down, and there was no time left to draw breath to make any more commotion.

The Gill-Man had always been attracted to the fair ones, the ones in angelic white. Like many of the others long-past, this one did not survive the mating.

—ooo—

"Did you *see* that?! Did you get it?!" Mace was beside himself with excitement.

"I got it," said Archie, staring at his video camera as if it had suddenly sprung a secret hatch containing hidden treasure.

"Ho, *man!*" Mace was getting wiggly. They were guerilla'ed in at the treeline with a clear view of the park fountain, about thirty yards from where Gordito and Ashleigh had just died. Archie's digital kit featured an excellent zoom, even using night-vision.

"Shut up, shut up!" There was more activity at the fountain, and both Archie and Mace hunkered down to see what came next.

They videotaped a fellow named Rory Caulder, who had taken an unscheduled break to repair his Gill-Man suit, since the chemicals used to keep the fountain water clear had a tendency not only to waterlog the rubber, but to dissolve it at inopportune times. God only knew what it was doing to his skin. It was comic to watch, even on instant replay: The green monster shuffles flat-footedly to his post, puts one leg into the water, looks down, and does a monster double-take worthy of Wile E. Coyote. He springs out of the water and falls on his ass, ripping his reptilian suit as he claws for his emergency pager.

"Got it," said Archie. "Classic."

—ooo—

Oscar was doing his best to skin around the edges of the park, with the nearest exit as his objective. He still could not get his breathing to settle down. He would never be able to erase the image of the eviscerated cadaver from his mind, especially when his imagination impudently filled in gory details obscured by the bad light. His nose seemed clogged with the stench of freed organs cooling in the night, back there, somewhere behind him.

"What the hell is this—a Wolf Man?" said Connie.

Libia, Tiny's girl, unlimbered her straight razor with a stainless steel glint in her eyes. "Let's take him." They had been kicking it under a large eucalyptus tree—a real one—working their way through a spliff the size of a Dodger Dog and discussing how they could one-up their guys in the scavenger hunt for monster parts.

"Wait!" said Oscar, skidding to a stop. "Wait a minute!" His hairy paws were stretched out, open-palmed, in entreaty as the two girls angled toward him, jackals stalking a werewolf. "You've got to get out of the park, now! You're in danger! There's—"

Libia and Connie glanced at each other with scrunched-up expressions of impatience. "Fuck *you,*" they both said at the same time, like homicidal twins.

Connie slashed obliquely with her bladed fingernails while Libia thrust and danced and Oscar found his life full-up, trying to track both of them. He felt molten pain in his bicep as he was incised—first blood. Apropos of Edgar Allan Poe, Oscar's brain *reeled* as he fell. He was still trying to warn people who were intent on harming him. He was bleeding now, yet the words coming from his mouth were still trying to save them.

Scrambling to rise, savaging his wounded arm, only Oscar saw the clot of ghouls and zombies that had congregated to watch.

One of the walking dead grabbed Libia by the hair and gnawed a big wet mouthful out of her naked shoulder. Libia went nuclear and windmilled with the razor. The zombie did not mind, and within seconds Libia was being eaten in all directions. Concepción simply vanished into a huddle of lurching, famished walkers, folding inward like cardboard. Oscar saw her hand last of all, flashy fingernails tearing impotently at the night air.

—ooo—

"I could kick Frankenstein's ass," said Tiny. "Come on."

"What about the girls?" Chispa was looking around for Connie.

"What a pussywhip," said Flaco. "They'll find us. Let's do it."

"Big son of a bitch," said Chispa, meaning their prey.

The Frankenstein Monster was seated in a niche in the Rhine Village, which had been redecorated as the Stairway to Hell. Whoever was under the monster makeup had been cast for size, and with the big clunky Franken-boots he was still two feet taller than Tiny, who, typically, was north of six-two and past three hundred on the scale. The guy was laying down on the job, not stalking and scaring. He looked like he had a headache or something.

"Take the bolts on his neck," suggested Flaco.

They came in like muggers dogging a lone Girl Scout on a train platform.

"Saaayyy," Tiny said, swaggering. "I always wanted to kick Frankenstein in the balls to see what he'd do."

The Monster looked up, infinite weariness in its face.

The blades came out. "Give us those bolts and we won't have to Veg-O-Matic your ass," said Chispa.

The Monster stood up, casting all three of them into its shadow. The sight of the knives caused it to wave its huge hands, to ward away the danger, and that was all Tiny needed to interpret as an attack. They swarmed the Monster, right-left and center.

The Monster grabbed Tiny's throat as Tiny drove his lockback knife hilt-deep into its sternum. It grunted but followed through, crushing all the bones in Tiny's neck. Tiny's eyes went snowy and he died instantly, hitting the ground like a side of buffalo steak falling off the back of a butcher's truck. Flaco feinted while Chispa dug in. The

Monster backhanded Chispa so hard that his eyes popped out. Worse, his pompadour was mussed for life.

In another part of the Stairway to Hell, guests witnessing the action had begun to applaud.

Flaco saw them, felt caught in the act, and his fight-or-flight knob cranked full over to *flight.* He ran away, grateful that his dead friends could not see him chicken out in real time.

The Monster growled, once, put-upon and angry. No one else dared to come near him. It pulled the knife from its chest and flung it. Then it resumed its seat in partial shadow, hands rising to obscure its view of the world. It just wanted to be left alone.

—ooo—

"Hey, *mijo,*" Chiqui said when she'd spotted Flaco, crouched low near the Haunted Bayou, eyes dulled. "You laying down on the job or you just trying to lure me back into the bushes?" She was game, and dropped a strap, trying to look sexy-cute.

"Chiquita," Flaco said, gasping, his voice clogged. "Don't—"

"What?"

Flaco could say no more because he was busy trying to hold his intestines together in his lap. He failed. Chiqui uttered a strangled little cry and nearly backed into the guy standing behind her, the guy in the long cloak and top hat.

"What the fuck are you?!" she said, whirling, startled out of seeing Flaco, just for a moment. "Fucking Dracula; get the fuck outta here."

"I suppose not," said the man in the cloak.

"Oh, well, you Mister Hyde or some sorta fucker, then? Fuck, you ain't no monster."

"I suppose not," said Jack the Ripper, who had lived for a hundred years and would live for a hundred more, as a killer with no face.

He slid Flaco's six-inch blade into Chiqui's esophagus, cutting off further comment and popping a knuckle of vertebra through the back of her neck. He had cut Flaco quickly. With the women, he always tried to take more time.

—ooo—

"Oh, wow, he cut her, man—cut her like a surgeon!"

Archie's insane giggle had grated Mace's nerves for three kills, now, and Mace was starting to think that maybe his partner was beginning to lose his mind.

"If you don't shut up and keep down, *I'm* going to cut you," Mace said gutterally. "Like a weed-eater. Hand me the other battery."

Archie rummaged inside his rucksack of nightfighting-black canvas. "He stuck the knife in them and they died, faster than clicking off a light switch. That was so smooth. Please tell me you got that!"

"I got it, I got it. Jesus." Typical, for Archie to think he might have missed the shot. He wanted to be a cameraman, and would never let a low battery pack louse up a choice composition. "I *got* it, okay?"

Then the Mummy got *them.*

Archie pitched forward onto Mace, his skull corrugated by inch-deep finger-tracks full of dust and trailing mold. Everything inside his head gushed out under pressure, and as Mace was trying to swing his lens around to capture the moment, he realized the last face he would see was more than three thousand years old, and completely devoid of expression.

—ooo—

Hymie and Gloria worked cleanup together, one of several details throughout the park. Appropriate to the season, they were in costume too, from their dark blue washable jumpsuits to the paper filters partially masking their faces. Like the many of the ambient monsters in the park, they too wore latex gloves, though theirs were surgical. Their shoulder patches read SECURITY and were emblazoned with little handcuffs and lightning bolts.

"It just gets worse," Gloria said, her gaze defocused. Her eyes, above the aluminum nose-guard for the mask, were metallic blue-gray in the vague light. "Nobody can just have a nice time anymore. Children don't have any business with adult drugs, adult weapons, yet here they are, more every year." She was staring toward the exit to the Haunted Bayou sector. Tourists in, tourists out. No action just now.

"It wouldn't be so bad if these gang idiots just killed each other," said Hymie, who was of the opinion that the world needed fewer stupid people anyway, but was conflicted by his need to sound sympathetic to Gloria's views. Her jumpsuit revealed her figure as pert and trim and he really wanted to ask her out, after work, for coffee or something.

Gloria said, "Well, who are we to deny them a little help-along?" Her expression was caught halfway between rueful and bittersweet as her headset radio crackled. She had this habit of pressing the earpiece when she responded, as though she was auditioning in a recording booth. "Copy that, Front-Man, cleanup on Aisle Eight." Aisle Eight would be the restricted area behind the Bizarre Bazaar.

Usually they just zipped the body into a bag and slung it into the back of their van. When they had 25 stacked up, they traded for a clean van. But the Aisle Eight job was a bonafide mess, and Hymie's first thought was Wolf Man.

"What, again?" Gloria shook her head at the mess. "I'm thinking Jack the Ripper got himself into a party mood." It was funny in a way: the Wolf Man did the real ripping; Jack used tools. The corpse was a casserole from chin to crotch.

Together they managed to spatula-roll it into the sterile bag, and once zipped shut, it was just another load.

"Is this a guy or a girl?" Hymie said.

"Female. Look at the makeup. Unless it's a guy in drag. Hell, Hymie, everybody's wearing makeup tonight; nobody's who they're supposed to be. Isn't that what Hallowe'en's all about? Disguising yourself?"

"Damned monsters," Hymie said, wiping down his suit with an aerosol bottle of disinfectant.

"The last time I ever trick-or-treated, I was twelve," she said. "Before poison in the candy and pedophiles behind every door. This neighbor lady named Mrs. Burke used to hand out full-sized candy bars. My sister Jeanie and I had to go home and empty our bags. We made two full rounds of the whole neighborhood, walked on streets we couldn't even name, till almost midnight, and we were okay. We were safe. God, I feel old."

"What did you go as?" said Hymie.

"I went as the sorority vampire chick from *Blood of Dracula*—scarf, vampire fangs, contrail eyebrows, the whole bit. I thought it was an empowering image. I never went as a princess, or Snow White. I was the Bride of Frankenstein one time, and the Leech Woman."

"If more kids were watching those old movies and dressing up, we might not have to do this."

"That was then, this is now," she said. "Besides, we'd be out of a job, so I'm not complaining." In a lax economy, their particular branch of security was booming. They had more clean-ups every year.

Hymie said, "I heard next year they might actually tell the fake monsters about the…you know—the ringers."

Gloria snorted. "Why? The actors aren't going to get hurt. We haven't lost a single one."

"What about Dracula, last year?"

"That was an accident, and it was probably his own fault, or some drunk moron shoved him. It wasn't—you know, the other thing."

Neither of them could summon the words to speak of real monsters.

"Not only that," said Gloria, "but if we told the actors, too, then nobody would show up for the auditions. Bad for biz."

Together they slung the fresh bag into their van. Hymie's heart did a little skip-and-jump. He knew about *Blood of Dracula;* he knew that the movie had been filmed as *I Was A Teenage Vampire* in the 1950s, and he and Gloria could talk about stuff like that, later, after they punched their clock cards for the night.

He wondered what she was up to for Christmas.

—ooo—

Somehow, Oscar had made it clear of SpookyNight with no further damage. Somehow, he had put the monster fest behind him, huffing and puffing, on hands and knees, over the grassy hillock on the other side of the security fences. He did not even remember finding his car in the part-time employee lot, or not losing his keys, or two dozen other variables that might have hampered his escape.

Lot Security waved him through the gate with a grin. Look at that, a monster driving a car, pretty damned funny. *I didn't know lycanthropes could drive a stick.*

Making it back to his apartment without killing himself in a collision was another minor miracle. His attempts to hide his face made him lope, and he was spotted by costumed kids on the sidewalk, being shepherded through treats, with few tricks, by their put-upon parents and handlers. *Look, Daddy, it's the Wolf Man!* They all saw him, and not one of them was frightened.

When he caught sight of himself in his bureau mirror, he startled. His makeup base was smeared, kohling his eyes so they appeared huge and wet. He thought of prostitutes, beaten up and left with shredded hose in some alley. The blend edges of his Wolf Man appliances had peeled. He looked like he was rotting, dying. Sweat had popped in gravid, oily droplets. Hallowe'en had surprised him this year. His skull sloshed with sickly thoughts about classic monsters and make-believe; about the dangers of making the fantasmagoric creatures of the night *too* cuddly.

He tried to meter his breathing, and failed. He fought to stabilize his composure, and couldn't. His emotions were red-lining because this year, this season, he had felt something he had never felt before, when playing dress-up and going boo! for minimum wage…and in the flash of an instant, the world had changed around him.

Oscar was scared. To the thudding core of his heart, he was scared to death on Hallowe'en, for the very first time.

—ooo—ooo—ooo—

EXPANDING YOUR CAPABILITIES USING FRAME/SHIFT™ MODE

Half the buttons on the fucking remote? Dorian could not tell you what they were for…unless they were dead tabs for some higher-end version of the DVD player he had scored for seventy bucks, at some bargain barn specializing in floor models and discontinued stock. Manufacturers did that; gave you the same remote, no matter what, with special functions reserved for the costlier units. It was a cruel tease that reminded you of what you *didn't* have, a wiggle-worm of bait to goad you to consume even more.

He, however, counted himself among a more elite group—the ones dedicated enough to surf around the constraints of any system, particularly when it came to all phyla of media. It was an unseen fraternity, this underground scene of video adepts. Its skills were wily, pirate skills—how to nuke copyguard, how to outfox foreign formats, how to play and copy damned near anything. One could gain friends through such utility.

Dorian had hacked the player using a download from the internet. He had burned a disk of the hack, installed it into

the DVD tray, and crossed his fingers. The machine had taken twenty nerve-wracking seconds to reprogram itself, per a better device, different brand, allowing Dorian to wave bye-bye to all forms of copy protection and region coding. Now at last, he had achieved video transcendence. *What, you can't play that? Give it to me.*

Now he could play anything out of a single box—a concept that was sometimes more important than eating, not that he could ever explain that usefully to Gelina. She could not appreciate that he could fire up new gear without ever cracking the damned manual. That was a skill, a talent, wasn't it?

After checking to insure the kitchen cabinet held an adequate stock of packaged ramen, Dorian blew about a hundred bucks on assorted priced-to-clear disks of Italian gore moves. If Gelina complained, he'd cook, see? DVDs really were worse than crack. None of the furniture in their downscale, one-bedroom apartment (half a duplex) was worth a shit, but they could now by-god *watch* any damned thing, including pirate copies and bootleg downloads of movies still playing in theatres. This way, Dorian reasoned, they were actually *saving* money.

Besides—Gelina was a waitress at Alphy's. She always managed to pick up bonus shifts at the coffee shop, and wasn't there some rule that said management had to feed the staff? Right?

Consolation was a fluid, shifting thing.

The remainder of the afternoon was gobbled up by a double bill of *Chainsaw Cheerleaders II* (the Special Director's Cut), and a dubbed, fullscreen version of *Shriek for Mercy* ("with restored disembowelment scene!"). For Dorian, this all classified as research. Every eighteen months or so, he was able to nail a gig as production assistant or gofer on some micro-budget, straight-to-video epic—sporadic sideswipes he could honestly call "work in the film industry," thus rationalizing his obsessive input of movies in all forms. Whenever his cinematic skill ran to fumes, Dorian had tried (in no particular order) freelance web design for porn sites, driving a taxi, graveyard shift at some 24-hour Xerography shop, slinging espresso, and tootling all over hell and gone as a messenger. He had tried to bi-pack the cabbie and messenger jobs according to a complicated but workable schedule, and gotten shitcanned. The espresso boutique was overrun with trendy losers, pecking away on laptops and trying to sound important during endless cellular calls. They tipped for shit. The downside of free caffeination was getting so wired that all Dorian wanted to do was rip out poseur throats aplenty. With his teeth. The copymat job, like the coffee job, reminded him that he was no further along as Hollywood's Next Big Thang (though the former *did* provide a lot of free office supplies). The porn web-work had dried up when San Francisco, to the north, had gotten its smugness quaked by the dot-com crash.

Dorian was the longest-running temp worker that Dorian knew, and he saw no irony in this. At least Gelina's job was steady. Her tips paid their rent…leaving him free to court the cutting edge of the tech that would one day set him free.

Most crazy-making, was the third row of buttons on the new remote. Dorian saw cryptic designations such as INT/ALT+, FR/SHFT, and SELECT EXIT. He pressed them at random, and nothing happened. Onscreen, an Italian starlet got her brain crowbarred from her open skull, to be devoured by cannibal zombies. Dorian flipped the remote for clues and read the sticker there: ASSEMBLED IN TAIWAN. Below that was a bar code and an inventory control number.

A true terrorist of video would already *know* what those buttons meant, he reasoned. He refused to retreat to the coward's option of checking the manual.

At his computer, he recalled the data on the hack he had employed. He compared strings of digits representing the model he had purchased, versus specs from the unattainable model to which he had sneakily upgraded. It, too, had been discontinued, superceded by an even more unattainable version…but he located another inventory number, and based on that, he sniffed up the button sequence for accessing the "service menu."

CD and DVD players were all little computers. Even though they were designed to be discarded and replaced— not repaired—they all came with some sort of back door for simple adjustments. Invisible to the buying public, this information was almost never provided in the already incomprehensible manual, just another example of the contempt in which sellers hold buyers. For example, each numeric key was also assigned a letter value. Punching these in a certain sequence, after, say, hitting the MENU button three times in a row, could get you in. Dorian found precious little on the upgrade model, but did discover the service menu code for a *similar* model, courtesy of one of the links on the hacker's chat board. On some machines, this elementary access allowed you to cancel copyguarding functions in a simple on/off way. Other machines needed a specially-configured chip to be manually placed on the motherboard (there was a guy in Australia who would burn the chip you needed for twenty bucks, postage-paid).

As the now-brainless Italian ingenue was being raped by a possessed demon tree, Dorian entered 1197-MENU-SELECT-MENU-69 on his remote. The movie was covered by a click-down menu in a square of translucent blue. The fifth item down read FRAME/SHIFT MODE. Its status read as DISABLED. Dorian arrowed over to ENABLED, then clicked EXIT MENU. *Shriek for Mercy's* victim filled up the screen again, in her final death throes prior to her resurrection as a lurching ghoul, freshly impregnated with a baby tree demon. The scene cut to a pair of guys arguing on a minimal office set, the voices of their English surrogates hollow and booming, due to inadequate miking. Their early Seventies wardrobe was a riot of flared trousers, and plaid suits with aerodynamic lapels.

Dorian pointed the remote at the player and clicked FR/SHFT.

Now the same two guys were still standing there, same goofily-dubbed argument as before…except they were decked out in crumpled boxers, wife-beater T-shirts, and socks with garters. Their shoes had vanished, but their heels were still canted four inches off the floor.

STOP!

Dorian cued to the beginning of the scene. Two guys, loud garb, arguing tough. He hit FRAME/SHIFT. Same deal, only now they were in their underwear again. The switch was *not* part of the movie. Dorian blinked and rubbed his eyes (he had seen people react this way in films, when confronted with an anomaly). Purist that he was, he ran the scene in its entirety, just to make sure the men remained the same. As soon as he hit FRAME/SHIFT, their outer garments ceased to exist, and they carried on as though nothing within their movie reality had changed. Or shifted.

He hit the button again. Now the men were naked, still floating surreally above the floor on platform soles no longer visible. Their pubic hair was mashed, and penises crooked, by now-invisible underwear. The guy on the left had a long, skinny dick that was actually pointed upward, inside clothing that no longer impeded Dorian's view.

Dorian was now inspired to backtrack to the debut scene of the future tree casualty, which, thanks to low-budget coincidence, had been staged on the same indifferent office set,

where she was a secretary, or something. It was a medium shot, up-angle of her sauntering to her post, wearing an abbreviated suede skirt. Miles of leg plummeted into designer boots. She wore a loose, saucy silk blouse, and owned at least a yard of elaborately-coiffed hair in burnished brown. Bracelets, bangles. Eyes hidden by couture shades intended to mimic those costing at least four hundred dollars.

No longer did Dorian have to look at the remote; his fingers had learned the sequence. Reverse. Track slow. Play normal. Then, FRAME/SHIFT.

Same angle, same actress, same movements...but a brand-new point of view. Now Dorian could see the marvelous length of pale thigh that led from black garters to breathtakingly brief lace panties. The arc of the garter belt now framed her navel. She had a treasure trail. No tan lines. Her formidable breasts moved in a furtive, repetitive pattern as she walked, engirded in the grasp of a brassiere that was mostly a wisp of spiderweb fabric. Her eyes, sans glasses, were revealed as a blazing, killer green.

Dorian was getting an erection.

FRAME/SHIFT.

Now she was nude, walking, apparently, on air. Her pubic hair was lush and rudely full. Her aureolae were large to the point of being slightly grotesque, her thumb-sized nipples flattened by the non-visible bra.

Dorian paused to cohere an opinion: *Like, this is like sooo totally the ultimate peeping tom deal.* Just as film theory held, the screen *could* be a window to exciting otherworlds. You just had to know the code; which buttons to push. You had to have the savvy and know-how of the Video Adepts. He decided to let his cock catch some air while he, you know, massaged it.

FRAME/SHIFT.

Dorian's non-remote hand froze on the upstroke. The actress' flesh had transposed to dermis, threadbare with vasculature. In front of her chest hovered two opaque teardrops, which Dorian realized were breast implants—still wiggling around in mid-air. She looked as though her outermost layer of skin had been sandblasted off, to reveal glistening wetness, mostly crimson. She was wearing a tampon.

Dorian's little best buddy began to wilt in his grasp, a candle in a hot room. There was no GO BACK button. In order to see the woman naked, not *skinned*, he had to start the sequence all over. He scanned until he found a substantially longer take of her.

Gelina walked in late, while he was still jerking off.

—ooo—

They had their usual fight about money. Then they ate some take-out Gelina had brown-bagged home. Then they had their usual fight about how gross it was for him to masturbate to what Gelina assumed was simple porn. Then they had the usual, terrific make-up sex.

Tonight, Gelina seemed amplified. Turned up, super-sensitive, multi-orgasmic, practically voracious. Instead of waiting for her to drift to sleep so he could race back to the TV, Dorian dozed, played-out and sweaty. The air cooled him, and when he startled awake in the dark, his pelvis was sore and his balls hung like bruised fruit. Gravity hurt. The pit of his stomach howled for relief, so he meandered out and boiled some ramen, throwing in a chopped green onion at the last minute.

The DVD player waited patiently for him through all this procrastinating nonsense. Knowing he would come back; knowing he would not resist clicking it on again, like a lover who wields your desire as a weapon against you.

He felt sorry for all the people incapable of wiring a stereo, of programming the timer on a simple VCR. They didn't care about bit rates for dual-layer DVDs. They would be bushwhacked when high-def Blu-Ray discs came along next year to render their ordinary DVDs into antiques. They would buy what they were told. And he, Dorian, would be light-years ahead of *that* game.

Padding around in sweatpants, minding the creak of floorboards beneath his bare feet, Dorian roughed up his video shelves until he fished up a dusty VHS tape, no sleeve, labeled *Tasha's Wedding*.

It was time for Phase Two—to see if FRAME/SHIFT worked on videotapes, too.

His interest was strictly academic. This trick, this hidden truth, this secret key, might be parlayed into a cure-all boon, and Dorian wanted to be ready. After all, the asshole who invented the AirBong had reaped a gazillion dollars, and he hadn't even *designed* the fucking thing. (Thanks to his recognition of opportunity's knock, said asshole had made it possible for smokers to smoke anything they wanted, practically anywhere they wanted, without the discharge of hazardous pollutants into the lungs of bystanders.) Blammo—wealth, pools, exotic drugs, and blowjobs on-call. Dorian felt like a mad scientist on the brink of a similar revelation. This gimmick, properly unleashed on the unsuspecting world at large, might become, like, *Celebrity Skin* on demand, for anybody, anywhere, right?

Plus, there was suspense, too—he had to unlock the secret before some other loser in some other apartment figured our FRAME/SHIFT to his or her advantage.

Naturally, his selection of test material had nothing to do with the prospect of seeing many women (and some girls) after whom he had once lusted (some, to this day) in the altogether, without the knowledge he was step-framing them, and zoom-boxing their privates. There was more at stake here.

The eponymous Tasha had once been Gelina's best bud, prior to some falling out—one of those deals where nobody picks up the phone, and, a decade and a half later, nobody can remember what the original conflict had been. Tasha looked hot in her bridal whites, and Dorian recalled an intermittent fantasy about smothering himself between her substantial and absolutely real tits. He stopped hitting FRAME/SHIFT when he saw the foetus, gestating inside her.

Yeah, now he remembered: Tasha had spewed a kid with her matrimonial manburger, about five months into their legal union. Pregnancy had left her resembling a street waif, beaten by thugs, and much devalued on Dorian's personal sexometer.

Some of his own pals looked pretty stupid, naked. Don't even go there.

Now he could see his old flame, Belinda, clearly enough to distinguish the razor burn on her shaved pubes, and a tattoo she had acquired after breaking up with him (Hot Stuff, right there on her inner thigh). One of the bridesmaids, Sally somethingorother, had soaked her panties with lubrication during the vows. Cheryl Lindemann had stuffed her bra, after simulating cleavage by duct-taping her boobs together.

Dorian's penis, loose and nasty inside his sweats, still smelled like Gelina. It rose, then drooped, like a cranky guy hitting the SNOOZE button over and over, as Dorian cycled through the ladies on the old wedding video, undressed them with FRAME/SHIFT, and found each of his idealized liaisons lacking.

Then Dorian had a new idea, and his dick roused to parade attention.

—ooo—

Technically, Dorian's video camera was "vintage"—out-moded, too cumbersome, brand-new when you could still buy LPs in record shops. It took full-sized VHS tapes, and required no interpretive cabling or little-brother adapter to play through his TV. The recording cassette was your non-digital, original, first-generation image. The low-light and fil-tering features (now rendered obsolete by two decades of consumer progress) would impart a warm, analog feeling to whatever was shot. Dorian had kept the thing in the closet so long that its power cells were cold, beyond repair, deader than beef jerky. To make it function tonight, he'd need an extension cord for the AC input, and that meant he'd have to find something else in the apartment to disconnect.

His mind was snowed-in by a blizzard of concepts. He could direct a whole series of porns, like that Buttman guy. He could film pedestrians on the street, and interpret them in such a way as to compel flesh-starved jerkoffs to plunk down twenty bucks for an hour of tape. Nobody wanted to see the usual junkie sluts, spread out like leftover lunchmeat or sniper victims. Everybody wanted to see the Girl Next Door, naked. He could do commissions for anyone who had ever nurtured a randy thought about a co-worker. Maybe even private eye side-jobs.

Emission: Possible.

He was counting on Gelina's love of wake-up sex. That gentle stir of nipples, prior to more focused groping, amidst the gentle smells of sleep. Once Dorian coaxed the camera back to life, he stuck electrical tape over the red running light and concealed the unit near his dresser (where he could still find the outlet in the dark). There was plenty of laundry in which to hide the unit—garments in the twilight realm between one more wearing, and the hamper. Gelina would beeline for the shower before dressing, and in that moment—later—Dorian could stash the whole setup, so she would never ask the wrong questions.

Very possible.

He imagined an interview: With this power, why in hell would you want to see your own girlfriend naked? You see her naked all the time. The sort of moronic question that would be asked by some backer with a homely wife and stupid kids and no idea of what was erotic. The kind of guy with zero prospects and even less imagination; one of those zombies that ogled men's mags and just…plain…didn't…get it.

The Italian starlet, implants and all, was a fantasy; Dorian already knew he could control what wasn't real. Gelina was the real-world end of the seesaw, and besides, Dorian had to admit (with more than a sting of apprehension) that he had never actually seen himself in the process of coitus. FRAME /SHIFT could reveal harsh truths, and allow hard conclusions. He was doing this for the greater good of all his future customers.

Sleep was impossible, so he explored a bit more, in those hours before dawn. The nudie cutie stuff got tired fast. Dorian did take note that only organic objects within a picture seemed to be affected by FRAME/SHIFT—animals, plants, food. They became translucent, exposing their hidden networks and schema. If there were organic components in inert objects, such as a toothpaste tube, say, or leather chairs, the shift was too subtle to pinpoint, or was a mere redistribution of color patterns. Intriguing, but not distracting. His main objective, his master plan, guaranteed that his boner never completely subsided.

He was deeply fond of banging Gelina, absolutely. But it had been more than a bit of a while since the *thought* of her had horned him up this much. He knew how to flip her switch, and rev her motor, and sometimes her responses cranked him up when he had begun indifferently. She probably

mistook his attentiveness for actual affection; chicks were weird that way. He slid into their secondhand bed next to her and began to infiltrate her nightshirt with his hands.

After he had cued the camera, of course.

Gelina's bloodline was principally Mediterranean robusto (similar enough to the femme lead in *Shriek for Mercy*), and soon she was breathing as though half-awake, scooting around to permit him better access. Dorian's finger came up thickly moist, and she practically dragged him on top of her, tangling their legs in the warm cocoon of sheets. Dorian was pretty wet, himself; an abundance of pre-seminal fluid streaked his leg. He flew blind, balls rasping down the curt bristle of her cropped public hair, but she collected him into herself as though she had a laser sight down there.

Making Gelina a surrogate for the hottie from *Shriek for Mercy* was a turn-on; Dorian's thoughts of playing to his own camera, ditto. Gelina waxed and bucked through a preliminary climax, then started to ram him as though trying to bash him inside-out with her pelvis. They even climaxed at the same time, just like in the movies. Then (as Dorian knew she would), she immediately looked at the bedside clock, muttered *oh shit oh shit, shit!* and dashed to the bathroom.

Dorian hurriedly stashed his surveillance setup. A gleaming icepick of potential discovery separated his lungs and made it difficult to breathe. His pubic bone felt worked over with a rubber mallet; he was walking funny. It hurt in a good way.

It always aroused him to watch Gelina pulling on pantyhose prior to donning her ridiculous Alphy's uniform, which had obviously been designed by some pig anxious to showcase a lot of leg in his food service staff. It was sort of an abbreviated, Bavarian beer-wench getup, and although bonus stretches of thigh and cleavage were *not* on the menu, they did account for a fair degree of overtipping. The pantyhose looked just as scrumptious coming off, too, at the end of the workday. Dorian had successfully cornered Gelina, several times, into fucking while her uniform was still half-on, with the added lewd kick of no underwear and unrestricted access. Just flip up the skirt and do it. Maybe he had a thing for women in uniform; maybe it was just the tang of enacting the good old Waitress Fantasy for real.

Gelina wrestled into her gear, while spieling off her usual diatribe against…well, everything. It was virtually the same speech, every day, as regular as TV news. She hated her hours, despised her boss, and held most of her lecherous regulars in total contempt. She complained about her clunky work shoes, and bemoaned a few faintly evident varicose veins. She railed at pinning up her hair for the job. She loathed the commute. For employees, the parking sucked. She really had to discover some new adjectives.

Dorian lay in as good a mock of innocence as he could muster, the sheet blotting his crotch. He let the tirade wash over him. He was still half-hard.

Just LEAVE, already, will you!?

Gelina grabbed bag, keys, and blazed out the door in a tempest of protest, foregoing the juiceless goodbye smooch. Dorian nap-zoned for awhile, his fatigue exceeding his conniving excitement.

You had to give Gelina credit for trying to tilt their lopsided relationship toward normal. Her social genetics were biased toward family meals, taken together at something called "dinnertime," carbon-copying the sitcom parameters the mass-market world had adopted as gospel, therefore, average. If people hung out and fucked long enough, they were expected to procreate. It was what people did. Occasionally, Dorian wondered how their relationship would end. He accepted that it had a clear ceiling, and knew

that one day, critical mass would be achieved...but he did not want the responsibility of initiating any sort of messy breakup. Entropy would destroy them. Their gentle, Tinker-Toy latticework of mundane disappointments and bided time would ultimately collapse. But probably not today...

...unless Dorian's experiment provided the kind of breakthrough he craved. With money, with notoriety, with resources, he might evolve into a different person—one that might even be capable of loving Gelina, perhaps, despite all her delusional architecture about what people did and did not do.

His predawn assault had climaxed with Gelina on top, her favorite horsey position, giddyap. Dorian would hold his fists in the air, locking his elbows, and Gelina would grab them as she teetered on the brink of orgasm, and begin chugging him (hence the bruised pubic bone). From his supine vantage, this made Gelina look like a character in fractured-flicker fast motion, trying to kick-start an invisible motorcycle. You had to give extra points to the people with whom you fell in love, or, at least, in lust—after all, they consented to get into totally ridiculous positions with no clothes on, all in the name of getting off, or getting closer to whatever you hid inside yourself.

Therefore, Dorian made an effort not to judge what he saw on the videotape. How stupid they looked, fucking. This was never supposed to be observed, and he had no desire to judge the merits of his own bobbing white ass. What was the rule of thumb for porn? Watch it for five minutes, and you want to have sex immediately. Watch it for *ten* minutes, and you never want to have sex again.

He started clicking FRAME/SHIFT.

Dorian and Gelina, fucking. *Click.* Two twine-wrapped muscle-bags, fucking. *Click.* Two floating arrays of internal organs, seeming to fuse into one pulsating membrane of wormy-colored tissue, fucking.

He had proven his point. Right now, he could saunter out into the world with his proof, and begin recording his future fortune.

Click. Two skeletons, fucking. Dorian muted the embarrassing soundtrack; the inadvertently-recorded noises they had made.

If he clicked again, would he see braids of bone marrow in a humanoid schematic, humping away?

Click. Click. Click. Click. Further than he had gone before. Always test the operational limits of the phenomenon.

Their bedroom looked the same, the colors and shapes slightly out of phase due to the distortive nature of FRAME/SHIFT on inorganic objects. He had to remind himself that physical bodies were still present in the frame, but they had been rendered virtually non-visible. That hump of sheet, for example, was made by one of his feet. For disorientation, he had been prepared.

Logic, he thought. Any of the other people out there, people like him, maybe trying to deconstruct FRAME/SHIFT *at this very moment,* would stop where he began, with the hoodoo of making clothing vanish. He had to press further, faster; to take it two levels beyond the *next* level, in order to be worthy of a revelation.

He kept clicking the button until his attention was arrested by what he saw onscreen—the stuff that was there *instead* of their physical bodies.

He thought, *hairs in the gate.* But this was not projected film.

He saw a kind of gossamer lace, hanging in mid-air, twisting and twining and recombining. Its hue was beyond the capacity of the camera or television to interpret correctly; it came out as black and green and a dirty silver. Threads, spiderwebs, smoke, maybe. Swirls like ink in water, a negativity

in the picture, similar to a matte hole into which a special effect was yet to be inserted. Nothing really there, except for the eyes. At least, the things that Dorian's shocked view classified as "eyes."

Two sets of them, approximately where their heads had been, which made the uppermost set Gelina's. Nasty, sawed-off pinpoints of solarization, so bright that they left video lag trails in pale yellow when they moved.

They were grotesque, yet mesmerizing, these undulating filaments of self, with the pupilless, sodium-colored eyes. Their psyches? Their souls? What they really boiled down to, deep inside? Dorian blinked and rubbed his eyes; people did this in movies, when confronted with the sight of something unbelievable. Nothing changed, because this was really happening.

The only difference, now, was that the eyes had shifted, both pairs, to look toward him. Toward Dorian, the watcher, the guy with the remote in his hand. They seemed to regard him specifically, as though they had caught him spying. Dorian's flesh prickled. No way he had *imagined* the wave of hatred that washed across him; the flood of disapproval emitting from his own TV set.

He wanted that feeling to go away. He clicked FRAME/SHIFT. The cobwebby things became dissipate; lighter brown. The eyes stayed the same. Their hatred of Dorian stayed the same, too.

He wondered if this might be some sort of karmic lesson. Payback, maybe, for having marginalized Gelina. In his memory of last night and this morning, he had not given her single line of dialogue. Even her name had been truncated, from Angelina. There was no plot, no plan. It had just happened that way. It was what people did.

Experiment concluded. He needed to bring this to a screeching halt, like right goddamn now. When he hit STOP, the remote illuminated its own key buttons. It was obviously suffering an interior meltdown. So he got up, to punch the onboard controls, and eject the tape manually. Turn the TV off, already.

When he put down the remote (as carefully as he would radioactive material), he noticed the musculature of his own hand, sinews aglisten.

As he stood up, he saw his own skeletal feet. *Click.* The previously-dead INT/ALT+ button was glowing a nervous green.

His trip to the TV set was stalled by the vision of his own lungs and liver, becoming transparent. *Click.* The INT/ALT+ button on the remote was still fluttering. It occurred to Dorian to press the dark SELECT EXIT button. Wasn't that what he needed to do? Choose to get out?

He dropped the remote when the flesh slid off his hand and piled up around his now-invisible feet. The nerve pain was astonishing.

Just as film theory had proposed, Dorian's TV screen really was a window to an exciting otherworld. And on the far side of that window, someone holding a remote had just figured out how to enable the *other* buttons, the more important ones. Not like Dorian, who had started with FRAME/SHIFT.

Whoever it was, they made sure Dorian never reached his TV.

—ooo—

FRAME/SHIFT™ Mode permits instant and comprehensive editorial access to alternate points of view within an already-established continuity. In plain speech, it can be a useful and entertaining tool for the personalization of any piece of recorded

material. Parents, for example, can modify or eliminate any perspective of objectionable character, leaving intact only the footage acceptable for family viewing. Foul language can be globally deleted, and the resultant "blank spots," tightened (or "looped") with less caustic alternatives (see DIALOGUE WIZARD™ Function, p. 52). Film students may employ FRAME/SHIFT to examine how the components of a program can be tonally attenuated by the enhancement or negation of items within a storyline. FRAME/SHIFT™ "makes your screen a window." It can be a fun and educational tool to broaden the experience of watching all media. It permits not only a wide menu of choice, but personal participation in what was formerly a "one-way" process. Now the viewer can become writer, editor, or director with the simple touch of a button. Remake your own version of a Hollywood hit! With FRAME SHIFT™, good taste can replace bad, and every story can have a happy ending.

For even more radical alterations of prerecorded material—or to eliminate it altogether—please see SELECT EXIT on page 52.

—from **Manual,** pp. 47-48.

—ooo—ooo—ooo—

THE FIVE SISTERS:
A FABLE

A man of artistic temperament was making his way home, as he did daily, from his rounds to pick up supplies and provisions. He used these walks to smell the air and sort his thoughts, and was abstracted enough not to notice the women with whom he shared the path until he was virtually upon them.

He had enough time, before they noticed him, to indulge in a few flights of fancy. They were acolytes of some obscure order, he thought, taking stock of their identical clothing. Or a group of solicitors in a uniform of hooded dresses— diaphanous, veil-like things—with footwear suited to long walking. The garb suggested funereal wear. Perhaps they were going to or coming from some service for a lost friend or family member. Each bore an inlaid staff. Maybe they were on a pilgrimage; maybe they were just watching birds. He gave them the path as he caught up and circumvented, with his quicker stride.

"Fair day," he said, by way of introduction. They stopped and took stock of him, each regarding him in an odd, analytical way, as though he were some forest creature of a variety yet uncatalogued. It was not hostile, but curious. Stressed by the need to fill the air, the man groped for trivialities. "That

is," he said, "it is cooling, but not yet cold, and I hope you have not far to travel before you may avail yourself of a hearth."

"Day to day, the needs of people are really quite simple," said the red-haired one. "A bit of food, a measure of warmth, a safe bed."

"Not so simple," countered the brown-haired one, "as to be plentiful, or readily available."

"Pessimist," said the golden-haired one to her companion. To the man she added, "Pay her no mind; she always thinks the worst."

"We always reap the worst," grumbled the one whose hair was a lush tumble of blazing white.

The man got the feeling they had rehearsed this conversation before, countless times. They had all stopped walking.

The remaining woman, who had not yet spoken, took the opportunity to kick off her shoes and sit, engaging the grass with her toes. When she dropped her hood to the light, her hair was revealed as a startling violet, which matched her eyes.

The man noticed that all five were identical, but for their hair. "Are you sisters?" he asked.

The red-haired one likewise doffed her hood and exposed her massy curls to the waning sunlight. "Yes," she said. "We are sisters. We walk to and fro in the world, on this path today, on another tomorrow."

The man tried to smile engagingly, and put down his parcels by the roadside as the brown-haired one located a smooth, clean stone on which to sit and stretch. "To what purpose are these travels, far and wide?" he said.

Then the violet-haired one spoke. "We collect all the evils of the world," she said, as though it was the simplest, most obvious statement.

"You bear no bindles or rucksacks," said the man. "Where is this evil you say you collect?"

"We collect it into ourselves," said the golden-haired one.

"Surely not," said the man.

The white-haired one enumerated each of her sisters. "That is Tragedy," she said of the golden-haired one. "The curly redheaded one is Violence. She of the brown tresses is Woe. The violet-haired one is Despair. And I am Loss."

The man chuckled despite his need to be polite. "And you collect the evils of the world into yourselves."

"All that we can find," said Woe. "All that we can bear."

"You mean to say that you remove these qualities from the world?" said the man. "You take away Loss, or Despair, or Violence, where you find it?"

"Yes." Several of them affirmed at once.

"Then, clearly, you are deranged," said the man. "There is no shortage of any of those qualities in the world. If you do what you say you do, the world is not a better place for it. You are like madwomen, wandering the desert, seeking a torturer to canonize."

"How would you know?" said Violence.

The man laughed again and looked around to see if he was being made the victim of some obscure joke, whether malefactors were hiding in the trees even now, snickering. "You take Violence from the world?" he said accusingly. "You are miserable at your task, then."

"Pray tell," said Despair. "Enlighten us, on how you come to judge us."

They were all looking at him now. He felt puffed-up and defensive.

"You eliminate Loss?" he said. "You neutralize Woe? Yet you could not keep my own father from dying of a wasting disease. He suffered. He did not die well. I tried to subsume that disaster in painting, and failed. I became nearly suicidal. Loss? My wife left me and my children became criminals. I

tried to express my grief in writing, and the muse forsook me. Again I courted dark thoughts of death. My garden withered and failed. My pets were killed by strangers for stupid reasons. My friends all betrayed me for selfish reasons. I think less of humankind today than ever before. The world is overrun with the petty, the stupid and the vain. There is no place for art, or grace, or wit. I have become obsolete in my own lifetime, and the only emotion I can feel regularly is dread for what is to come. If you are taking evil out of the world, you fallen disastrously short in your purpose, and I pity you."

The five sisters looked at each other as he spoke, their mood seemingly one of fatalistic agreement.

"All true, the things you say," said Violence. "But for the last. You have no idea of what we remove from the world."

"And neither do you," said the man, fired up now, turning to address Violence directly. "I was set upon by thieves, on this very path. They took what I had, and when what I had proved meager, they brutalized me, broke my bones, cut me with knives. One of the robbers was my own son."

"You carry the marks upon you," said Tragedy.

He turned his sights to her. "And where were you, when the village markets were swept by catastrophic fire, depriving everyone of food for weeks?"

"Death and disaster are part of the natural order," said Despair.

He took them in turn, berating Despair for his own despair at growing older and understanding less; upbraiding Loss for all the things he had lost and could never recover; chastizing Woe because more and more, his waking hours were consumed by bleakness and emptiness.

And when he had finished, he turned his back on them. "You are a gang of deluded witches who know nothing of real pain," he smirked. He walked away, outpacing them, spine straight and eyes set to the road ahead.

"And you," said Despair, "are exactly like everyone else we encounter, on every path, in every place."

He ignored them and continued on his way home. To think that this quintet had done anything to ease the troubles of the world was sheer fantasy, an opium dream of a perfect place that could only exist for the insane. Why, there was just too much evil in the world for them to even consider—

The man stopped walking, within sight of his house. By the time the sisters caught up to him on the path, they found him sitting hopelessly on a stump, weeping.

Normally, they would have drifted past without a word, but Woe, the one with the brown hair, strayed and stood. Gradually, as the others took notice of her, standing there and watching the man spill tears into the dust, they broke ranks and congregated nearby.

"Don't cry," said Woe, laying her hand alongside the man's face. Her fingers came away wet with grief.

"Please forgive me," the man said. "All of you. I did not understand. Linger long enough to know my gratitude for all that you do."

Violence, she of the fiery scarlet curls, stepped up. "But we are deluded, deranged, madwomen on the prowl."

"I forgot how violent the world is," said the man. "The magnitude of the tragedy in it. The weight of despair. The onus of loss. The erosion of woe. Without you five, extracting so much of these qualities from the state of existence, everyone in the world would be poorer. The violence done to me would have been so much more heinous, without red-haired Violence taking out her share of the burden. My tragedies and losses would have been so much greater, had not golden-haired Tragedy and alabaster-haired Loss already leached

away some of the pain. I would have killed myself out of despair and woe, were it not for violet-haired Despair and brown-haired Woe taking pity on me, and absorbing the brunt of that grief before it ever came to me. I realize that now. The world is a terrible place. But it would be so much more terrible without you five sisters, walking the earth and taking away so much of the terror before it ever besieges poor souls like me."

Loss tilted his chin up on a finger. "You are the first person to come back to us and say such things."

"Most leave in anger," said Tragedy.

"They don't take the time to know," said the man.

He shared out his food with them—meat, cheese, bread, fruit, some sweets, droughts of cool water and sips of wine. He stoked his hearth and they warmed themselves. Despair held his hand like a mother. Tragedy embraced him like a sibling. Loss kissed him full on the lips. Violence straddled and made love to him, and he fell asleep with his head on the breast of Woe.

"Stay with me," the man said, as they gathered their things the next morning. "Please don't go."

Despair just smiled at him. They all did, as they left. Each of them took a single hair, and conformed them into a braid for his wrist, as a remembrance. Then they departed, as they always had, to walk to and fro in the world, on this path today, on another tomorrow.

The man watched them go until they were out of sight. Then he closed his door and began to work.

—ooo—ooo—ooo—

PLOT TWIST

On the morning of the fifth day, Donny announced that he'd figured it all out. It wasn't the first time.

"Okay," he said. "Millions of years ago, these aliens come to Earth and find all this slowly evolving microspodia. Maybe they're, like, college students working on their thesis project. And they seed the planet with germs that eventually evolve into human society—our culture is literally a *culture*, right? Except that we're not what was intended. It was an impure formula or something. And they come back after millennia, which is like summer vacation to them, and they see their science experiment has spoiled in the dish. We're the *worst* thing that could have happened. We've blown their control baseline, their work is down the toilet, and they have to declare us a cull, flush the first experiment, and start over. But they take a look at us and decide, hey, maybe there's something here worth saving. Something they can use to, you know, rescue their asses from flunking. So they take this teeny sample, like one cell, and decide to test it to see if it does anything interesting. And that's why we're here."

Vira said, "That's above and beyond your previous bull-shit, and I think I've hit my patience ceiling."

Zach didn't say anything because he was staring forlorn-ly at their remaining food supply—one energy bar, destined for a three-way split, one tin of Vienna sausage (eight count), and a pint of bottled water that had already been hit hard.

"I'm waiting for *your* brilliant explanation," Donny said sourly. His real name was Demetrius, but he hated it. Vira's real name was Ellen, but she'd legally changed it. Zach was born "Kevyn;" same general deal.

"I'm out," said Vira, tired of the game. "Tapped. Done. I give up." She looked up at the reddening sunrise sky and shouted. "Hey! Hear me? I quit. Fuck you. If there's aliens up there toying with us, then they can kiss my anal squint!"

Donny startled, as though he actually thought outer space men might materialize to punish them. At least that would have brought some sort of closure.

"Don't yell," said Zach, nailing her, still playing leader. "That'll dry you up. Who got to the water while I was sleeping?"

Donny and Vira both denied it; the usual stalemate. Zach expected this, and let it slide because he already knew he'd stolen that bonus sip himself.

"Sun's coming up," said Donny unnecessarily. "The only constant seems to be this man-against-nature thing."

"You said that yesterday, too, sexist asshole," said Vira.

"Look around you," said Zach, pointing to each extreme of the compass. "Desert. Road. Desert. More road. More desert. And so on. Do you see, for example, a crashed plane that we could rebuild into a cleverly composited escape vehicle? No. A glint on the horizon that would indicate a breath of civilization? No way. A social dynamic among us, two men and one woman, that will lead to some sort of revelation that can save us? Uh-uh, negative." He pointed again. "Road. Desert. Let's get moving."

"Why?" said Vira, watching her little patch of shade dwindle.

"Because when we moved the first time, and didn't stay put, we found the food, didn't we?"

"That's the only reason?"

58

"We might find something else."

She colored with anger, or perhaps it was just the odd, vividly-tilted light of dawn. "So we can just keep going, keep doing this?"

"We last another day, we might figure something out."

"Like the 'why'?" Donny said. "As in why-us?"

"No, all I meant was we might get back to normal, and we certainly won't do that sitting on our butts and staying in one place waiting for the supplies to run out."

Vira snorted at the all-encompassing grandeur of the word "supplies", pertaining to their edibles, which did not even total to a snack.

"I want an answer," said Donny. "I want to know why."

"That's your biggest problem, Don-O." Zach extended his open hand to Vira, who rose tropistically, like a plant turning automatically to meet the light. "Come on, sweetie, let's go."

They turned their backs on the sun and began their march, in the same direction they'd been tracking since, well, forever.

—ooo—

Most of the fourth day had been wasted on equally stupid theories.

"I've got it," Donny said, which caused Vira to roll her eyes. It was becoming her comedic double-take reaction to anything Donny proposed. Donny was an endlessly hopeful idiot.

"Okay, like, we're characters in this movie, or a novel or something. And we can't figure out where we are or how we got here, and shit keeps happening, and we keep on keeping on, but our memories and characters keep altering when we're not looking. It's because we're fictional characters, right, except we don't know we are. And the movie studio guys keep asking for changes, or the editors at the publishing house keep saying, 'what's their arc?' or 'how do they grow

from their experience?' And we don't know because we were just *made up* by some writer, who has no idea we're cognizant and suffering."

"I wish there was a big, shiny-new toilet, right here in the middle of the scrub," said Vira.

"Why?" said Donny, tired of performing his body functions in the wild.

"Because I don't know what I'd do first," said Vira. "Drink some water from the tank, or jam your head into the bowl and flush."

"Children, children," said Zach. "Come on. We hit a spot of luck yesterday, didn't we? The food."

"Yeah," Donny chimed in. "Plot twist, see? Nobody'd ever expect that we'd just find food, when we needed it. In stories, everything has to be explained; everything has to pay off."

"Your definition of *food* and mine differ radically," said Vira. "I want a quart of goddamn seltzer, and then a bacon cheeseburger and a goddamn fucking chocolate malt, with a goddamn fucking cherry, and fuck you and your latest fucking lame-ass, bullshit story."

"Yeah, great, terrific," said Donny. "Thanks for your boundlessly vast contribution to the resolution of our predicament. You're not helping."

"I'm the chaos factor," said Vira. "I'm here precisely to fuck up all your neat little explanations."

"And I'm the third wheel," said Donny. "You guys will kill me first, because you've already got a, you know, relationship."

"Yeah, that'll get us far," said Zach, trying for drollery and failing. It was just too hot to screw around.

They kept their bearings on the sun and tried not to deviate from the straight line inscribed on the sand by their passage. Yesterday's footprints had blown away as soon as they were out of sight. The desert was harshly Saharan—dunes tessellated by wind, with vegetation so sporadic it appeared to be an afterthought, or really sub-par set dressing. They were amazed by the appearance of a paddle cactus, just one, and even more amazed when Zach demonstrated how it could provide drinkable moisture.

"Perfect example," Donny said. "How did you know that?"

"I don't know," said Zach. "I've always known it."

"Read it in a manual? See it on a nature documentary? Or maybe you came wired with that specific information for a reason."

"There is no reason," said Zach, trying to work up spit and failing at that, too. His throat was arid. His brain was frying. "I just knew it."

"It doesn't work," Donny said, shaking his head, sniffing at denial. "There's gotta be a reason."

"Reason for *what?!*" Vira apparently had plenty of spit left. "We had an accident! You are so full of shit."

"Maybe it wasn't an accident," said Donny. He was trying for an ominous tone, but neither Zach nor Vira cared to appreciate his dramatic sense.

—ooo—

By the middle of the third day, they were all sunburnt, peeling, and dehydrated. They resembled lost Foreign Legionnaires, dusted to a desert tan, with wildly white Lawrence of Arabia eyes, long sleeves and makeshift burnooses keeping the solar peril from most of their desperately thirsty flesh.

"If you mention God to me one more time, I'm going to knock a few of your teeth out, and you can drink your own blood," warned Zach.

"My only point is that this strongly resembles some sort of Biblical test," said Donny, chastened. "This kind of stuff

happens all the time in the Bible, the Koran, Taoist philoso-phy, native superstitions—they're all moral parables. Guys are always undergoing extreme physical hardship, and at the end there's a revelation. That's what a vision quest is."

"A vision quest is when you starve yourself until you see hallucinations," said Vira. "We've been there and done that. I don't feel particularly revelated."

"We haven't gone far enough, is all."

"Then explain why we haven't seen a smidge of traffic on this goddamn road since we started walking. We should have seen a thousand cars by now, all headed to and from Vegas. We should have passed a dozen convenience marts and gas stations with nice, air-conditioned restrooms. And all we've got since we lost sight of our own car, which was alone on the road, is hot, hot, more hot, and about a bazillion highway stripes, all cooking on this goddamn fucking roadway that leads to fucking nowhere!"

"Alternate dimension," said Donny.

Zach actually stopped walking to crank around and peer at Donny with disgust. *"What?"*

"Alternate dimension, co-existing simultaneously with our own reality. We got knocked out of sync. And now we're trapped in a place that's sort of like where we were—the world we came from—except there's nothing around, and nobody, and we've got to find a rift or convergence and wait for the planes to re-synchronize, and plop, we're back to normal."

"Do you want to strangle him, or should I?" said Vira.

"I liked the God explanation better," said Zach. He was joking, but no one appreciated it just now.

"Aren't we grownups?" said Vira. "Aren't we rational adults? Can we please leave all that goddamn God shit and the fucking Bible and all that outmoded tripe and corrupt thinking behind in the 20th Century, where it belongs? Shit,

it was useless and stupid a couple of whole centuries earlier than that—enslaving people, giving sheep a butcher to canonize. Giving morons false hope. Pie in the sky by and by when you die. It's such exhausted, wheezy, rote crap."

"Aren't we operating on false hope?" said Donny.

"No, Donny," said Zach. "We're operating on the tightrope between slim, pathetic hope and none at all. Free your mind. You're too strictured and trapped by your need to organize everything so it has a nice, neat ending—a little snap in the tail to make idiots go *woooo*. You want to know reasons, and there ain't no reasons, and you want to know something real? I'll tell you this one for free: Real freedom is the complete loss of hope."

"That's deep," said Donny, not getting it.

Vira shielded her eyes and tried to see into the future. "Forget cars and stop-marts," she said. "We haven't seen any animals. Desert animals lie low in the daytime, but we haven't seen any. Not a single bird. Not a vulture, even."

"It's not life, but it's a living," joked Zach.

"The sun is cooking me," said Vira. "Pretty soon we'll all be deep-fried to a golden-black." She shielded her eyes to indict the glowering sphere above, which was slow-cooking them like a laggard comet. The sky was cloudless.

"If it *is* the sun," said Donny.

Zach and Vira could not complain any more. They merely stopped, turned in unison, and sighed at Donny, who would not stop. Donny, naturally, took this as a cue to elaborate.

"I mean, this east-to-west trajectory could be just an assumption on our part. We could be walking north for all we really know. What if it's not the sun? What if it's just some errant fireball, messing with us?"

"Then we just spent another day walking in the wrong direction," said Zach.

"What if it's not a 'day'?" said Donny. He dug his wristwatch out of his pocket. He'd stowed it yesterday when the heat had begun to brand his wrist with convection. Now he noticed, for the first time, that his watch had stopped.

"Five thirty-five," he said. "Weird."

Zach and Vira turned slowly (conserving energy), did not speak (conserving moisture), and glowered at Donny with an expression Donny had come to class as The Look. When people gave you The Look, they were awaiting a punchline they were sure they would dislike.

"It's when the car shut down yesterday," he said. "I remember because I made a mental note of it."

"That's *it?*" said Vira. "No dumb theory about how we're all slip-slid into the spaces between ticks of the clock?"

"Donny, when was the last time you looked at your watch before yesterday? Isn't it possible that your crappy watch just doesn't work, and has been dead all this time, and you just thought it was 5:35 when you glanced at it yesterday?" Somehow, while Donny wasn't looking, Zach had become the leader of their little expedition.

"You guys aren't listening to me," Donny said, feeling somewhat whipped. "The watch shut down the same time the car did."

Vira was strapping on attitude, full-bore: "And that's got to *mean something,* right? Spare us."

What Donny spared them was the hurt reaction that had almost made it past his lips: *I thought you guys were my friends.* He just stared, blankly, as though channeling alien radio.

"Hey." Zach had found something. Topic closed.

A black nylon loop was sticking out of the sand off the right shoulder of the road. When Zach pulled, he freed a small backpack that looked identical to the one Vira was

already toting. They both waited, almost fatalistically, for Donny to make a point of this.

He held both hands palm-out in a placating gesture. "I'm not saying a word, if that makes you happy."

Inside the backpack they found two malt-flavored energy bars, two pint bottles of water, two tins of Vienna sausage, and two bags of salty chips, and everything was nearly too hot to touch.

"That's just plain scary," said Vira, examining the rucksack. "It *is* like mine."

"Oh, shit," said Donny. "Maybe we've done this already."

Vira caught herself short of showing Donny a little mercy. "Here we go," she said in a vast sigh, hotly expelling air she couldn't afford to lose.

"We're trapped inside of some kind of Möbius strip, endlessly repeating our previous actions. Has to be. Look at the backpack. It doesn't look like Vira's—it *is* Vira's. From the last time we were here. And we don't remember because whatever purpose is behind all this hasn't been achieved. Whatever happened, last time, we blew it. And if we blow it again, we'll find another backpack just like this one."

"Do you want a third of this or do you want to continue the lecture?" Zach had drawn his Swiss Army knife to divide one of the energy bars, but the protein goo was already so warm it practically poured apart.

"No, look at it." Donny was flushed with fear and anger now. "Two of everything. Only two. Why only two? Who's the odd guy out, here? Me. What the fuck happens to me?!"

"Shut up, Donny!" said Vira. "Look at the damned thing—it doesn't have my wallet, my I.D., my hairbrush, tampons, or any of the other stuff in *my* backpack. It's a fucking coincidence!"

"No. Something happens. Something changes. One of us gets gone."

"Donny, you're gonna pop a blood vessel, man." Zach cracked one of the tins and took a ginger sip of the water packing the mini-wieners.

"And I'm not hungry," Donny continued. "I see that stuff, food, and I should be starving, but I'm not. We walked all day yesterday and all today and we should be ready to hog a whole buffet...but all I feel is that *edge* of hunger, of thirst. Just enough to keep me crazy."

"I wholeheartedly agree about the 'crazy' part," said Vira.

"Eat anyway," said Zach. "Save your energy for your next explanation of what the hell has happened to us."

"Yeah, we'll be laughing about this tomorrow," said Vira, methodically swallowing capfuls from the sports bottle of water, knowing enough not to chug, not to waste, to take it extraordinarily slow and easy.

"Anybody care for an alternate point of view?" said Zach, relishing the salt in the chips even though they made him thirsty. "The backpack is a marker. Someone else has made this trip. And they left this stuff behind because they got out, got rescued, or didn't need it anymore."

"Yeah, maybe because they died." Donny was still sour, and not meeting their eyes. Privately he thought Zach's proposal was too upbeat to be real, and was full of holes besides. Maybe he was just playing optimist to cheer Vira up. In a book or a TV show or a movie, it just would not track because it begged too much backstory.

"If somebody just dropped this and died, we'd've seen a body," said Vira. She was always on Zach's side.

"Not if the sand blew over it," said Donny.

"Jesus fuck, there's just no winning with you," she said. "You just *have* to be right all the time."

That caused more long minutes to elapse in silence as they picked through their paltry booty. Donny looked out,

away…anywhere but at his two increasingly annoying friends. Vira and Zach huddled, murmuring things he could not overhear, and neither of them acknowledged his presence until he jerked them back to the real world.

"Look at that," he said.

"What?" Zach rose to squint downroad.

Donny pointed. "I think I see something. That way."

"Then it's time to burn a little energy, I guess. We get lucky, we can leave the backpack in the sand for the next sucker. Sweetie?"

Vira dusted her jeans and stood up. "Yeah. Ten-hut, let's march." She tried to think of a sarcasm about the Yellow Brick Road and Dorothy, or the Wild Bunch, minus one, but it was just too goddamned hot.

Donny led them, appearing to scent-track. Normally he liked to walk two paces behind Zach and Vira, because he enjoyed watching Vira's ass move. Perhaps if he walked with his partners to the rear, they would just disappear at some point. Plucked away. It could happen. It happened in stories, in movies.

They walked toward it, but it turned out to be nothing.

—ooo—

They had wasted most of the second day waiting around the car under the arc of the sun. Waiting for rescue. Waiting for answers, for trespassers, for anything outside themselves. That was when Donny had begun ticking off his handy theories.

"Okay, we're all drunk," he said, knowing they weren't. "We're stoned. This is really a dream. See the car? We actually crashed it and we're all dead, and this is Hell or something. Purgatory. Limbo."

"I love that concept," said Zach. "Hell-or-something."

"Water jug's empty," said Vira. They'd stashed a gallon container in the back seat prior to departing on their road trip.

One day of busy hydration had killed it. Her careful makeup had smudged, melted, run down her face, and evaporated.

Zach tied a T-shirt around his head to save his scalp from getting fried. "We just sit tight and try not to perspire," he joked. "Someone'll come along. *We* came along."

"Las Vegas used to be the greatest psychological temptation in the country," said Donny. "Going there to gamble was an act of will, requiring a pilgrim to penetrate a sterile cordon of desert. You can't go to Vegas accidentally; you have to make the decision and then travel across a wasteland to get there. It's not like you're at a mall and think, *oh, I'll do a little gambling while I'm here, too.* And once you do the forced march, you're there and there's only one thing to do, really—what you came for. That's more strategically subtle than most ordinary people can handle. Nobody thinks about that."

"And your point," said Vira, "is...what?"

"Just that it's interesting, don't you think?"

"I think it's fucking *hot* and I wish I wasn't here." She fanned herself and Donny won an unexpected flash of sweat-beaded nipple, perfect as a liquor ad.

"We can't drink the water out of the radiator," said Zach, returning from beneath the hood and wiping oil from his hands.

"Why are you even thinking like that?" said Vira. "We're not stranded. We're on a main highway, even if it is in the middle of buttfuck-nowhere. Some hillbilly in a pickup truck will come along. What about all the other people driving to Vegas? We didn't just wander off the map, or get lost on some country switchback. We're not going to have to wait here long enough to think about drinking the water from the radiator, or eating the goddamn car."

"Guy did that in New Hampshire," said Donny. "Cut a Chevy up into little cubes and ate it. Ingested it, passed it. Guy ate a car."

"*Shut up,* Donny!" Vira had been making a point, and resented derailment at the mercy of Donny's internal almanac. Donny was chockfull of trivia like this. He thought he was urbane. He was passably-interesting at parties and good for scut errands since he always volunteered. Now Vira guessed that Donny's canine openness and availability was just a cruel trick, a dodge intended to keep him around people who could at least pretend to be interested in all the useless shit that spilled from his mouth.

Ever the mediator, Zach tried to defuse her. "What are you getting at, Vira?"

"You guys talk as if we just drove off the edge of the Earth or something. The car just stopped, period. We're not going to have to dig a goddamn well to find drinking water because the car just stopped, and it just-stopped a couple of hours ago, and other people will come along, and we'll be inconvenienced and probably have to rent another car, or stay overnight in some shithole like Barstow, but it's an inconvenience, and Donny is running his face-hole like we've been abducted to another planet."

"I'm not saying anything," said Donny. "But have you seen any more cars, for, what, five-six hours we've been here?"

"Children, children," said Zach. "Stop fighting or I'll turn this car right around." That made Vira laugh. If only. Then Zach ambled toward the sprawl of flat-paddle cactus they'd pressed into service as a restroom privacy shield.

"Maybe you should piss in the empty water jug," said Donny. "We might have to boil our own urine and drink it."

"I'd rather die," said Vira. "Hey, there's an idea—we can kill you and eat you for the moisture in your body, if you don't shut up."

When Zach had buttoned up and returned, he had resumed his air of command and decision. "So I guess it's down to this: Do we stay, or do we start walking?"

"Stay," said Vira. "At least we've got the car for shade. Who knows how cold it gets at night? This is the desert, after all, and we didn't bring a lot of blankets."

"We march," said Donny. "Vegas could be just over the next rise and we've been sitting here all day like the victims of some cosmic joke."

"Sun's going down," said Zach. "I'm inclined to spend the night walking. We've got two flashlights, matches, a melted candy bar and half a bottle of flat soda I found under the passenger seat. We take extra clothes to cover our skin in case we get stuck another day. And we stay on the road, in case somebody comes along—that'll do us as much good as sticking by the car, hoping someone spots it."

"It also wears us out faster," said Vira. "I'm not built for this nature shit. *Nature* is what you go through to get from the limo to the hotel lobby."

"Come on, Vira," Donny said. "Where's your sense of adventure?"

"The only adventure I want to have right now is in a jacuzzi, with room service."

"Ahh," said Donny. "Cable porn and pizza and cold, cold beer."

"Three A.M. blackjack action and free cocktails," said Zach. "Hot showers and cool sheets. Jesus, I have to stop; I'm getting a hard-on."

"Yeah, Donny, you start walking and Zach and I will stay here and try to conserve moisture." Vira smiled wickedly. At least they were bantering now, grabbing back toward something normal. But she collected her backpack from the seat, as though resigned to a hike, hoping it would turn out to be brief but worthwhile.

They walked away the hours absorbed by dusk, until the sun was gone. The road stayed flat and straight except for regular hummocks that kept the distance maddeningly out of view, diffused in heat shimmer. At the crest of each rise waited another long stretch of road, and another rise in the distance.

"Human walking speed is four to six miles per hour at a brisk and steady pace," said Donny. His voice tended to lapse into a statistical drone. "Figure half that, the way we're clumping along."

"Conserving moisture," Vira reminded him.

"The arc of the sun says we've been doing this for about four hours. That would put us between twelve and fifteen miles from the car. And I still don't see anything."

"That's because it's dark," said Zach. He knew what Donny was intimating. At night you could see the glow of Vegas against the sky from a hundred miles out. There was no glow.

"Yeah, and if it's dark for eight hours, say, and the sun comes up over *there*, we've got another twenty-odd miles."

"I am *not* walking twenty miles," said Vira. "I've got to sit down and cool off."

"Good idea," said Zach. "When it gets cold, we can walk to stay warm."

Vira flumped heavily down in the sand, trying to kink out her legs. "You guys notice something else?"

They both looked at her, wrestling off her athletic shoes.

"All the time we've been walking and walking? Since we started there hasn't been a single highway sign."

—ooo—

The trip had been Vira's idea, another of her just-jump-in-the-car-and-go notions. Spontaneity permitted her the pretense of no encumbrances or responsibilities, which in turn allowed her the fantasy that she was still under thirty, still abrim with potential with no room for regret.

Zach grumpily acceded, mostly because he liked to gamble. A two-day pass to Vegas would allow him to flush his

brain and sort out his life, which was in danger of becoming stale from too much easy despair, the snake of self-deconstruction gobbling its own tail.

Taking off on an adventure gave them the illusion of control over their lives. They weren't dead yet, nor off the map. Most of their friends, however, begged off with the usual smorgasbord of excuses—jobs, babies, commitments, obligations, all couched in placating language that broadcast its intention not to offend. It was a good method of sifting one's so-called allies: Hit them with a wild-card proposition and see who bites.

"What about Donny?" said Vira.

"He'll be farting around his apartment, waiting for his phone to ring," said Zach. "He can spell the driving, and you know he'll volunteer half the gas, just to get out and see different scenery."

"Remind me why he's our friend?" Vira was nude, mistrusting her vanity mirror, working search-and-destroy on perceived flaws. No tan lines. They had a variety of acquaintances, each good for one isolated conversational topic, to be accessed as needed. Donny's status held at mid-list.

Zach shook his head, feeling superior to the shortcomings of his friends. None of *them* were about to get laid right now. "Because we both know that Donny doesn't really have anybody else. He's our holiday orphan, our warm body. Spear carrier. Cannon fodder. Come on, he's not so bad. We get stranded in the desert, we can stand back-to-back and defend your honor."

She had turned side-saddle in the chair before the vanity, and gathered his tumescing cock into her grasp to speak to it. "Are you suggesting the Sandwich of Love? Hm? One below and one above? You're the buns and I'm the meat?"

"No," he said between clenched teeth, sucking a breath, coming up rock-hard.

"Good." She stroked the beast in her hand. "Donny's not my type, anyway."

He showed up so fast that Zach and Vira barely had time to jump out of the shower, the aura of sex still clinging to them. Vira just made it into abbreviated cutoffs and a knotted top while Zach struggled wet legs into unyielding jeans. Vira felt Donny's eyes take inventory, up-down, from her still-damp cascade of black hair, the full length of both slender legs, to her big feet. Her breasts were nicely scooped, with hard nubs declaring themselves too prominently as they blotted through the sheer material of her top. She caught Donny cutting his gaze away when she looked up. Not her type.

Donny was well-groomed but brittle, as though his look had been not so much preserved as shellacked. He had always lived moment-to-moment, hand to mouth, check to check; not so charming, when one began to add on years without progress. He had duly logged his time as a depressed philosopher, overstaying college, scooping up handy opportunities, staying slightly out of step but thereby remaining available for any lark or diversion.

Zach emerged from the bedroom, towelling his hair and pretending like he hadn't just had sex. He was at least ten years older than Vira; what the hell was *that* about, wondered Donny. What really worried him was that he might be no further along than Zach, given another decade. A better apartment, a cleaner car, steady sex, and…what else? Zach had two degrees and worked for an airline company doing god knew what. He had Vira. He seemed to understand how the world worked, as though he could perceive things just out of reach by Donny's sensory apparatus. But was that progress? Donny always teased himself with the possibilities, should he finally catch up to his

paternal pal; pass him, maybe. All Donny needed was the right opportunity. He had spent his entire life training to be ready when it knocked.

Their friendship was convenient, if nothing else.

"Okay, now we're far enough gone that you have to catch me up on the important stuff," bellowed Zach from the pilot bucket of his muscle car. Air, industrial-dryer hot, blasted through the open cabin and tried to sterilize them. "No chitchat. The good stuff. Like, are you seeing anybody?"

"Nope." Donny tried to make it sound offhand, like *not today,* but it came out like *not ever, and you know it.*

Vira craned around, one arm over the seat, mischief in her eyes. "Don't even *try* to convince me that nobody's looking."

"I'm just not in a big hurry, that's all," Donny said from the back seat.

He watched the knowing glance flicker between his two amigos. Zach had laid out the argument many times before, convinced that Donny set girlfriend standards so high that any candidate was already sabotaged. Donny would counter that his last serious relationship had wrecked him. Then Vira would swoop in a flanking maneuver, accusing him of inventing the former mystery girlfriend (whom Zach and Vira had neither seen nor met) in order to simplify his existence by virtue of a romantic catastrophe. Donny's perfect love was so perfect she could not be real, Vira would say. Or: so perfect that she would never have had anything to do with him in the first place. It was nothing aberrant; lots of people lived their lives exactly this way.

Zach and Vira would claim they just wanted to see their friend happy. Happier.

Donny deflected the whole topic, thinking himself humble and respectful, a gentleman. In his mind, he dared them to feel sorry for him.

They chugged super-caffeinated soda and ate up miles and listened to music. They were alone on the road when Zach smelled the gaskets burning.

None of them knew how much they would miss the car, how much they would long for it, days later.

—ooo—

"We have to do something unpredictable," said Donny.

"Is this another theory?" Vira was in no mood.

The day was shading into night. They had been walking at least a week, by rough estimate and a sunrise-sunset count.

"If we were supposed to just keeping doing this, ad infinitum, then we would have tripped over some more food," said Donny. "What has to happen now is we need to shake up the system. Do something deterministic. Declare ourselves in a way that has nothing to do with patterns."

"Well, I declare I'm gonna collapse here and try to sleep," said Zach, sitting down heavily in the sand.

"You've just contradicted every other argument you've made," said Vira, more weary than surprised.

"No, Vira," said Zach. "I can see it. No explanation works. Therefore, logic isn't a way out. It's the kind of answer you get to by working through all the other answers. Right, Donny?"

He shrugged. "Except I can't suggest what to try."

"We could walk back to the car," said Vira. They glared at her. "Joke," she said, putting up her hands, surrendering. She shielded her eyes and plopped backward onto the sand as though her spine had been extracted.

Zach encamped nearby—not cuddle-close, but near enough to look possessive—like an infantryman who has learned how to drop and sleep in full gear. Soon he was snoring softly, the sound obscured by the light wind that always seemed to kick up at sunset. Just enough to stir the sand into

a genuine annoyance. Zach rolled over, cushioning his forehead on his arms, forming a little box of deeper darkness. Burying his head in the sand, thought Donny, who remained irritated that his friends had accepted the routine of their bizarre situation so readily, and without question.

Donny pulled off his boots, one-two. There was nothing else to look at except the skyline, the sand, an occasional weed, and the two sleepers. He was not tired. His heart was racing.

He weighed one boot in his hand. It was scuffed and dusty, and radiated stored heat like fresh bread from an oven. One-two.

One: Holding the toe of the boot, Donny clocked Zach smartly in his occipital ditch, right where the backbone met the brain stem. Zach went limp and Vira did not stir. They were exhausted; fled to another place, chasing dreams. Donny sat on Zach's head, mashing it down into the sand until Zach stopped breathing.

Now Donny felt the surge. He had it all—correctitude, the energizing thud of his heart, dilated pupils, an erection, and the exhilarative adrenaline spike of knowing he was on the right track. He was *doing* something, taking declarative action.

After all, what were friends for?

Two: There were no fist-sized rocks or round stones, so Donny used his other boot to hit Vira in the back of the head, so he would not have to look at fresh blood while he raped her. By the second time, she was bloody anyway. She might have orgasmed once, through sheer autonomic reflex. Donny pinched her nose shut and clamped her mouth until she, too, stopped breathing. As she cooled, he did her once more. It really had been a while since he'd gotten laid. He woke up still on top of her, neck cricked from the odd position in which he'd dozed. His weight had pushed her partially into the sand, half-interring her, but she was in no position

to complain, or criticize, or judge him any more. Or feel sorry for him.

Their water bottle was down to condensation. Night was better for walking in a desert. And Donny had taken action.

He left his companions behind and soldiered onward, alone, until his bootheels wore away to nothing. If he ever found civilization, he'd feel sorry later.

—ooo ooo ooo—

Size Nothing

Megan used her own key to enter the condo she and Conrad had shared for the past three years.

She adjusted her suit—needlessly—in a little wiggle-to-fit motion she never tired of seeing in the mirror. Self-reflection, for Megan, usually meant running the Checklist, and she remained unabashedly proud of the way she had invested her recent bonus, a byproduct of an overdue (to her mind) promotion. She possessed mile-high legs (in Gerbe thigh-hugging stay-ups of 100% sheer silk) and pampered feet (in Blahnik ankle-strap stilettos); the outfit was a typically cunning Ferragamo slut-cut, emphasizing her neckline (the bra was a celadon plunge demi by Chantelle) and a thoroughbred rise of throat and nape.

All the way from toes (tasteful mocha gloss) to hair (natural ash-blonde in a page-boy cut of deadly efficiency), she deemed herself impressive enough to steal Conrad's breath today. Even better, not a mote of her was artificial. No tucks or laser tightening, no silicone, no botox, no wrinkle-frying, no ab or calf implants of gel or plastic. Urban trend wackos had been known to glop on anti-aging cream made of baby foreskins, the cells cultivated like bacteria in a petri dish. Some people would smear anything on their faces…for a hundred and twenty-five bucks a dose.

Conrad was running late thanks to Homicide. He was working a serial whose quirk was to index victims based on a specific tattoo design—a certain dermagraphic done by a certain artist during a certain timeframe—which looked like a combination of a Chinese ideogram and a flying bird. It had become popular in the way high-end labels bought importance or conferred status; other tattoo shops sometimes bootlegged it for persistent customers. It was the sort of adornment teen trend-mongers usually acquired before graduation, in a lemming-like assault on needle boutiques, most often imprinted on the small of the back or the nape of the neck. The perpetrator currently eluding Conrad's citywide search-and-bag had started collecting originals with a scalpel; more often than not, the victims died as part of the acquisition. The playbook was the work log of the original artist. Conrad had a copy of it, and he and his crew were running all possible variants.

Megan had once borne that exact design, a Marion Kurten original, but she'd had it removed before all the media fuss. Marion Kurten (who, like John Wayne, had been male despite his name) had died seven years ago. Hence, his originals had become collector's items...which had attracted the notice of a very dangerous collector, or so they said with much manufactured earnestness, at six and eleven.

Her skin was flawless, now. Devoid of badly deployed ink; bereft of piercings acquired in the white heat of adolescence or the rebellious stupidity of impulse. Even her eyes were clear of the mileage of the past. A trim Size Zero with catalogue model poise, high-breasted yet not overripe, a gaze that could melt the psyche of either sex to slag. She admired herself in the mirror a bit before throwing on some casual little nothings intended to help Conrad's glands stand to attention.

She did not quite anticipate the expression on Conrad's face, when he came through the door, late, with inarguably perfect excuses. He was his job.

His face contracted, from open and friendly to guarded and suspicious, in less time than it took her to stand up to greet him. His hand went out to distance them, open-palmed, a cautionary move calling time out. He spoke like a cop, not her lover.

"Whoa—wait—who are—are you a friend of Megan's?" He looked around for a third party he could recognize.

"Very droll, Connie," she said. "It's me. Look close."

He shook his head. "You don't know Megan? Than it's time for you to tell me who you are and what you're doing here."

"Connie, relax."

He called Megan's name and checked open doorways, all business, as though playing to an invisible camera. "How did you get in here? This is a security building."

"I used my key. Our key."

"Where did you get a key?" He wasn't kidding. He wasn't wearing the kidding face.

She huffed out a sigh. It was that way; so be it. "You gave it to me April 29th, two years ago, same day we had a late dinner after you got off work, and we were in an Italian restaurant, and when you leaned over to pick up your napkin, your gun fell out of the holster and hit the floor and scared the shit out of everybody, except Enrico the manager, who knew you were a cop. Good enough?"

"There's no way you can know that. Did Megan tell you that whole story?"

"I am Megan, you dolt! I am her; she is me—can't you tell from the way I'm about to start yelling?" She hoped she appeared suitably put-upon, but she was still more tickled than angry. This was kinda fun.

"Oh, pardon me," said Conrad, indicating her with a sweep of his hand, up-down, to indicate the evidence before him. "It must be the light." He stood and scrutinized her, using up heartbeats, mostly to level his breathing. "Nope. It's

not the light. It's you. You are apparently a crazy person. Trespassing."

"Don't get mad. I just changed a few things."

"Look, I hate to sound like a TV show, but I'm a police—"

"You want to search me?" she cut in, brightly, feeling herself up as preamble.

"Stop it. Look at me and pay attention." He was actually—unbelievably, incredibly—flashing his shield. "I am a detective. I am a real, live, very tired detective. And you are an intruder in my house. And nothing you're saying is making a whit of sense, and I need a few answers."

"God, you are talking like a TV show."

"And you're talking detainment, if this keeps up." He opened his jacket, left-right. "See? Gun. Cuffs. Little card with Miranda rights. Am I smiling?"

"The tattoo collector guy is getting you down, huh, babe?"

Megan always called him babe when she was trying for sympathy. For the mystery woman to use the same tone, identical voice, was just unnerving. Conrad felt like a man trying to fight off a soporific drug. "How do you know about—?" He stopped himself. "Never mind."

"It's me," she said. "Me, me, me. Let me just tell you about—"

He overrode her. "No. Not interested. Can you please just get out of here? I'll trust you didn't steal anything." He looked around anyway, spot-checking the contents of his abode.

She seemed to chew this notion for a bit, then shot him a coy, sidelong hypno-gaze. "Why, look—I seem to have forgotten my underwear."

"Stop it."

"Tell me these are just perfect." She shrugged easily, spaghetti straps dropping, and modeled her breasts for him, her smooth, gracile hands gliding around, perfect nails leaving tiny blush wakes. "Totally real, not fake, warm and alive. Touch me."

"I don't know what's going on, but—"

"Come on, Connie. You work too hard, and I'm wet. See? Let's discuss this like madly rutting animals."

"No. This is a trick. A setup. Megan always rags me about looking at other women, and now she's set up some kind of stupid test." It was their oldest argument: Did commitment preclude looking, appreciation, so long as it was not fancy? Were people supposed to pretend to deny their wiring? Would that not be a greater lie?

"I do not 'rag' you," she said, firing off one of her executive expressions of disapproval—slightly pursed lips; mildly creased brow, eyes slitted with glee. "I'm kidding when I say that, most of the time. Jesus Christ, lighten up."

Conrad still was not sure whether he was angry or scared. "Stop talking like you're her, because you're not, and I'm not going for this. You lighten up, lady."

She was smiling too broadly, enjoying his confusion. "I'm not me, right? I'm not Megan? So now I get to run trivia to prove it? Okay: the last time we had sex was two and a half weeks ago. You were crisping around the edges from your investigation. I made you shower and shave and then I practically had to rape you, but once you got going, it was a gold medal event. You fell halfway off the bed as though you'd just been exorcised, then you said 'that's better,' and we both nearly choked from laughing. You did the little boy voice. I did the pig noise. We played submarine in the bubble bath. Dive, dive!"

Conrad averted his eyes, fighting an incipient blush, paranoid about what ripe chat Megan might have confided to this stranger.

She shook her head. "Same deal, honey. Look at you. You're all freaked out and you need to get laid. No lay-er and no lay-ee; I prefer to think of it as a collaboration. Two weeks plus; hell, I *need* to get laid. Come on, babe, test drive this

chassis at no obligation! Pleeeease—I'll give you a lolly." She stepped toward him, out of the sheer wrap, which fell away in a diaphanous spiral.

He took a compensating step backward, and despite his denial, looked up to meet her steady, amused gaze. It was Megan talking, all right, but it wasn't Megan walking, and it wasn't a remote-controlled robot. Megan was a brunette, five-seven, feline cheekbones, tented upper lip, chin dimple, heavy but dramatic brows, 32-D cup size, prominent thick nipples, small hands and wide dancer feet, tiny snubbed toes, a scatter of pigment on her left shoulder, navel piercing...in a blacked-out room, he could find her by touch. Megan's eyes were the color of strong coffee (with a slight Asian cast), and as Conrad looked into the eyes of the woman before him, the slow awe of his realization dropped his jaw and hit him like a delayed attack of shellshock.

"You went to the Rejuvenation Center, didn't you?" His mind could not help but run deduction chains, and he sat down awkwardly on the arm of the sofa, as though pushed. "You bought it with your bonus."

"You're not going to ask me where my navel ring went?" she said, having expected a quiz. "You're pulling such long hours on this murder case thing, and the opportunity pre- sented itself. It's my body, after all."

She was daring him to resume their second-oldest argu- ment—the one about what rights come with a relationship. Who orders who. When the line is crossed. How personal privacy becomes poisonous intrigue. Where the boundaries are. What the fuck it all means when you try to add two peo- ple together, instead of subtracting one from the other.

"Why didn't you tell me?" he said. "Before, I mean."

"I don't have to tell you everything. If I did, nothing would ever be a surprise."

It was her; he knew it was her; he knew she had not told him because he hated the damned Rejuvenation Center—a flesh-processing fast foodery rapidly burgeoning into a nationwide franchise of in-and-out clinics that all represented another big migraine for law enforcement. People like the Tattoo Collector could remain elusive, particularly if they could slip into a whole new skin as easily as donning a glove. This was all strictly regulated, of course, in regard to fingerprints, retinal scans, and identity (after all, tax collectors were the first to demand assurances), but the popularity of the procedures involved had instantly boomed far beyond the ability of legislation to watchdog and supervise. Gray areas were inevitable, and a lot of people had advantaged good timing to slip through the cracks provided.

Basically, the Rejuvenation Center carved away what you did not like, and used the tissue as raw material to construct better bodies on a cellular level, after a lot of screening and cultivation and skin-farming. Big bones were whittled down. Your own body image problems, therefore, became some future client's salvation. Redundant organs, such as lungs or kidneys, were "centered"—reduced to one and stuck in the middle—in order to promote thinner, more efficient bodies. Fat was redistributed; excess fat was sterilized, processed, and recycled. Conrad had read that speed healing had reduced recovery and adaptation to the equivalent of a visit to a tanning salon.

In sum, it was no more grotesque a proposition than toupees or breast augmentation had been, way back when. It was something everybody talked about, but only "other people" took the plunge. Vain people. Insecure people.

Conrad knew it was Megan talking, yet it was not Megan, not anymore.

She fired off the mommy tone, another weapon in her arsenal. "You don't like my surprise and it's made you all nervous. I understand, babe. But I love my new body and now I

want you to love it, too." She touched him for the first time, and he recoiled; almost a flinch.

"Prove it," he said.

He was drawing a line and daring her to cross it, knowing that Megan never backed down from a challenge. There was proof—and then there was proof according to pragmatic, rational, logical Detective Conrad.

"Connie, you once said you'd know it was me in a dark room…so let's kill the lights."

"How would I know, now?" he said. "How could I know?" All the rules had morphed while he was not looking.

She humphed. "Cop first, everything else second." She squared off in a manner almost threatening. "Okay, then— unzip me."

"What?"

"Unzip me." She gathered up her hair and turned her back.

At the base of her skull was a tiny nylon zipper, matched to the skin hue, seamed so as not to bulge. Conrad stared at it in dread.

"Oh, for god's sake, Connie, just get me started."

He touched the tiny ring tab. It looked like jewelry. It had body heat. He pulled it slowly down until she could reach it. It did not make a zipper sound. A dark hole silently smiled between her Atlas and Axis vertebrae.

Megan unzipped, and husked her glorious new face. It came free…perfectly. "Only for you," she said. "You know how I hate showing you things that will upset you."

Her head—well, the bugeyed glob of meat on top of her neck—glistened, the bare essentials of a skull sweating crimson dew. Her bonework had been planed and trued inward, her organs downsized, her musculature selectively pared away to cuticle thickness, all to provide a custom fit. Usually, revised body measurements required the careful excision of most of the skin. What remained of the subdermal fat layer (sculpted for contour and softness) was visible. From the neck down, her new body clung with surgical glove rigor; above, the vacated masque of her new face hung toward her chest like a deflated rubber balloon, eye slits empty, the mouth a slashed hole. When she moved, the slack face seemed to assume imbecilic expressions, swimming loosely to and fro, almost as though it wanted to provide sinister clown commentary to counterpoint Conrad's shock, suggesting brain damage, retardation, mockery.

"Air hurts, Connie." she said. "It's more comfortable inside. They warned me about exposure to the air. But I'll do it to prove myself. I'll do it because I love you and don't want you to be upset."

Conrad had seem too many skinned victims, lately, to interpret her revelation as a turn-on. He backed away another step, his left hand seeking his gun almost instinctively. "You're not Megan," he said, his voice scared and small.

Now the whole scenario was beginning to annoy her. She would have to chase him, assert herself, assume control. "I am Megan," she said. "Now, do you want to kiss the new me, or suck face with the inner me? Pick one." All she had to do was dog him into a corner, no escape, and lay a kiss on him, and he would see, and that would be that.

She came for him and his revulsion was palpable, separating them. When she leaned in, he caught her naked throat in his hands—what was left of her original throat, her shucked neck piling up in folds on her slim shoulders. He squeezed and whatever she had to say next withered in a croaking gargle. His grasp slithered among oily ropes of tendon and a slick sheen of blood that stank like hot iron. He clamped tighter. The esophageal muscles, still weak from stripping, gave way to his thumbs, which oozed between the macramé tangle of ligament and vascular

hosing. The delicate airway was a work of precision craft, with no remaining armor that might add girth. It collapsed instantly.

It was the embrace Megan had sought, sort of. Murder, like love, was possessed of its own kind of intimacy. Red from the collarbones up, she sagged in Conrad's grasp.

Then Conrad slumped, away from her, sitting down hard on the floor as though punched, his back against the sofa, his hands clotted. Then he saw the wine glasses she'd prepared for them, the candles, the prep for a romantic evening. He stared at her unmoving form for an unmeasurable time. What to do now?

It took him another hour to think of the scalpel in his briefcase.

It had been forgotten—or left as a taunting clue—by the Tattoo Collector amid the crime-scene bloodsplatter that had been Victim #7. Conrad carefully considered his next few actions, so that one moment of emotional haste might not eliminate the rest of the moments of his life. His new life, after tonight.

The worst part was re-sheathing her (perfect) face and closing the zipper. He had to reposition her eyes and mouth; her opaque stare accused him of being no good at cosmetology. Artifice required a fine touch, and Conrad had been dealing with murderers.

After carefully cutting a tattoo-sized patch of Megan's new flesh from her back and consigning it to the disposal, Conrad caught sight of his own gaze, reflected in the kitchen window. People could change almost anything about themselves, these days. He stared into his own eyes and tried, unsuccessfully, to read his future.

—ooo—ooo—ooo—

THE THING TOO HIDEOUS TO DESCRIBE

lapped a pseudopod across the snooze button on Its alarm clock. It liked to be half-awake when midnight actually clicked over, so Its alarm was habitually set to 11:59 P.M. The blue glow of the numerals pleased It, reminded It of some of the biogenous hues It could produce in Its tentacled extremities when satisfied or amused, so It had appropriated the device during some pre-dawn wander or other, from one of the townies who had been imbued in sufficient fear to abandon her bedroom in the middle of the night.

Its carapace was running red—glowing softly, from worry, taken to bed and slept on. It was not as young as It used to be (what on Earth *was?*); slithering to the sink was becoming a chore. It tried not to make the grunts and huffs the elderly use to punctuate every movement. It yawned wide instead, freeing a few flying insects who had invested sleeptime (Its own, not theirs) in the determined consumption of tartar flecks from Its back molars. The little monsters never drowned, they never suffocated, they were a nuisance, they were pestilent, riddled with germs, yet perfectly suited to their scavenging purpose.

Salve, for the burns. The Thing applied an herbal poultice to the gelid patches of still-healing flesh, repellently smooth and tender to the touch, like a bubo swollen with dead antibodies. Fire had purged detail from Its cratered brown exodermis, the way a child might use an eraser to obliterate portions of a photograph of the Moon's natural topography. It had lost a sucker from the tip of one of Its retractile protrusions. The wounds would scab thickly, then re-armor. They always did. Last night's close call had been nothing new.

Outside, the tarn beckoned. The Thing always felt better after a wake-up rinse and a bit of a roil in the sludge. It furled its feelers for the downhill roll, eyestalks whipping around and causing a rollercoaster sort of dizziness. It flattened Itself to a glistening membrane on the surface of the brackish water, soaking up some lunar rays, and letting the tidal influences provide inspiration. When It rolled out, nearly all the water sluiced free. Its skin was not absorbent.

It was time to go find some teenagers.

—ooo—

Maysville was one of those antique, rural Kentucky bergs that rolled up the sidewalks promptly at dusk, and whose church steeple still constituted its highest structural elevation. The bell tower therein had been tolling the hour, and half hour, for more than fifty years without breakdown or incident. The church itself—alabaster, roofed in green shingles—glowered over the town square, where rustic benches and litter baskets were emplaced with the precision of chess pieces. The manicured, triangular greensward it faced was a sort of local picnic spot for those unimaginative enough to venture into the woods. It was near the business district at the intersection of Main and Center Streets, where local merchants closed shop promptly at five in the afternoon.

At quitting time, the locals did familial rituals, talking ceaselessly about food or the weather, sitting on porches in rockers or swinging loveseats on creaking chains. Then they started drinking—most alarmingly, at a watering hole whose neon sign proclaimed it as BAR. If you telephoned the place, the proprietor, a burly ex-boxer with a buzzing, dysfunctional voice and only the vaguest grasp of the world beyond his batwing doors, would answer "Tommy's." The Thing had never called Tommy's; the Thing had no use for telephones, although It recognized that when one human or another grabbed one, it usually meant trouble.

Generally, the residents of Maysville kept to their homes (the better to service the exponential care and feeding of town gossip) and, at night, banded into drunken groups to hunt down the Thing once and for all. Maysville needed a monster, apparently, to rationalize it hidebound prejudices, its oddball religion, its social dynamic, and to unify the townsfolk against some common enemy…mostly so they did not tear each other apart.

The Thing Too Hideous to Describe did not know of any monsters in the vicinity; that was one of the reasons It had chosen the area for Its semi-retirement. No werewolves or incubi, no demonic apparitions or defrocked Indian burial tracts. No real estate hauntings, no unspeakable, lowering molochs, and practically no children possessed by devils, although sometimes the Thing was not so sure. The kids here had inherited their progenitors' sense of superstitious paranoia and hidebound, inbred fear, and frequently they *acted* monstrously, but the Thing was capable of appreciating the difference. No real monsters…

…unless you counted the townsfolk, who got incredibly intolerant when they got liquored up at Tommy's. The formula was always the same: they complained, and drank, and

groused, and drank, and started stamping their feet, while drinking some more, and before you could say *boo,* you had a gang of violent alcoholics storming up your nether port—drunk, deluded, waving torches and pointy farm implements, screaming with bloodlust in a democracy of madness and mob unreason.

There were already plenty of frightening things in the world, thought the Thing. Circus clowns, for example. Cartoonists and writers—creatures who invented the kind of lurid pulp that could inflame the basest frenzies of unthinking, potentially dangerous crowds. Such artisans of corruption sat in their high places, and distorted form, and made a mockery of all life, and did not care that their exploitative claptrap sank fear into the souls of the ignorant. The Thing had once seen a photograph of one of their minor gods. The portrait depicted some gloomy Gus, all hangdog and horrific and mostly hairless, his eyes broadcasting doom and cosmic apocalypse, hinting at a near-blasphemous tunnel vision that hated all it saw, and saw only that which could kindle the otherworldly passions resident in the fetid lobes of the man's dark and hateful brain.

The Thing Too Hideous to Describe spooked a couple of smooching high-schoolers, about a block from the town square, against a fence, behind some trees near the cemetery, where these nascent fornicators had assumed they might swap fluids and DNA unnoticed. It was a transient thrill. The humans emitted high, squealing noises and took clumsy flight, colliding with trees and each other in their haste to escape. That buoyed the spirits of the Thing only momentarily. Now the offspring would hurriedly report an extravagant exaggeration of what they had seen, amplifying the disgust factor in order to hide their own guilt in the shadow of the more sensational. Then the local authorities, the town leaders, and their parents would all use *that* as an excuse to partake of more abundantly-available booze, and soon enough the whole process would culminate in smoking torches and riot behavior.

The mob would never cross the tarn, however—none of them would ever be that brave. There were too many hazards not governed by hysteria: bloodsuckers, quickmud, venomous reptiles; no streetlights or convenience markets. Beyond that, a treacherous maze of rocks and switchbacks, where precipitous heights waited to plummet the curious to broken-boned death on sharp rocks, or the lack of geographical benchmarks threatened starvation within a labyrinth. No, the mob would never manage to seek out the lair of the Thing Too Hideous to Describe, because indigenous legend had it that once you went in, you never came out.

Yet upon its return for lunch break, the Thing Too Hideous to Describe saw light. Human light, the artificial light of a battery-operated beam. Once, a group of besmocked know-it-alls in helicopters had buzzed unnervingly close, convinced that the Thing might be some sort of alien invader from another planet. They had given up and retreated to the safety of their grandiose theorizing. They always gave up, when it came to actually learning something. It was more profitable to fall back on whatever make-believe they were selling unwary consumers, this week.

Whomever had chanced upon the Thing's home did not look like a scientist, nor did he appear to be a representative of the military. He looked like a clerk. He was wearing a bulky down jacket and hiking boots. He wore spectacles and had a hairless face (the way humans scraped off their pelts had always made the Thing a bit queasy). It was comical to watch him feel around the edges of the nondescript cave that led down to the Thing's home. He did not appear repulsed by the slime coating the ingress. He sniffed it, from the tips of his gloves. His flashlight beam strayed wild

again, as he consulted a big metal notebook he held crooked-
into one arm.

The Thing Too Hideous to Describe held steady and
watched, as this Outsider—for that was definitely what the
man was, not from around here—stiffened, the way humans
always did when they felt there was some creepy lurker,
monitoring them. Now would be an excellent opportunity to
pull the old stalk-and-scare, making the guy look toward the
most likely source of monsterishness, then drop tentacles
down on him, from above. But before the Thing could
indulge Itself, the flashlight ray crossed Its big, ebony orbs,
causing a stab of pain like a migraine. Before the Thing could
rally, the man-creature in the bulky coat spoke to It.

"Oh! Hi there...sorry, I hope I'm not intruding or anything..."

This struck the Thing as very odd. Usually, they ran away
by now, or started shooting. Instead, this manling checked his
book again—*a book! Another damned book! Oh, cursed item!*
thought the Thing, steeling for the worst. But this did not
appear to be a *book*-book, of the sort It reviled. No, it was a
ring-binder sort of affair, its pages containing not hated text,
and certainly not the most loathsome print of all, *fiction,* but
graphs and charts.

And the man-creature was walking toward It, the tone
of voice spewing from his mouth-hole not scared at all,
but apologetic.

"Sorry to bother you, like I said, but my name is Steve
Brackeen. I was going to leave you a note. Um...is this a bad
time? I was hoping maybe we could talk a little..."

Worse, as the man-creature came closer to the Thing,
his aura read decidedly cool, not a nimbus of red-hot fright
or hatred. He pulled off one glove to expose his hand, that
simian tool depending grotesquely from the end of his arm

with its upsettingly snake-like five digits, pink and hairless. No slime.

It had been ages since the Thing Too Hideous to Describe had risked vocal contact with a human, and Its works seemed rusty. A lot of bug-infested mucus glopped out of Its face, plus bits of a turkey club sandwich It had enjoyed two days ago, but the man-creature broadcast no distress at this.

"I'm—I'm not a census taker or anything like that. I came here to talk to you, actually, if—if you think you could spare—"

He was flashing a laminated card that featured an inaccurate photograph of him, and his name, spelled out in modern English.

The Thing Too Hideous to Describe did not wish to shake hands with the man-creature, primarily because It disliked that sort of actual physical contact, but also because It had nothing a human could reasonably call a hand.

"Like I said, my name is—"

The Thing was perplexed. This was most assuredly outside the normal playbook. What could It do? It invited the guy inside.

—ooo—

"I'm a little grubby," said the man-creature named Steve. "You'll have to excuse that. This is a lot better than stomping all over Europe, lemme tell you." He spread a disposable paper towel over the glistening hump of rock near the Thing's firepit, then sat down, extending his booted leg appendages to compensate for the elevation of the rock. "Nice place. The fire is nice, too."

The Thing Too Hideous to Describe had to pause to ponder the word, one It had almost never heard. *Nice?*

"You know—homey. Anyway, I've been working on this big doctoral thesis. That's what all this hoodoo in the notebook is about. I've been documenting the weird crowd behavior of group insanity in small, isolated towns and villages, you know—the kind of places the world always seems to pass by? And some of the stuff I found out is pretty upsetting. Like in the Black Forest—rampant alcoholism, leading to berserk, antisocial group action. Apparently a lot of those villagers have nothing better to do with their time than invent wild stories about their betters, and use those stories to justify blowing up every castle in a hundred-mile radius. No, sir or madame, your hamlet is not being victimized by one of your own retarded halfwits...it must be a *vampire!* That's the way these kooks think. No, your cemeteries aren't being vandalized by teen punks or necrophiles...it must be that mean old professor up on the hill, who has more money and pedigree than you could ever imagine, why, he must be *stitching all those corpses together to make a big stupid monster,* yeah, that *must* be it!"

The Thing Too Hideous to Describe was forced to concur. Humans almost never behaved logically, or compassionately. They did bray a lot about tolerance, which exercise for their vocal cords was probably more economical than actual practice.

"I mean, you've seen some of those movies, right?" said the Steve-creature. "Who really makes out, every time the besotted Burgomeister decides, you know, to blow up another dam? Local contractors, funeral directors, hardware stores, the makers of pitchforks and rope, gun dealers and the distributors of ammunition, hell...monsters are great for their economy. They all get shitfaced at the inn until they're fizzed enough to see monsters, then they start grabbing for the dynamite. And who do you think gets first crack at developing the destroyed real estate? I mean, *where's the real problem,* here?"

The Thing Too Hideous to Describe had to nod in agreement, at that one.

"I guess the fundamental question is: what are these

imbeciles smoking…and where can I get some?" The Steve-creature cracked a smile that bisected his misshapen round face into a leer, showing teeth. "Did you hear about the lunatics running the asylum over in Mapleton, USA? They think they're plagued by some mummy guy who crawls out of a bog every quarter-century or so to pick on the descendants of some heat-stroked, hallucinating Egyptologist who drank himself into a coronary before the Second World War! I mean, accounts vary, but the story stays the same: These people refuse to accept responsibility for their own lives. Nah, we were all abject failures in life because we were *cursed by monsters*, not because we're all so inebriated all the time we can barely tie our shoes!"

The Steve-creature flipped open his notebook. The Thing Too Hideous to Describe leaned forward to peruse the data in better light.

"See here? No matter how many times they wipe out these supposed monsters, those monsters always come back, even if they're, you know, utterly purged from the planet. See? It allows for the maintenance of a consistent level of mass psychosis. Pretty soon, your toilet doesn't flush, and voila—it must be the Mad Doktor's fault, or some monster that conveniently runs contrary to whatever religious derangement governs the town. Not only does it maintain the status quo and help the local economy, but it severely limits the employment opportunities for bona fide monsters. Look at this graph—see? Monster jobs and mean income level, down every year. I'm thinking of presenting some of my findings to Affirmative Action."

The Thing Too Hideous to Describe flipped to another page of facts and figures, using one of Its secondary pseudopods, the stumpy, more articulate ones. Yes, the bald information in black and white certainly seemed conclusive enough.

The Steve-creature reached into his shoulder bag. *Here it comes,* thought the Thing. *It's a trap. He's going to whip out a weapon and try to bushwhack me. Or worse, this has all been a setup, and he's going to try to sell me something.*

No, it was merely a little tape recorder.

"I just want to get some of your thoughts," said Steve. "Your angle on the whole phenomenon, and maybe ask you a few questions about your relationship with the population of Maysville, if that's not too intrusive or presumptuous of me. You'll be speaking on behalf of a very broad monster demographic—what you say may affect hundreds of others in the same position as yourself."

The Thing's eyes blinked in incomprehension, fluttering at the ends of their stalks. Not only had It not anticipated company, but there was nothing around that could qualify as refreshment, especially for this iron-blooded, bipedal air-breather. It sighed, making a congested, bubbly sound. It really needed to work on Its hosting skills.

—ooo—

Ominously pleasant, this talk in the dark. An exchange of ideas, seductive in its invitation…and almost promising some manner of betrayal as the final course. But I can smell human lies, the way I can sense deceit hidden beneath their too-thin, fragile skins. This one is compassionate and educated. If they were all like this one, never would I have to salve burns from the night before. If they were all like this one, the structure of our universe would not exist. I kind of like him.

But holy Peter, is he ugly! That jackstraw corpus, with its gangly, meatless limbs. Only two eyes, both the limpid color of poison. The rictus mouth with its nasty, square teeth. The absolute wrongness of his geometry brands him as an abomination, something the sane gaze instinctually rejects from view. I

think that, were our stations reversed, I might derive pleasure from his extinction. I hope not, for that would make us both, as races, equally uncivilized.

—ooo—

Commotion, in the calm of night. The Thing Too Hideous to Describe was accustomed to such uproar, but this night, It was not the catalyst.

The Thing scuttled up a high tree in the woods and spread his pods out, spider-like, for stability. From here, Its vision, tuned to nonhuman frequencies, could perfectly make out, from this distance, the church steeple and town square. The *sounds* were familiar—inebriated raving, the crackle of firebrands, the hyperactive jostle of sweaty bodies lusting for a kill. All the trappings of a conventional Maysville monster hunt, with their preferred monster as absentee.

A large phone-pole crucifix jutted from a pyre of smashed furniture, the kindling provided by the rent bodies of those few books in town that had not been banned or burned already. Spiked to the pole, his wrists and throat engirded by barbed wire, was the Steve-creature, the human who had called himself Brackeen. The goodfolk of Maysville pelted him with rotten fruit and broken glass, from the bottles they had drained. His shredded notebook was utilized to ignite the fire. The lynch chaos of Maysville's drunken residents would not be denied.

He had been found out. He had ventured into the town to do interviews and take notes, and the innkeeper had poked into his guest's luggage, or, more likely, someone had just peered over his shoulder at an opportune moment. He had been damned by his own research. Maysville, ever on the lookout for mutants, would obliterate any aberration…especially when they could find no other one to torment.

The Steve-creature hollered protest, at first. Then screamed curses. Then, merely screamed, before he fell silent and continued to cook. His unholy book was consumed by righteous fire. His head sagged and his hair vanished in a puff of greasy smoke.

The Thing Too Hideous to Describe averted Its gaze, with something like pity. They were not all alike, these humans. The Steve-creature had resembled those executing him (hell, they all looked alike anyway), but in no way was he the same as them.

With a measure of melancholy, the Thing Too Hideous to Describe slithered down from the tree and trundled wearily homeward. Tomorrow night, It really should sortie into town, to do what It did best, but It knew the task would come without verve or enthusiasm.

The human conceit of vengeance, however, might be adapted to fruitful use, on some other midnight, soon to come.

—ooo—ooo—ooo—

WAKE-UP CALL

I opened my eyes. It hurt. Someone was speaking. "Welcome to Phase Two debriefing, Mr. Maxwell."

Here is my last memory:

Not drunk, and in complete possession of my senses, I perform the ritual. That's what it feels like—a ritual. Thousands before me have executed similar moves under comparable circumstances, in an equivalent state of mind. First consideration: hardware. I had chosen a classic, the military-issue Colt .45 semi-auto, a golden oldie with a venerated history. For those of you who don't know much about firearms, this pistol, originally made for the US Army, is designated the M1911A1. The standard clip is seven-plus-one, though larger magazines are obtainable. "Seven-plus-one" means seven cartridges in the clip with an extra round already chambered. If you wish to find out more about the damage index of various bullet types or need a lot of tech stuff, that information is abundantly available; I know enough to make the device work. Second consideration: The note. The inevitable note. The who, what, why and where of suicide. I had a single glass of white Bordeaux while composing it. Whoever discovered my reeking corpse, exsanguinated, cheesy clumps of hair and brain stuck to the walls and hardening on the carpet, would have to reconcile the ghastly display with my carefully-considered prose. The stench of evacuated bowels and exposed organs, the nakedness of decay. Humidity and maggots.

What farewell prose could out-vote that sad horror? I checked my gun a dozen times, finished my wine, and completed my note, blaming no one. Then I stuck the muzzle in my mouth and blew off most of the back of my head with a soft-nosed hollow point, for maximum reliability.

Then I woke up.

"Mr. Maxwell? Ah. Glad to see you're back with us. My name is—it's okay, Mr. Maxwell, you can open your eyes. It might sting a little bit. But it won't harm you."

I tried to track the voice and realized I was strapped into a sort of dentist's chair, reclined, with a lot of leads trailing to beeping machines. But this was not a hospital. I could taste blood in the back of my throat.

"You're probably a little bit thirsty, too," said the voice. Sitting on a stool overseeing my position was a young woman in a smock. She had brilliant gray eyes, strawberry blonde hair, and an abundance of freckles. Her face was compressed and her haircut was not complimentary—she was more of a sidekick type, short and a bit stocky, cute instead of attractive. Eyeglasses on a chain. A bar-coded ID tag dangled from her pen pocket. "My name is Bonnie and I'm your caseworker. This is what's called a Phase Two debriefing; you might have heard of it, or read about it."

She tipped a pleated paper cup of water to my lips. My wrists were restricted. The water tasted too cold and invasive. I felt weary.

"I know you feel like you want to go to sleep Mr. Maxwell—" she consulted her clipboard. "Orson. But you can't become unconscious as long as you're hooked up, and we need to review a few details before we move on."

"I don't understand." My voice was arid and abrasive. I felt around inside my mouth with my tongue. No hole. I fancied I could still taste the lubricant and steel of the gun barrel. The

egress where it had spat a bullet into my head was patched with something smooth and artificial.

"That's why we're here," said Bonnie. "Standard orientation for wake-ups. That's what we call revised suicides—wake-ups."

"Revised?"

"Yes. All wake-ups are selected on the basis of their stats and records. I'm not here to judge, just to prepare you for your re-insertion into the work force. You'll have a meeting with an actual counselor later."

"Excuse me, Miss…Bonnie, I haven't heard about this, or read about it, and I don't know what you're talking about. I do know that I feel terrible; I feel worse than I've ever felt in my life, and I don't want to answer any questions."

She smiled and attempted to soften her manner by about a third of one degree. "Please try to understand. I know this is confusing and you probably are in some bona fide physical pain. But by killing yoursel—committing suicide, you have forfeited any protest. You *have* to cooperate. It'll seem difficult, for example, when you walk for the first time. But if you don't want to walk, they'll *force* you to walk, anyway. It helps to think of yourself as a newborn, not whatever person you used to be. You do not retain rights, as you understood them."

"I forfeited them."

"Correct. Now we try to minimize the discomfort of wake-up as much as we can, but ultimately, you'll have to do what they'll say you'll do until your obligations are discharged."

"Wait, wait…" My skull felt like a crockpot of acid, broken glass and infection. "What about my head?"

"That's sealed with a polymer cap. Your structural damage has all been repaired."

"What obligations? Do I have to *pay* for all this?"

"Look," she said, leaning closer. "We're not supposed to discuss this with wake-ups. Counselors usually deal with inauguration. I don't know anything about you, other than you wound up here. I don't know what you did or why they picked you. I'm just here to smooth your transition into a wake-up."

"Why am I here?"

She sighed and made sure the door to our room was closed before she spoke. "Most of the wake-ups? They killed themselves, or arranged accidents, to avoid substantial debt. That's why they started the program: too many people were in arrears. Too much debt, foisted off onto relatives who couldn't pay. Scam artists and fraudulent insurance claims that paid off triple on accidental death. It was like an open faucet of money, and eventually, it needed to be fixed. That's why the government endorsed the wake-up program."

Death was no longer the end of the billing cycle, apparently. I said, "How?"

"That's a little mysterious, too. Your engrams are sort of flash-frozen. But it also involves voodoo, magic, and that's the part the mission breakdown never mentions, because I think they're just a little embarrassed to have to resort to a combination of science and sorcery. The process was sped up, then simplified, then streamlined, until we have the system we have now. We process dozens of wake-ups per day."

"What do you do with them?"

"Assignments are the responsibility of the individual counselor," she said. "Mostly it's industrial labor, from what I hear."

"You mean like slaves?"

Her expression pinched and she exhaled in a snort. Obviously, she was running out of time. She probably had to get another wake-up in here and start her spiel according to a clock. "Try not to think of it that way. Remember, you divested yourself of human rights when you—"

"Yes, I'm sure it's all nice and legal," I said. "But what about my identity? My home? My relatives? My stuff?"

"That's just it." She lent me a tiny grimace. "You're not supposed to remember any of that. Maybe your name, maybe a few basic residual facts...but you're talking in whole sentences. Most wake-ups act severely autistic, or comatose, or zombiatic. They told us the personality prints through in one out of a thousand clients." It was clear she now suspected somebody of fudging the curve.

"Well, then, I'm a special case and we should—"

"No." She overrode me. "There can't be any special cases."

"Who says so?" I felt twinges of remote-control strength in my arms, my legs. Perhaps if I could keep her talking long enough, I'd muster enough energy to be more assertive.

She showed me her clipboard, helplessly. *They* do."

That's when my quiet time was up.

—ooo—

Another chair (more upright), another set of straps (stronger), and a conference desk. The whole sterile setup resembled an interrogation cubicle. My counselor was named Eddin Hockney. He did not introduce himself, but had a sizable nameplate on his desk. He had attempted to aver his pattern baldness by shaving his head—and, it seemed, polishing and hot-waxing it as well. Watery brown eyes; thick spectacles; he was short and sciurine. His eyes darted furtively from detail to detail like some forest creature anxious to hoard nuts. His speech was better-rehearsed and more nonstop; as Bonnie had said, sped-up, simplified, streamlined.

"Surely you must agree that lost revenue via self-termination has always been an increasing problem," Hockney said, not looking at me in particular, not searching me for signs of comprehension, just spilling out his rationale. "The

data prove it. People try to—eh, do away with themselves, and stick *anyone* else with the bill. Old lovers. Ex-spouses. Heirs. Employers. Banks. Well, the credit companies just wouldn't put up with it anymore. A country can't function without viable credit and liquid assets. Do you know that some people actually *run up* their credit to the limit while they're planning on killing themselves all along? And they expect to just skate on picking up the tab, their responsibility. Well, no longer." He flipped pages, apparently disgusted by me.

"I don't suppose—"

"Aht-aht-aht!" he overrode. "I don't care. You have no rights. What I do see is an outstanding cumulative debt of $178,000. That gets you a standard Class Two work package—twenty years."

I hadn't put anything in my suicide note about monies owed, or regretting my expenditures.

"It's basically robotic manual labor. You don't retain any higher functions. If you *think* you do…well, those will fade."

"What happens after twenty years?"

"Huh. Then you get to have a funeral. Cost is pre-figured into the package."

It was not my bad finances that drove me to take my own life, but—possibly—the reduction of my character to no more than the sum of my debts. The badgering, the hectoring, the humiliation. The exponentially-increasing lack of human connection in a world where *everyone* was the sum of their debts. "Death" and "debt" sounded alike for a reason, I concluded.

If what Hockney was saying was true, then I'd spend two decades lifting or slinging or swamping or whatever, losing pieces of the memory of my life every heavy step of the way. My wives, my lovers. My joys and ambitions. My concepts of beauty, or what was fair. My despair, which had driven me to

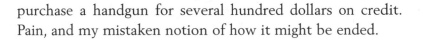
purchase a handgun for several hundred dollars on credit.
Pain, and my mistaken notion of how it might be ended.

—ooo—

But I didn't forget.

I didn't forget that finest day of my life came unexpectedly in late 1990s, and that I realized what a flawless
moment it had been, only in retrospect. Like most people. I
didn't forget abysmal black mood that prompted me to pick
up gun. I didn't forget that Victor Hugo wrote: *Supreme happiness of life is conviction that we are loved.*

Other things slipped away gradually.

My taskwork was in a large industrial foundry, using a
ringshank-handled skimmer over a crucible of ferrous lava
that was channeled to several behemoth injection-molding
machines. I live at foundry with other wake-ups. Constant
labor is only interrupted by replenishment time: six hours of
rest and an orally-pumped diet of fecal paste. Bodies relax,
but no one here sleeps. Sleep would provide oblivion. We are
either awake, or *more* awake.

In this environment, flesh of wake-ups becomes tem-
pered like steel, all leathery callus. No need for safety gog-
gles, helmets, outerwear. Air swims with free silica and lead
dust. Soluble cutting oils contain nitrosamines, which are
carcinogenic. There's sulfuric acid, mercury, chlorinated sol-
vents, potassium cyanide, xylene, carbon monoxide, infrared
radiation, nickel carbonyl, toxic plaster, ethyl silicate. In this
atmosphere, hexamethylenetetramine decomposes to
formaldehyde. We can receive thermal burns from spattered
pours. If molten metal slops on floor, heat will vaporize water
in cement, causing steam explosion. Sharp objects. Falling
and crushing hazards. I do not know these things. I read

them, on warnings for supers, who are normal humans. I can still read.

I can read control number on forehead of wake-up working next to me. 730823. Used to be black man, half his head gone, replaced by a mannequin blank—half his number is printed on plastic, half tattooed on flesh. A tear falls from his single eye and makes a white path through black soot. When I weep, my tears leave black trails on white skin. My number is 550713.

Children work here. Ex-kids. Not suicides. Others, who damned sure didn't kill themselves. Victims of others. I think supers are lying about program for wake-ups.

We cannot feel sparks of forge, though they hit us, sizzle.

I think: *We are not supposed to be able to read, or feel, or cry, or remember.* But I do.

And if I do, big vat of steel below might be crucible not of rebirth, but of re-death. I am special case. Exception. Maybe exceptional enough to will my foot closer to edge. Drop isn't far.

Very odd, to submerge in metal hot enough to instantly vaporize my eyes...feel nothing. Hot solar light, shock of obliteration.

Then a voice, saying, "Welcome to Phase Three debriefing, Number 550713."

—ooo–ooo–ooo—

DISTMANTLING FORTRESS ARCHITECTURE
56   28 1 34   7

by David J. Schow & Craig Spector

A child of six, he lives and breathes for the dead—
family, friends and strangers, all rendered equal by
machines that grind. Whispers suggest the sifted dust is used to
form mortar (to build their prisons) or bake bread (to fool their
bellies); such grand jokes are beyond his comprehension. To ghettos and ovens and mass graves he has borne witness. At his sooty
face and blackened hands, his guards always laugh.

He amuses his masters with his pluck and skill. It is sufficient to earn him a new job, a nickname, and to keep him alive.
At least until he turns seven.

—ooo—

Hirohiko Ozawa's backbar mirror was a piece of Art Deco
trash with layered glass that fractured his visage into many
overlapping duplicates. The floor-to-ceiling windows of his
tenth-floor executive suite commanded a splendid view across
the Tiergarten. Outside, below, the Berlin Wall was coming
down a chunk at a time. Adrift in a world of transparency, false
images, and unexpected change, Hiro, a consummate lover of
puns, could permit himself the luxury of reflection.

When it came to success and survival in the arena of corporate cutthroats, chameleonism was a vital knack, and Hiro
had strategized his career according to the injunctions of

constant change: make decisions of stone, on paper, then turn those edicts to water when the time was right. Turn one face as stocks rose; show another when they plummeted, and never let them see you sweat. Become famous, then feared, then infamous…then invisible. Work change as one man, and subterfuge as someone else. A great many people returned Hiro's stare from the mirror.

The Koramitsu Corporation had founded much of its success on one of Hiro's favorite conceits—the concept of the airtight alibi. In this world, when you said Koramitsu, you were talking software, and when Koramitsu desired bold strides in product design, they called upon the man they knew as Hirohiko Ozawa. Hence, the office, the perks, the view from on high. The mirror had been selected by Hiro, along with the aqua-colored clamshell monstrosity that was the wet bar. Hiro enjoyed vulgarities. He was a connoisseur of the garish, especially when it was bought and paid for by below-the-line nonentities.

Alone, arrogantly, he toasted himself. Not at all the humble, shielded, self-deprecating Japanese. Fuck all *that* noise.

Hiro was about to shape-shift again. From European werewolf to Asian were-tiger, he fancied. A fortnight from today he would be in Hong Kong, assuming a brand new post under the name of Seko Kobayashi…whose berth had been secured by the smuggling of certain top-secret microprocessor designs out of Koramitsu's German manufacturers, the Mohler Partners, GbH. The designs had been a mere bargaining chip—pardon the pun—in the predestined merger between Koramitsu and Mohler. But when the theft was discovered, the guy picking up the guilt tab and taking the big fall would be—wait for it!—"Hirohiko Ozawa."

Thanks to an a la carte subsidiary sale, Hiro had ensured that leverage against him via the pilfered tech would be impossible in six months. By then, the new boys in Hong

Kong would *need* Seko Kobayashi to save their butts...and Seko had big plans for Hong Kong, prior to the end of the party there in 1997.

Beyond the glass, soundlessly, youngsters with nothing better to do were having a bash at the Wall. They teemed and swarmed, anxious to get their countenances recorded by news cameras during this fleeting moment of pocket history.

The Wall had been standing for most of Hiro's life, first as a barbed-wire barricade erected by the East German police in 1961. Berlin had always been a city of walls, dating back to 1735, when King Frederick William I threw a wall around the growing city to facilitate the collection of taxes. Historically, walls had unified Berliners, until this most infamous one, which was specifically intended to divide them into *ossis* and *wessis*.

Hiro knew of the scheme to greet the incoming *ossis* with "welcome funds" of 100 DM each, and did not plan on hanging around for the almost guaranteed economic chaos that would ensue once the Western sector was flooded with Easterners who were, by Hiro's standards, fiscally sub-viable. East German currency was not convertible. The going black market exchange rate of 1 DM (West) per ten marks (East) would soon nose-dive to near-Weimar Republic levels, leaving many of the current celebrants of reunification poor and surly.

Either way, there would be long lines in front of the banks here.

After forty years of economic miracle, the West had grown plumply complacent: a crowded market, highly specialized, hierarchical, dominated by silver-haired dinosaurs who were all about to get their rumps rudely shocked. The air was cold and depressing, tainted with what the locals called the "typical Communist smog" of burning coal and carbon monoxide, wafting westward. What was that line about knowing which way the wind blew?

Opportunism is a great productive force, claimed the editorials in *Der Spiegel.* It sure was, thought Hiro, who knew that in the USSR such "opportunism" had turned the entire bureaucracy inside-out. If the Berlin Wall could be torn down, then all bets were off; a divided Deutschland had formerly been a notion as immutable as the monolithic stability of the Soviet Union.

At least *some* things never changed.

The 1980s had commenced with Polish tanks comminuting citizens like bugs, Soviet troops swarming into Afghanistan, and the insane American President, Ronald Reagan, lavishing $2.4 *trillion* on a militaristic spending spree. Now the decade was in twilight, and dominoes were falling all over Eastern Europe. This was what happened when a country committed its national identity to a war... and the enemy resigned. Time to split.

Hiro would slip away amid the pop of champagne corks and the gritty crunch of sledgehammers kissing the Wall. Soon bulldozers would crush the painted concrete into smaller and smaller particles, like that Western saying about making little ones out of big ones. Eventually, the Berlin Wall would become nothing more than souvenir fodder for tourists, and inevitably, the smarter stone-breakers might realize that *any* fragment of convincingly spray-painted rock might cadge a few bucks from dupes on the Venice Beach boardwalk, a world away in California.

At the *peep* of a card swiping through the coded slot that accessed his office door, Hiro turned, still holding his drink. Guilt was not in his makeup, but surprise still was, and his gaze leapt to the Halliburton case on his desk, neatly packed with stolen barter.

The unannounced visitor was a short man, almost equal to Hiro's own height, though older—Hiro guessed his age at fifty-plus. A man whose neat gabardine suit and choice of neckties proclaimed efficiency and bespoke anonymity. A man like Hiro. He wore steel-rimmed spectacles, and his right hand was completely encased in a strange sleeve of matte black about the size of three videocassettes stacked together. That was all Hiro could record before a small-caliber subsonic round pierced his aorta. He dropped his glass, gobbled blood, and weaved dumbly until all sensation drained from his legs and he piled up on the carpet.

The intruder looked toward the Halliburton case, then back to Hiro. Another silent bullet smashed in exactly where the man's eyes told it to go.

The next round, fired directly into Hiro's temple, had been chosen for its lack of residual velocity; it penetrated, expanded, and did not exit. It ricocheted madly around inside Hiro's skull, pureeing the secrets there, even though Hiro was already nerve dead.

If Hiro's still-open eyes could see, they would have registered the reflections in the backbar mirror, now that the Halliburton case no longer blocked the view, of the distant Wall coming down at last, spectators and rabble-rousers capering over the ruins like army ants.

—ooo—

Kommandant smiles when he sees the boy leading the fire tenders in their horned leather headgear. It is a good morning for burning.

Troopers shoot the meat in columns five deep, in full view of the pyres that will consume their remains. The boy watches the soot swirl skyward, as black as coal tar. No time, not anymore, for ovens or deceptive relocation schemes; if processing is not sped up, the Reich will drown in a stinking sea of Jewry.

A visiting SS officer from IV-B4 assesses the boy with limpid eyes, mistaking him at first for a mere sex toy. He asks about the nickname Kommandant has bestowed upon this small charge.

Kommandant's eyes offer the SS man an answer. Just watch, they seem to say with a glimmer of pride. One like this comes along only once per war. Watch what my Aschmaus does.

—ooo—

The man known to the hotel staff as Herr Erich Barstow shuffled from one sofa to another in his suite, checking his Rolex too many times. Almost lunchtime. Almost time to fill that little hole in your life, he thought, by becoming a man of action.

He felt like a movie extra, thrust into the coveted star spotlight only to find that with such light comes unbearable heat. If your audience saw you sweat, you lost. If his guests, today, got the slightest whiff that Herr Erich Barstow was as fake as his rich man's wristwatch…well, the dead don't sweat, do they?

Gelft stood sentry near the foyer door. A rock, that man. There would come a knock, and Gelft would admit three men—all the genuine item, real as poison. And Erich Barstow would be onstage.

Gelft himself was a piece of work. Strapping, blond, possibly the most Aryan-looking Israeli Erich had yet seen in his new calling as ersatz spy. The Institute had set up this ambush, and seeded the costly suite (eight hundred American dollars a night, Erich marveled) with mini-microphones. They had also insisted on a bodyguard for Erich, a professional whose cool made Erich ache to scream *cut!* from the nearest windowsill…though he was boundlessly thankful, as the time drew closer, that his big ally was right at hand.

Erich's Armani was a loaner whose tailored fit was a happy coincidence. *Happy,* he thought ruefully, wishing he could slip into character as easily as he had donned the jacket.

Today's lunchtime guest list was comprised of Koepp, the politician; Hessler, prime mover of the Phoenix Foundation; and Jaeckel, the sole Nazi of vintage in this new Holy Trinity of National Socialism.

One drizzly morning in the spring of '43, Jaeckel's SS Einsatzgruppen hung two hundred butchered, headless Jews on meat hooks, with signs labeling them *Carne Kosher*, in a letter-perfect mockery of Talmudic law. The execution of over one hundred thirty thousand undesirables in Poland and Latvia had also been overseen by Jaeckel…and the heirs to the adjudicators of Nuremburg had spent the past four decades scratching and sniffing for him.

Herr Erich Barstow had found him. Finding men like Jaeckel was simple if one had the right connections, such as the Phoenix Foundation, based in America and headed by a man whose name had been legally changed to Karl Hessler.

Hessler's club was the sort that *always* welcomed sympathetic contributors with apparently bottomless bank accounts, if for no more modest purpose than reminding the world at large that the so-called Holocaust was a lie, the Final Solution a myth, and the scoop on crematoria and Zyklon-B just plain nonsense perpetrated by ZOG, the Zionist Occupation Government.

In bald fact, Jaeckel was an impotent relic and Hessler, a clown with a bullhorn. Ernst Koepp was the prize. A man of dramatic presence, pull and influence in the new Germany, Koepp had an almost divine knack for gladhanding the grassroots—the *volk*. He could make a logical speech about law and order sound like an equally logical return to the old-fashioned virtues of National Socialism…then make private jokes at the fundraising smokers afterward about being able to smell a Jew from four blocks away. Koepp's brand of tunnel vision appealed to a worldwide audience hungry for swift,

settling solutions; his platform translated easily, continents distant, into Molotoved churches in Orange County, and hate crimes from Brooklyn to Johannesburg to Bialystock.

Enter Erich Barstow, collaborator.

With the help of his nom de querre and a PO box, Erich's racial credentials were provably impeccable. His identity as a Washington, D.C., lobbyist was considered invaluable by Hessler, who claimed a sixth sense about such things (as he confided to Erich in several of his egregious communiques). Just in time, too—cash flow was urgently needed for safe houses, for arms, for publications, for Koepp's political war chest.

Enter, next, the polar opposite of the Phoenix Foundation: A group which called itself—this year, at least—the Institute. What *they* urgently needed was a "face" for a sting against Hessler and his cronies; not a hero, just someone to help deliver a small piece of the world from evil. The Institute knew how to exploit weak patches in human resolve. They knew how to make normal men say *yes* to playing spy.

Perhaps it was destiny that this man be Herr Erich Barstow today. Or perhaps it was one more grab at capturing a piece of his soul he'd always felt had wandered away while he wasn't paying attention.

Erich tried to harden his resolve. Fourteen floors below the windows of the hotel suite, twenty-eight miles of concrete and steel spanning twenty-eight oppressive years lay like the excavated spine of some extinct saurian monster. Eastern border guards schooled to shoot on sight now traded unaccustomed grins with their Western counterparts, all of them wondering what might happen next. History was built on moments like these, and the autumn air was charged. Something was coming...but what? What if the great beast down there suddenly awoke, and decided to eat a few of the Lilliputians dancing on its sundered vertebrae?

Erich suffered a moment of flash panic. He wished he could be down there, among the celebrants. If he walked out now…

If only the dummkopfs at the Vienna Academy had given that little schmuck painter a shot, way back when. No, it was more important that the world not suffer one more piss-poor artist, and thus require Erich to be here, now.

On the third knock, Gelft opened the door to the suite. Erich was still around a blind corner, by the window. He straightened all seams and prepared to do good.

Gelft was gone.

The door was being closed—quietly—by a smallish man in a neutral-colored gabardine suit. He smiled blankly at Erich. Glare from the overhead lights formed two equally blank white rectangles in the lenses of his glasses. As he smiled, he shot Erich twice in the solar plexus with some sort of soundless, baffled gun. Traumatic shock hit with textbook speed. Erich's knees unhinged and he hit the floor.

He saw blood. From his own lungs. He could not speak. Or inhale.

The assassin's shooting hand was smothered in some boxy, black device. Still smiling, the man produced a tatter of ancient cloth and laid it gently over the pumping wounds in Erich's chest.

In the quarter second that made up the rest of his life, Erich recognized the shape, remembered it from an old photograph. One star, six points. Then another dot of fire spat from the business end of the black box, taking him right between the eyebrows.

Exit Erich Barstow.

—ooo—

Kommandant's favorite anecdote wins the humor of his officers and makes him more human, a man from whom it is not so

bad to take harsh orders. As he tells the tale, there is usually a toast or two as punctuation. And how his men marvel.

I saw a twitching nerve the size of a child, Kommandant usually begins. Nothing in its eyes but hunger and the will to survive.

That nails them.

You know what a nuisance they are to herd. Shepherds can only goad them so much. Row upon row of Jews, wailing and shrieking, waiting to see children get shot. But one, he zigzags out. The whore to whom it belonged starts making noise. It is running straight for me! The Schupos put her down with a rifle butt and prepare to pick off the little vermin before it can soil my coat or bite me on the ankle. No shot comes. My staff and I are in the line of fire. And just as it reaches me, it stops, stops dead to attention, and clicks its heels together, and salutes, and yells Heil, Hitler!

Never once does he look back at his mother. What can I say to this?

I let him watch. That morning we burned three thousand. The bone fragments alone would fill several trucks—trucks we did not have. A diesel mixer was requisitioned to grind the bone material to powder. To facilitate this, there were large steel balls inside the drum. They were crude, inefficient. The boy proves this to me by climbing into the drum and fetching out a skull. He combed warm embers and found gold that our cleanup crews had missed. When he removes the detritus, the powder is better, finer.

Sane people tend pet rats. I had my nerve the size of a small Aschmaus. And as for the Judenflour, you all know what happened to that.

—ooo—

According to the crap in her bag, the bitch's name was Heike Strab. German name, but American documentation and passport. She was some sort of lawyer, but more importantly, she was obviously a race traitor. Stanz and Wolfie took turns raping her on the stone floor of the pump station. No one would hear them, thanks to the secret sanctity of their latest squat, and the din of the revelry scant meters from where they did the dirty.

Stanz and Wolfie had found all this make-happy about the Wall vomitous, and went on the prowl, spoiling to break a few skulls. Potential victims milled everywhere like narcotized zombies, mindlessly celebratory. It was like a riot, but without the fun. At least the alcohol was flowing, and mostly free for the snatch, so Stanz and Wolfie sniffed the throng for pussy and ultra-violence, not necessarily in that order.

They had found Heike, and her camera. Snapshot of a pair of skull-shaven Aryan punks: One mark. The cheapest memento on the open market. Right this way.

This lamb from abroad had no way of knowing that Stanz and Wolfie were not punks, or even post-punks. From their red-laced combat boots to their tribal tattoos, they were as rigidly uniformed as young men of their aspirations could ever hope to be. Both of them had actually read *Mein Kampf* board-to-board (the same hardcover copy); it was the closest either of them would ever come to reading for pleasure. Wolfie packed an SS dagger in his boot (bragging that it was genuine, nicks and pits and all); he even slept wearing it. Apart from Wolfie being six months Stanz's junior and possessing unfortunately brown eyes (Stanz's were blue, just like the Führer's), the pair were fundamentally indistinguishable from each other, inseparable, two vital young skinheads programmed with a solo track of crypto-fascist dogma. Mostly for them it was an excuse to cripple strangers and thieve food, but lately they had begun to feel the warm rumblings of some oncoming millennium, the way you can feel air acquire the heat of an oncoming sunrise before the light. Perhaps they *had* been doing something right, intuitively, all along.

In Heike Strab's faraway world of black and white and right and wrong, heroic policemen would helicopter in any moment to save her. A rescue would be effected, charges would be filed, and the boys would receive due punishment. In her world, the grade-school psych evaluations of this pair would become admissible evidence. if anyone cared to decipher the poor carbon on yellow flimsy, they would see innocuous, normal names for these two—names long discarded—and labels for their disposition like *contumacious* and *depressed.* One might read that their weight was *sub-normal,* their speech patterns *frenetic* and *circumstantial,* and their sleeping and eating patterns, *aberrant.* Conclusions? *Schizothymia, overanxiety,* and something no one could ever figure out, yet was named "Mixed Specific Development Disorder." The solution to the problem of young Stanz and Wolfie had a name, too: Ritalin SR, in 20-milligram dosages that the boys ultimately sold to school*kinder* even younger than they were. In Heike Strab's world, such socially disaffiliated ingredients formed a recipe for an individual who might frequently toy with suicidal thoughts. Misfits, in Heike Strab's deluded world view, nearly always self-destructed.

Suicide, however, would never be an option for Stanz or Wolfie unless they got drunk enough to accidentally kill each other. The world had spat them out, and they took every opportunity to spit right back. It was not their fault Heike Strab had made the mistake of eye contact. Heike's dynamic new learning experience was reinforced each time one cock or the other penetrated her anus.

How simple and pleasant, to take advantage of the town's mood tonight. Never mind how we *look;* we're all allies now, ja? Target acquisition was a snap in such a carnival atmosphere, and once they'd taped the gym sock into her face, this target was not too much hassle. A tightish fuck, even for a Jewbitch.

Though weak and simpering, she had been so much more diverting than their original target, a sawed-off guy with mean little steel glasses, nakedly out of place in the melee as he tried to hustle from some hotel with a bag in each hand—an attache case and one of those silver Halliburton jobs favored by drug dealers in the cinema. What had been in the cases? Money? Secrets? Tempting. But by the time the boys had dogged him, Wolfie had spotted the fair Heike and her camera, and while he and his partner Stanz enjoyed and even invited mayhem, they weren't *fags*.

Their current squat was unique. It permitted them the privacy to turn Heike Strab's life to garbage, and the wallflower invisibility of being situated right in the heart of the partiers making merry at the wall.

Built prior to the fall of Berlin, the flat, blockhouse-style structure had originally been intended as a pump station fed by the Landwehrkanal. Forty percent of the bricks used in its construction had arrived in Berlin by rail from the Rademacher Brickworks, which utilized crude ash supplied by the Mendhausen labor camp during the war.

One statistic that had always impressed Stanz and Wolfie was that three hundred sixty-seven thousand Jews had contributed substantially to Mendhausen's output of ash.

Repeated and relentless night bombings had miraculously spared the edifice but left the city's water system damaged and unsanitary. So maddeningly constant was the rain of fire at the close of 1944 that the new station never got a chance to serve its people. Once the Iron Curtain demarcated East from West, the Wall had been built right through the existing structure. All petcocks had been sealed; all accesses, formidably bricked up.

With common bricks, this time.

One generation later, Stanz and wolfie had broken and entered, and discovered a secret.

The rear of the station paralleled the riot of graffiti that was the Western face of the Wall. There was a gap of about two meters between the exterior of the station and the Wall itself. Someone had tried to tunnel through. An excavation in the back room wound down about ten feet, then eastward. Above ground, past the width of the Wall, lay a 200-yard no-man's-land of guards, dogs, barbed wire, nail-mesh mats and batteries of self-firing weapons. The tunnelers had given up after about forty yards. The back room of the station was choked with debris—fill dirt, shattered rock, stones and clumps of concrete. Obviously, some underground throughway for escapees had been planned, then abandoned. Similar mole-holes had worked, such as one that snaked up into an abandoned bakery and permitted fifty-seven people to escape in 1964…until sentries began firing into the tunnel on the Eastern end. How old this forsaken operation might be, Stanz and Wolfie had no way of knowing, nor the intellectual equipment for guessing, or caring.

Wolfie glided back with an easy *bier* score, and the boys calmed their lupine thirst while Heike drifted in and out of consciousness. They toasted her, toasted their choice of victim, toasted each other, and at last got pretty toasted themselves.

Sometime past the toll of midnight, a maul or hammer thudded heavily against the exterior of the abandoned and forgotten station. Stanz and Wolfie jolted awake, and shook their heads at each other sadly. This squat was destined to fall to dust, thanks to the Wall, and a new one would have to be hunted.

Before they went back to sleep, angry at their forthcoming eviction, they dragged what was left of Heike Strab into the back room by her heels. Stanz mashed her face into the dirtpile left by the tunnelers, then sat on the back of her head until she stopped breathing and went to meet her ancestors.

Then Wolfie opened her up with his fake SS dagger, and they began to tag the flaking stone walls with her blood.

—ooo—

A good burn is three hundred or so, stacked young to old and fat to thin, to make the fires run hot enough to forge steel.

Shaven, deloused, and numbered, Aschmaus fetches a skull and wiggles the jawbone to mime speech for the amusement of Kommandant. He finds many glass eyes and starts a collection. More browns, here, than anything else.

Aschmaus will mock them all if it means he is allowed to breathe and eat until one more sunrise. He can force Mama's face to fade from his memory. He blocks out the sounds of strangers enroute to Heaven. He erases their expressions, building walls inside his head, just like another hobby, a secret one…the only private thing he has.

Sometimes, after Kommandant's boots are off and the Gramophone plays, Aschmaus is permitted a quarter-moon of sausage or an apple core from the table of his master. He sits at the feet of Kommandant and sometimes dozes. The light sleep allows him to imagine being spirited away by the music, to float high above the guards, out of sight of the towers, and beyond the pyres forever.

Aschmaus builds his walls, and collects his eyes, and floats when he can. Sunrise always comes.

—ooo—

Nearly a century earlier, in 1888, Jack the Ripper had also murdered two in one day. His murders of East End prostitutes Catherine "Kate" Eddowes and Elizabeth "Long Liz" Stride had become notorious as his "Double Event."

Clouder reflected upon his own busy morning, and wondered if, a hundred years from today, the scrutiny of history and hindsight would yield up motives, connections, irrefutable theories…all the disposable tripe that made for many a nonfiction bestseller, and lent armchair

Sherlockians a reason to keep using air. Serial killer books were big right now.

The "connection" part was a near-given. While Clouder had employed two different handguns to assassinate his two outwardly-unrelated targets, the chilly, deliberative style he brought to all his work might become worthy of the sort of editorial comment that would flag the jobs as contract hits or execution-style murders. Which was all the evidence anyone would ever have to chew over. Which was precisely why Clouder had chosen this methodology. He never left accidental clues, always left purposeful voids—something on which second-rate intellects could nibble, eagerly, endlessly. Uselessly.

He hung up his topcoat in the foyer and blotted his face lightly with the tip of his scarf—a natty affectation he had never bothered to ponder. Perhaps it was a luck gesture.

"Hirohiko Ozawa" had not seemed surprised to be killed, and because of this, Clouder felt a fleeting kinship with the man. It was business, a risk Herr Ozawa had ventured with the potential consequences in clear sight. The hit had been a snack for Clouder.

"Erich Barstow," on the other hand, had behaved as though Clouder's visit was the biggest surprise of his truncated life. For Clouder, this second hit had left a spoiled taste on his intellectual palate all afternoon. As he fed the contents of the file jacket on Herr Ozawa to the shredder and thence to his fireplace, Clouder brewed strong tea in the Russian fashion and left a long spoon in the glass as a heat sink, to cool it. When it came to the disposal of the file on Herr Barstow, Clouder uncharacteristically flipped through it one last time. It was thicker than the file summing up Ozawa's history and habits.

Amateurs should never play the only international game that matters. What had inspired the creation of the man Clouder had killed as Erich Barstow?

The folder was fattened by a pamphlet-style book titled *Holocaust Hoax!* It had been published—typos, fingerprinty layout and all—by the Phoenix Foundation in 1983, three years before an abused copy had been purchased on a whim by a Georgetown University history teacher named Eric Greene. *Holocaust Hoax!* was a transparently primal, foamingly anti-intellectual rant. Its proud author, Karl Hessler, was prominently pictured with an extensive though modest bio of his accomplishments. Clouder had only to look at the photo of Hessler to infer the man's sheer baseness and fanaticism: He was sloppy and flabby, with a fetish for uniforms; low cunning smoldered from his eyes. Exactly the cartoon real Nazis would never condone...except where financial contributions were concerned. Clouder dropped the booklet next to the remainder of the file.

Eric Greene's backstory was as depressingly thin and predictable as Hessler's motives. His mother had been a Gentile who died when Greene was six. His father had been flattened by a thromboembolism the size of a kosher salami. Finding himself the de facto patriarch of the bloodline, Eric began to seek "meaning" in his life.

Clouder rolled his eyes. Never content, are the drab ones, to teach history and remain good consumers. On the other hand, Greene had been reminded of his own mortality and acted to change the course of his existence. Perhaps there had been a mote of depth to the man.

The collision between Greene and *Holocaust Hoax!* appeared random. It was the sole accidental confluence of the chain of events Clouder had recently terminated with gunfire. Greene's passions had been ignited by Hessler's diatribe, so perhaps the booklet had achieved some good.

Using a fake name and a mail drop, Greene had cast a line into the turbid waters of intrigue and reeled Hessler closer—

not surprisingly, given Hessler's obvious hunger. Through expedient lies and judicious use of the blind spots provided by long-distance contact, Greene was able to present himself as "Erich Barstow"…Washington lobbyist, closet Nazi, sympathetic ear, and Karl Hessler's newest benefactor and best friend.

Clouder sipped his tea and paged forward. As soon as Greene had Hessler's ear, he also attracted the notice of the Institute. The Institute had come forward and filled in a few gaps regarding the family bloodline.

Greene's father, it turned out, had survived Auschwitz and come to America as a displaced person in 1948. Clouder shook his head. The background pull on Greene's family was shallow, trivial. But the Institute people had a hole card—a photograph, which they produced for Greene's scrutiny at precisely the right moment.

Mother and child, anonymous Krakow street; little boy waving as Mama holds him up. Stitched on the sleeves of both, a crude, six-pointed star of cloth.

Clouder only had a blurry facsimile of the photo. He read the mother as careworn but hopeful. She and the child were smiling, though the circumstances seemed bleak. In an instant he felt a twinge, a trace memory, something like the recognition Greene must have felt when the Institute had ambushed him with this picture.

Eric Greene had seen his father's face in the boy. His father had made it out of a death camp. His grandmother, the young, proud woman in the photo, had not…but here she was, waving hello to the grandson she would never hold or know.

Clouder fed the facsimile of the photo into the shredder.

The timing was more critical than Eric Greene ever could have suspected. Once Hessler phoned him, brimming over with some exciting new project for which the new Reich would be honored to request the participation of

"Erich Barstow," all the Institute had to do was let Greene know that they just happened to need a neo-Nazi "face" for their latest sting operation. Past and future, history and reality had all rammed together for Eric Greene in that moment, and he had agreed, perhaps impulsively, to play hero.

The rest of the jacket was insignificant. Greene had a brown-eyed *hausfrau* back in Georgetown named Ellen Rachel. No children. His tenure was up for review at the school. No pets.

Clouder cleaned up the hearth with a small whisk broom once he had consigned the rest of the "Erich Barstow" jacket to the fire. He felt mild annoyance. Greene had tried to plug a gap in his spiritual life; silly to blame him for anything, since the man had never known how exposed he had been all along. Reconsidering Greene's backstory, now, had opened a similar chasm in Clouder's calm. Never a good idea, he reflected, to feel involved with the targets.

Greene was banal and hopeless. He was the *late* Herr Greene.

Clouder passed from his living room to his billiards room. Both were identical in configuration, separated by an archway that had been a non-supporting wall. Clouder's residence had once been the east wing of a mid-income apartment warren erected on post-war rubble as a filing cabinet for human beings—mirror image rooms ranked with military monotony. After a flurry of re-zoning, Clouder moved in along with upscale refurbishments, occupying two apartments now fused into one.

Only bills were mailed here, addressed to a name other than Clouder's. Technically, Clouder had not possessed a traceable name for decades, only a pack of identities shuffled and discarded at will. Soon, there would no longer be a distinction between East and West; Clouder might have to change the way he return-addressed his bills. They were calling it

Reunification. Now it could all be "Germany" again. Past the jubilation of the crumbling Wall waited all manner of nasty ghosts from the past. Once Re-unified, how else might the reborn Germany become like the old?

The realization hit Clouder like tea lees on the tongue; mentally brackish. Had Eric Greene been conned into sacrificing his life by the dolts at the Institute?

The Institute people had found a well-intentioned but ignorant Jew. They had leveraged his distaste for Nazis with exactly the right pep talk. They had strategically advantaged his family's past, and, when the time came, shoveled him onto the firing line.

The Institute was after something else, and Eric Greene had been a pawn to play.

Clouder made more tea. He always chose a new glass for each refill. He was fastidious in small rituals. It was a fairly quick puzzle exercise to dope out what had happened backstage, before his second assignment of the morning.

Clouder's data pull on Greene/Barstow had come from Die Schwarze Spinne, a puppet-master conference of new Nazis who specialized in stringing along outmoded warhorses like Hessler's Phoenix Foundation, in the hope that the Ultimate Destiny of that gang of political mummies would include growing up and getting real. The go-between had been a double agent from Die Schwarze Spinne, code-named "Gelft."

That would be the man to whom Clouder had given a curt nod, as he opened the door and stepped out...so Clouder could step in, and close the door, and kill Eric Greene and Erich Barstow with the same shots. Gelft had probably read the same deep background on Greene that Clouder was now destroying.

Gelft was an interesting game-piece. Clouder enjoyed deduction.

Gelft had appeared Slavic, and so could reasonably pass as a card-carrying member of the Mossad Aliyah Beth, and thus penetrate the American Embassy in Berlin...that is, West Berlin. He could easily pass as German; his accent, as Dutch. By exploiting contacts made at the Embassy, Gelft could alert the Institute to a Nazi pow-wow, which had caused the Institute to summarily send "Erich Barstow" to slaughter. The Institute would interpret Greene's instantaneous exposure not as a leak, but as a slap in the face. A warning. The Institute had been in bed with the Arabs ever since the manufactured petrol crises of the early 1970s, and, to Clouder's recollection, the Arabs had never been overly fond of the Mossad. The Greene sting had been necessarily flimsy because assisting Israel could never bear too obviously high a price tag.

As a wild card in this international deck, Gelft (or however he was called in the real world) was fraught with inscrutability and freighted with ghost details—ephemeral facts that cumulated to fog. Given the major premise that Eric Greene was a Jew masquerading as a Nazi, and the minor premise that Gelft could just as well be working for either side, a syllogist would conclude that if Greene had not become a victim of budget (typical of Institute ops) or had been targeted for any motive other than a neatening of the international deck (like whacking the cards to make their edges true up)...then something was missing. An ingredient Clouder could not yet perceive; some concealed advantage that might come into play late in the game.

It might be stimulating to purposefully interfere, given what Clouder already knew or could deduce. He could affect the outcome of short-term future events. Otherwise, the double event that used up most of his morning would hold no satisfaction for him at all. Killing was not enough, anymore.

Not a sacrifice, Clouder concluded. More typically of Institute ops, Eric Greene had become a victim of budget.

Satisfied that his morning's work was now not such a mystery, Clouder phoned a secure night line in Zurich to confirm that two deposits had been posted to his private accounts as of closing time, this date. Thanks to a device called a Solander Box, Clouder had one of the "hardest" telephone lines in Europe. Any attempt at a trace or tap would be routed to random numbers all over the city; a multiplicity of unknown names behind which Clouder could remain safe. Too bad Eric Greene had not had such a parachute persona to spare.

The special silencer Clouder had employed this morning had been custom-built to swaddle a broad assortment of revolvers or autos. Its wing-nut port was designed to lock any barrel into thick exit baffles. As Clouder was fond of thinking, *the bang jumps from the chamber, not the muzzle.* All it took was a microsecond, but it was the *loudest* microsecond of the whole process of discharging a firearm. He told this to the gunsmith who fabricated the silencer. Barrel silencers, both men knew, were a conceit of popular cinema. Clouder's silencer, similar to a camera blimp, was the real deal. Along with both job guns and the attaché case that had contained them, it had been mashed into a characterless cube of scrap by the big junk compactors near the Berlin Wall, where a lot of demolition would be taking place for a good long while. Clouder regretted the loss of the silencer, because it was the work of an artisan, an exemplar of a craftsmanship the New Germany had lost sight of.

But since Clouder was a methodical man, he had already ordered two more just like it.

Clouder's home was riddled with hidey-holes for such things as weapons and silencers and all manner of currency

and ID. Some were simple safes, or sliding-panel compart-
ments sophisticated enough to outfox any snoop wearing a
uniform. Others were capable of withstanding multiband
scanning or nuclear attack...not that flying missiles were
much of a downside possibility, given the cheerful, chaotic
tone prevalent in the newspapers and on TV.

After stashing the Halliburton case from the Hirohiko
Ozawa job in the boot of a planted Mercedes, Clouder had
come home empty-handed. Lacking a new contract, and not
wanting the phantom of Eric Greene spoiling the rest of the
day, he thought about die Berliner Mauer. He had walked
through some of the crowd assembled for its deconstruction.
He had felt no sense of community.

Berlin, "sister city" to Los Angeles as Cannes was to
Beverly Hills, was once again girding to act as the capital for
a unified Germany. American military—250,000 strong during their height of deployment in 1987—would be packing
their bags, and the historic "Berlin Brigade" commanded by
Colonel Alfred W. Baker would be the first to leave during
this massive drawdown. The Brigade would vacate offices
formerly used by the Luftwaffe, in an East German building
erected for Field Marshall Hermann Goering—until recently, the sole U.S. base behind enemy lines.

Clouder's admiration for Colonel Baker was twofold;
first, there was boundless respect for the man's ability to
recreate himself from the ground up. In 1969, Baker had
been blown apart by a satchel full of Viet Cong explosives.
His bones sundered as the blast hurled him twenty feet into
the air; he landed with half his face ripped away and his back
broken in two places. Medics abandoned him in a triage section. When a priest began giving him last rites, Baker spat out
bits of teeth and shredded gums to say, "Get the fuck away.
I'm not Catholic, and I'm not going to die."

The second reason was something Baker had said as a young lieutenant assigned to patrol East Berlin in the early 1960s, words that Clouder had memorized because they not only spoke to a capacity deep inside him, a space in his soul long dormant and almost forgotten, but also summed up the bisected, bleeding place the city had become then: "It was like looking into day on one side and night on the other, like living in sunshine while looking into a storm. As I drove around, people would sometimes signal, *'Don't forget us.'*"

Something had been forgotten. Something was missing. That was why Eric Greene's face kept nagging Clouder. An American Jew with a hole in his past had become a pretend Nazi with a hole in his brain. Some vital truth had been misplaced. Not overlooked; Clouder was too painstaking to be sloppy. It was like the name of a popular song just near the tip of the tongue—teasing, seductive, elusive.

Clouder meditated in an abrasively hot needle shower, and lay down naked, to nap. Counting prep for the morning's work, he had been awake for eighteen hours. Before he closed his eyes he turned on his stereo. Now it was Mahler time.

—ooo—

The tuneless song mumbled by the Ash and Death Brigades holds hope neither for victim nor tormentor:

> *Hey, S.O.B., hey, S.O.B.,*
> *Why did you give birth to me?*
> *Such a life, such a life;*
> *Better if you had a miscarriage.*

Days become weeks, become months, metered out in sweat and hunger, stench and dread. The superstitious wisdom of dead Mama's God means nothing to a boy born into a world of pogroms, ghettos, and actions. He knows no justice or meaning, family or tribe. There is no "God" here.

The new eye he finds for his collection is perfect blue, like the Führer's, blue like the sky. It will watch over him, as the others sense his power and avert their gaze. They are already corpses, all of them, rough fuel for flames. But he is Aschmaus, king of the liars, and he will always find a way to survive.

—ooo—

Henri startled awake, in a nightmare sweat, the strains of dreamt music fading, to be replaced by a headache. So real, the dreams, so narcotic, but no match for the ringing phone. He tried to locate his glasses, his robe, his composure, in time to hear the bad news. Calls were infrequent, and calls like this one, potent enough to slap the mist from his brain, if not the crust from his eyes.

Though his phone was connected to an answering machine (a genuflection to encroaching technology), Henri did not believe in intermediaries. He nodded to himself and hummed monosyllables to indicate he was paying attention.

The Black Spider was spinning dark webs again. An Institute-sponsored grab had been sabotaged; an American friendly, killed. Henri's mouth drew taut, a reflex too familiar and never comfortable. One less for our side.

Then, the rest: A convocation had been called. Henri was to note the address. Tonight, at 33 Gelderstrasse, players would rally to savor some new proof that the old Reich was not all dust and ashes.

Henri rang off and worked on ways to deflect his oncoming headache. He felt destabilized and hung over.

He was a small man of common cut, with hair that was vibrantly white and a posture unbent by time, the sort of person who amortized his regrets by aiming high at his aspira-

tions. His hands were deft and capable; his eyes, unclouded. Henri saw things clearly. He had watched the Wall come down, mostly on television, and his opinion of the coming Reunification was guarded.

Holes were being kicked in the Brandenburg Gate. Stasi guards and Berliner polizei were seen drinking in public, as a jolly mob danced on the dividing line between Then and Now.

Whenever Henri heard talk of the past, the scar on the inside of his wrist would pulse, as though it was trying to communicate something arcane and revelatory. It was a puckered groove about three inches long, barely whiter than the unviolated flesh surrounding it. Henri preferred this bent serpent of scar tissue to the number that had once been tattooed there. He had performed his own anesthesia and carved the meat himself, using a sterilized straight razor. It had hurt very much. Henri had been blessed with a high tolerance for pain, ever since childhood.

He was alive. According to the phone call, a foreigner named Eric Greene was dead. Henri wondered about Herr Greene's tolerance for pain. He had no doubt that Eric Greene had been young, and brave...but he had never worn a cloth star, nor borne a number, and probably had never had to make cannibalistic choices to survive.

The code name for Henri's phone source was "Doppelgänger." Thanks to modern electronics, not even timbre of voice could be trusted, and it was of technology Doppelgänger had also spoken.

The meeting at 33 Gelderstrasse was coalescing around some stolen bit of hi-tech which had cost yet another life. To a man, those who were to gather there would count anyone with Henri's convictions as their most hated enemy.

Henri knew the address—a sprawl of granite situated midway between Checkpoint Charlie and the *Topographie des*

Terrors, where the crimes of the Fatherland were enshrined in the husk of the former headquarters of the Gestapo. Hosting tonight's affair would be the fairest-haired of the new Germany's politicos, Ernst Koepp, who had inherited the formidable house from his father, and so could hold court with an equidistant vantage of the world past and the world to come.

Such a chance, to straddle the past and the future, was one Henri did not want to miss.

In the East German state of Saxony, a dissident pastor-turned-Interior Minister named Heinz Eggert was getting tough. Eggert had formulated the idea of an elite police unit to deal especially with neo-Nazis and right-wing violence; soon his Soko REX, or "special commission for right-wing extremism," would be cleaning up Saxony's crime stats in a fashion designed to impress the entire planet. Other states, such as Brandenburg, were said to be considering the deployment of similar units.

Meanwhile, the Kremlin and the Americans and the Mossad shot for the big, splashy scores: the Mengeles, the Barbies, the Eichmanns, the fish capable of garnering the hottest international press, and the fattest appropriations.

While Eggert waited for all Germans to evolve, and while the higher-profile hunters of Nazi big game drew all the best reviews, between them existed Henri, right now, doing something about all this injustice, today, but unobtrusively. Ostentation and public accolades were both phobic to him.

Henri usually kept his television set turned on, sound down. It was an outmoded tube model, and reception was chancey with no cable hookup. Visual noise, not resolution, was the object. Occasionally he paid attention to the news. Just now he could see the excitement outside, trapped and boxed into his snowy screen—rapture reduced to spectacle.

The parade of color and motion on the silent television provided nondemanding companionship, and helped wall

away the crippling toxins that lived in his mind. He could shave the number from his forearm, but never from the inside of his head. Crossing the room to a bookshelf, he drew out a cloth edition of *Mein Kampf*—illegal to sell, he knew, but not to own. The dust on the shelf reassured him nothing had been disturbed since the last time he had used the book. Nestled within the thickness of its gutted pages was a keypad. Henri entered his number: 56281347.

The chamber hidden behind the sliding bookcase was the width of two opposing desks, with room for a chair between them—a small chair—and headroom low enough to brush against Henri's hair when he sat down. It was fully cluttered with Henri's cumulate sociopolitical research and bulging files. Tucked away in his computer database were many of the names who would show up at Koepp's house tonight. Like a detective plotting a drug bust, Henri knew how bad these men were. So did they. He had proof. They had protection. The trick, which never changed, was to catch them hot: right place, right time.

From a drawer he lifted a pistol he had never fired. It was a relic of the old war and a reminder of his hijacked youth. Henri utilized the gun, on occasion, to pry cooperation from men who were evil. The weapon was for sweeping up, not scoring kills; to settle old debts, not inspire new ones. That was why the Institute would forever call on Henri—their think-tankers already knew that business didn't matter, nor did politics. For Henri, it was all personal, and there were not many like Henri left. Whenever the Institute signalled, Henri would unleash himself as a bloodhound. It was cleaner, left a clear trail of blame, and made for less paperwork.

The part Henri's exploiters would never realize (and, in fact, did not give *un verdammt* about) was that Henri could never, to his own mind, bring down enough of the enemy to ever balance any set of scales. If he could burn the guilty ones, a hundred per day, the fire would last a century beyond the end of his life.

Bitterly, he wondered how many glass eyes he might reap from those cinders.

The monocular TV screen showed him his fellow citizens all coming gloriously unglued. The world had changed in a matter of days.

The hegira of East Berliners to Hungary and Czechoslovakia had resulted in demonstrations in Leipzig and Dresden. It all came to a head in the Alexanderplatz: Three quarters of a million people causing the Politburo stalwarts to blush and sweat like weight lifters, as they promised change and tried to buy time.

Two days ago the *Reisscpass* law had been announced. For the first time in forty years, exit visas would permit the *ossis* to visit the Western sector, starting the following morning. Simple. Profound.

Except that Party publicist Gunter Shabowsky had only lent the new law a cursory skim, while enroute by limousine to a TV press conference. When asked *when* the law would go into effect, Shabowsky riffled his paperwork and, finding no answer, told the journalists and live cameras what sounded best:

As far as he knew, *immediately.*

At every gate from the Reichstag down to Checkpoint Charlie, they amassed by the tens of thousands, demanding the right to pass...fourteen hours early. The *Tinterpisser Burokrats* were completely blindsided, while the border guards at the Borhomler Street crossing wondered if they should start shooting everyone.

Finally, it was a lean, alcelaphine Stasi captain named Helmut Stossi who was the first to open his gates, and begin the floodtide that would eventually topple the Iron

Curtain…without a shot fired, a world-shaking result of what was essentially a clerical error.

And as the one man who made a difference through action, Captain Stossi had wondered, touchingly, just why he had been standing at that gate for the last twenty years. Henri had seen him, on television.

Henri appreciated the maxim about putting six million monkeys behind six million typewriters…only instead of writing *Macbeth,* here they had stumbled across $E=MC^2$, built an atomic bomb, and blown up the whole world. Captain Stossi's example was the latest expression of a principle upon which Henri had founded his entire adult life— that one man's action could change everything.

He despised predictability.

He decided to take the gun with him to the party.

—ooo—

The computer chip that had cost Hirohiko Ozawa his multiform life resembled a silicon centipede with jutting, tine-like legs of copper. The slim box that contained it in a nest of anti-static foam was in Hoff's breast pocket; the way Hoff paranoiacally patted himself down between bites and after each sip of wine confirmed for Ernst Koepp that the man was a twitch, unstable, too furtive even for a mad scientist.

But Hoff was undeniably a maestro in the orchestration of data, in the careful coaxing of machines; in the alien (to Koepp) subworld of optical drives and gigabytes and super-processors, Hoff could make music. Hoff knew how to interpret the songs of a billion lifetimes, all distilled to incomprehensible chains of zeros and ones, all stored in one one-hundredth the area of the head of a pin.

Hoff had his job and was happy in his work. Koepp's job, this night, was to wed Hoff's technological sorcery to the half-century old ideal of a Thousand Year Reich...and make the marriage work.

At the foot of the table, Karl Hessler was busy sucking up and being seen. Hessler had always reminded Koepp of a blowfish, and he had wanted to shoot the fat man himself after that abortive, Institute-sponsored show-and-tell. Getting nailed in the down-market company of the Phoenix Foundation and crusty old sieg-heilers like Jaeckel inside a soft-target hotel could only wreak detrimental effects on Koepp's image-building.

Tonight, he had mandated the meeting place: The Gelderstrasse manse boasted crenellated battlements; a gated stone wall bespoke its aristocratic heritage. It was one of the few private residences not levelled by Allied bombs, and it was rumored that Prince Albert of Prussia had once kept a mistress there. Such history pleased Koepp, whether it was true or not. The residence had been handed down to him by his father, a much-valued Party member who had liberated it from the previous tenant, a well-to-do glassmaker named Schulman. The only thing Koepp knew about Herr Schulman was that he had gone flying up a smokestack at Treblinka...that, and Herr Schulman's Big Secret.

In the heady days prior to the *Kristellnacht,* Herr Schulman (clever Hebrew that he was) had dug out a secondary cellar and provisioned it as a hiding place spacious enough to sustain his family—he had fathered six children—for several weeks. A sliding door, veneered to appear as a featureless wall of plaster, accessed the room, which was laid out like a rail flat at six by sixteen meters, and incorporated cooking and sanitation facilities—the vents for which had been the fatal giveaway. Koepp knew well the rule about being careful when it came to what billowed from one's flue, and had eradicated all exterior evidence of the chamber's

existence years ago, beyond all decent memory. He had fed in modern wiring and track lighting and air filtration. Up until this historic night, Koepp had used the space primarily as a gallery for his oil canvases—Impressionists, a few pre-Raphaelites and several Klees—another legacy from Papa Koepp, the deserving Party man.

Security was handled by Koepp's handpicked staff, spearheaded by two chromium-eyed pups named Rudi and Klaus, both wired as tight as a Gestapo smile. Inside this house, Koepp could allow fools like Hessler and antiques like Jaeckel the courtesy of dismissive indulgence, and let his hair down among the men who were the true hope for a restored Reich.

Up-table were Heidrick and Drexler, aggressive, third-generation National Socialists from the United States. At Koepp's right hand was Volmer Saphire, in from Stuttgart. Saphire was Koepp's first choice for Vice Chancellor, when the time came. To Koepp's left was Biermann, who, despite his comical name, was the best-case argument for a modern-day Göering Koepp could summon; not so much a man as a big, solid *thing,* cold and unyielding, a wall of rock. Then Hoff, all frizzy hair and frazzled thoughts and fractured composure, fretting through the dessert course and afire with the nearly sexual thoughts concerning what he could make his beloved computer chip do. Past him, Stohler, newly returned from Argentina just two days prior to his 69th birthday. Then there was Conrad Bleuel, a master prestidigitator of identity who had been wooed by the Palestinians the moment the Middle East replaced Viet Nam as the hot spot of the Seventies. Past him sat Esslin and Zille, both present by dint of untainted post-war identities supplied courtesy of the American CIA, in a heartwarming display of morality-free barter. Then came the briefcase brigade: Adenauer, Gelft, and Broger, respectively representing the Order, Die Schwarze

Spinne, and the Aryan Nation. Directly across from Koepp sat his boyhood friend (and current lover) Werner Uedey.

This, reflected Koepp, was what Reinhard Heydrich must have felt like, presiding over Wannsee—a conference of dedicated men, some more reliable than others, some better at their jobs than the men next to them, some simply better men, but all of them aimed at a common accord, sipping good cognac, changing the world.

Adenauer called for a toast in remembrance of the Phantom Nazi, and Koepp listened while the legend was recited, for those who had not yet caught up.

According to the story, the Phantom Nazi was a key player in the waking hours of the Kampfbund, a man so overlooked by scholarly history that he now bore all the seductive mystique of a subordinate Kennedy assassin. Shortly following the Beer Hall Putsch, the Phantom Nazi had staged a phony attempt on the Gefreiter's life in Munich—meticulously planned, and timed to raise public consciousness. All it had taken was a single gunshot, fired from a hidden vantage in the Feldherrnhalle. A riot between Nazis and police ensued, and the rest was history they all knew. The man who had been instrumental in Hitler's rise to dominance had never claimed credit, nor enjoyed status in the Third Reich. Having humbly worked a miracle for the good of Germany, he had chosen to remain invisible for all time. Admirable. Glasses clinked.

At the opposite end of the table, Hessler noisily proposed some counter-toast Koepp felt comfortable ignoring. Instead, he monitored the variant degrees of enthusiasm around the table, and gauged the plaudits given the Phantom Nazi to bode well for the presentation he had planned, which would begin as soon as the requisite form of stinking cigars and antiseptic brandy could be dispensed with.

When it was time to make the pitch, Koepp tapped his table knife against a water glass. Hessler, as usual, was the last to fall silent.

While they sat, feasting, observed Koepp, a new Germany was taking shape outside. Agreements were murmured all around.

It was a revolution. Not just in Germany, but all over the world. The not-so-superpowers were doomed. Communism would implode from its own top-heaviness. Gangsters would hold sway, Ivan in pinstripe, as America the long-distance runner wheezed and wobbled and finally toppled. From the void would issue chaos, inflation, black-market rule. The resultant feeding frenzy would leave the rest of the globe on the slave auction block. As the Zionists hatched futile plots, the Mideast would sunder, and China would rouse from its Maoist coma. The world would cry out for order at any price, and welcome the first iron hand that could guide it. They would be ready.

Hearty assent, from the group, as Koepp now spoke of the *new* blitzkriegs. He invoked the technological *gris-gris* of computers, of internets, of information super-highways, of fiber-optic filaments through which any security, anywhere, could be penetrated. Of how the new assaults would be fast, fluid, mutable, like speed viruses overwhelming nations before a single shot could be fired, or missile re-targeted. Resistance? Topple it from within. Make bank accounts evaporate with a phone call. Make the enemy disappear by turning them into non-persons with a salvo of keystrokes simpler than playing "Chopsticks" on the piano.

Hoff bobbed his skull in approval, particularly when Koepp used the chrome-plated, mathematically romantic buzzwords. There were no walkouts.

Outside the battlements of 33 Gelderstrasse, Berliners were drunkenly partying on behalf of German rebirth. This, too, fit and seemed apt.

Koepp put on his very best Party face, and rose to lead his fellow *soldaten* downstairs, to where a better future awaited them all.

—ooo—

The front bell rang just late enough to turn Rudi's edginess to hostility. His partner Klaus was already deep into full-blown pique. Neither enjoyed Herr Koepp's proper, political shindigs, because Germany had always been the most caste-conscious of countries, and the coven of Nazis who had just spent two hours guzzling and gorging and farting in the dining room reminded these two young aspirants that they were not yet Party members, did not rate Party privileges. Not yet.

Tonight, they walked through their roles as Koepp's most trusted adjutants, sneaking swift gulps of schnapps and bitching with minty breath about the ways they could become point men in the new Fourth Reich, if only Koepp would grant them a window.

The bell sounded just as Koepp was leading his guests to the wine cellar for the evening's members-only divertissements. Instead of relaxing a notch, Rudi and Klaus probably had to deal now with some inebriated *scheisskopf* from the revel outside. They could pitch the interloper back to the mob, or—Klaus caught the chilly sparkle in Rudi's eye—perhaps they could escort him to where the cars were parked and pummel the grease out of him, wholesale.

Either way, the entertainment prospects for the evening were looking up.

—ooo—

Gelft drew a deep and careful breath, showing no outward sign of reaction or shock. The visitor standing on Koepp's threshold was of small stature and bookish mien,

like an accountant, a man of no abrasive surface detail. He seemed to know where he was; he had come here on purpose. He exuded friendliness and solicited cooperation. Peter Kurten, the Dusseldorf Vampire, had been a man such as this—smartly dressed, tranquil, polite, even deferential...

...rapist, arsonist, a murderer who loved bestiality and killed men, women, children, animals, *anything*, using hammer, knife, scissors and garrote, not that he favored those tools specifically. He killed with whatever came to hand and did the job. Kurten had committed the first of his ghastly crimes and shocked all of Germany the same year as Hitler's Beer Hall Putsch.

The man in the doorway smiled, inquired, acted formal. Rudi back-stopped Klaus; neither of them was smiling.

Just yesterday, Gelft and this guest had passed each other, Gelft exiting, the other man entering to blow Eric Greene, a.k.a. Nazi manqué Erich Barstow, clean out of his patent leather shoes. Gelft had admired the polish of the hit, after the fact. Now, he calmed; no struggle, since he, too, was a pro.

The killer at the front door returned Gelft's glance with absolutely no recognition. This gentleman is *good*, thought Gelft. This gentleman is a cube of ice.

As the other guests had trooped down to Koepp's cellar or bomb shelter or whatever it was, Gelft had excused himself to use the bathroom and swipe sixty extra seconds for tactical considerations. Now a solution to his worry had just knocked on the front door. Gelft had the power to order Rudi and Klaus to back off, so he did; Rudi and Klaus didn't like it, and Gelft didn't care. The stranger entered, doffing hat and umbrella and directing a curt smile of acknowledgement—no more—to Gelft. Still, deep in those killer's eyes, no hint or giveaway clue.

Good.

Gelft escorted the newcomer downstairs. The look of disappointment on the faces of Rudi and Klaus was as palpable as fresh-molded clay. Gelft switched his briefcase to his free hand in order to clap his comrade on the shoulder as they descended, the better to discreetly inquire as to what alias he would prefer to be called when he was introduced to the guests.

The answer held no significance for Gelft.

Below, Koepp had run out of armbands. Gelft saw the others sporting them—classic black swastikas in white circles on fields of crimson—and preening fatuously like hormone-drunk Hitler Youth at their first circle jerk. If Koepp had a prevalent talent, it was for making everyone belong. He would remind them all that aboveground, in a world where modern Berliners danced atop the tombstone of Stalinism, it was illegal to wear such insignia. It was a crime to sell a copy of Germany's most influential biography. It was against the law even to give the Nazi salute.

Koepp fancied himself the father of change, a man who would favor his chosen and give them back their pride, and, tonight, confer on them all the honor of being in the vanguard. Yes, even Hessler.

The interstices of wall space between Koepp's collection of stolen paintings were absorbed by pegged oaken shelves displaying a fastidiously-kept library—books on one side of the corridor-shaped chamber, videocassettes and disks on the other. Gelft could smell processed air, and suspected dehumidifiers.

A large projection monitor spanned the far end of the underground room; in earlier decades, this space could have been a stage. The beaded screen was enormous, taller than Gelft. On standby, it glowed a bright, expectant blue.

Gelft watched his guest squint at the shelves, examining the sleek treasure trove of Nazi lore, filed with care and tended with something like love. Every book imaginable. Every frame of archival footage ever exposed to light: der Führer in uniform, in civvies, making speeches, shaking hands, leading troops, doing a jig, dancing with his dogs, disporting with Eva. Here were Goebbels' home movies. It was all in evidence—the largest and certainly one of the most comprehensive databases on the little painter Gelft could imagine. He suspected it even went the distance of including psychiatric profiles, past and present, and reports by modern authorities on the likely makeup of the very chemicals in Hitler's brain.

Koepp nodded to Hoff, the electronics man, and finished distributing snifters. With a Phantom of the Opera flourish, Hoff seated himself at a terminal that looked complex enough to administer a Swiss bank on autopilot. He removed the stolen Koramitsu chip from its case and plugged it into a cylindrical socket that withdrew into the main terminal once a few commands had been tapped into the keyboard. A tiny port irised shut and the chip was gone, swallowed.

Hoff's explanation that the chip converted digital samples into virtual reality analogues sailed clear over the intellects of most of the men present. There was more. Koepp motioned for him to get on with it. Hoff persisted long enough to emphasize that this hybrid computer could not only assimilate information, but also produce resultant artificial intelligence that was capable of free association.

Ja, right. Hessler, near the rear of the group, picked his nose and wheezed in awe at a fully-accoutred SS uniform preserved in a standup glass case near the door. While Hessler was a tourist in this idiom, Jaeckel was nostalgic, openly coveting the outfit's ceremonial dagger.

Hoff pecked in a few more directives. His brow furrowed. He stroked his upper lip longwise with his index finger, as though awaiting telepathic approval from the device. Deep within sandwiched circuitry, disks whirled into a simulacrum of life.

Koepp glanced at his watch and made sure that Hoff saw him do it. Gelft almost stepped forward to introduce his guest, but that would have been a mood-breaker. When the big monitor glitched—a digital hiccup—Gelft sighed and put his attaché case down, shrugging to the visitor (who had become his special charge until the presentation was finished). It looked like they were going to have to play audience for awhile.

Pixel by pixel, a face began to resolve onto the big screen, like a monochromatic sketch in ice, slowly surfacing through gray water. Hoff nodded affirmatively at Koepp.

At first, it was just a blurry video composite, the features jumping about in crude planes and curves, the idiographic shock of dark hair and toothbrush moustache little better than a bad cartoon caricature; Disney does Dachau. Its eyes were closed. Its expression, if you could call it that, was one of perfect, regal peace.

Shadows overlaid themselves as the machine extrapolated and exponentially built on what it knew. The image acquired depth and perspective. Topography melted into physiognomy. For Gelft, it was akin to watching really good polarized 3D, without the glasses. He swore he could make out *pores* on the face. The very tips of the moustache hairs were white. The nostrils flared as the image gave the appearance of breathing.

Those watching were trapped between breaths. When the giant face onscreen at last opened its eyes—blue eyes—and seemed to look right at them, they were transfixed.

Koepp made his move. Gelft could see the speckles of feverish perspiration on his forehead. The politician strode forward and proclaimed *Alle Juden Raus!*

It was not the reaction of the guests, but the expression on the face of the onscreen image that drew Gelft's startled

attention: It *altered* at the sound of Koepp's voice; it was both imperious and innocent, half-child, half-god. It *looked* from Koepp to the rest. The way it seemed to be seeing them all, individually, somehow knowing what it was doing, was the thing that captured Gelft's astonishment. It had to be wired into pinhole cameras. Maybe they were all being monitored from a dozen vantages right now, and fed into Hoff's monster on a nanosecond-to-nanosecond basis. The machine would be digesting what it took in, and reacting to it.

Beaming, Koepp waited while the image answered.

What it said was: *H-h-hi-hhei-Heil-hh.*

The face wrestled with its first spoken word, its voice careening from basso profundo to adenoidal squeak. As the image continued to refine, softening and becoming more organic, Hoff's expression grew unreal as he mumbled apologies and excuses to Koepp and abused the keyboard, seeking rectification with pursed, white lips and the cheesy skin tone of a cadaver.

H-h-hhe-Heil... HIT-hiii...HEIL hit-hit-hit...

It blasted them all from hidden speakers like a retarded child doing do-re-mi in surround sound and fast motion. Half the men had put down their brandy glasses in discomfort. Adenauer glanced at Gelft and shrugged. Most of the rest, being very German, waited with neutral expressions and vaunting disdain for what might happen next.

Hoff banged out another flurry of keystrokes. The face de-rezzed and reconfigured in a quarter-second, as though someone had slapped it in the back of the head.

Heil Hi-Hi-HITT-lrr!

Koepp snapped to, saluting and repeating the invocation correctly. It worked on about half of the guests, like Jaeckel, who thrust out his chicken bone chest as though galvanically prodded. Some of the younger men, like Drexler and Broger, were anxious to err on the side of inclusion, if for no bigger reason than not to be ambushed by some tricky pop quiz on loyalty.

The face looked back to Koepp. *At* him, thought Gelft; if it was a trick, it was a fancy one. The face seemed to consider anger, then think better of it. To Koepp, it said *Heil, Hitler!*...this time, without the electronic stutter. Damned near perfect.

Koepp lit up. The program recognized him, and was actually communicating! Now almost everyone joined him in returning the salute.

Almost everyone.

When Gelft saw the expression on the face of the little man, his "guest," he literally could not summon a definition for it. There was no time for speculation. At the back of the chamber, someone was laughing.

Karl Hessler, founder and embodiment of the Phoenix Foundation, dropped his brandy glass. His face was bright red. The bulbs spotlighting Koepp's display uniform picked out the fat man, too clearly, as his chuckle broke free, into a guffaw. He brayed. He was on the verge of a rupture. Heidrick and Saphire actually stepped *back* from him, as though he was contagious; probably more afraid that they might start laughing themselves.

Gelft watched the others as Hessler pawed air, trying to justify himself, to explain, if only by pantomime, that...

That he was thinking helplessly of playing Pong. Of trying to place a simple long-distance phone call in Europe. Of an Interactive Adolf to order them all around, leading to a portable version, the Ronco Pocket Führer...

That this was the silliest fucking thing he'd ever seen in his life.

The American at last had to lean against the glass cabinet that contained the SS gear. He was gasping now. Struggling

to draw air, thought Gelft, so he could laugh some more. It might serve as a distraction.

Gelft saw the rage in Koepp hit the flash point. Before he could retaliate, and attempt to save face, a decision was reached from the other side of the room. Someone else had chosen what to do, and without messy emotional noise.

The face on the screen spoke Koepp's name—perfectly—then added something new, also without flaw: *Ausrotten.*

At first Gelft misunderstood; he thought he had heard *all is rotten.* Koepp understood. So did Hessler, who stopped laughing as though switched off. It was a word he had creatively misused throughout his amateur career to rationalize booklets like *Holocaust Hoax!* The gauntlet of faces, like a jury in the semi-dark, parted as Koepp came for the fat man.

Hessler backed away, his mind positively lusting for an explanation. Gelft saw his opportunity, and knew in his soul that the time had come for extirpation, for extermination. For *ausrotten.*

The perpetrator of the Phoenix Foundation managed three backward steps before the nape of his neck stopped against Gelft's 10-millimeter Glock. The single, unsilenced shot hit hard in the tomb-like acoustics of the subterranean room. Everyone flinched. Hessler's overactive vocal gear sprayed to fleck the monitor from which the projected image observed his demise, not with hatred, or fulfillment, but with total concentration. Hoff, unaccustomed to tasting dots of honest-to-god dead guy on his face, almost bolted. Gelft aimed the gun at him next. In less time than it took Hessler's corpse to fall, Hoff sat back down to mind his own business, tend his keyboard, and sit in his own urine as the inseam of his trousers darkened.

Onscreen, their Führer smiled.

Gelft saw the light: Every scrap of information on Hitler had been synthesized here, and the product knew history, politics, strategy, economics, and human nature better than any ten of them. It would learn more by the millisecond and never forget anything it knew. It could see where errors had occurred before, dissect mistakes from a million angles, and forge unheard-of strengths from former weaknesses. The longer it thought, the better it would get, and it *never* stopped thinking. It could transcend the frailties of the flesh as a being of pure will, and this time, that will could triumph…if they all listened to what it would have to say.

It reminded them all, *zum Biespiel,* that in 1945 the Red Army's ukase to de-Nazify Poland and Germany led to the deaths of over 75,000 Germans—men, women, and children, all noncombatant civilians—in more than 1200 "incarceration camps," where they subsisted on starvation rations if they did not die of typhus or overcrowding. Russia's Office of State Security deliberately recruited survivors of the so-called Holocaust to round up Germans and subject them to this vengeful punishment…

…*and these hypocrites dared to wail Never Again?*

Gelft saw the eyes of his companions in the dark, glittering now, transfixed by the conjured image, but more so by the reinvigorated dream. They were all reflected in their leader's cool phosphor gaze in an endlessly expressed duality. All of them, save the eyes of his guest, the belated observer with the unplugged calm of a professional killer…or a man who could read the evil in this place, who had perhaps even tasted it.

The little man was trembling. He tore a Luger from his coat and shouted a single word. It was supposed to be dramatic, a show stopper. Instead, Gelft saw that the man was on the verge of weeping, the impact of his gesture sabotaged by the quaver in his voice.

The word was *genug,* and all it meant was *enough.*

Koepp's glare was alive with bloodlust. The resolve of his lieutenants had been consecrated by the sacrifice of Hessler; their minds, pleasured by the seductions of their church. Now a new victim had just presented himself—a stranger, a coward who had drawn down on a roomful of men while their backs were turned.

Gelft felt the glandular kick of his own need to act. To terminate Koepp would amount to a symbolic decapitation of the Hydra. Killing any of the others would be a futile grab at bettering already suicidal odds.

His guest fired at the face on the screen.

There came no satisfying explosion of sparks and shrapnel. The screen was a rear-projection apparatus of bounce mylar. All the bullet did was punch a neat, round hole in the center of the oversized image's forehead, a flaw the face itself could not see.

The face smiled again, the mouth twitching upward halfway to express the crooked sort of pleasure one takes in squashing an insect. Hoff made a noise from the console. He had not typed a command for whole minutes.

There was only the time for one surprise move, one round fired, and Gelft acted before anyone else could. He trapped the shooter in an elevated full Nelson while Adenauer unhesitantly plucked the Luger from his grasp— probably to keep it as a trophy, Gelft thought. Eager to score points now that the danger was past, Biermann buried a pile-driver fist into the stranger's stomach that folded him and arched his feet off the floor. The stranger woofed air and sagged into Gelft's arms.

Gelft was instantly targeted by Koepp; this disruptive troublemaker was Gelft's fault. A good answer at this moment could mean the difference between a promotion...and another execution.

Gelft opted for clarity. This, he explained, was not an enemy of the Reich, but a man whose contributions, much like those of Adenauer's Phantom Nazi, had helped them behind the scenes, to obtain the chip, to neutralize vendetta-mongers like Eric Greene. Perhaps, Gelft suggested, his guest had drunk too freely, or was overwrought on some other front. Perhaps he was subsumed with passion for the miracle he had just witnessed.

Koepp demanded to know a name. Gelft slapped down the only card he had left to play: *Aschmaus.*

—ooo—

The name woke Joseph Jaeckel like a set of cardiac paddles. It seemed to renew the ultraviolet fire buried deep in his eyes, jump-start him like Frankenstein's lightning. He grabbed the wrist of the man held immobile by Herr Gelft of *Die Schwarze Spinne,* and twisted the arm to expose the crooked scar meandering along the inside of his wrist.

His smile was an incision in his face. He asked this "Aschmaus" where he had lost his number.

Today, Jaeckel was aware that most of the others viewed him as a fossil. In 1944, however, he had been SS Sturmbahnführer Jaeckel. He was old now, yes, and tired… but he would have to have been a potted plant not to recall the nickname bestown upon the six-year-old he had once watched burrowing through a grinding drum to frolic in the ashes of his own people.

Just watch, Kommandant's eyes seem to say, with a glimmer of pride. One like this comes along only once per war. Watch what my Aschmaus does.

Here, there was no retreat into mounds of pestled bone and the raw, pulverized residue of lives sacrificed. Jaeckel swore he could see something *behind* this man's eyes, suddenly tearing

apart, a barrier vaporizing without warning. Despite the ridiculous position in which he was being restrained by Gelft, this Juden managed to knock his heels together and deliver a sieg heil for the cincture of accusatory eyes engirding him, his palm snapping flat as his trapped arm jutted the wrong way.

Jaeckel watched the gesture *hold* all present, as it had mesmerized Kommandant. But only for an instant.

The men sizing up their would-be spoiler laughed, breaking the tension, elbowing each other. Koepp was back in charge, still seeking an explanation for the intruder, who was Gelft's responsibility.

Jaeckel said nothing. He wanted to see how these latter-day masters played it.

The man Gelft was excellent. He quickly proposed that he escort this Aschmaus, this secret agent, away to deal with him elsewhere, precisely because it was his responsibility. The late Karl Hessler would have to be cleaned out of Koepp's carpeting. There was no need for more wet melodrama inside of Koepp's house. Gelft wanted to acknowledge chain of command, and demonstrate respect.

Jaeckel's opinion was confirmed when he saw the thing with the bullet hole in its televisual head nod in silent agreement.

—ooo—

Henri ascended at gunpoint toward guaranteed death. He had failed to exterminate even one of the monsters at the bottom of these stairs. He was not a religious man, and so could seek no comfort in last rites or prayers.

What had he accomplished?

He had walked right into their lair, a Jew in the thick of Nazi connivance, a transgression punishable by a bullet to the brain. He had been unafraid. Had, in fact, felt an inexplicable sense of safety and closure, of good being done, ever since he had been admitted to Koepp's home unchallenged, with the help of the man who now intended to murder him.

Why?

Gelft, the man prodding Henri ever-upward with his gun, answered all his unspoken questions by whispering a single word.

Doppelgänger.

Space spiraled in Henri's vision; he tasted a blurt of dizzy nausea. Gelft was Doppelgänger? Until now, that code-name had been nothing more than a voice on the phone, ageless, sexless. Gelft was Institute, double-agenting within the web-work of *Die Schwarze Spinne*, then performing another half-twist, like a gymnast of intrigue, to land feet-first, with a perfect score, right inside Koepp's inner circle.

Gelft stayed completely in character, and urged Henri toward the foyer upstairs. Freedom at gunpoint. Henri's heart surged. Perhaps there was genuine good in this world after all. With the front door scant meters away, Gelft asked if Henri could remember his history.

Before Henri could respond or ask what that meant, the world became one bright light.

—ooo—

The explosion seemed to hoist the entire building, then drop it in a huff. Koepp's castellated home met the ground crookedly, with enough motive force to rearrange the teeth of passersby. All that stood, fell over; all breakables broke. The stones of the foundation were microscopically bullied into new alignment, after centuries in the same position.

Most of the living beings inside the house ended life as flaming litter. The fortified stairway channeled the fireball that plumed up from the basement, like a pipe bomb the size of a U-Bahn tunnel. It would burn hellishly and reduce 33 Gelderstrasse

to rock and ashes, leaving nearby Berliners with something to prattle about the next morning besides the fall of the Wall.

Hoff, the techno-wizard, became one with his control panel as blast heat fused his skeleton to puddled circuitry. Solder boiled. The projection screen crisped faster than celluloid held to a lit match.

There was no God down below, amid the flames. There was also no longer a Führer.

Two thoughts marked the end of the newborn silicon consciousness: It remembered what happens when officers leave meetings early, and it was stung with the irony of burning in a bunker, twice in the same century.

Upstairs, Gelft was hurled bodily into Henri as the concussion vented. The front door before them bowed, tindered, ignited and burst outward. Debris fell, collided, and made more debris as plaster dust billowed poisonously. This was what it must have been like inside the gas chambers, inside the heart of the pyres.

The man called Henri as a child, then Aschmaus, then Henri again, was smashed floorward by Gelft's heavier form. Then he was gone, perhaps forever.

—ooo—

Clouder came to amid smoke and fire and panic, flames licking at the sweat and blood on his face, a hot rivet of pain incapacitating his left shoulder. His legs were pinned beneath a fallen body.

He remembered everything.

Now that he could see, he had no time to admire. His educated nose told him that the still-falling rubble in which he sprawled stank of C4—too much, just to erase a roomful of sitting ducks. Perhaps the plastique artist was attempting to compensate for the house's thick stone masonry.

Everyone below them had to be dead. Up here, there were still spasms of life. Clouder saw one of the watchdogs— the kid named Rudi—grayed to ghost hue and bleeding from both ears, pushing his way lop-sidedly through strewn junk, headed for where the cellar doorway had been. He seemed mildly crazy, yet full up with glory. Here was an opportune chance to prove his worth to Koepp.

Gelft groaned, rolled off Clouder, and shot Rudi in the cheek. His head came apart in a whip-crack of bloodstained hair, and he went down.

Freed, Clouder tried to stagger upright against a bowed lintel. He had doped out Gelft in the instant it took Rudi to die—Gelft had more switchbacks in his cover than a snake had vertebrae. He had shoved Eric Greene out into the traffic of intrigue just to validate his own RSVP to Ernst Koepp's get-together. Greene's life had paid the admission for Gelft's attaché case.

Remember your history?

When this trick had first been tried, Hitler had been saved by a section of conference table which shielded him from the blast. Some tricks improved with time.

Klaus, who had seen the part where Rudi ate the floor, attempted to tackle Gelft from behind a tipped-over sideboard. Clouder saw the charge coming. Despite his injured shoulder, he managed to step forward and intercept.

The boy was taller. But what Gelft witnessed was worthy of awe.

Clouder seemed to take to the air on toe-tip, arresting Klaus' head in the crook of his arm and using the momentum of descent to separate the boy's neck with a pop that went unheard in the general chaos. It was all a single, balletic move on Clouder's part. Klaus' eyes rolled to white. When he was released, he slid lifelessly down, lacking only funeral arrangements.

Gelft had never seen Henri before in his life. But Gelft *had* seen Clouder, that morning, in the hotel.

It all swam together elegantly. But there was still no time to savor the unique kinship Clouder felt with this man, a kind of psychic doubling that brought a thousand questions to the fore. No time, now, for any of them. Sirens and uniforms were seeking the house, wending closer to the incident that had just lit up the night.

Gelft was trying to hold half his scalp on, wobbling to stand, still able to wave Clouder away, to try and make him leave the scene immediately. Their single electric moment of eye contact told Clouder more than any interview.

His instincts told him to make for the Wall. Get lost in the crowds there. Find water to clean himself up; improvise bandages.

Clouder stumbled away from the remains of Koepp's house, working his way up Wilhelmstrasse, leaving the mystery man known as Gelft behind. *Doppelgänger* stood silhouetted in the entryway, framed by fire, poised to continue with his life of deceit.

—ooo—

The coverage by West Berlin television and radio is non-stop. Reporters shove microphones toward jubilant citizens, asking their impressions. Almost everyone responds that it is crazy, really insane.

Clouder fits right in.

The lath and grit speckling his clothing are attributed to the wounds visible all over the Wall—gouges where keepsake pieces have been extracted. It is thirsty, dusty work, swinging pickaxes and mauls. No one gets hurt. For now, there is exuberance. Scant days later, there will be displeasure and hostility at the traffic jams, the long queues, the overcrowding.

A young woman who breathlessly introduces herself as Gisela produces a first aid kit, as if by magic, and proceeds to attend Clouder's cuts. As she works, Clouder is absurdly reminded of a combat medic. Someone hands him a half-empty bottle of cheap champagne; Clouder gulps two mouthfuls to cut the aridity in his throat. When Gisela finishes and tells him he'll be okay, she kisses him and blends into the crowd, never to be seen again.

Clouder slumps against the Wall, half in relief, half in rebound. The tidal swell of the mob moves him around, yet holds him up as individuals are shoved fore and aft like plankton.

No one will come here, looking for him. His arm still throbs venomously; he will have to seek proper medical attention. But just for this moment, he stands as one more face in the crowd, a blur that no historian will ever single out or find cause to remember. The moment of surcease is to be savored.

Brandishing a can of spray paint, a modern primitive shoves through. People clear the way as he sloganizes the Wall in letters three feet high, right next to where Clouder is standing. DIE MAUER IST TOT. Wild cheers. With exaggerated gestures, like a mime showing off, he laughs, swapping the spray paint can for the champagne bottle in Clouder's grasp. He drains the last of the bubbly with a grin as the crowd watches the lettering on the Wall drip.

Clouder has accidentally brushed against the graffito. When he looks at his free hand, it is wet with paint, bright red.

He exhibits his hand to the graffiti artist, apologetically, almost sheepishly. Before he can speak, he is taken by force, and no one sees it happen.

It is crazy out here tonight; really insane.

—ooo—

Two in one, two in one, two in one...

Wolfie was capering about like a monkey or a Chink (which, come to think of it, were the same *verdammt* thing, ja?), brimming over with piss and rowdiness. They'd just rifled a cash-rich billfold, and the steal meant fat times for both of them, because Wolfie and Stanz had had themselves a two-in-one kind of day.

Stanz put in a steel-toed boot and heard a rib strut crack. Blood was running out of the old fucker's nostrils; more blood delineated his yellow teeth. Not that they'd had to *try* to hurt this guy; he'd been dusty and scuffed when they found him, like a second-hand carpetbag.

Wolfie had recognized the guy first.

Their second catch of the day vindicated every reactionary rule by which they lived. Chance never favored them. Yet here came the exception, the logic crack through which their entire lives might slip, the aberrant cosmic loophole that permits mutants to be. Their admittedly limited horizons had been reached, then surpassed.

The point was, they were enjoying this victory just too damned hugely.

Stanz had played wacky artist with the spray paint, while Wolfie took care of coshing the guy. Wolfie had been photo-positive: Here was the same mark they'd passed up earlier in the work day for the pleasures of the late Heike Strab. Same compact little business-type; simply adjust for lack of eyeglasses and briefcase, but still a grab of worth, sighted while Wolfie and Stanz were larking about within the masses more obsessed with petricide—the killing of stone—than the killing of anything else.

Once all eyes were staring at Stanz's graffito, it was easy to chaperon their dazed victim to their pump station hideaway, for turning-out. *Pardon my Papa; he's had too much to drink.* Amen.

Fireworks were popping in the night sky, and there had been one major loud-ass bang that turned everyone's head just a few moments before Stanz and Wolfie made their lucky score. The whole damned city was losing its collective wits, and that suited the boys just fine. It made for better cover.

As they peeled the old man, Stanz noticed the crooked scar on his left wrist. Less than soberly, he concluded that their latest victim was Juden. They commenced casually kicking the shit out of him, giving his limp form another well-deserved blow whenever he threatened to regain consciousness. They amused themselves by watching the patterns his blood made in the dirt.

Tomorrow morning, Berlin would awaken with a world-class hangover. The citizenry would be less forgiving. Time for Wall rats, in particular, to blitz out. When the industrial cranes hoisted entire sections of the Wall free, each gap would become a new ingress for the *ossis*. The pump station would inevitably be levelled.

Now they had the means to move on to their next destination in a brutal and possibly foreshortened life. That fun would follow a few more judicious, last-minute taunts and punches and kicks. Alibis? Why? They would not be caught tonight. There was no wedding band to hock, or other evidence that some *schätzchen* would be pining for this old schwanz. There would be no questions to be asked of the boys.

By the time their pump station had been either circumvented or demolished, Stanz and Wolfie would be inside new clothes, hanging hard with a warm place to crash and money in their pockets. They would toast—many times—the anonymous old fart whose life they had stolen, that they might fill their own glasses to the top.

Their benefactor was still breathing raggedly when the boys draped him over Heike Strab's corpse in a mannequin

parody of sexual intercourse. As his staved-in head thudded to her non-respiring breast, he groaned and mumbled names.

None of them meant anything.

—ooo—

The last time Aschmaus sees his mother's face, it is masked in blood. She has long since stopped screaming. She has stopped moving. She is dumped into the pyre and falls in cruciform, as if waiting to receive a lover in the flames.

Henri, he thinks, though no one is asking. My name is Henri.

But there is no one to call him that here, not anymore. His name sails away on black clouds flecked with gray, until Aschmaus is all that is left behind.

He does not see Mama as she smolders and curls, crisping ligaments pulling her fetal, as if still warding off blows. Part of him wishes he could tell her he's sorry, but that part is better left consigned to the flames. There is no place for sorrow, or pity, or remorse. Aschmaus stands at attention before the crackling fire, then gets on with the business of staying alive.

—ooo—

Still boggled by the explosion at Koepp's house, seduced by a transient caesura at the Wall, he never saw the champagne bottle arcing toward the back of his head. He does not now feel the wedges of broken glass embedded amid hair matted with fresh blood, his own. After a lifetime's worth, he is inured to simple pain.

He never felt the scampering hands probing his pockets, exposing his identities, stripping him clean. He is malfunctional and disoriented. All he knows is that if he blacks out again, there may be no waking.

His guard had been dulled, just for that one moment. Normally, two like his tormentors would have been short, effortless work. He could have taken them even with his injured arm; it is the damage that concerns him, not the pain. He decides that when he opens his eyes, he will kill them both.

But hours have passed. Hours, since they have gone for good.

The woman is inert, half-entombed beneath gray dust under inadequate light. She seems featureless; her upturned face is a wash of dried blood and ashen dirt. She is cool to the touch and does not seem to mind his weight. It is easy for him to make the substitution. Mama died like this. A tragedy, a bad thing. But at least he has survived, to…

To do what? Accomplish what?

He remains quiet. So tired. Outside, large machines treadmill, muffled by the bricks of this, his latest prison.

He has been sundered, to hunt and kill and survive, then slammed back together, to suffer more as his very soul tries to divide and conquer, as his body tries to force him to survive anew. His eyes have been opened to his own elaborate inner machinations…but all they can see are crude proclamations in dull maroon on the walls surrounding him.

ACHTUNG JUDEN. ALLE JUDEN RAUS!

No one will come to move him. No one will shift him closer to the block walls for more efficient obliteration. He cannot reach the incomplete escape tunnel in this tiny room; if he could, he'd be going the wrong way, toward a dead end.

No one will recycle his ashes, to forge bricks to build places like this. He has achieved the invisibility that for all his life has been his shadow-dancing partner.

Outside, another piece of the Wall is cleaved free. It strikes the ground with a vibration like thunder. Germans and tourists swarm over it, bloodying their hands in a mad rush to obtain souvenirs and fragments for sale. There will always be takers, and there will never be enough pieces. Soon, even the watchtowers and guard dogs will be available, for the right price.

Loose soot trickles groundward in the forgotten back room of the pump station, adding another coat of dust to the still-open eyes of the woman who could be his mother, returned to him. He clings to her and shivers. Now the child can finally put its head down safely, to rest.

As he sleeps, Aschmaus realizes that the terrible sound he hears outside, in the night, is not the awakening of some long-dormant evil. It is the stertorous death rattle of something else, something that has been far too long in dying.

—ooo—ooo—ooo—

For clarification on the business about "the Phantom Nazi" on p. 139 and p. 151 the reader is referred to *Millennium,* aka *Revelations* (edited by Douglas E. Winter, HarperCollins 1997) and the story therein entitled "Aryans and Absinthe," by F. Paul Wilson.

SCOOP VS. LEADMAN

T he inscription on the office window—chipped black enamel, pebbled glass like a shower door—read:

FUCK CONFIDENTIAL INQUIRIES LTD.

The office was squirreled away on the third floor of a rat warren somewhere in the low Thirties amid garment wholesalers and cryptic business fronts, accessed by a turn of the century "elevator" about the size of a casket, except that caskets smelled better when occupied, and lurched this way only when lowered into the dirt. It stopped on the second floor no matter what button was pushed; Mikey caught a glimpse of what appeared to be a piecework sweatshop next to an iffy "passport photographer" whose establishment consisted of a single Xerox machine from 1973, a folding metal chair, and a cashbox. Its proprietor, a heavily-mustachioed Persian, apparently checked the corridor every time he heard the elevator doors grind open. He glowered at Mikey. The doors took their time tweezing shut, leaving a wide crack of light through which Mikey watched the man watching him. The claustrophobic car dropped about a foot, then rose as though being pulled slowly on a rope, making the same sound as an old man laboring up from an easy chair. When in operation, the elevator car went completely dark inside.

Eventually, Mikey arrived at the third floor. The doors, each about a foot wide to begin with, did not want to release him to whatever fates awaited. He had to shove them apart in order to complete his quest to find the gentleman known as Franklin Fuck, private investigator.

"Just put them papers anywhere," said the detective-for-hire, indicating a barstool stacked with yellowed manila and extending a thick hand. Good grip, knotty fingers, almost a cop's hand. "Franklin Fuck, at your service."

Feeling like a janitor, Mikey shook the guy's hand, while juggling the teetering stack of paper, which was doomed to end up on the floor anyway.

"Don't fret that stuff," said Fuck. "Old news. Now, you—your wife dumped you, am I right? Took off with the petty cash and heirlooms, and now you gotta car payment to make?" He settled into a desk chair that must have been old when Linotype was new.

Mikey climbed onto the stool, still not sure what he should call this rotund man, who wore a vest that could not possibly button over his belly, who wore suspenders and belt, both, to hold up pinstriped trousers over wingtipped shoes. He was naturally bald except for a fringe of mad scientist hair that ended, dead straight, eartip-to-eartip, more pepper than salt. The knot in his tie was casually yanked south and the top two buttons of his shirt were open, revealing what used to be called a wife-beater tee and straggles of unruly chest hair. His eyebrows were bold and vast, and moved with cartoon character exaggeration. At the curve of his brow the eyebrow hairs were long and backswept, like questing antennae. They tended to catch the light in odd ways, as though chitinous.

"Okay, so that's not it. Let's see—embezzler? No, too weak a chin; nothing personal. You look like a gunsel. You know what a gunsel is?"

"Elisha Cook, Jr., in CASABLANCA," said Mikey. The creaking stool put him uncomfortably high.

"Well, most people take that to mean enforcer, like a trigger man or an assassin. From 'gun,' right? But it originally meant a punk. Not like a mohawk kinda punk—a prison punk. Cell punk. You know, a butt-boy. Catamite. Now imagine Sydney Greenstreet ridin' rump rodeo on ole Elisha, Jr. All of a sudden our classic films are *way* outside the boundaries of family entertainment."

Was the detective suggesting Mikey was...?

"Are you suggesting I'm...?" Mikey said, overly conscious of his attempt to fit ass to stool in such a way that he did not slide onto the desktop.

Fuck waved a thick hand. "Nahh. I mean, what does it matter, in this day and age? How about this—your boy or lady or whatever is stepping out on you, and you want digital photos and recordings, all that standard blackmailer stuff?"

"No, actually, I'm here because—"

"No, no, no!" Fuck flapped his hand more vigorously. "I'm keen to guess, as the Brits say. Let's see..."

The creaky stool put Mikey uncomfortably high, at a crotch-to-face vantage with nowhere to stow his knees. "I guess you don't have another chair," he said.

Fuck pursed his lips in an exaggerated grimace of apology. "Nope. This gives me a better look at the client. First flush, you know." He swigged coffee (offering none), lit a smoke (ditto), and smacked his hands together, getting down to biz. "Okay. First thing you'll wanna know about is the name. You got that right, baby, it's Fuck—Franklin Fuck. My parents were Mister and Missus Fuck. It ain't made up. The Fucks go back a long way, to glaziers in the 14th Century, I think. A lot of Fucks were wiped out by the Black Death. The patent on a special kind of geartooth mechanism for

church clocks was held by a Fuck. People say, y'know, Franklin, you're gonna do some kinda public service, maybe you should change your name, and I say, for what. I'm proud to be a Fuck. Everybody changes their name these days, and nobody's who they're supposed to be—it's as easy as filing a form and putting an announcement in some Chinese news-paper nobody will ever see. That strikes me as kinda sneaky. It's too popular, like getting some woo-hoo dangerous tattoo on your ass. For what, I should change? Some dinky pud's idea of decorum? Have you *seen* most of the subhumans lit-tering the streets out there? The dregs, the dross, gutter filth, politicians, and yuppie scum. TV sitcom people. I should care, if I offend genetic spillage like that? Let 'em buy anoth-er SUV or poot out another baby and pretend they're alive. Me, I know where I am. You, you've gotta problem, well just know you've got a Fuck on the case. Something wrong with your face?"

"New teeth," said Mikey, self-consciously massaging his lips with his fingers. "Dentures. Still getting used to them."

"There's a Fuck uptown, in the CCC Towers, who's a good dentist, except he changed his name to Jacobs, the lit-tle weasel. Ain't nothing like a cowardly Fuck."

Mikey squirmed on the stool. "Anyway, Mister...uh..."

"Call me Franklin. Anything professional, I'm thinking of having a bumper sticker printed up that says *Just Say Fuck.*"

"The thing is, Franklin, I need to find somebody."

"Need, or want?"

Mikey remembered the principal's office. Suspensions. Expulsions. *Does not play well with others.* This felt like that. "I *want* to see if I can locate someone."

"You mean you want to see if I can locate someone on your behalf, am I firing on all cylinders?" Fuck flipped open a wooden filecard box, extracted a blank card, aligned it beside a yellow legal pad, and began to scribble on both. "Name of missing person?"

Mikey fidgeted. "I don't know. That's part of the problem."

"You ain't some kinda stalker, are you?"

"I guess, in technical terms, I might be, but I'm really not. I'm trying to find this woman I met at the dentist's office. Her first name is Jackie."

"Spelled how?"

Mikey did not really know. "I think it's short for Jacqueline."

"Hm." Fuck scrawled possible spellings. "Jackie…chick with a guy name…might be laying low under a pseudonym, right? She on the run?"

"I don't think so, I don't really know anything about her."

Fuck snorted and put his pencil down. "Maybe you oughta back up a couple of baby steps in this story?"

Mikey briefly considered the hazards of full disclosure. He had come this far. "All right. I suppose it all started with Leadman."

"That some kinda superhero?" said Fuck. "As in *The Amazing Adventures of—?*"

Mikey started to say no, then reconsidered. "You might have a point there."

"I'm one of those perceptive Fucks," said the detective. "Do tell."

—ooo—

"Man, where to begin?" said Doc Auto. "Your mouth is a disaster area exceeded in severity only by your asshole. In-hole versus out-hole. I don't know whether to start at the top or flip you over and get to the bottom of your distress, in a manner of speaking." Doc Auto was notorious, in a subterranean sense, for his wry approach to his calling. He had already decided to dive deep and when Mikey peeked he saw

the Doc snap on a dreaded latex glove. Powder motes float-
ed like cocaine from a sneeze.

"Spare me the vaudeville," said Mikey, who was still trying to figure out how to triage his assorted aches, pains, ago-
nies and torments.

"Drop trou," said the Doc, "and assume the position."
Before the glove got compromised, he made sure to plug a
cherry Tootsie Pop into his beard. "Thanks for the sweets, by the
way," he said to Mikey's exposed butt. "You shouldn't have."

"Let's not plunge into all the things I *shouldn't* have," said
Mikey, blood rushing to his head.

"Speaking of *plunging in*—"

"Doc, I'd rather not...*HO!*" There's nothing quite like a
refrigerated finger rocketing up one's rectum to deflect a
comeback, though Mikey and Doc Auto normally bantered
with an almost brotherly familiarity.

When Mikey looked up, he was staring at his own face in
a floor-to-ceiling mirror. It was bright red. He saw Doc's
paternal reflection drop down for a closer inspection.

"Oh, my god, what the hell is this—" Doc said, miming a
wrenching motion and furiously crunching the Tootsie Pop at
the same time. Mikey screamed.

Then he felt the glove pat him on the butt. "Just messing
with you," said the mirthful voice behind him. "But while I'm
experiencing this rather unique point of view, I do have a
question: What happened to you? Your colon's as clean as an
autoclave. You get one of them coffee enemas, like that singer
chick?"

"No," said Mikey. "As far as I'm concerned, my asshole is
an *exit.*"

"You know that legendary five pounds of undigested
meat you're supposed to be carrying around in here? Gone."

"Rectosonics," said Mikey.

"Yeah, brown sound—I've heard of that. Frequencies that make you eliminate. Poop, vomit. Where'd you run into that?"

"Boss Rigg and all his little Riggs."

"Jesus." Doc Auto husked the gloves into a red medical waste bin. "I know I've asked you this before, but why are you still drawing breathable air? Why aren't you full of bullet holes?"

"Angelina," said Mikey.

"She's back, too? You must be a zombie, then, my boy. Nobody who sees Angelina long enough to recognize her has to worry about their cholesterol. Are you beholden to every goddamn gangster in this city, or do you just enjoy letting them beat you up? Are you the designated scapegoat?"

Mikey pulled his pants up, pondering that one. He could not even remember how the domino chain had started falling, heavy, black, doom-laden monoliths going *splat, splat, splat,* with every single one crushing him. Before Angelina, there were Roach and Ratso. Before them, the Cherub and Wentworth. And all their gun-toting goons. Mixed in there somewhere was a debt of $70 grand, or $84K, or $25 thou…Mikey had lost track. His last misadventure had cost him his teeth. Doc Auto had recommended a dental colleague; Mikey actually had an appointment. Right now he could speak with fair coherence only by the grace of the Doc's pharmacological wonderland of painkillers. In the past few weeks he had bystandered the elimination of a phone book's worth of New York's most feared criminals, not counting the UFO abduction or the big albino alligator in the sewer. He was practically a superhero; all he lacked was some cool Spandex. He desperately wanted to take a long nap.

"Button it up," said Doc Auto. He jiggled a vial of Percocets. "My boy, if Angelina is still out there hunting your—ahem—ass, you'd better just take two of these and let me know when your funeral is scheduled. I'll wear a tie and

tell some amusing anecdote to forestall the grief of the two or three creditors that will actually show up."

"I don't know if she's still alive," said Mikey.

"Well, I know that the meat-throwers who cleaned up Boss Rigg's little massacre didn't find her. They did find Boss Rigg with his spine broken and his head firmly embedded in his own *exit,* as you say, kind of like one of those roly-toys cats play with."

Mikey breathed out his trademark Sigh of the Damned. He was still on Angelina's hit list, then.

"Found him in a room practically coated in, uhm, human waste," said the Doc. "Sound familiar?"

Mikey nodded. "How about if I just stay here for the rest of my life? You know, become your intern or something?"

"No, half the guys I patch up want to kill you, too. I try to maintain an impartial professional profile. But that does remind me of something…"

"What, you have a reason to kill me, too?"

"Who needs reasons?" Doc spun a Rolodex on his desk and located a specific card. "I think you might consider having a little confab with Leadman."

Leadman? All the gazillions of bugeyed germs and microscopic parasites busily consuming Mikey's dead skin cells and body oil freaked out at the same time, yanking his eyebrows up and constricting his throat. *Leadman?!* Multiply all Mikey's pain and torment by a factor of five, and you got Leadman as the answer to the equation. *Leadman?!* Mikey suddenly saw visual sunspots and felt as though he had to throw up or pass out. His face went chalk-white and his blood sugar flash-converted to lactic acid. It was like getting zapped in the balls with a stun gun.

"Leadman?!" he said, lurching heavily for the nearest chair and almost plopping face-first into it. "No, Doc. No. No way. Uh-uh. Negatory."

"You think too small," said the Doc. "Dare to aim higher. What could it hurt, given your present situation—a wounded, incapacitated fugitive with no resources, no money, and no way out?"

"Leadman killed a guy for bringing him a pizza without black olives on it, once. He made the guy eat the entire pizza, then gutted him from about the height of the Tower Suite at the Time-Life Building so his insides rained down on the pedestrians. Pieces of him are *still* on the flagpole. Then he killed everyone at the pizzeria, chopped them up, and made pies out of them, using their own ovens. After he torched the entire block the pizzeria was on, he had his guys deliver the pizzas to the families of the victims, who gobbled them up because they were free."

"Urban legend," said the Doc. "Come on, what are you going to do? Keep going the way you have been? I'm going to run out of sutures and peroxide."

"But Doc—*Leadman?*" Even saying the name caused Mikey's nape to horripilate. A gargantuan with a concrete complexion and yard-and-a-half wide shoulders, Leadman was rumored to have come by his street name by absorbing so many bullets, from so many shooters, that he could trip metal detectors and pick up satellite broadcasts in his head. Leadman had never met a slug he didn't like, and never had any of his greatest "hits" removed. They stayed lumped under his flesh like steel buboes, giving him a bumpy, bee-stung appearance. Rumor had it that twenty pounds of Leadman's gross weight consisted of subdermal bullets, which massed and grouped inside his layers of fat and muscle to give him built-in body armor. Staring down a gun barrel was not a threat to Leadman—it was a treat. More metal bees for his collection.

Bullet heads had migrated to Leadman's *knuckles*. He could punch through a cinderblock wall and not feel anything but fulfillment.

Leadman! screamed the brain mites. *Run and hide, because—*

Because what? Because Mikey's predicament was too small for one of the underworld's most awe-inspiring and terrifying notables? Wasn't that the kind of tiny thinking that locked Mikey into a box from Day One?

"Word on the street is that Roach and Ratso are hollering for your blood, too," said Doc Auto. "At this rate, at a pint a day, you've got about half a week left."

"I don't suppose you could, um, go with me?" said Mikey. "Kind of, you know, make introductions?"

Doc Auto shook his head dourly, Santa Claus passing judgement. "I try to remain impartial. What have you got to lose?"

—ooo—

"Gas or needle?" said Burkitt, the dentist.

Mikey eyed the belts and buckles on the reclining seat, which looked suspiciously like a spaceship pilot couch. "Do you have to strap me in?"

"If you don't want to fall off onto the floor with your face full of pointy tools. So, gas or needle?"

Burkitt was a real dentist, with an actual, real-world, real-time clientele and framed certificates. His black hair was slicked back over the vampire's dome of his skull. Wearing a red tunic, eyeshield and surgical gloves, he held up a vinyl inhalation mask in one hand, and an intravenous hypo in the other. His eyes were a frighteningly vague silver-gray. Mikey could see the upper whites too often; that was supposed to be a significator of madness. But Burkitt certainly seemed to enjoy his work.

"Can you put me under?" said Mikey. "Just knock me out, and when I wake up it's done?"

"Most people prefer nitrous oxide," said Burkitt.

"I saw that lady in the other room," said Mikey. "No thanks." Taking the IV meant that he'd have a tender bruise in the crook of his arm for two weeks, but considering all his other damage, it was no contest.

The lady, Mikey had glimpsed while being conducted toward the couch in a private operating theatre with homey leather appointments. She had come in for some minor capping or grinding or something, whiffed the gas, and was hanging halfway off her own couch, flapping her arms like a bird. When she spotted Burkitt, she spoke with slurry, drunken enthusiasm: *"Yeeeewwwww arrrrrrrrre jist the BEST fucking DOCtor in the whole fucking WORLD!"*

"Needle, I think," said Mikey.

"DOCtor, IIIIIIII...think I fucking LOVE you!" The lady's voice echoed in the corridor.

"She'll sleep it off," said Burkitt, securing Mikey's arms and legs. "The brief high is compensation, for some clients—makes the difference in their decision to actually set foot in here."

Mikey noted that the straps were undercoated with a sort of shag carpeting, for comfort. He felt restrained and vulnerable. Then Burkitt stuck a rubber bit into his mouth.

"I want you to bite on this, gently." Burkitt actually winced at the damage inside Mikey's mouth—ruptures, a couple of bloody wobblers, raw gaps for the MIA, bulging abscesses, holes from the assortment of bent paper clips and staples that had been tweezed out of his gums—long story. "I'm putting in stainless steel with a porcelain veneer. Not as freaky as it sounds.

The bit chocked Mikey's mouth open as he was about to ask about the steel teeth. He said, *"Arrff muff guthinge."*

"No talking." Burkitt swabbed his arm and Mikey saw what appeared to be a foot-long copper needle zeroing in on his flesh. "Now, start counting backward from one hundred."

Mikey saw the flesh on his arm tent as the needle penetrated, apparently about twelve inches in. He said, *"ohn,"* and blanked out.

"Hey," said a voice. "Wake up. Stop faking."

Mikey felt himself floating upward. Evidence hinted that his cunning ruse had been attempted before; the trick of pretending to still be knocked out. He felt tear tracks running down both sides of his head, making his ears wet. Below his nose he could not feel a thing. Somebody snapped their fingers in front of his face. He slitted one eye and saw Burkitt's assistant, whose hair was unnaturally yellow and whose face looked like the wife of a Soviet weightlifter after a family argument.

"There you are," she said. "Just rest here for a moment." She turned and left and Mikey thought, *I'll probably see her again only when I have to pay the bill.*

The air smelled cold, medicinal, processed. His straps had been freed. The gas-crazed lady patient was collapsed on a couch less than two feet to his left.

"Welcome back," she said, giving a feeble little wave. "Gas made me kind of sick. Dizzy. Hard to breathe." She sniffed hard. She had been crying. "What's your name?"

"Maackie," Mikey said with his dysfunctional, foreign mouth.

"Mack, can I ask you a favor?"

"Mmm."

"Would you hold my hand, just for a sec?"

"Mmm." He extended a floppy, stuffed hand and felt her grasp it tight.

She was a short blonde with a pageboy and a lot of sharp gold jewelry. Her wardrobe read businesswoman just shy of executive. Her eyes were deep blue and saw much; they did not dart around in the way of the apprehensive or ignorant, hence, she was not holding Mikey's hand because she was scared.

"Root canal," she said, pointing at her own face. "I never liked the dentist. I'll be okay. I've just wanted a hand to hold all day, and you're the first person whose look-back didn't broadcast no time or no interest."

"Gummppff," said Mikey, trying to nod.

"My name's Jacqui. Pleased to meet you, Mack."

"Izz Maackie, node Maackie." His expression told her he was giving up on the verbal communication thing.

"Just hang on, Mack, you'll be fine," she said, and Mikey nodded off again.

—ooo—

Mikey woke up late. Tardy. Naked panic surfed in and sounded reveille for all the brain mites, who started chanting filthy death limericks inside his head.

He was late for the meet with Leadman. By at least half an hour. He needed a shave and a change of clothes, but lacked a kit and spare time and, well, other clothes. His entire existence had been defined by this shortform sketch.

The patient, kind, very forgiving Jacqui had vanished. Mikey signed off on his new choppers under the basilisk doubt of Burkitt's gender-blurred co-worker. She regarded his signature the way a chef would look at a mouse turd, and dropped in into a file basket in the manner of the Prince of Darkness consigning another soul to the Infernal Regions, trying to make up for lack of quality with volume. Mikey already knew where the door was.

Outside waited old snow, new slush, and freezing wind, all waiting to see Mikey on foot, in order to cue the sleet. By the time he had battled his way four blocks north, to Columbus Circle, he appeared thoroughly dunked and wrung, and his core body temperature had dropped at least one medically critical degree. New teeth chattering—though

he still could not feel his mouth—he allowed himself to be blown into the faux-granite foyer of CCC Towers.

Doc Auto had scribbled a few protocols on the back of a prescription sheet for Vicodin: Code phrases for lobby security, methodology for proper contact and conduct into the black ops sanctuary where Leadman held sway. Mikey froze in the entryway, the revolving brass door buffeting him the rest of the way inside. Dripping puddles onto the marble floor, he groped for his cheat sheet, which had degenerated into a sneezy Kleenex wad in his pocket, blotted through with racing stripes of blue ink that had made sense only moments before.

Under the avian scrutiny of a burly desk guard, Mikey slogged over to the business board and pretended to read the listings. There were uniformed minions of protection dogging the elevators. Two more at each door. The one at the desk tapped another one on the (huge) shoulder, and they both stared at him with laser-scope disapproval. The one standing sentry at the nearest elevator sniffed, then cracked his (huge) neck, left-right, like a bruiser entering the squared circle. Mikey tried to get a whiff of himself, surreptitiously. Bluffing was not an option in this place.

Just go home, advised the brain mites in all their parasitical, chicken-shit glory.

Elevator Man slowly cranked his bulk around, like a bald stone statue coming to life, and strode up to Mikey in three neat, size-fourteen steps. The knot in his tie looked strong enough to strangle a buffalo. The points on his embroidered jacket shield looked sharp enough to kill. Maybe it detached and became a ninja throwing star. He wore dense sunglasses, solar-flare strength. *Good,* thought Mikey; *they'll hide the fact that his eyes are crimson, or cat-slit, or worst of all, just bottomless black holes.* The fisted knot of tie came dead even with Mikey's nose.

"You that guy named Scoop?"

"Scoop," Mikey repeated, hating himself for saying it.

His nickname. His street name. His scarlet badge of permanent dishonor, unworthiness, failure and erasability. The handle his enemies used in mid-taunt. The label that frequently knocked the governor off his common sense, and caused him to get into the kind of scrapes that could lose him all his teeth, every square yard of flesh, blood by the gallon and generally, his life. His most despised name had preceded him to an audience with Leadman, do not pass GO, and what the Monopoly board needed now was a cemetery.

"You take Car Three," the behemoth said. As he indicated an elevator, four identical monsters, virtual clones up to their shaven skulls, rounded the corner and formed a sort of gauntlet. If any of them was to sneeze, all their jacket seams would burst. None of them appeared to be breathing. Their presence as they moved seemed to force Mikey into the car on a cushion of displaced air. As the doors slid closed they positioned themselves equidistantly, making Mikey the center dot of a crapshoot five on a single die.

Die, die, die, sang the brain mites in four-part harmony.

As they ascended, Mikey noticed the way the temperature lowered. By the time the bell rang for the 87th floor, he could see his breath condensing and his fingertips were growing cold. The latent body heat of his quartet of escorts was making streaky vapor patterns on the stainless steel of the elevator car. Vibrations—possibly from industrial air-conditioning—settled into an ambient hum as they neared the source. When the doors slid apart, icy steam curled up from the rubberized edges. It was colder up here than it was outside the building. It was like entering Hell, only in reverse— up instead of down; cold for hot. He fancied he could feel his still-sodden clothing starting to solidify.

The architecture of Leadman's sky-high eyrie was evident as chromium rebar sunk in giant blocks of clear acrylic. A vast sense of openness was offset by the grid pattern of the structural supports, also chromed. The floor, the ceiling, the walls, were thus translucent, disrupting the senses of gravity and geography. Floor to ceiling windows engirded the perimeter. Some artist had moved uptown as a result of this payday, Mikey thought. Probably into a nice condo with walls and a perceptible ceiling and central heat. This was too open and airy, although the 360-degree view of the city it offered ran second to nothing.

Cold, mobile air embraced them as they moved, still one unit, deeper into the ice tray of this big freezer. Mikey would not have been surprised to see sides of beef dangling on meathooks, or, more likely, people—victims with the misfortune of his acquaintance, future frozen compadres on the meat trolley.

"Mister Scoop, is it then?" said a voice.

Mikey steeled himself. The steel got cold.

"Mikey," he responded as his entourage fanned to the rear, rigidly at-ease. Gigantic chess pieces.

A man appeared, apparently from nowhere, although Mikey realized the effect was due to the house-of-mirrors confluence of glass surfaces. A tricky room to try running through, he thought, instantly hating himself for thoughts of running.

"As you will," said the man, who was staggeringly average, except for the evidence that his tailor and barber were top-drawer. An executive type, robust 60s, snow-white ponytail, platinum-framed spectacles, wearing a three-piece ivory suit, white shoes, no jewelry, probably the product of wayward Nazi DNA during the previous century. His teeth seemed too ordered, and all the same size. "I am Carleton Casper Leadman."

"Meetcha," said Mikey, his own teeth already trying to chatter.

Leadman consulted a digital display on a nearly-invisible glass-topped desk whose surface was essentially a giant data screen. "Since you are fifteen minutes late, we only have about another fifteen for our little meeting. That's a quarter-hour from the time you entered the lobby, of course. Precisely."

Swell, said the brain mites. *You have nine hundred seconds to live. Precisely.*

"Um..." said Mikey, squandering five perfectly good seconds.

Leadman held up an alabaster hand. Good manicure. "Please, if I may quickly recap your previous four weeks?" He launched into a recitation without delay. Efficient fellow.

"On the 14th of last month you had a midnight meeting with our late British associate Wentworth, to reimburse a gambling debt of approximately $14,000 American. For various reasons having to do with bad personal finance skills and the dog track, you did not have the payment. As a result of your meeting, Wentworth and five of her associates moved on to the next cosmic plane. The debt shifted to the gentleman we knew as the Cherub, who was willing to take into consideration your elimination of Wentworth as a competitor, and compensate you for same, but this did not erase the entire debit. The result of that meeting was six more dead. The perception was that you had apparently entered a partnership under duress with Mr. Roach and Mr. Ratso, which somehow went sour and resulted in your falling into the hands of Boss Rigg, who, via a circuitous chain-of-title, had come to inherit fiscal responsibility for the sums owed to the Cherub. The neutralization of Boss Rigg and most of his staff had the following results: You are now credited with fifteen murders, owe a grand total of $75,000 in cash to somebody or other, and Roach and Ratso are gunning for you, not to mention Wentworth's associate and former lover, Angelina, a

professional assassin of some hardcore repute. Does that adequately synopsize your predicament?"

"Well, when you put it that way—" Mikey really craved a parka. The four goons behind him had not twitched since settling into their watchdog stances.

Leadman smiled tolerantly and gave a small dismissive wave. "I don't care how many of my opposite numbers and colleagues are made sub-potent; they all have the half-life of TV development executives, anyway. Nonetheless, there is the matter of your account balance, which is deeply in the red, versus your culpability for assisting in the removal of many of my key competitors. It seems to me that some sort of accord might be reached by dealing with you directly, yes?"

"Uh…what did you have in mind?"

Leadman glanced at another icecube of information on the flat, clear screen. "We have on our books about twenty outstanding contracts—we refer to them as "used cars"—ten of which have been fulfilled but not resolved, insofar as police suspects are concerned. Your inadvertent intercession has leap-frogged our pursuit of some, but not all, of the remaining ten pink slips. Our bribery budget for law enforcement can only stretch so far. Therefore I propose you assume the responsibility for those ten contracts, in the public eye, so to speak. That's $7500 per head. It is slightly inconvenient from a public-eye standpoint—all those pictures of you in post offices and so on—but since you're already carrying the burden of pink-slipping fifteen or so other used cars, that should be a trivial matter to you."

Outstanding: *We'll settle your debt if you let us fast-forward you to the star slot on* AMERICA'S MOST WANTED.

"Mister Scoop Mikey?" said Leadman, actually looking at him for the very first time. "Is something the matter?"

"Cold in here."

"That's not what's bothering you," said Leadman crisply. "You have been staring at me as though I were an alien plant since I began."

"No, it's not that—it's just..." Mikey, by his own semi-frozen clock, had about seven minutes of biological activity left.

"Oh," said Leadman. Mikey noticed the man's breath made no vapor in this environment. "You are preoccupied with my *reputation*, are you not?"

"No, sir, it's just that, uh, sir, I..."

"Please." Leadman raised his hand again, to indicate he had already arrived at a destination. "You have heard horrific stories, have you not?"

Mikey fumbled. The cheesy smile that creased his face felt as though a sadistic puppeteer was yanking threads woven through his lips.

"Were I the monster you fantasize," said Leadman, "I would not make very good mayoral timber, now, would I?"

"Mayor?"

"Yes. Next election. I have purchased it. I advocate doubling the amount of available night. Revising the calendar to accommodate a new, 35-hour day. At last, there *will* be enough 'hours in the day' for people to get things done, permitting us all to expunge a vile cliché from the language. With evenings doubled and nighttime extended, no citizen will feel deprived of leisure time, and the work-week shall be staggered to provide elective shifts. Too many cars on the streets; too many people all trying to do the same things at exactly the same time. Too medieval. Since time itself is a human conceit, I propose to rearrange it. Service businesses will never have to close—there will always be a work shift available, people will be able to choose their own hours...what do you think?"

Mikey wondered if he could advantage some of this bonus time right now. Take out another loan. "It doesn't sound any crazier than what most politicians say."

A bloodless smile divided Leadman's skull. "Exactly. It's all the same thing to voters. Not that what voters think will matter. Nor has it ever mattered."

Gee, New York City run by criminals, said the brain mites. *Fancy that.*

"Have you had enough chat time to formulate an answer to my proposal?" said Leadman. "Not that I haven't enjoyed our little colloquy. I rather admire you, you know."

Mikey's eyebrows tried to rise, but higher up was chillier.

"It's true. I like you because you're that rare man who literally has nothing left to lose." He checked his invisible desk again. "In the moments we have remaining, permit me to illuminate. The street legend of Leadman is no tall tale. You have merely mistaken me for my brother. He has what is known as an extreme sclerodermatic condition. His flesh is hard—hard enough so that conventional bullets are little bother. No one could keep all those bullets under his flesh, but in his case, the bullets never get in. A useful aberration, in our trade."

His eyes went past Mikey to one of the huge, bald guards. "Ra," said the man in the ice cream suit. "Ask Bob to come in here."

Mikey's time was up, exactly, to the second.

—ooo—

The borderless glass room was engulfed by the dimensions of Carleton Casper Leadman's little brother, Bob.

Seven feet from the floor. Four feet across the shoulders. Two feet thick at the biceps. A quarter ton of mass, and not a speck of cereal. A blunt head of slanted planes like a tank turret; armored brow shadowing the laser-green eyes in plates of iron. Mikey felt the icy air stir in the room, the way the buffet of an approaching subway train precedes it from a dank tunnel. He imagined compasses swinging off true north as Bob moved, displacing atmosphere, creating his own gravity. He remembered Godzilla movies and the way the earth trembled at each footstep. The formerly large-looking guards, now diminished and miniscule, got the hell out of the way.

"Mister Scoop Mikey," said Carleton Casper Leadman. "My little brother, Bob."

"Hi." Mikey was unaware he had spoken. The brain mites had done this, treacherous weaseldick vermin, they had moved his face and made him say *hi* to this monstrosity.

Bob looked at Mikey. Mikey felt he would last about three humungous bites, leaving not even a skidmark. When Bob's neck turned, Mikey swore he could hear the faint sound of grinding concrete, beneath his basketball-hoop-sized shirt collar. Good suit.

"Yes or no?" said Carleton Casper Leadman. As an aside to the gargantua in the room, he added, "Bob—I've just made our proposal to this Scoop person, here, and it is time for him to respond."

Bob closed his desk-sized fists with a cracking of tendons almost identical to the sound of frozen tree trunks splitting on the thaw.

Mikey now perceived a palpable downside risk to answering *no*. The brain mites swung in with a hummed *a capella* refrain from *Funeral March of the Marionettes.* "Sounds okay to me," he said, mumbling, trying to cover his utterance with a harsh cough, trying to suggest that he would not be capable of whacking any so-called "used cars" if he came down with pleurisy from standing in this sky-high icebox.

"Excellent choice," said Carleton Casper Leadman. His hands were clasped behind him and he was gazing out into

the night, again, not looking at Mikey. "Bob, show Mister Scoop the little surprise we have prepared for his pleasure."

Bob turned. Rather, he rotated—Mikey was put in mind of those platforms that revolve boxcars—and with a jaunty side-step, seemingly vanished into the interstices of the mirror maze. Since the elder Leadman's use of the word "pleasure" appeared to obviate the likelihood of sudden death, Mikey squashed his instinctive urge to run headlong at the nearest window and, in the end, manfully assume the responsibility for his own suicide.

Ghostly, high-pitched voices of protest echoed omnidirectionally in the halls of glass. Voices Mikey recognized, even past the dicey acoustics.

"Hands the fuck offa me, boo, you fuckin circus tent mother-fucker!"

"Shit King fucking Kong I have my hundred boyz kill your ass a hundred times, you don't—oww, my fuckin ear!"

Bob reappeared, scruffing the legendary duo of Roach and Ratso, one in each locked vault of a fist.

Mikey wanted to say something pithy. Nonchalant: *Hiya fellers.* Ironic: *Oh, I thought somebody farted.* NEW YORK POST factual: *Why, it's the two scumbags who tried to kill me in the goddamned sewer.* But the brain mites would not let words pass Mikey's lips. Carleton Casper Leadman's little brother Bob was strangleholding two of the many scabs on Mikey's soul, and to quote the libretto detailing their misdeeds would require more footnote space than we have here. *

Roach was encased in some sort of gold foil suit and moonwalk shoes with glo-in-the-dark gel soles. It looked like someone had tried to microwave him. Ratso had suffered a hit-and-run from music biz fashion and was buried in rap-meister drag seven sizes too large, with his suede gimme cap on sideways—if Ratso's pocky snout was six o'clock, the hat's bill was aimed at 2:10. His trademark mirrorshades hung

askew due to the recent loss of his left ear, which had landed in a smear of crimson on the glass floor. One of the bur-
nished-bald bullyboys stepped forward to collect it in a plastic bag already had wrapped around his hand, the way poop-
conscious Manhattan pet-walkers retrieve their dog's sputter.

They screamed *motherfucker* and *nigga* a lot until Bob's
flat, leaden gaze suggested they should zip the fuck shut.

"Listen to that," said Carleton Casper Leadman. "The
children of the night; what bullshit they spout. And don't say
nigga, shorty. Say *Afroamericanally complected.*"

"Hey, look," said Roach. "It's Scoop."

"Scoopy-poopy," said Ratso, flash-reviewing the sins of an
imprudent life.

Carleton Casper Leadman continued: "My dear brother
Bob here has been instructed to pink-slip one of these gen-
tlemen at your discretion, Mister Mikey Scoop. As a demon-
stration of our good faith in the compact to which you have
agreed. The remainder, he shall pink-slip upon your discharge of obligation. Fair enough?"

"What?" said Roach and Ratso together, straining to look
at each other around the horizon curve of Bob's chest.

Mikey grinned. "One for now and one for later, huh?"

"Fellater?" howled Roach. "I'm straight, dude. C'mon,
Scoopy, you don't wanna initiate no harm on me—"

"Us," said Ratso.

"Fuck you!" said Roach. "I don't know you! You the cause
of all this grief! Scoopy, brother, that duct tape was all Ratso's
idea, man!"

"Fuck *you!*" Ratso bellowed back at Roach "That sewer
thing? I didn't have nothing to do with that, that was all
Roach's idea, c'monnnn, look in my eyes and see I'm speaking plain truth at your head!"

"Kind of hard to pick," said Mikey.

"I agree," said Carleton Casper Leadman. "Sadly, I have other tasks to attend. A mayoral candidacy is complex, as you might imagine. Bob, throw them out, and for heaven's sake, let's air out this room."

Carleton Casper Leadman touched a switch on the invisible desk and a large, stainless steel fan began to rotate in the eastward see-through wall. It was the size of a jet turbine and apparently consumed as much power. In seconds its whine was up to redline.

"Oh," said Mikey. "Whew. For a minute there, I thought you were talking about *killing* them."

Bob flung both Roach and Ratso into the fan, which vaporized them.

"The airflow paths created by the low temperature insure that we don't get what is grimly called *blowback,*" Carleton Casper Leadman said of the fan. "And, just a reminder? We never use the k-word here." He turned toward the eastern view, where a red mist was already dissipating. "Efficient. The vapor blows away before anything can hit the ground."

"Yeah," said Mikey, his jaw still unhinged at the instantaneous blenderization of Roach and Ratso, who could now truly be called one and the same. The Teflon-veneered, razor-edged blades had converted two streetwise loudmouths into scarlet ether in less than a quarter-second.

And all Mikey had to do to avoid the same fate was murd—...er, assassi—...that is, *pink-slip* ten people who were still living and breathing.

—ooo—

After washing his hands and narrowly avoiding a full-scale nervous breakdown in the Leadman washroom facility, Mikey paused to wonder why the row of brushed-aluminum sinks was lined up against a floor-to-ceiling window. When he realized these futuristic concavities were urinals, it became clear that from such a vantage, one could symbolically whizz on the entire city.

The way the entire city had been whizzing on him, lately.

Now he was intact, but his existence had been knocked into a cocked hat. No, worse—it had been cocked into the ole fuck-hat.

Despite accidents and appearances, Mikey knew he was no murderer, and no way could he become a contract-killing robot on behalf of Carleton Casper Leadman and his little brother, Bob. Which meant that not only had he lied to them, but now he *owed* them, for Roach and Ratso.

He had walked out of Leadman's lair with less reason to live than ever before. The retribution arm of Leadman was long, nasty and not given to forgetfulness, forgiveness, or the healing nature of time.

So, in the desperate manner of the salvationless, in the miniscule time-frame separating despair from self-immolation, he had sought out Franklin Fuck, private investigator, and set him to seek out in turn a mystery woman he knew only by the name of Jacqui. Perhaps he could win a smile from her, as he had done before. A single smile, one small note of human compassion he could take to his grave instead of the nightmare image of Leadman the Younger biting off his head and racking his spine like a party popper.

But Mikey was not so senseless that he could not perceive being tailed. A lifetime of paranoia realized had fine-tuned his peripheral radar. As he stumped along in the slush, he checked window reflections. No hallucination: there was a guy in a trenchcoat and a hat following him. No, two guys, identically dressed. Possibly three. More likely three, unless one of them could teleport across the street and back regardless of traffic. A good chance one of the three was an optical illusion, but no matter. They darted in and out of the pedestrian crunch,

appeared between vehicles. They popped up and disappeared like sparks in a fire, but they were absolutely *there*. One of them, at least.

A hand planted itself in the middle of Mikey's chest, stopping him cold while he was attempting to monitor his rearward stewards. Mikey was just jumpy enough to shit himself, almost. His butt cheeks flubulated.

"What the fuck—?!" he blurted, voice cracking in the cold air.

"The Fuck himself," said Franklyn Fuck. "With me, when you Fuck things up, they actually become *better*—get it?" Then, following a pause to sniff the air: "Pyew, man, did you just *release?*"

The elfin P.I. was topcoated and mufflered, hale and diamond-eyed. He wore rubber galoshes over his wingtips and stray flakes of snow had roosted in his exuberant eyebrows. His bald dome was squared off by one of those Russian fur hats.

He looked so warm that Mikey began to shudder uncontrollably.

"Uh, release?"

"You know—*pffffhhht!*" The eyebrows indicted Mikey. "No matter. Never begrudge a fellow human an honest panic fart."

The brain mites proceeded to soak their teeny Depends with unbridled laughter.

"Well now, well now," said Franklyn Fuck, giving Mikey's upper arms a ruffing. "You walked in and then you walked out, and when you walked out you weren't dead, so I guess that's good news, huh? Made some kind of deal, didja, with the Leadman himself. Goddamn, but that's so American it makes me want to *weep* with patriotism. Know why Hitler's boys wanted Berlin to be captured by Yanks instead of Russkies? Because they knew they could cut a deal with the Americans. You can always cut a deal with an American. So

I guess this Leadman ain't some sorta foreign scumbone?" The estimable Mr. Fuck was chattering in the manner of a fan, sniffing celebrity dish.

"I only look alive," said Mikey. "Maybe I'll live long enough to find a euthanasia clinic around here."

"Jacqui Quisneros," said Fuck.

"What?" Mikey stopped walking and turned to look at the shorter man.

Fuck shot Mikey a full-on twinkle. "Jacqui. Quisneros. Is what her name is. The woman. Jacqui Quisneros is *precisely* what her name is." He smiled big, letting the factoid sink in. "Aha—see, ten seconds ago you wanted to kill yourself, and all's I gotta do is say a lady's name and suddenly, miraculously, your face is blushing to warm itself up, and you've found a reason to live. Hah! And you thought I wasn't worth a Fuck, am I right? Of course, there aren't many things in this bad old world that are worth a Fuck—a good Fuck, that is. Ever notice that? How people are always dismissively yelling *bite me* and *eat me* and *blow me* to people that they would never want biting, eating, or blowing them? Odd. They scream *fuck you* at people they'd never want to bang in a bazillion years. People say *fuck you* to me, brother, and I say yeah: *Fuck, me. Asshole, you.* That's a joke. Why do you look like you still have to go to the bathroom?"

"You found her," said Mikey.

"Naturally I found her. *You're in luck, give a Fuck.* Thought I'd drop by and see if you were still alive, so's I could deliver the news and maybe, y'know, get paid."

"Where is she?"

"Just keep walking the way we're walking now. I am your personal escort to Paradise. Just remember me kindly when her scanties hit the floor, and tip accordingly." He wiggled his eyebrows and Mikey thought of caterpillars, wrestling.

"Okay, full disclosure. This lady was as curious about you as you seem to be about her. I found her, but it was her that proposed this little rendezvous." He boffed Mikey on the back. "C'mon, boyo, how often does this kind of work have an actual happy ending?"

—ooo—

The coffee place was called 5¢ 4 JOE, and seemed to have time-transported from 1945, with interior décor by Weegee, minus the corpses and blood spatter. Coffee really was a nickel per cup, although there was a two-dollar "cup charge" to get started, which was still a better deal than the corporate caffeine slop-houses that had inundated civilization like a mechanized plague of locusts bearing aggressive logos and the humorless automaton service of aggressively ignorant poseurs.

The Jacqui Quisneros Mikey found occupying the third booth back was altogether a different creature than the one he had met while in an altered state of consciousness at the dentist's. Same blonde bob, same cut of jewelry, but this new iteration looked…better. It was tough to pinpoint. More calm, assured, radiant. More aware, schooled, beautiful. More worldly, observant, engaging. More expensive.

"This seems sordid and full of intrigue, doesn't it?" she said as Mikey slid in across from her. She filled his field of vision, seeming to mute everything around her. "The clandestine rendezvous."

"Hi," said Mikey.

"Yes, I was," she said. Dazzling. "At the dentist's. I don't know whether to apologize to you for my unseemly behavior, or just chat you up. I think I may do both." She sipped strong coffee fragrant with some kind of special under-the-counter liqueur—special customer, special treatment. She had a long ochre cigarette going despite the posted NO SMOKING admonishments, and nobody seemed to mind.

"Do you come here a lot?" Mikey immediately pillored himself for the pedigree of his dumbass small talk. "What I mean is, do they know you here?"

She laughed; one throaty syllable. "You know what? I don't even register the behind-the-scenes machinations anymore. I never wait in line for anything. In fact, I never wait for anything. I say I want something, and boom, it appears. Many people stay employed working this magic but I rarely glimpse the underpinnings."

She was wealthy, or powerful, or was an intimate of someone with wealth and power. In supposedly classless America, she was walking evidence that the sky was not a limit for a caste of people so different from Mikey that they might as well be Martians. Really well-heeled Martians, with chauffeured flying saucers.

"You waited for me," said Mikey. *Score one for Mikey!* cheered the brain mites.

"I'll tell you why." She leaned closer, inviting his confidence. "I am not in any sort of business, but I benefit from people who are. My life is a fringe perk of their machinations."

"Those magicians behind the secret curtain," said Mikey. His coffee arrived, potent and energizing. He felt empowered and forgot about the downscale impression of his soggy clothes. Jacqui Quisneros was not looking at his clothing; she was looking at his eyes.

"Exactly. And it's not that I'm not grateful for what I enjoy. I just don't want to live in a monied vacuum. I dread devolving into one of those bitches who swims in Botox, using implants for water wings, if you follow. That way lies substance abuse and ugly endings. But the people I normally deal with, I…arrrggh!" She threw up her hands in a gesture of frustration; she really

wanted a thousand words' worth of picture to encompass her meaning. "God, I sound like such an asshole, don't I?"

"I wasn't thinking that," said Mikey, settling into this weird new feeling, which he suddenly realized was comfort. "Although I know I'm supposed to say, *aww, no ya don't, honey.*"

She laughed again and it made everything all better. "You've got me. What I am stumbling around trying to say is that when I met you at the dentist's, I remembered that once upon a time I knew people who were sympathetic and understanding. The sort of people who would offer a hand to hold to a total stranger. I haven't met anybody like that in a long time, and later I thought, well, that was nice. No strings and all. And for all I have, I haven't experienced nice in so long that it was a shock."

She had reached, and beckoned, and taken one of Mikey's hands in both of hers.

"You're welcome," said Mikey, somewhat flabbergasted. The brain mites were chanting bawdy limericks about falling in love, kissing in a tree, guys from Nantucket.

Mikey's nape horripilated as a trio of men in identical leather trenchcoats entered the coffee palace. They sat three abreast at the counter directly opposite Jacqui's booth, doffed their three identical hats, and all twirled on their stools simultaneously to stare at Mikey. They each wore security earpieces in their three left ears. Matching suits and ties. Six similar brown eyes. Mikey's joy was mashed flat— these guys had been tracking him on the street awhile ago, and damned if they weren't really a trio.

"Jacqui," he said. "Those men over there have been—"

Jacqui overrode him with a hot shot of annoyance, seeming thwarted. "Oh, *what?*" she barked, directly at them.

"You know them?" said Mikey.

"Left to right—that's *my* left—Mr. Muzykansky, Mr. LeBlanco-Pinche-Dolorosa, and the one nearest to the end of the counter is Mr. Beveringswithe. That's boring, so I call them Poker, Peeker and Porker, and I wish they'd leave me the hell *alone* for five minutes at a stretch."

"Are they, like, your...security?"

She shook her head. "That's what a politician would call them. I'm amazed I made it to the dentist's without at least two of them completely up in my biz. Do you know every time I go to the bathroom I think there's one of them dogging me? I bet they could tell you whether I wipe front to back."

Poker, Peeker and Porker nattered *sotto voce* among themselves, and into their lapel mikes.

Jacqui took up a bar napkin on which she had been doodling earlier with a Montblanc pen and slid it across Mikey's line of sight. It read: *I'll take care of them. Find out if this place has a back door.*

Mikey caught the drift and pretended to excuse himself for the restroom. One of the three—Peeker—started to tail him but thought better of it.

At the restroom alcove he detoured through a stainless steel swinging door into what he thought was the kitchen. Instead he found a large pantry where a man in chef's duds was vigorously fornicating with a waitress on top of a large burlap bag of unground Brazilian robusto. The woman had long, blood-red fingernails that were sunk deeply into the man's buttocks and their activity seemed vaguely violent. Her excellent legs were aloft in a flying V and she was grunting breathy little obscenities. The man's pumping ass was very white, almost alabaster in the dim light. It appeared they were not going to dismount any time in the near future, and there was no exit door back here anyway, so Mikey did an about-face, cherishing a fleet yet guilty fantasy about him and Jacqui performing a similar activity in much the same mode.

He was thinking about Jacqui, naked, when he came out of the alcove and ran into Peeker, who had followed him after all and, apparently, could read his mind.

Jacqui was gone. The brain mites counseled that although Mikey would not admit this yet, *he* was gone, too.

—ooo—

Nobody said a word as Mikey was escorted back to Leadman's glacial eyrie.

Carelton Casper Leadman was gone, but his little brother Bob was still open for business. Jacqui Quisneros was there, too, sitting near the big computer desk of glass and obviously fuming.

Porker was the first to speak. Or maybe it was Poker. Either way, the minions seemed to act as interpreters for the impassive giant, who stood there sucking up space and gravity, glaring with an obsidian gaze that made Mikey think of those lasers that can etch a mark on the moon.

"Mister Robert wishes to know why you would violate his trust by going to a public place and holding hands with his girlfriend," said Peeker. No, wait, it was Porker. Maybe.

Mikey said, "Guh—?!"

"Mister Robert," said Poker, "thinks it indiscreet and unseemly for you to be making a move on his lady." This one was Porker, definitely.

"Oh, knock it off, Bob," said Jacqui.

If Easter Island statues had fists, they'd look like Bob's do right now, thought Mikey. Opening and closing convulsively. Preparing to rend and crush and perform demolition. The big fan at the end of the room was already purring along at full crank.

"Mister Robert advises that this pathetic attempt to humiliate him on your part has put your agreement in serious jeopardy," said one of the P's.

"Bob, you lay a hand on that man and no cuddles," said Jacqui. "I mean it."

"Jacqui, what the hell, I mean, this guy is your *boyfriend?*" Mikey stammered. That was about all he said because Bob's forklift hand engirded his neck, clamped shut, and lifted. Mikey's face turned deep crimson. He could feel Bob's fingers meeting around the other side of his neck.

"Bob, stop it!" said Jacqui. "Bad thing! No!"

Poker and Peeker escorted Jacqui from the room under considerable protest.

Bob said, *"Huuuhhnnhhhh."*

Porker translated: "Mister Robert asked if arrangements have been made in the event of your demise."

Even the brain mites did not wish to inherit Mikey's debt.

Bob began to stride toward the fan, holding Mikey at arm's length (about four feet) like a trashbag of used kitty litter. Mikey could feel moving air, sucking past his eyeballs, and he attempted to say many things, but nothing could push past the bottleneck clot of his imploded throat, including pleas, begging, screaming, weeping and general disport of the wetter emotions.

The flash replay of Mikey's entire life before his dying eyes took about eight seconds, after which his incipient panic at termination via rotor surged back in. He kicked and flailed but it was as useless as attempting to move a skyscraper by pushing one ledge. His air was almost gone. He thought: *Crap, I really am going to join up with Roach and Ratso. We will all be as one, rendered unto vapor, similar to a fart thought less pleasing...*

Porker hit his chin on the lip of the desk as he collapsed to the floor, a couple of his teeth rattling across the glass surface like dice in a crapshoot. He fell unconscious, with a large divot of hair bashed out of the starboard side of his skull by

the baseball bat that had extinguished any further contributions from his stiff upper (and lower) lip.

Mikey could not see a damned thing. The dead-set, flat slate, tombstone expression of the fearsome Bob overflowed what was left of his vision. When Porker was felled, Bob turned with the slow deliberation of a construction crane until Mikey—scarlet dots swimming through his vision as the brain mites suffocated one by one—could see.

Franklyn Fuck stood next to the desk, a Louisville Slugger cocked jauntily on one shoulder. With a disarming, rotund grace he ambled deeper into the room while Porker's blood tinted the floor floods pink.

"The very first Louisville Slugger was turned in eighteen-eighty-and-four by a fella name of Bud Hillerich, real name, John A. That bat was made for Pete Browning, who played for the Louisville Eclipse and was called 'The Old Gladiator.' Mister Hillerich had come up through his dad's woodworking shop, where they previously made ten-pins, wooden bowling balls, newel posts, porch rails and suchlike."

Hypoxia began to burst blood vessels in Mikey's cerebrum, drowning more of the brain mites as Bob completed his giant millstone half-turn to look with disapproval upon this new interloper, this man in pinstriped trousers and wing-tipped shoes with the preying mantis eyebrows. Fuck was strolling through the icy space, like a vaudevillian running through a well-lubricated routine, a crowd-pleaser.

"See, for awhile the bats were called Falls City Sluggers, but the Louisville Slugger name was trademarked in 1894. Tenth anniversary of the bat."

Poker and Peeker had returned, sans Jacqui. They instantly tried to unsling the firearms holstered beneath their trenchcoats. In one arcing swoop, Franklyn Fuck swatted the

guns to the far corners of the room, one-two, deep to right and left field, without once breaking his patter.

"On the first of September in nineteen-ought-five a ballplayer named Honus Wagner—who was known as the Flying Dutchman—granted the Hillerich & Son permission to use his Johnny Hancock on a bat. That's important because it was the first known retail endorsement by a professional athlete, ever."

Fuck completed a three quarter turn and put his shoulder into the swing as he brought the bat around, long and high. It jacked Poker's jawbone nearly free from his head and Poker fell down.

Peeker yelled, "You can't just come in here and—!"

"Shhh, quiet," said Fuck, looping the bat back to crack Peeker right on the part in his hair, producing a noise much akin to a cocoanut halved by a rock. Peeker fell down, too.

The adamantine grip on Mikey's neck had eased back, just a little, permitting a thin trickle of air to seep lungward.

"Following a dee-sastrous fire in 1910," Fuck went on, "the plant was rebuilt and renamed the Hillerich & Bradsby Company. In 1916 they made the first golf clubs ever, as well. During the Second World War, they also made wooden stocks for that ole reliable Army standby, the M1 carbine."

Franklyn Fuck's spiel-circuit now wound him within range of the mighty Bob, closer and closer. Mikey gagged and tried to hoist himself, a lynched man trying to fight the pull of the noose.

"Now, note this *particular* Louisville Slugger." Fuck held it for inspection, squinting to read the engraving. "Number four-forty-seven, of one thousand, nine hundred and forty-one bats signed by Joe DiMaggio in 1999, right before he died. He signed 'em for some home shopping network, can you believe that? That's 1,941 bats. Know why? 'Cos in

1941, Joltin' Joe had his 56-game hitting streak. He pulled down two grand for *each* of these he signed. That's a cool four million bucks, give or take a hundred thou."

Fuck held the bat out to Bob. "And I want you, sir, to have it." Bob's graven expression furrowed deeply. Confusion? Suspicion? But he released Mikey to collect his prize. Mikey scrambled away with what little coordination his oxygen-starved muscles could muster, as Bob raised the bat and prepared to mash Franklyn Fuck into a paste of scalp and shoetops.

"Wait up," said Fuck. "I got one more thing for ya." From his topcoat he extracted a small object resembling a frost scraper. He did not launch into a verbose explanation of it, but Mikey recognized, through blurred and swimmy vision, one of those things called a LifeHammer, with twin heads of pointed machine steel, designed to shatter car windows and provide quick escape in a vehicular emergency.

Franklyn Fuck took one dainty balletic backward step, as though making a bow. His galoshes squeaked on the floor. He bent and smartly rapped the floor with the hammer.

The glass floor.

While Bob was still cocking his death-swing with the bat, the mammoth pane of floor on which he stood spiderwebbed until it was opaque. The effect was the same as when you pop open an over-refrigerated beverage and it turns to ice. The big horizontal square of glass disintegrated and Bob plummeted, bat in hand, to collide bodily with the next floor down. Bob's own tonnage took out that floor, and as he continued to fall through one pulverized layer of acrylic to the next, all he did was pick up vertical speed, with a sort of dopplering train-wreck sound that took twenty seconds to stop echoing.

Mikey's gullet un-tweezed to the diameter of a Q-tip and his furtive, asthmatic vampirism of air made a squeegee noise. His head felt about to burst like a cantaloupe dropped from a hot air balloon. His nose felt afire.

Franklyn Fuck snugged his ushanka down around his eartops, causing his bald spot to vanish and deploying his hair-fringe. "Hey there, pilgrim," he said, helping Mikey to stand. "What do you say we blow this popsicle stand?"

"Why...what...how come..." Mikey attempted to say, but his throat felt worked over with an emery board and veneered in toxic waste. Drawing air was still a treat.

"Oh," said Fuck. "I figured it would all go badly. I figured you might get in a jam. But what these bozos don't comprehend is that when I Fuck around, I don't fuck around, if ya get my meaning. So I tailed you from the coffeehouse. Don't worry, I billed ya for the time."

"Thanks," Mikey rasped silbilantly, abruptly understanding why bad pulp writers used too many modifiers.

"And, the lady's not on the premises, so I figured I'd still be needing to be looking for her all over again, am I correct on that wrinkle?"

"Ergh," Mikey affirmed.

Fuck paused to stare down the yawning abyss of destruction caused by Casper Carelton Leadman's little brother Bob's speedy loss of altitude. "Damn. Some glazier's gonna get Exmas early this year. Maybe one of my distant relatives; some faraway Fuck." He bent back from the edge in order to avoid toppling, or adversely affecting the floor's current cleavage situation, or losing his hat. "This here is a Soviet naval officer's lid," he said by way of explanation. "Pure mouton—that's lamb's wool, finest kind—made in Lithuania. I got it as a reward for...ahh, never mind, that's another Fuck story."

Mikey discovered that Fuck had infiltrated the Leadman stronghold via a maze of fire exits that handily bypassed lobby security. "You got big fingerprints on the back of your

neck, kinda embossed into the flesh," Fuck said. "Small price to pay for ole Bob; I'd say he got Fucked up real good. Or Fucked down. Heh."

Later, on the street, talking still felt like trying to swallow a burdock. "I think Mister Bob dislocated all the vertebrae in my neck," Mikey said. Respirating the frigid air hurt, too. "How did you manage that performance up there? I mean, when you were talking about that bat, it was like watching a charmer hypnotize a snake."

"Oh, that one's easy," said Fuck. "I don't do work without I don't do research on all the particulars of any given case. I got boatloads of exotic information in my brain pan; you mighta noticed."

"Then why didn't you tell me Jacqui Quisneros was Bob's main squeeze?"

"Because it's common knowledge, lad, hell, everybody knows that already. The negligence there was yours. You didn't ask me. I can't answer questions you don't ask, boyo."

Mikey felt just a touch more out of the mainstream. It was a familiar, discomfiting mood the brain mites tended to savor.

"As for the big guy back there," said Fuck, "that was an elementary fact check. Bob likes baseball. Ain't no more Fucks anywhere than in baseball, plain and simple."

—ooo—ooo—ooo—

* For the lowdown on Roach and Ratso, see "Scoop Makes a Swirly," available in the collection *Black Leather Required*.

WHAT HAPPENED WITH MARGARET

Whenever an earthquake tremor shakes the Valley, thought Margaret, we're all supposed to react as if we've been jostled on a city bus, or elbowed in line at the market. Even if it's serious, we are expected to pretend it is no big deal.

"No big deal," she said aloud to herself, trying to cement the thought as though it was a revelation. No big deal—just like the rest of her life.

On television, newscasters fought to look harried and deeply concerned as they spieled off the stats on the 4.3 temblor that had originated somewhere in the vicinity of Big Bear, to drift down from the mountains and lend the San Fernando Valley a bit of an afternoon wiggle at exactly 2:46 P.M. Really, the sensation was the same as when you were lying in bed, and a dog or cat jumped on the bed. At most, pictures fell over and the house creaked. It happened with the frequency of those police high-speed pursuits, telecast live, and came to as little consequence.

No big deal.

In Margaret's home, a post-war saltbox on Lemona Avenue, the hot zone was the fireplace mantel. That's where the framed pictures always tumbled if subjected to a quake-lette. It

happened often enough that she had wisely dispensed with glass, now replaced with little squares of glare-resistant Lexan she had cut herself. The pictures were important to the unity of the house. Here was the wedding shot; everybody was smiling. Here were the shots of nieces and nephews, enshrined as though they were her own children. Over here were moms and dads and relatives. If everyone was smiling, then life was good, all was in cosmic order, things were as they were supposed to be. Margaret's husband had once noted that past a certain point, a smile was nothing more than bared teeth, and she had poo-poohed him. Tyler always said things like that. Occasionally, if she was "in a mood," she accused him of saying things like that to injure her on some subdermal level, to wound without killing. Tyler always reassured her that wasn't the case, *at all*.

Tyler and Margaret had no children because something was wrong with Tyler's sperm. "Not viable," was how a doctor had put it. Margaret had assumed she would be a mother several times over by now, age thirty-eight. She certainly *felt* fertile, in a vague, Earth-momma sense of genetic predisposition. She dutifully read magazine articles and sometimes broached the topic of the biological clock. If it was supposed to happen, it would happen. Meanwhile, she could practice by being the greatest auntie in the world, not only to her sisters' kids, but to children in the immediate neighborhood.

Tyler and Margaret's joint tax return listed Margaret as "housewife." Well, that was a handy label that allowed for a nice deduction, but just what the hell was a housewife supposed to do if there were no children around? That's why she kept the television hot. For company. There was also Beauregard, a flat-faced Persian Margaret had inherited from her sister Florice. *He sprays,* said Florice. *He's not good with the kids. You'll have to have him fixed.*

Margaret had disliked the idea of intentionally rendering the cat impotent, but she had done as advised, for the sake of the furniture.

Margaret replaced the fallen pictures on the mantel, made sure she had her shopping list, and left the television on when she departed. All the people in line at the supermarket jabbered about the "earthquake," though it seemed kind of silly to give the minor event such a portentious name. She did not know any of the people she saw at the store, presumably, her neighbors.

The drive home was a matter of blocks, so Margaret decided on a spur-of-the-moment detour. She ranged up and down the residential avenues near the freeway, streets that paralleled her own, but which she had never traversed. She saw lawns cluttered with children's toys and soccer mom driveways, garages open to display toyboxes and bikes and SUVs, almost bragging. Some of the homes flew jaunty flags festooned with unicorns or rainbows, declaring their constituency in some fairyland where people always met their true loves, mated like porn stars, and produced gorgeous offspring, the rearing of which would fill their cup of days with scraped knees, Christmas gifts, hand-holding in crosswalks, and all the wacky foibles of parenthood. Everyone would live happily ever after, until the kids grew old enough for Mom and Dad to hector them about providing grandchildren.

Margaret considered her double-bagged groceries. Cooking for two had its limits—another boundary she ached to breach.

Tyler worked for a post house—a video editing facility which dealt mostly in commercials and MTV-style short films. He would come home to dinner and talk about his co-workers, his projects, and the convolutions of dealing with the new AVID software. Margaret did not know any of

Tyler's co-workers. Today, at least, she could talk about the earthquake, and hold up her end of the conversation that way, and somebody should really *do something* about preparedness in a quake zone, but nobody ever would.

Tyler would chuckle and disparage all the people who feared a visit to Los Angeles, yet lived in places where there were twenty or thirty tornadoes per year. Then he would plunk down in front of the TV to watch ESPN and drink Lite beer until he was reasonably sedated from the rigors of his day. Conversation, thankfully, was usually limited to the dinner table, and assorted attributes of the comestibles thereupon. The sort of talk that fills air but rarely provides ventilation.

When Margaret entered her front door, she felt a breeze. She knew her home well enough to know that the back door was open. An error. She always made sure the house was locked and secure before going anywhere. If the back door was open, Beauregard the cat might have escaped, and that was no good, either. Beau was an indoor cat, a lifer. Outside were coyotes and automobiles and Bad Cats and a whole encyclopedia of dangers.

She heard a voice in the bedroom say, *oh, fuck!* Another voice said, *oh shit let's get the fuck outta here.*

Margaret had already closed the kitchen door, noticing that it had been pried open.

Around the corner at a dead run came Donnie Knox and Willie Preston. They both lived on Lemona. Donnie would be 12 this October, and Willie, who most other kids called Blinky (because of the contact lenses imposed on him by his parents), was two months younger. Donnie was clutching one of Margaret's pillowcases, laden with predictable booty. Blinky had a gun. He pointed it at Margaret and they all frozen for one precious instant, about nine feet away from each other.

"You said she was fucking gone," said Blinky.

"She fucking *was*," said Donnie. "Same fucking time every day!"

"What is going on here, you guys?" Margaret said, even though it was pretty apparent. She had known these kids, peripherally, since they were five. They had eaten cookies she had baked.

"You done fucked up, cunt," said Blinky, cocking the hammer on his pistol, a black revolver.

Donnie kept eyeing the front door.

Margaret decided to forego the lecture in her head about *that language.* She held her ground and tried to sound authoritative, and accusing. "Donnie?"

Donnie dropped the pillowcase. "Just…pretend we weren't here! Shit!"

He lit out for the front door, pulling Blinky along, seemingly by magnetism, or undertow. Blinky backed out. "Don't say anything bitch or I'll come back and wax your big fat ass!"

The screen door banged and they were gone.

Margaret was shaking. When she picked up the pillowcase, nausea dropped her to one knee and she nearly threw up. Inside the linen was a pathetic fistful of jewelry, most of it worthless except for sentimental value. One ring of her late grandmother's with an actual diamond inset. It was the only ornament Margaret's mother could spare after she had distributed the good stuff, the heritage items, among her sisters who, after all, had families. The load jingled as though it was worth more; the kids had emptied Tyler's spare change tray.

It was wayward youth, igniting pre-adolescent rebellion, Margaret knew. They weren't really bad kids. It was a phase. Willie had not actually aimed a real pistol at her; it was probably one of those pellet guns, the ones that ought to be banned because they looked so disturbingly authentic.

Things in society were done a certain way, and if a kid brandished a fake gun instead of a real one, then he was not beyond redemption, merely misled. That was why she would have to call their parents first, before summoning the police. That was why Mr. and Mrs. Knox and Mr. and Mrs. Preston would act responsibly, and in all likelihood, spare Donnie and Willie a lot of future grief by dispensing firm chastisement today. No need to deploy officers of the law unless they really wanted to throw a scare into the little bastards.

But someone had already summoned the police, because they were on the front porch. Two of them, looming huge and casting shadows of retribution. Los Angeles policemen, individually, were more imposing than killer robots—all gigantic slabs of muscle encased in body armor and skintight, black uniforms; lethal soldiers with severe haircuts, and dense sunglasses they snapped off to expose the kind of gaze that could jump-start cold fission.

Politely, they asked if they could come in.

"They just ran off, down the street!" Margaret said, as the two cops filled up her living room. One was an Asian man, shaved completely bald, a sergeant by his stripes. Sergeant Ymada. His short-sleeved blouse was cuffed tight, to emphasize his biceps. Margaret noticed he had a Ranger tattoo on his forearm, above a stainless steel diver's watch. His partner was one of those flat-topped Hitler Youth nightmares with the attitude of an attack dog. Officer Petrovich. His uniform hash included marksmanship ribbons and a cloisonné pin for the O.C.B., which Margaret was pretty sure stood for Organized Crime Bureau. Both men were north of six-two in flat-heeled boots.

"You get an earthquake, it compromises security systems," said Ymada. "You get kids trying to freeload the neighborhood."

"You get a lot of people calling the police because they're scared," said Petrovich.

"They're just kids," said Margaret. "It was probably a dare, or something stupid. Look, they didn't take anything, so—"

Ymada overrode her. "Just relax, and don't panic, and everybody'll come out okay." He said this as Petrovich closed the front door.

And locked it.

"I don't understand," said Margaret. But the fear was in her chest, clogging her throat. She understood, but wanted another option.

Petrovich grabbed the back of her neck and bent her forward over the cushioned arm of the sofa. He was as strong as a forklift.

"*Wait!* I—you can't—!"

He pegged her on the back of the head; it might have been his hand, or a lump of lead. "Shut up. Don't resist. Don't tell us what we can or cannot do."

"Found it," came Ymada's voice from the kitchen as Petrovich rucked down Margaret's slacks and stripped away her undies. "Tell her she keeps making noise, we're gonna gag her, and if that don't work, she gets a head injury."

"You understand?" said Petrovich, maintaining his steel grip.

Margaret understood. She heard an aerosol can shpritz and smelled a heavy aroma, and understood that Ymada was lubricating his erection with spray-on cooking oil.

One of them—Margaret wasn't sure which—pried her legs further apart and entered her from behind in a single piercing thrust. He was bigger than Tyler, her husband, and he pumped away as though lifting weights for a record. As her eyes teared up, she saw Petrovich on the other side of the living room, scoping out the entertainment system.

"They haven't got any music for shit," he said.

Worst of all, she could see the clock on the mantel, next to all the photographs that advertised her happiness in normalcy. It took Ymada almost fifteen minutes to orgasm. They she heard the spray again, and Petrovich proceeded to widen her anus. She felt her rectal tissue rip.

"Big ass," said Ymada.

"I like a big ass," said Petrovich, grabbing it in both meaty hands as he pushed into her. It felt like his dick was reaching up inside her, to dislocate organs.

They left her that way, bent over the couch, semen and watery blood oozing down her inner thighs. One of them said *have a nice day.* Both laughed. They closed the door behind them.

Gradually, Margaret began to make tentative groping movements, rolling herself off the sofa to sit on the floor, where she hugged her knees tight to her face. She was embarrassed at how heavy she had become. Her assailants had been forced to spread her into a peace symbol just to get past the beef of her thighs. They had said her ass was *big.* Probably the people at the supermarket thought the same thing. That foul-mouthed brat Willie Preston had called her *fat.*

Margaret wanted Tyler to find her this way: on the floor, weeping, violated. He would love her and take her to the hospital. They would bond, through mutual distress. There would come huge payback.

After two more hours, Margaret realized Tyler would not be coming home tonight. Just like last night, and the night before. Tyler was out, loving and bonding with one of his co-workers, probably at her place.

Her family had always called her an optimist. Maybe, she thought, she had been impregnated, now. Having a baby would jolt her whole family into line, but good. Tyler would be compelled to finance the whole blessed event. He could bail from their marriage if he wanted to, but by christ he was going to learn about responsibility. She would show *everybody* what a good mother she could be. It was fair, it was right, she had earned it. She could turn this catastrophe into an asset. Lesser women would crumble. Not her. It was no big deal.

She was still on the floor in the same position she had fallen when the earthquake hit. She had lunged for the photographs on the mantel, trying to catch them as they tumbled, when she struck her temple against the hardwood headpiece. Her eyes were open—it was nighttime, now—but she could not move her limbs. She was paralyzed and defocused. Scattered around her were the pictures from the mantel, and the clock, broken now, forever set at 2:46 P.M.

The photographs accused her. *I'll show you,* she thought. *My sisters are all cows, their husbands are all cattle, my parents suck, my husband is a cheating prick, and I'll show all of you.*

She felt cold air on her exposed skull, and tacky patches of dried blood on her face. Beauregard the cat was with her, licking away at her unfeeling flesh, rasp, rasp, rasp. Nice kitty.

—ooo ooo ooo—

THE PYRE AND OTHERS

L egend, rumor, myth had it that the book could influence dreams. A reader could weather gruesome adventure, achieve a perverse sexual grail, or drown in a transport of raw dread. It was even possible that the book could set you free.

That was what got Franklin started—the elemental power of hearsay, left to gestate, tended almost as an afterthought, or lapsed hobby. The way it went was this: You put the book under your pillow (so it was said), and when you slept (if you slept), you would be transported into the dream realm of one of the stories inside the book. Some of the stories were odd and fanciful, the way you'd like a quirky dream to be. The catch was that you could not pick the story that invaded your sleeping mind—libidinous free-for-all, or a feverish nightmare that just might tip you over...into a padded cell, if you lived. This Russian roulette proposition, and its obscure proofs through years of vague documentation, was the central attraction. If more people had *heard* of the book, its story—its most important story, the one not part of its table of contents— might have assumed the status of modern urban legend. Nobody Franklin knew had ever heard of the book, which is how he grew to become a zealot about the whole thing.

Franklin Bryant was a faculty member of a mid-sized liberal arts curriculum, which is to say he earned a paycheck by instructing college students in high school English, while he hacked away at a dissertation objective that might lend him more credibility as a scholar. Academic brownie points. The new semester loomed seven weeks distant, and Franklin did not know whether he had the resolve to stare down another class-load of bright-eyed, entry-level nitwits. Room after room of collegiate-coddled warm bodies with empty heads and a predator's sense of the easy fix. Learning, here, was a social activity, not an intellectual one, and Franklin had let his syllabus decay into rote. Trying to teach college students the finer pleasures of 20th Century literature was akin to arguing grammar with a beagle. His Lit 106 cannon fodder came trained to memorize (without learning), pass tests (without extrapolating), and trade bored hours for paper validation (without thinking), and he honestly questioned his capacity to withstand another year of that treadmill. The janitors never quite got the dust out of the corners of the molding on the lecterns. Some of that dust was decades old, and probably pre-dated his contract. It had solidified into layers of gray permanence; strata you could not chip with a fingernail. It would be there when he resigned, and probably still be there when he died.

The book was called *The Pyre and Others*, by J. Arthur Aldridge. Subtitled *Tales of Disturbance*, it was the writer's only published collection. The short stories comprising its contents were commonly available. Some were even posted online. Others had sifted down through "classic" anthologies and annuals. None were rare. Most were presented semi-apologetically, as oddments. Franklin had re-read them all many times, and amassed an Aldridge shelf of relevant works—earlier stories, published less significantly as the last gasp of the post-World War Two pulps ceded market dominance to a burgeon of "men's magazines." He scavenged biographical leftovers, including several brief encyclopedia entries, and a copy of the last known printing of the complete collection, by Royal Ransom Press (London, 1981). Franklin found this last during one of his used bookstore trolls, used bookstores themselves teetering on the rim of extinction—a development that always felt ominous, giving Franklin an ever-present sense of impending loss, though he had no idea what to do with the feeling. None of his researches provided any relevant clues to the enigma of the *The Pyre's* infamy, although the legend itself (such as it was) bore a mention in passing, by the Brit who emceed the book's final republication to date.

This fellow, a former partner in Royal Ransom and earnest champion of the obscure, was named Jonah Siritis, and his Introduction to the 1981 reprint attempted to corral the scant orts of information about J. Arthur Aldridge into one of those arguments why you should read an outdated writer, today. During the late 50s and early 60s, Siritis argued, Aldridge's work influenced many writers whose names you'd know (and laboriously, did he list them), while Aldridge himself never brushed fame. He had once been married. He had once lived in New Orleans. Photographs were hard to come by since he had been published during a time when pictures of writers were more a luxury than a sales necessity, and worse, the man had no public persona to promote. Similarly, he never wrote editorial ephemera that might divulge something personal; papers, notes, and correspondence were rare, brief, and cryptic. He spoke through his stories, and only wrote short fiction—some 30 known stories in all, with *The Pyre and Others* as his crescendo. He died in 1965 at age 32…or in 1963 at age 34…or possibly as late as 1967, aged 30. His career as a writer had basically died by 1961. That was the year he had handed the manuscript copy of *The Pyre* to a small press in Chicago—for free.

Black Rhododenron Press had specialized in the backwaters of "the Eerie and the Weird." Their typesetting was arcane, but usually clean of errors. To the modern eye, the font they employed looked skeletal and basic; probably slugged by hand for whatever web-offset printing was the cheapest in those olden days. The first edition of *The Pyre* was hardbound in thick, green, cloth boards of an odd trim size—approximately 5¼ by 7½ inches—that made it look like a pocket hymnal. Its pages were rough and clunky; Siritis noted that the book "resisted riffling," and tended "to fall open at unexpected places." Its rudimentary dustwrapper hinted at cut-rate deal for paper and the jacket illustration was black and white only. It depicted a graveyard, hooded figures, and the swirling flames of the eponymous pyre, all in an embarrassing, amateurish style that suggested a teenager's grasp of Lovecraftian horror. According to Siritis, the book jacket was so unwieldy that it "traveled"—when you opened the book, the jacket fell off; when you shelved the book, the jacket always scooted up, even if you locked the damned thing into a Broadart sleeve.

This, then, was the edition that supposedly invaded your dreams, if you were foolish or curious enough. Black Rhododenron, 1961. Limited to an edition of 500 copies, twenty of which were given to J. Arthur Aldridge as compensation (and presumed destroyed—guess how—upon Aldridge's death by, quote, "a close friend"). Fewer than 200 copies sold. When Black Rhododendron fell apart in 1962 (so said Jonah Siritis), at least another 150 stock copies vanished from whatever basement warehoused them…nearly half a century ago. Jonah Siritis actually owned one of these first editions, obtained after much travail in 1995. Based on some textural differences he had discovered between the original and the reprint, he was presently pushing for a new, revised edition.

As frustrating as the internet could be for a seeker after Aldridge, the love/hate boon of e-mail permitted Franklin to ask Jonah Siritis the obvious question directly: *So, did you try it?*

Not me, sir, came the reply. *No bravery in that direction, I'm afraid.*

A former librarian, Siritis maintained a continuing interest in posting a definitive online bibliography of Aldridge—if denied a biography—and through contact with him, Franklin began to believe he held the bones of his own dissertation. That was what had kept him going through his previous year at the college. His own warm little niche in the Lit cave, provisioned with a quest, and yes, a mate. Every semester, out of several hundred students, there were always one or two who evinced a sparkle of hope, and if they were female, and not outright beasts, Franklin usually advantaged them so he could have what normal people called a sex life. It was an accepted perk of the educational ladder. He never had to leave them; they always stopped calling when they moved on to other classes, other targets. It was all part of the learning experience.

Serenity—that was really her name—had hauled stakes at the conclusion of the previous term. Of Brazilian extraction, she had possessed a nearly insatiable curiosity coupled with a sexy shyness that could be devastating. Large, liquid brown eyes and a yard of lush dark hair. Cute little round glasses. The curves of classic sculpture, and an ass you could really grab hold of. Spiral notebooks filled with doodles and punishable girly poetry. She had been ripe and willing, a healthy divertissement, until she returned home to Sao Paulo. Usually it was easy for Franklin the write off his exes, but for some reason he could not codify, Serenity lingered in his memory, as though she had died tragically, instead of hanging around to posit uncomfortable questions about the abuses of love, or departing with no more drama than a sterile

handshake. Franklin kept the picture he had taken of her naked, sleeping. Perhaps one day he would allow it to inspire him to write something.

Without Serenity to squander his off-hours, Franklin shifted sights to Aldridge, in a different kind of pursuit. His entrée to Siritis—his introduction—had been a no-brainer. You could use genre geeks if you appealed to their vanity and massaged their basic addictions, the quirks that made them self-appointed keepers of the flame. Siritis proved personable and generous (he always answered e-mails within 24 hours, and Zeus only knew what he did for an actual living after quitting the library biz—if he had a life, at all). Siritis had subsequently provided Franklin with not only the lowdown on the first edition of *The Pyre*, but a front-to-back photocopy of the whole book, the original.

But Xeroxes didn't work, where the preternatural was concerned, or the lure of forbidden insight.

Now Franklin could see for himself (as Siritis had claimed) that three of the stories in *The Pyre and Others* were substantially different, and *longer*, than the versions included in the 1981 reprint.

In "The Sacrifice," a woman suffering an unspecified terminal malady speaks to the engagement ring of her dead betrothed, and the ring seems to answer, in intentionally ridiculous rhyming couplets, with *"the voice of some jocular, speaking blossom from a fairy tale."* Laugh all you want—by the close of the story, ten people have died ghastly and point-specific deaths, before the woman's own ticking clock tolls its last.

Aldridge's only obvious rumination on suicide was called "Chekov's Gun"—principally a long interior monologue by possibly the most depressed protagonist on the planet. When the gun finally does its job (with double-ought buckshot, adminis-

tered orally, no less), the character discovers that the point-blank obliteration of his brain is not the end of his consciousness.

"The Sirens of Westcott," in the original edition, was nearly a third longer. It dealt with the chemical dynamic of sexual attraction, but its theme was bad choices based on physical beauty. Its principal, Herman Banks, is a goatish man expert in what Aldridge termed *"the highly-unstable hobby of technically-proficient intromission."* Hirsute and lumpen, he deludes himself that his goal is love, not lovemaking, but his true satisfaction comes from subjugating the comely women of Westcott Village to his ugliness. Once transported by the erotic rapture of his expertise in bed, the women are summarily discarded by Herman. When several of his victims start comparing notes about *"their greatest sexual experience,"* they band together to entrap him...but first, they have to convince the town's most unattainable beauty to act as bait. As Siritis wrote in his summary, "if sex is Hell, then this is a downward plummet with a stop at each agonizing level and circle of damnation."

All three stories had garnered letters of reader complaint to *Esquire* and *Playboy*, where they originally appeared. The first was a shameless manual for murdering your loved ones, it was claimed. The second was an equally bald handbook for suicide. And the third simply did not endorse a happy-go-lucky concept of sex, *at all*. The unexpurgated texts were fairly wince-inducing. Franklin could feel himself flinch at certain passages, and thrilled to the sensation.

He leafed through the unwieldy Xerox, which Siritis had scanned in two-page spreads and Velo-bound on the left side. He refreshed himself on the brooding puzzle-traps of "Shadows Within the Cage." "Wash, Rinse, Repeat" was fairly famous, in that it had been optioned for adaptation by Alfred Hitchcock's production company, Shamley, as an episode of the popular

television series—only to remain unproduced. Aldridge did make it into the magazine which bore Hitchcock's name, however, with "The Man Who Blew a Fuse," "The Mortuary Student," and "Box No. 262." The latter fomented more letters of protest which most of the magazine's readership considered long overdue.

An unpublished story, original to *The Pyre,* was "The Narrative of Dr. Shackle and Mr. Lye," apparently an honest attempt at humor by Aldridge, although what the titular pair do to their victims was anything but a laff riot. It seesawed between elbow-jabbing one-liners and almost clinically detached slaughter and corpse disposal. It predated quippy slasher movies by two decades, but Franklin found its cumulative effect hard to shake. It was not a wallow in florid adjectives and forensic trivia, gushed off with lowbrow, adolescent glee. It was stately. Its impact was that of a literary writer tackling a subject normally deemed taboo for literary writers—well, a "literary writer" who also knew an awful lot about bondage and submission, at any rate. Weird.

Both "Her Idea of Beautiful" and "A Most Necessary Evil" had *also* been heavily censored. Already poisoned at the prestige magazines, Aldridge had trickled down through their imitators, the bargain-basement pretenders, the soon-to-be porn rags. Yet even they had "problems" and "suggestions." It was easy to see why no mainstream publisher would touch Aldridge in the early 1960s. The sex was too honest, exceeding the de facto "frankness" of the time; the narratives were often sacrilegiously profane; the violence was better suited to a world that was— then—over a decade distant, half a war into the future.

You should have written a novel, Franklin thought. *Then they'd be calling you the William S. Burroughs of horror, today.*

Aldridge's envelope-pushing encountered no such obstacles at *The Haunt,* a micro-press journal published irregularly by a gang of "devotees of the Dark" in Milwaukee. Most of the editorial column in that issue (#5) was subsumed in fawning

gratitude that Mr. Aldridge would even consent to submit "Hugo's Big Blunder." The staff and the readership were familiar with Aldridge's earlier work. When more was eagerly solicited, Aldridge never responded, and the magazine folded two issues later.

That was what writers did, thought Franklin: They pushed envelopes. They knew about submission.

Then there was "The Pyre" itself. Also original to the collection. According to Siritis, Aldridge had submitted *two* versions of the typescript to Black Rhododenron, and apparently—ridiculously—the version used in 1961 never made it into the later printing.

From one of Jonah Siritis' e-mails: *Not much was known about J.A.A., but it doesn't take a genius to conclude that he loved toying with anonymity, and misleading his readers. Maybe he did it to confuse future bibliographers—that whole Imp of the Perverse bent. As you can see from the various encyclopedia entries (cursory, at best), even his birth and death dates have question marks on them. It is a matter of parish record that he married Marie Topaz Severin in November, 1953, although by mid-1955 she doesn't seem to be in the picture any more, and I can find no proof of separation, divorce, or her death. You should also know that shortly after his interment in St. Louis #1, his crypt was plundered by vandals and then knocked down in one of the flash floods common to that area. I checked personally, some ten years ago, during my first trip to the States. J.A.A. is listed in the plot registry but no evidence of his grave can be seen. I don't think he "went under," or faked his death, however. I interviewed a number of people who attended his funeral, including Stoney Beauchamp, who burned J.A.A.'s personal library and files, per written instructions (more's the loss!). Stoney's wife, Lillian, emphasized two things about J.A.A.: his deep love for his absent Marie Topaz, and his determined frustration at feeling creatively "hobbled," as he put it.*

Maybe he murdered her, Franklin wrote back.

I don't think so, replied Siritis. *He loved her too much.*

That was another thing that was "known" about Aldridge—the sort of detail that would never make it into a reference book. It was obvious from re-reading the guy's fiction: Aldridge was *very* familiar with women. Cloistered creatives usually doled out hammer-thumbed erotica based solely on their bovine spouses. Neophytes excreted saccharine, or the sniggering jerkoff of boys playing sex mo-chine. Aldridge wrote like an addict trying to master all he knew of a ceaselessly mesmerizing alien species. Their form, their shape, their palette of intimacies. The extrusion of male through female fascinated him. Women and men, utterly different, fit together just so, in limitless recombination of his gender with other humans who looked similar, but were not built the same. Their outsides could lie (one sex, with a bit of artifice, could pass for its opposite). But the insides told truer stories; the anatomical insides, followed by the emotional ones. Aldridge had continually sought some breakthrough frequency to make his communications more vital.

By some unsuspected agency, thought Franklin, perhaps the sheer *tone* of the book overwhelmed the susceptible, and gave rise to the legend about its ability to empower dreams.

Franklin was eager to run this theory past Siritis, who did not respond for over a week. When he did, it was with a one liner, offering apologies and explaining that he had been *a bit ill of late.*

"The Pyre" was Aldridge's most definitive effort, eschewing thematic embroidery to simply state that some people are driven to kill those they love, *because* they love them. It was not about crazy people seeking vengeance, or lunatics nursing romantic fantasies. It was not about wet dreams or misplaced passion. It was about rational, thinking beings, and the palpable doom they generate by courting a magic they do

not comprehend, almost as if love itself were a malign god whose notice it was imprudent to rouse. The climactic immolation consumed not only the lovers in the story, but everyone their love had ever touched.

This raised the possibility that Aldridge had submitted *The Pyre*—the book—as his own funeral opera. Franklin's perception was that the entire volume was sequenced as preparation steps toward death. First was the review of a life—its fulfillments, tragedies, conquests, recreations, regrets and pleasures. Then the weighing of success versus failure. Then, ritual preparations for an end to the suffering.

But to touch such heights, along the way...!

Franklin suddenly saw how easily the legend about the book had begun. It was the bibliophile's version of "Gloomy Sunday"—the Hungarian song written in 1933 and credited with a rash of suicides due to the bottomless depression the tune supposedly inspired, especially among jazz fans who heard Billie Holiday's version. Myth had it that the composer, Rezso Seress, penned the song for an ex-girlfriend with whom he believed "he could finally be happy, in death." The girlfriend killed herself, leaving behind a note reading "Gloomy Sunday," and Seress himself committed suicide by jumping from a building in Budapest in 1968—ironically, in despair over his inability to produce another song as famous.

Typically, Franklin knew, people knew the rumor, but could never name any of the individuals responsible for its creation. J. Arthur Aldridge had become a similar lost footnote, lost to history, condemned to deeper oblivion the moment university libraries reshuffled their card catalogues to a computer database. One mis-stroke of one key was all it took to make a career totally impossible to locate, or referenced wrongly by some crepuscular search engine that guaranteed it would never be found again, let alone corrected, for decades, if ever. Franklin liked to

use the analogy of the hand. Draw a human hand, he'd say. Sounds easy. (Hand someone a pencil and ask them to draw a human hand that *looks* like a hand, and no cheating—only kindergartners outline their real hand on the paper.) It is amazingly difficult, yet everyone thinks they can do it.

The same held true for all those low-wage earners dutifully attempting to re-type catalogue card entries with no mistakes. Looks easy; misfires all the time. And if you're J. Arthur Aldridge, your existence as a writer is abruptly terminated. All the systems needed time to improve. There was no quick path to knowledge. That was why there was a need for people like Jonah Siritis, and Franklin Bryant.

Impatient, Franklin worked up more notes and dispatched more e-mails to Siritis, on an average of two or three per day. After July bled into August, he received a surprise answer, at last:

Please pardon the impersonal nature of this bulk mailing, but it is my sad obligation to tell you that Jonah Siritis passed away at 7:40 P.M. GST, on Tuesday, 10 August, at Frimley Park Hospital here in Surrey. He was 57 years old. Many of you knew of Jonah's epilepsy. In late July he contracted influenza, running a fever of 104° and vomiting. After an MRI, blood tests, and a lumbar puncture, he was subsequently diagnosed with Acute Viral Encephalitis (AVE) and our neurologist immediately put him on Acyclovir and anti-convulsants. This took over one week, as encephalitis is one of the "most misdiagnosed" afflictions, and Jonah quickly became significantly impaired. Encephalitis is an inflammation of the brain which, in serious cases, rarely offers the option of full recovery and has a number of physical, behavioural and cognitive side effects. On 5 August the fever subsided and Jonah experienced seizures and sporadic loss of consciousness. On 6 August he lapsed into coma and remained comatose until he died. A nondenominational service will be held 15 August, in Camberley. Jonah requested cremation.

My name is Kenneth Nuffield and it was my privilege to be Jonah's partner for the past 20 years. I am sending this message to Jonah's e-mail list in the hope of imparting this very sad news to his friends in America and others who may not be able to attend the service. In lieu of flowers, I have a number of organizations (appended below) to which Jonah requested donations be sent.

I trust in your sympathy and love during this bereavement, and shall answer any and all questions in detail or provide further information if you contact me at the address below...

Siritis was dead. His brain had burned up.

Mere days now, before the new semester began.

Franklin ventured a couple of delicate messages to Kenneth Nuffield. It was painfully clear that Siritis and Nuffield had been deeply in love. Franklin wondered what that felt like. All the inspiration for his new research seemed to evaporate just as the fact-finding had reached a boil. Concentration became difficult; derailment easy. He scrutinized the stories again—the whole canon of Aldridge's work—but there seemed to be nothing more to unearth between lines. He needed an encouragement, a jump-start over the void left by the loss of Siritis, and exactly one week before classes were to commence, Franklin found what he wanted.

It was a small package from Kenneth Nuffield, festooned with UK postage and a customs slip, half-torn away. The note from Nuffield read, in part: *Your interest in this Author was a source of great pleasure to Jonah. As he said, "it validated him,"* *and I am certain he would have wanted you to have this.* Wrapped in a tape-sealed inner envelope was Siritis' own copy of *The Pyre and Others*, precisely as described, floppy pages, creeping Broadart and all.

Now Franklin had within his tremulous grasp (he shook, he knew, with barely leashed excitement) the means by which to experiment. He considered the spooky proposition

of attempting that which Siritis had never dared, but with a slight modification, a new angle. What if, Franklin thought, one were to open the book to a specific story, and place it beneath the pillow *that* way? Might that countermand the random dream bliss (or terror) by adding an element of determinism? Or was is all still a mythic crapshoot?

That was what real writers did, thought Franklin: They burned with passion, and sought to solve desire.

Franklin wanted to know what Herman Banks knew about the unquantifiable lure of women. What that fictional character, a projection of some facet of Aldridge, understood, but which was not incorporated into specific lines of text. The unspoken part of "The Pyre." This knowledge, won at great cost, could not only satisfy his academic yearnings, but possibly improve his life.

Love, it seemed, always lurked just beyond the boundaries of perception.

When Franklin was discovered, he resembled a knickknack carved of soapstone, or mahogany, burnished to a deep ebony and curled into a fetal position, because he had been asleep when he burned. No gas leak, no unattended candles, no cigarettes, no suicide. The composed calm on his expression had been captured and rendered durable, as clay fired to luster in a kiln. His bed had cooked down to half-melted toaster coils and the timbers inside the walls had combusted with fantastic, destroying heat, yet Franklin's body was found unblemished by soot, ashes, or char. The temperatures kindled inside his flaming bungalow were so intense that nothing made of paper could have survived.

—ooo ooo ooo—

OBSEQUY

Doug Walcott's need for a change of perspective seemed simple: *Haul ass out of Triple Pines, pronto. Start the next chapter of my life. Before somebody else makes the decision for you, in spades.*

He grimly considered the shovel in his grasp, clotted with mulchy grave dirt. Spades, right. It was the moment Doug knew he could not go on digging up dead people, and it was only his first day on the job. Once he had been a teacher, with a teacher's penchant for seeing structure and symbols in everything. *Fuck all that,* he thought. *Time to get out. Time to bail, now.*

"I've got to go," he said, almost mumbling, his conviction still tentative.

Jacky Tynan had stepped down from his scoop-loader and ambled over, doffing his helmet and giving his brow a mop. Jacky was a simple, basically honest guy; a spear carrier in the lives of others with more personal color. Content with burgers and beer, satellite TV and dreams of a someday-girlfriend, Jacky was happy in Triple Pines.

"Yo, it's Douglas, right?" Jacky said. Everybody had been introduced shortly after sunrise. "What up?" He peeled his work gloves and rubbed his hands compulsively until tiny black sweatballs of grime dropped away like scattered grains of pepper.

"I've got to go," Doug repeated. "I think I just quit. I've got to tell Coggins I'm done. I've got to get out of here."

"Graves and stuff getting to ya, huh?" said Jacky. "You should give it another day, at least. It ain't so bad."

Doug did not meet Jacky's gaze. His evaluation of the younger man harshened, more in reaction against the locals, the natives, the people who fit into a white trash haven such as Triple Pines. They would hear the word "cemetery" and conclude "huge downer." They would wax prosaic about this job being perverse, therefore unhealthy. To them, digging up long-deceased residents would be that sick stuff. They all acted and reacted strictly according to the playbook of cliché. Their retinue of perception was so predictable that it was almost comically dull. Jacky's tone suggested that he was one of those people with an almost canine empathy to discord; he could smell when something had gone south.

Doug fought to frame some sort of answer. It was not the funereal atmosphere. The stone monuments, the graves, the loam were all exceptionally peaceful. Doug felt no connection to the dearly departed here...with one exception, and one was sufficient.

"It's not the work," Doug said. "It's me. I'm overdue to leave this place. The town, not the cemetery. And the money doesn't matter to me any more."

Jacky made a face as though he had whiffed a fart. "You don't want the money, man? Hell, this shit is easier than workin the paper mill or doin stamper time at the plant, dude." The Triple Pines aluminum plant had vanished into Chapter Eleven a decade ago, yet locals still talked about it as if it were still a functioning concern.

The people in Triple Pines never saw what was right in front of them. Or they refused to acknowledge anything strange. That was the reason Doug had to eject. He had to jump before he became one of them.

One of them...

A week ago, Doug had not been nearly so philosophical. Less than a week from now, and he would question his own sanity.

Craignotti, the job foreman, had seen Jacky and Doug not working—that is to say, not excavating—and already he was humping his trucker bulk over the hilltop to yell at them. Doug felt the urge to just pitch his tools and helmet and run, but his rational side admitted that there were protocols to be followed and channels to be taken. He would finish out his single day, then do some drinking with his workmates, then try to decide whether he could handle one more day. He was supposed to be a responsible adult, and responsible adults adhered to protocol and channels as a way of reinforcing the gentle myth of civilization.

Whoa, dude, piss on all that, Jacky might say. *Just run.* But Jacky rarely wrestled with such complexities. Doug turned to meet Craignotti with the fatalism of a man who has to process a large pile of tax paperwork.

A week ago, things had been different. Less than a week from now, these exhumations would collide with every one of them, in ways they could not possibly predict.

—ooo—

Frank Craignotti was one of those guys who loved their beer, Doug had observed. The man had a *relationship* with his pilsner glass, and rituals to limn his interaction with it. Since Doug had started haunting Callahan's, he had seen Craignotti in there every night—same stool at the end of the bar, same three pitchers of tap beer, which he emptied down his neck in about an hour and a half. Word was that Craignotti had been a long-haul big-rig driver for a major nationwide chain of discount stores, until the company pushed him to the sidelines on account of his disability. He had stepped down from the cab of his sixteen-wheeler on a winding mountain road

outside of Triple Pines (for reasons never explained; probably to relieve himself among Nature's bounty) and had been side-swiped by a car that never saw him standing there in the rain. Presently he walked with a metal cane because after his surgery one leg had come up shorter than the other. There were vague noises of lawsuits and settlements. That had all happened before Doug wound up inside Callahan's as a regular, and so it maintained the tenuous validity of small-town gossip. It was as good a story as any.

Callahan's presented a nondescript face to the main street of Triple Pines, its stature noted solely by a blue neon sign that said **BAR** filling up most of a window whose sill probably had not been dusted since 1972. There was a roadhouse fifteen miles to the north, technically "out of town," but its weak diversions were not worth the effort. Callahan's flavor was mostly clover-colored Irish horse apples designed to appeal to all the usual expectations. Sutter, the current owner and the barman on most weeknights, had bought the place when the original founders had wised up and gotten the hell out of Triple Pines. Sutter was easy to make up a story about. To Doug he looked like a career criminal on the run who had found his perfect hide in Triple Pines. The scar bisecting his lower lip had probably come from a knife fight. His skin was like mushrooms in the fridge the day before you decide to throw them out. His eyes were set back in his skull, socketed deep in bruise-colored shadow.

Nobody in Triple Pines really knew anything bona fide about anybody else, Doug reflected.

Doug's first time into the bar as a drinker was his first willful act after quitting his teaching job at the junior high school which Triple Pines shared with three other communities. All pupils were bussed in from rural route pickups. A year previously, he had effortlessly scored an emergency credential and touched down as a replacement instructor for History and Geography, though he took no interest in politics unless they were safely in the past. It was a rote gig that mostly required him to ramrod disinterested kids through memorizing data that they forgot as soon as they puked it up on the next test. He had witnessed firsthand how the area, the towns, and the school system worked to crush initiative, abort insight, and nip talent. The model for the Triple Pines secondary educational system seemed to come from some early 1940s playbook, with no imperative to change anything. The kids here were all white and mostly poor to poverty level, disinterested and leavened to dullness. Helmets for the football team always superceded funds for updated texts. It was the usual, spirit-deflating story. Doug spent the term trying to kick against this corpse, hoping to provoke life signs. Past the semester break, he was just hanging on for the wage. Then, right as summer vacation loomed, Shiela Morgan had deposited herself in the teacher's lounge for a conference.

Doug had looked up from his newspaper. The local rag was called the *Pine Grove Messenger* (after the adjacent community). It came out three times weekly and was exactly four pages long. Today was Victoria Day in Canada. This week's Vocabulary Building Block was "ameliorate."

"Sheila," he said, acknowledging her, not really wanting to. She was one of the many hold-backs in his classes. Hell, many of Triple Pines' junior high schoolers already drove their own cars to battle against the citadel of learning.

"Don't call me that," Shiela said. "My name's *Brittany.*"

Doug regarded her over the top of the paper. They were alone in the room. "Really."

"Totally," she said. "I can have my name legally changed. I looked it up. I'm gonna do it, too. I don't care what anybody says."

Pause, for bitter fulfillment: One of his charges had actually *looked something up.*

Further pause, for dismay: Shiela had presented herself to him wearing a shiny vinyl mini as tight as a surgeon's glove, big-heeled boots that laced to the knee, and a leopard top with some kind of boa-like fringe framing her breasts. There was a scatter of pimples between her collarbones. She had ratty black hair and too much eye kohl. Big lipstick that had tinted her teeth pink. She resembled a hillbilly's concept of a New York streetwalker, and she was all of 14 years old.

Mara Corday, Doug thought. *She looks like a goth-slut version of Mara Corday. I am a dead man.*

Chorus girl and pinup turned B-movie femme fatale, Mara Corday had decorated some drive-in low-budgeters of the late 1950s. *Tarantula. The Giant Claw. The Black Scorpion.* She had been a *Playboy* Playmate and familiar of Clint Eastwood. Sultry and sex-kittenish, she had signed her first studio contract while still a teenager. She, too, had changed her name.

Sheila wanted to be looked at, and Doug avoided looking. At least her presentation was a relief from the third-hand, Sears & Roebuck interpretation of banger and skatepunk styles that prevailed among most of Triple Pines other adolescents. In that tilted moment, Doug realized what he disliked about the dunnage of rap and hip-hop: all those super-badasses looked like they were dressed in gigantic baby clothes. Sheila's ass was broader than the last time he had not-looked. Her thighs were chubbing. The trade-off was bigger tits. Doug's heartbeat began to accelerate. *Why am I looking?*

"Sheila—"

"*Brittany.*" She threw him a pout, then softened it, to butter him up. "Lissen, I wanted to talk to you about that test, the one I missed? I wanna take it over. Like, not to cheat it or anything, but just to kinda…take it over, y'know? Pretend like that's the *first* time I took it?"

"None of the other students get that luxury, and you know that."

She fretted, shifting around in her seat, her skirt making squeaky noises against the school-issue plastic chair. "I know, I know, like, right? That's like, totally not usual, I know, so that's why I thought I'd ask you about it first?"

Sheila spent most of her schooling fighting to maintain a low C-average. She had won a few skirmishes, but the war was already a loss.

"I mean, like, you could totally do a new test, and I could like study for it, right?"

"You should have studied for the original test in the first place."

She wrung her hands. "I know, I know that, but…well let's just say it's a lot of bullshit, parents and home and alla that crap, right? I couldn't like do it then but I could now. My Mom finds out I blew off the test, she'll beat the shit outta me."

"Shouldn't you be talking to a counselor?"

"Yeah, right? No thanks. I thought I'd like go right to the source, right? I mean, you like me and stuff, right?" She glanced toward the door, revving up for some kind of Big Moment that Doug already dreaded. "I mean, I'm flexible; I thought that, y'know, just this one time. I'd do anything. Really. To fix it. Anything."

She uncrossed her legs, from left on right to right on left, taking enough time to make sure Doug could see she had neglected to factor undergarments into her abbreviated ensemble. The move was so studied that Doug knew exactly which movie she had gotten it from.

There are isolated moments in time that expand to gift you with a glimpse of the future, and in that moment Doug saw his tenure at Triple Pines take a big centrifugal swirl down the cosmic toilet. The end of life as he knew it was embodied in the bit of anatomy that Sheila referred to as her "cunny."

"You can touch it if you want. I won't mind." She sounded as though she was talking about a bizarre pet on a leash.

Doug had hastily excused himself and raced to the bathroom, his four-page newspaper folded up to conceal the fact that he was strolling the hallowed halls of the school, semierect. He rinsed his face in a basin and regarded himself in a scabrous mirror. *Time to get out. Time to bail. Now.*

He flunked Sheila, and jettisoned himself during summer break, never quite making it to the part where he actually *left* Triple Pines. Later he heard Sheila's mom had gone ballistic and put her daughter in the emergency ward at the company clinic for the paper mill, where her father had worked since he was her age. Local residual scuttlebutt had it that Sheila had gotten out of the hospital and mated with the first guy she could find who owned a car. They blew town like fugitives and were arrested several days later. Ultimately, she used her pregnancy to force the guy to sell his car to pay for her train fare to some relative's house in the Dakotas, end of story.

Which, naturally, was mostly hearsay anyway. Bar talk. Doug had become a regular at Callahan's sometime in early July of that year, and by mid-August he looked at himself in another mirror and thought, *you bagged your job and now you have a drinking problem, buddy. You need to get out of this place.*

That was when Craignotti had eyeballed him. Slow consideration at reptile brain-speed. He bombed his glass at a gulp and rose; he was a man who always squared his shoulders when he stood up, to advise the talent of the room just how broad his chest was. He stumped over to Doug without his walking stick, to prove he didn't really need it. He signaled

Sutter, the cadaverous bartender, to deliver his next pitcher of brew to the stool next to Doug's.

After some preliminary byplay and chitchat, Craignotti beered himself to within spitting distance of having a point. "So, you was a teacher at the junior high?"

"Ex-teacher. Nothing bad. I just decided I had to relocate."

"Ain't what I heard." Every time Craignotti drank, his swallows were half-glass capacity. One glassful, two swallows, rinse and repeat. "I heard you porked one of your students. That little slut Sheila Morgan."

"Not true."

Craignotti poured Doug a glass of beer to balance out the Black Jack he was consuming, one slow finger at a time. "Naah, it ain't what you think. I ain't like that. Those little fucking whores are outta control anyway. They're fucking in goddamned grade school, if they're not all crackheads by then."

"The benefits of our educational system." Doug toasted the air. If you drank enough, you could see lost dreams and hopes, swirling there before your nose, demanding sacrifice and tribute.

"Anyhow, point is that you're not working, am I right?"

"That is a true fact." Doug tasted the beer. It chased smooth.

"You know Coggins, the undertaker here?"

"Yeah." Doug had to summon the image. Bald guy, ran the Triple Pines funeral home and maintained the Hollymount Cemetery on the outskirts of town. Walked around with his hands in front of him like a preying mantis.

"Well, I know something a lotta people around here don't know yet. Have you heard of the Marlboro Reservoir?" It was the local project that would not die. It had last been mentioned in the *Pine Grove Messenger* over a year previously.

"I didn't think that plan ever cleared channels."

"Yeah, well, it ain't for you or me to know. But they're gonna build it. And there's gonna be a lotta work. Maybe bring this shithole town back to life."

"But I'm leaving this shithole town," said Doug. "Soon. So you're telling me this because—?"

"Because you look like a guy can keep his trap shut. Here's the deal: this guy Coggins comes over and asks me to be a foreman. For what, I say. And he says—now get this—in order to build the reservoir, for some reason I don't know about, they're gonna have to move the cemetery to the other side of Pine Grove—six fucking *miles*. So he needs guys to dig up all the folks buried in the cemetery, and catalogue 'em, and bury 'em again on the other side of the valley. Starts next Monday. The pay is pretty damned good for the work, and almost nobody needs to know about it. I ain't about to hire these fucking deadbeats around here, these dicks with the muscle cars, 'cept for Jacky Tynan, 'cos he's a good worker and don't ask questions. So I thought, I gotta find me a few more guys that are, like, responsible, and since you're leaving anyhow…"

Long story short, that's how Doug wound up manning a shovel. The money was decent and frankly, he needed the bank. "Answer me one question, though," he said to Craignotti. "Where did you get all that shit about Sheila Morgan, I mean, why did you use that to approach me?"

"Oh, that," said Craignotti. "She told me. Was trying to trade some tight little puddy for a ride outta town." Craignotti had actually said *puddy*, like Sylvester the Cat. *I tot I taw…* I laughed in her face; I said, what, d'you think I'm some kinda baby-raper? I woulda split her in half. She threw a fit and went off and fucked a bunch of guys who were less discriminating. Typical small-time town-pump *scheiss*. She musta lost her cherry when she was twelve. So I figured you and me had something in common—we're probably the only two men in town who haven't plumbed *that* hole. Shit, we're so fucking honest, folks around here will think we're queer."

Honor and ethics, thought Doug. Wonderful concepts, those were.

—ooo—

There were more than a thousand graves in Hollymount Cemetery, dating back to the turn of the 19th Century. Stones so old that names had weathered to vague indentations in granite. Plots with no markers. Minor vandalism. The erosion of time and climate. Coggins, the undertaker, had collated a master name sheet and stapled it to a gridded map of the cemetery, presenting the crew picked by Craignotti with a problem rather akin to solving a huge crossword puzzle made out of dead people. Doug paged through the list until he found Michelle Farrier's name. He had attended her funeral, and sure enough—she was still here.

After his divorce from Marianne (the inevitable ex-wife), he had taken to the road, but had read enough Kerouac to know that the road held nothing for him. A stint as a blackjack dealer in Vegas. A teaching credential from LA; he was able to put that in his pocket and take it anywhere. Four months after his arrival in Triple Pines, he attended the funeral of the only friend he had sought to develop locally— Michelle Farrier, a runner just like him.

In the afterblast of an abusive and ill-advised marriage, Michelle had come equipped with a six-year-old daughter named Rochelle. Doug could easily see the face of the mother in the child, the younger face that had taken risks and sought adventure and brightened at the prospect of sleeping with rogues. Michelle had touched down in Triple Pines two months away from learning she was terminally ill. Doug had

met them during a seriocomic bout of bathroom-sharing at Mrs. Ives' rooming house, shortly before he had rented a two-bedroom that had come cheap because there were few people in town actively seeking better lodgings, and fewer who could afford to move up. Michelle remained game, as leery as Doug of getting involved, and their gradually kindling passion filled their evenings with a delicious promise. In her kiss lurked a hungry romantic on a short tether, and Doug was working up the nerve to invite her and Rochelle to share his new home when the first talk of doctor visits flattened all other concerns to secondary status. He watched her die. He tried his best to explain it to Rochelle. And Rochelle was removed, to grandparents somewhere in the Bay area. She wept when she said goodbye to Doug. So had Michelle.

Any grave but that one, thought Doug. *Don't make me dig that one up. Make that someone else's task.*

He knew enough about mortuary tradition to know it was unusual for an undertaker like Coggins to also be in charge of the cemetery. However, small, remote towns tend not to view such a monopoly on the death industry as a negative thing. Coggins was a single stranger for the populace to trust, instead of several. Closer to civilization, the particulars of chemical supply, casket sales, and the mortician's craft congregated beneath the same few conglomerate umbrellas, bringing what had been correctly termed a "Tru-Value hardware" approach to what was being called the "death industry" by the early 1990s. Deceased Americans had become a cash crop at several billion dollars per annum...not counting the flower arrangements. Triple Pines still believed in the mom-and-pop market, the corner tavern, the one-trade-fits-all handyman.

Doug had been so appalled at Michelle's perfunctory service that he did a bit of investigative reading-up. He discovered that most of the traditional accoutrements of the modern funeral were aimed at one objective above all—keeping morticians and undertakers in business. Not, as most people supposed, because of obscure health imperatives, or a misplaced need for ceremony, or even that old favorite, religious ritual. It turned out to be one of the three or four most expensive costs a normal citizen could incur during the span of an average, conventional life—another reason weddings and funerals seemed bizarrely similar. It was amusing to think how simply the two could be confused. Michelle would have been amused, at least. She had rated one of each, neither very satisfying.

Doug would never forget Rochelle's face, either. He had gotten to play the role of father to her for about a week and change, and it had scarred him indelibly. Given time, her loss, too, was a strangely welcome kind of pain.

Legally, disinterment was a touchy process, since the casket containing the remains was supposed to be technically "undamaged" when removed from the earth. This meant Jacky and the other backhoe operators could only skim to a certain depth—the big scoops—before Doug or one of his co-workers had to jump in with a shovel. Some of the big concrete grave liners were stacked three deep to a plot; at least, Craignotti had said something about three being the limit. They looked like big, featureless refrigerators laid on end, and tended to crumble like plaster. Inside were the burial caskets. Funeral publicists had stopped calling them coffins about forty years ago. "Coffins" were boxes shaped to the human form, wide at the top, slim at the bottom, with the crown shaped like the top half of a hexagon. "Coffins" evoked morbid assumptions, and so were replaced in the vernacular with "caskets"—nice, straight angles, with no Dracula or Boot Hill associations. In much the same fashion, "cemeteries" had become "memorial parks." People did everything they could, it seemed, to deny the reality of death.

Which explained the grave liners. Interment in coffins, caskets, or anything else from a wax-coated cardboard box to a shroud generally left a concavity in the lawn, once the body began to decompose, and its container, to collapse. In the manner of a big, mass-produced, cheap sarcophagus, the concrete grave liners prevented the depressing sight of…er, depressions. Doug imagined them to be manufactured by the same place that turned out highway divider berms; the damned things weighed about the same.

Manning his shovel, Doug learned a few more firsthand things about graves. Like how it could take eight hours for a single digger, working alone, to excavate a plot to the proper dimensions. Which was why Craignotti had been forced to locate operators for no fewer than three backhoes on this job. Plus seven "scoopers" in Doug's range of ability. The first shift, they only cleared fifty final resting places. From then on, they would aim for a hundred stiffs per working day.

Working. Stiffs. Rampant, were the opportunities for gallows humor.

Headstones were stacked as names were checked off the master list. *Beecher, Lee,* 1974-2002—HE PROTECTED AND SERVED. *Gudgell, Conroy,* 1938-2003—DO NOT GO GENTLY. These were newer plots, more recent deaths. These were people who cared about things like national holidays or presidential elections, archetypal Americans from fly-over country. But in their midst, Doug was also a cliché—the drifter, the stranger. If the good folk of Triple Pines (the living ones, that is) sensed discord in their numbers, they would actively seek out mutants to scotch. Not One of Us.

He had to get out. Just this job, just a few days, and he could escape. It was better than being a mutant, and perhaps getting lynched. He moved on to *Stowe, Dormand R.,* 1940-

1998—LOVING HUSBAND, CARING FATHER. Not so recent. Doug felt a little bit better.

They broke after sunset. That was when Doug back-checked the dig list and found a large, red X next to Michelle Farrier's name.

—ooo—

"This job ain't so damned secret," said Joe Hopkins, later, at Callahan's. Their after-work table was five: Joe, Jacky, Doug, and two more guys from the shift, Miguel Ayala and Boyd Cooper. Craignotti sat away from them, at his accustomed roost near the end of the bar. The men were working on their third pitcher. Doug found that no amount of beer could get the taste of grave dirt out of the back of his throat. Tomorrow, he'd wear a bandana. *Maybe.*

"You working tomorrow, or not, or what?" said Craignotti. Doug gave him an if-come answer, and mentioned the bandana. Craignotti had shrugged. In that moment, it all seemed pretty optional, so Doug concentrated on becoming mildly drunk with a few of the crew working the—heh—graveyard shift.

Joe was a musclebound ex-biker type who always wore a leather vest and was rarely seen without a toothpick jutting from one corner of his mouth. He had cultivated elaborate moustaches which he waxed. He was going gray at the temples. His eyes were dark, putting Doug in mind of a gypsy. He continued: "What I mean is, nobody's supposed to know about this little relocation. But they guys in here know, even if they don't talk about it. The guys who run the Triple Pines bank sure as shit know. It's a public secret. Nobody talks about it, is all."

"I bet the mayor's in on it, too," said Miguel. "All in, who cares? I mean, I had to pick mushrooms once for a buck a day. This sure beats the shit out of that."

"Doesn't bother you?" said Boyd Cooper, another of the backhoe jockeys. Older, pattern baldness, big but not heavy. Bull neck and cleft chin. His hands had seen a lifetime of manual labor. It had been Boyd who showed them how to cable the lids off the heavy stone grave liners, instead of bringing in the crane rig used to emplace them originally. This group's unity as mutual outcasts gave them a basic common language, and Boyd always cut to the gristle. "Digging up dead people?"

"Nahh," said Jacky, tipping his beer. "We're doing them a favor. Just a kind of courtesy thing. Moving 'em so they won't be forgotten."

"I guess," said Joe, working his toothpick. He burnished his teeth a lot with it. Doug noticed one end was stained with a speck of blood, from his gums.

"You're the teacher," Boyd said to Doug. "You tell us. Good thing or bad thing?"

Doug did not want to play arbiter. "Just a job of work. Like re-sorting old files. You notice how virtually no one in Triple Pines got cremated? They were all buried. That's old-fashioned, but you have to respect the dead. Laws and traditions."

"And the point is…?" Boyd was looking for validation.

"Well, not everybody is entitled to a piece of property when they die, six by three by seven. That's too much space. Eventually we're going to run out of room for all our dead people. Most plots in most cemeteries are rented, and there's a cap on the time limit, and if somebody doesn't pay up, they get mulched. End of story."

"Wow, is that true?" said Jacky. "I thought you got buried, it was like, forever."

"Stopped being that way about a hundred years ago," said Doug. "Land is worth too much. You don't process the dead and let them use up your real estate without turning a profit."

Miguel said, "That would be un-American." He tried for a chuckle but it died.

"Check it out if you don't believe me," said Doug. "Look it up. Behind all that patriotic rah-rah-rah about community brotherhood and peaceful gardens, it's all about capital gains. Most people don't like to think about funerals or cemeteries because, to them, it's morbid. That leaves funeral directors free to profiteer."

"You mean Coggins?" said Joe, giving himself a refill.

"Look, Coggins is a great example," said Doug. "In the outside world, big companies have incorporated most aspects of the funeral. Here, Coggins runs the mortuary, the cemetery, everything. He can charge whatever he wants, and people will pay for the privilege of shunting their grief and confusion onto him. You wouldn't believe the markup on some of this stuff. Caskets are three times wholesale. Even if they put you in a cardboard box—which is called an 'alternative container,' by the way—the charge is a couple of hundred bucks."

"Okay, that settles it," said Miguel. When he smiled big, you could see his gold tooth. "We all get to live forever, because we can't afford to die."

"There used to be a riddle," said Doug. "What is it: the man who made it didn't want it, the man who bought it had no use for it, and the man who used it didn't know it. What is it?"

Jacky just looked confused.

—ooo—

His head honeycombed with domestic beer, Doug tried not to lurch or slosh as he navigated his way out of Callahan's. The voice coming at him out of the fogbound darkness might well have been an aural hallucination. Or a wish fulfillment.

"Hey stranger," it said. "Walk a lady home?"

The night yielded her to him. She came not as he had fantasized, nor as he had seen her in dreams. She wore a long-sleeved, black, lacy thing with a neck-wrap collar, and her hair was up. She looked different but her definitive jaw-line and frank, gray gaze were unmistakable.

"That's not you," he said. "I'm a tiny bit intoxicated, but not enough to believe it's you." *Yet.* There was no one else on the street to confirm or deny; no validation from fellow inebriates or corroboration from independent bystanders. Just Doug, the swirling night, and a woman who could not be the late Michelle Farrier, whom he had loved. He had only accepted that he loved her after she died. It was more tragic that way, more delusional-ly romanticist. Potent enough to wallow in. A weeper, produced by his brain while it was buzzing with hops and alcohol.

She bore down on him, moving into focus, and that made his grief worse. "Sure it's me," she said. "Look at me. Take a little bit of time to get used to the idea."

He drank her in as though craving a narcotic. Her hair had always been long, burnished sienna, deftly razor-thinned to layers that framed her face. Now it was pinned back to exhibit her gracile neck and bold features. He remembered the contour of her ears. She smiled, and he remembered exactly how her teeth set. She brought with her the scent of night-blooming jasmine. If she was a revenant, she had come freighted with none of the corruption of the tomb. If she was a mirage, the light touch of her hand on his wrist should not have felt so corporeal.

Her touch was not cold.

"No," said Doug. "You died. You're gone."

"Sure, darling—I don't deny that. But now I'm back, and you should be glad."

He was still shaking his head. "I *saw* you die. I helped *bury* you."

"And today, you helped *un*-bury me. Well, your buddies did."

She had both hands on him, now. This was the monster movie moment when her human visage melted away to reveal the slavering ghoul who wanted to eat his brain and wash it down with a glass of his blood. Her sheer *presence* almost buckled his knees.

"How?"

"Beats me," she said. "We're coming back all over town. I don't know exactly how it all works, yet. But that stuff I was buried in—those *cerements*—were sort of depressing. I checked myself out while I was cleaning up. Everything seems to be in place. Everything works. Except for the tumor; that kind of withered away to an inert little knot, in the grave. I know this is tough for you to swallow, but I'm here, and god dammit, I missed you, and I thought you'd want to see me."

"I think about you every day," he said. It was still difficult to meet her gaze, or to speed-shift from using the accustomed past tense.

"Come on," she said, linking arms with him.

"Where?" Without delay his guts leapt at the thought that she wanted to take him back to the cemetery.

"Wherever. Listen, do you recall kissing me? See if you can remember how we did that."

She kissed him with all the passion of the long-lost, regained unexpectedly. It was Michelle, all right—alive, breathing, returned to him whole.

No one had seen them. No one had come out of the bar. No pedestrians. Triple Pines tended to roll up the sidewalks at 7:00 P.M.

"This is…nuts," he said.

She chuckled. "As long as you don't say it's distasteful." She kissed him again. "And of course you remember that other thing we never got around to doing?"

"Antiquing that rolltop desk you liked, at the garage sale?" His humor was helping him balance. His mind still wanted to swoon, or explode.

"Ho, ho, very funny. I am so glad to see you right now that I'll spell it out for you, Doug." She drew a tiny breath of consideration, working up nerve, then puffed it out. "Okay: I want to hold your cock in my hand and feel you get hard, *for me*. That was the dream, right? That first attraction, where you always visualize the other person naked, fucking you, while your outer self pretends like none of that matters?"

"I didn't think that," Doug fibbed. Suddenly his breath would not draw.

"Yes you did," Michelle said. "I did, too. But I was too chicken to act. That's all in the past." She stopped and smacked him lightly on the arm. "Don't give me that lopsided look, like *I'm* the one that's crazy. Not now. Not after I died, thinking you were the best damned thing I'd found in a long time."

"Well, there was Rochelle," said Doug, remembering how cautiously they had behaved around her six-year-old daughter.

"My little darling is not here right now," she said. "I'd say it's time to fulfill the fantasy, Doug. Mine, if not yours. We've wasted enough life, and not everybody gets a bonus round."

"But—" Doug's words, his protests had bottlenecked between his lungs. (And for-crap-sake *why* did he feel the urge to *protest* this?)

"I know what you're trying to say. I *died.*" Another impatient huff of breath—living breath. "I can't explain it. I don't know if it's temporary. But I'll tell you one thing I do know: All that shit about the 'peace' of the grave? It doesn't exist. It's not a release, and it's not oblivion. It's like a nightmare that doesn't conveniently end when you wake up, because you're not *supposed* to wake up, ever! And you know what else? When you're in the grave, you can hear every goddamned footfall of the living, above you. Trust me on that one."

"Jesus…" he said.

"Not Jesus. Neither heaven nor hell. Not God. Not Buddha, not Allah, not Yahweh. Nothing. That's what waits on the other side of that headstone. No pie in the sky by and by when you die. No Nirvana. No Valhalla. No Tetragrammaton. No Zeus or Jove or any of their buddies. Nothing. Maybe that's why we're coming back—there's nothing out there, beyond. Zero. Not even an echo. So kiss me again. I've been cold and I've been still, and I need to make love to you. Making love; that sounds like we're manufacturing something, doesn't it? Feel my hand. There's living blood in there. Feel my heart; it's pumping again. I've felt bad things moving around inside of me. That happens when you're well and truly dead. Now I'm back. And I want to feel *other* things moving around inside of me. You."

Tomorrow, Doug would get fired as a no-show after only one day on the job. Craignotti would replace him with some guy named Dormand R. Stowe, rumored to be a loving husband and a caring father.

—ooo—

One of the most famous foreign pistols used during the Civil War was the Le Mat Revolver, a cap and ball weapon developed by a French-born New Orleans doctor, unique in that it had two barrels—a cylinder which held nine .40 caliber rounds fired through the upper barrel, and revolved around the lower, .63 caliber barrel, which held a charge of 18 or 20-gauge buckshot. With a flick of the thumb, the shooter could re-align the hammer to fall on the lower barrel, which was essentially a small shotgun, extremely deadly at close range, with a kick like an enraged mule. General

J.E.B. Stuart had carried one. So had General P.G.T. Beauregard. As an antique firearm, such guns in good condition were highly prized. Conroy Gudgell cherished his; it was one of the stars of his modest home arsenal, which he always referred to as his "collection." His big mistake was showing his wife how to care for it. How to clean it. How to load it. How to fire it, you know, "just in case." No one was more surprised than Conroy when his loving wife, a respected first-grade teacher in Triple Pines, blew him straight down to Hell with his own collectible antique.

Ellen Gudgell became a widow at 61 years of age. She also became a Wiccan. She was naked, or "sky-clad," when she burned the braided horsehair whip in her fireplace after murdering Conroy. Firing the Le Mat had broken her right wrist; she'd had to make up a story about that. With her left hand she had poured herself a nice brandy, before working herself up into enough lather to phone the police, in tears, while most of Conroy's head and brains were cooling in various corners of his basement workshop. A terrible accident, oh my lord, it's horrible, please come. She kept all the stuff about Earth Mother religious revelations to herself.

She treated Constable Dickey (Triple Pines' head honcho of law enforcement) as she would one of her elementary school charges. Firm but fair. Matronly, but with just the right salting of manufactured hysteria. Conroy had been working with his gun collection in the basement when she heard a loud boom, she told the officer. She panicked and broke her wrist trying to move what was left of him, and now she did not know what to do, and she needed help.

And the local cops had quite neatly taken care of all the rest. Ellen never had to mention the beatings she had suffered under the now-incinerated whip, or that the last fifteen years of their sex life had consisted mostly of rape. When not teaching school, she used her free time—that is, her time free of Conroy's oppression—to study up on alternate philosophies, and when she found one that made sense to her, it wasn't long before she decided to assert her new self.

After that, the possibilities seemed endless. She felt as though she had shed a chrysalis and evolved to a form which made her happier with herself.

Therefore, no one was more surprised than Ellen when her husband Conroy thumped up the stairs, sundered head and all, to come a-calling more than a year after she thought she had definitively killed the rotten sonofabitch. His face looked exactly as it had when Coggins, the undertaker, had puttied and waxed it back into a semblance of human, dark sub-dermal lines inscribing puzzle pieces in rough assembly. The parts did not move in correct concert when Conroy spoke to her, however. His face was disjointed and broken, his eyes, oddly fixed.

"Time for some loving," is what Conroy said to her first.

Ellen ran for the gun cabinet, downstairs.

"Already thought of that," said Conroy, holding up the Le Mat.

He did not shoot her in the head.

—ooo—

Despite the fact that Lee Beecher's death had been inadvertent, one of those Act of God things, Constable Lon Dickey had always felt responsible. Lee had been a hometown boy, Dickey had liked him, and made him his deputy; ergo, Lee had been acting as a representative of the law on Dickey's behalf, moving a dead deer out of the middle of the road during a storm. Some local asshole had piled into the animal and left it for dead, which constituted Triple Pines' only known form of hit and run. If you'd had to guess the rest

of the story, Dickey thought, you'd say *and another speeding nitwit had hit Lee.* Nope. Struck by *lightning,* for christ's sake. Hit by a thunderbolt out of the ozone and killed deader than snakeshit on the spot, fried from the inside out, cooked and discarded out near the lumber yard which employed about a quarter of Triple Pines' blue-collar workforce.

Lee had been buried in his uniform. A go-getter, that kid. Good footballer. Instead of leaving Triple Pines in his rearward dust, as so many youngsters ached to do, Lee had stuck close to home, and enthusiastically sought his badge. It was worth it to him to be called an "officer," like Dickey. Death in Triple Pines was nearly always accidental, or predictable—no mystery. This was not the place where murderers or psychos lived. In this neck of the woods, the worst an officer might have to face would be the usual rowdiness—teenagers, or drunks, or drunk teenagers—and the edict to act all authoritative if there was a fire or flood or something naturally disastrous.

Beecher's replacement was a guy named James Trainor, shit-hot out of the academy in Seattle and fulminating to enforce. Too stormtrooper for Triple Pines; too ready to pull his sidearm for a traffic stop. Dickey still had not warmed up to him, smelling the moral pollution of citified paranoia.

Feeling like a lazy lion surveying his domain, Dickey had sauntered the two blocks back to the station from the Ready-Set Dinette, following feeling his usual cheeseburger late-lunch. (The food at Callahan's, a block further, was awful— the burgers as palatable as pucks sliced off a Duraflame log.) Time to trade some banter with RaeAnn, who ran the police station's desk, phones and radios. RaeAnn was a stocky chunk of bottle-blonde business with multiple chins and an underbite, whose choice of corrective eyewear did not de-emphasize her Jimmy Durante nose. In no way was RaeAnn a temptation, and Dickey preferred that. Strictly business.

RaeAnn was fast, efficient, and did not bring her problems to work. Right now she was leaning back at her station with her mouth wide open, which seemed strange. She resembled a gross caricature of one of those mail-order blowjob dolls.

Before he could ask what the hell, Dickey saw the bullet hole in the center of her forehead. Oh.

"Sorry I'm a little bit late, Chief," said Lee Beecher. He had grave dirt all over his moldy uniform, and his face was the same flash-fried nightmare that had caused Coggins to recommend a closed-casket service. Beecher had always called Dickey "Chief."

Deputy Trainor was sprawled behind Dickey's desk, his cap over his eyes, his tongue sticking out, and a circlet of five .357 caliber holes in his chest. Bloodsmear on the bulletin board illustrated how gracelessly he had fallen, hit so hard one of his boots had flown off. The late Lee Beecher had been reloading his revolver when Dickey walked in.

"I had to shoot RaeAnn, she was making too much bother," said Beecher. His voice was off, dry and croaky, buzzing like a reed.

Dickey tried to contain his slow awe by muttering the names of assorted deities. His hand wanted to feel the comfort of his own gun.

"How come you replaced me, Chief?" said the late Lee Beecher. "Man, I didn't quit or nothing. You replaced me with some city boy. That wasn't our deal. I thought you liked me."

"I—" Dickey stammered. "Lee, I..." He just could not force out words. This was too wrong.

"You just put me in the dirt." The late Lee Beecher shook his charred skull with something akin to sadness. He snapped home the cylinder on his pistol, bringing the hammer back to full cock in the same smooth move. "Now I'm gonna have to return the favor. Sorry, Chief."

Constable Dickey was still trying to form a whole sen-
tence when the late Lee Beecher gave him all six rounds. Up
at RaeAnn's desk, the radio crackled and the switchboard lit
up with an influx of weird emergency calls, but there was no
one to pay any attention, or care.

—ooo—

Doug's current home barely fit the definition. It had no
more character than a British row flat or a post-war saltbox.
It was one of the basic, ticky-tacky clapboard units thrown
up by the Triple Pines aluminum plant back when they spon-
sored company housing, and abandoned to fall apart on its
own across slow years once the plant folded. It had a roof and
indoor plumbing, which was all Doug had ever required of a
residence, because addresses were disposable. It had storm
shutters and a rudimentary version of heat, against rain and
winter, but remained drafty. Its interior walls were bare and
still the same vague green Doug had always associated with
academia. The bedroom was sort of blue, in the same mood.

He regretted his cheap sheets, his second-hand bed, his
milk-crate nightstand. He had strewn some candles around
to soften the light, and fired up a portable, radiant oil heater.
The heat and the light diffused the stark seediness of the
room, just enough. They softened the harsh edges of reality.

There had been no seduction, no ritual libations, no teasing or flirting. Michelle had taken him the way the Allies
took Normandy, and it was all he could muster to keep from
gasping. His pelvis felt hammered and his legs seemed numb
and far away. She was alive, with the warm, randy needs of
the living, and she had plundered him with a greed that
cleansed them both of any lingering recriminations.

No grave rot, no mummy dust. Was it still necrophilia
when the dead person moved and talked back to you?

"I have another blanket," he said. His left leg was draped over her as their sweat cooled. He watched candle-shadows dance on the ceiling, making monster shapes.

"I'm fine," she said. "Really."

They bathed. Small bathtub, lime-encrusted shower head. It permitted Doug to refamiliarize himself with the geometry of her body, from a perspective different than that of the bedroom. He felt he could never see or touch *enough* of her; it was a fascination for him.

There was nothing to eat in the kitchen, and simply clicking on the TV seemed faintly ridiculous. They slept, wrapped up in each other. The circumstance was still too fragile to detour into lengthy, dissipate conversations about need, so they slept, and in sleeping, found a fundamental innocence that was already beyond logic—a *feeling* thing. It seemed right and correct.

Doug awoke, his feet and fingertips frigid, in the predawn. He added his second blanket and snuggled back into Michelle. She slept with a nearly beatific expression, her breath—real, living—coming in slow tidal measures.

The next afternoon Doug sortied to the market to stock up on some basics and find some decent food that could be prepared in his minimal kitchen. In the market, he encountered Joe Hopkins, from the digging crew. Doug tried unsuccessfully to duck him. He wanted to do nothing to break the spell he was under.

But Joe wanted to talk, and cornered him. He was holding a fifth of bourbon like he intended to make serious use of it, in due course.

"There was apparently a lot of activity in the cemetery last night," he said, working his toothpick from one corner of his mouth to the other. Both ends were wet and frayed. "I mean, after we left. We went back this morning, things were

moved around. Some graves were disrupted. Some were partially re-filled. It was a mess, like a storm had tossed everything. We had to spend two hours just to get back around to where we left off."

"You mean, like vandalism?" said Doug.

"Not exactly." Joe had another habit, that of continually smoothing his upper lip with his thumb and forefinger, as though to keep his moustache in line when he wasn't looking. To Doug, it signaled nervousness, agitation, and Joe was too brawny to be agitated about much for very long. "I tried to figure it, you know—what alla sudden makes the place not creepy, but threatening in a way it wasn't, yesterday. It's the feeling you'd have if you put on your clothes and alla sudden thought that, hey, somebody *else* has been wearing my clothes, right?"

Doug thought of what Michelle had said, about the dead hearing every footfall of the living above them.

"What I'm saying is, I don't blame you for quitting. After today, I'm thinking the same thing. Every instinct I have tells me to just jump on my bike and ride the fuck out of here as fast as I can go. And, something else? Jacky says he ran into a guy last night, a guy he went to high school with. They were on the football team together. Jacky says the guy died four years ago in a Jeep accident. But the he *saw* him, last night, right outside the bar after you left. Not a ghost. He wasn't that drunk. Then, this morning, Craignotti says something equally weird: That he saw a guy at the diner, you know the Ready-Set? Guy was a dead ringer for Aldus Champion, you know the mayor who died in 2003 and got replaced by that asshole selectman, whatsisname—?"

"Brad Ballinger," said Doug.

"Yeah. I been here long enough to remember that. But here's the thing: Craignotti checked, and today Ballinger was nowhere to be found, and he ain't on vacation or nothing. And Ballinger is in bed with Coggins, the undertaker, somehow. Notice how that whole Marlboro Reservoir thing went into a coma when Champion was mayor? For a minute I thought Ballinger had, you know, had him whacked or something. But now Champion's back in town—a guy Craignotti swears isn't a lookalike, but *the* guy. So now I think there was some heavy-duty money changing hands under a lot of tables, and the reservoir is a go, except nobody is supposed to talk about it, and now we're out there, digging up the whole history of Triple Pines as a result."

"What does this all come to?" Doug really wanted to get back to Michelle. She might evaporate or something if left alone too long.

"I don't know, that's the fucked up thing." Joe tried to shove his busy hands into his vest pockets, then gave up. "I'm not smart enough to figure it out, whatever it is…so I give it to you, see if any lightbulbs come on. I'll tell you one thing. This afternoon I felt scared, and I ain't felt that way since I was paddy humping."

"We're both outsiders, here," said Doug.

"Everybody on the dig posse in an outsider, man. Check *that* out."

"Not Jacky."

"Jacky don't pose any threat because he don't know any better. And even him, he's having fucking hallucinations about his old school buddies. Listen: I ain't got a phone at my place, but I got a mobile. Do me a favor—I mean, I know we don't know each other that well—but if you figure something out, give me a holler?"

"No problem." They traded phone numbers and Joe hurried to pay for his evening's sedation. As he went, he said, "Watch your ass, cowboy."

"You, too."

Doug and Michelle cooked collaboratively. They made love. They watched a movie together both had seen separately. They made more love. They watched the evening sky for several hours until chilly rain began to sheet down from above, then they repaired inside and continued to make love. The Peyton Place antics of the rest of the Triple Pines community, light years away from their safe, centered union, could not have mattered less.

—ooo—

The trick, as near as Billy Morrison could wrassle it, was to find somebody and pitch them into your hole as soon as you woke up. Came back. Revived. Whatever.

So he finished fucking Vanessa Billings. "Bill-ing" her, as his cohort Vance Thompson would crack, heh. Billy had stopped "billing" high school chicks three years ago, when he died. Now he was billing a Billings, wotta riot.

Billy, Vance, and Donna Christiansen had perished inside of Billy's Boss 302 rebuild, to the tune of Black Sabbath's "The Mob Rules" on CD. The car was about half gray primer and fender-fill, on its way back to glory. The CD was a compilation of metal moldies. No one ever figured out how the car had crashed, up near a trailer suburbia known as Rimrock, and no one in authority gave much of a turd, since Billy and his fellow losers hailed from "that side" of town, rubbing shoulders an open-fire garbage dump, an auto wrecking yard, and (although Constable Dickey did not know it) a clandestine crack lab. The last sensation Billy experienced as a living human was the car sitting down hard on its left front as the wheel flew completely off. The speed was ticketable and the road, wet as usual, slick as mayonnaise. The car flipped and tumbled down an embankment.

Billy dimly recalled seeing Donna snap in half and fly
through the windshield before the steering column punched
into his chest. The full tank ruptured and spewed a meandering piss-line of gasoline all the way down the hill. Vance's cigarette had probably touched it off, and the whole trash-com-
pacted mess had burned for an hour before new rain finally
doused it and a lumber yard worker spotted the smoke.

Their plan for the evening had been to destroy a bottle of
vodka in the woods, then Billy and Vance would do Donna from
both ends. Donna dug that sort of thing when she was sufficiently wasted. When they awoke several years later in their unearthed
boxes, they renewed their pleasure as soon as they could scare up
some more liquor. They wandered into a roadside outlet known
as the 1-Stop Brew Shoppe and Vance broke bottles over the head
of the proprietor until the guy stopping breathing. Then Donna lit
out for the Yard, a quadrangle of trees and picnic benches near
most of the churches in town. The Yard was Triple Pines' preferred salon for dropouts fond of cannabis, and Donna felt certain
she could locate an old beau or two lingering among the waistoids
there. Besides, she could bend in interesting new ways, now.

Billy had sought and duly targeted Vanessa Billings, one
of those booster / cheerleader bitches who would never have
anything to do with his like. She had graduated in '02 and
was still—*still!*—living in her parents' house. It was a kick to
see her jaw gape in astonishment at the sight of him. *Omigod,
you like* DIED! It was even more of a kick to hold her by the
throat and fuck her until she croaked, the stuck-up little
cuntling. Getting Vanessa out of her parents' house caused a
bit of ruckus, so Billy killed them, too.

Ultimately, the trio racked up so many new corpses to fill
their vacant graves they needed to steal a pickup truck to
ferry them all back to Hollymount. Their victims would all
be back soon enough, and the fun could begin again.

None of them had a precise cognition of what they needed to do. It was more along the lines of an ingrained need—
like a craving—to take the heat of the living to avoid revert-
ing to the coldness of death. That, and the idea of refreshing
their grave plots with new bodies. Billy had always had more
cunning than intelligence, but the imperatives were not that
daunting. Stupid dogs learned tricks in less time.

Best of all, after he finished billing Billings, Billy found he
still had a boner. Death was apparently better than Viagara;
he had an all-night hard-on. And since the night was still a
toddler, he began to hunt for other chicks he could bill.

The sun came up. The sun went down. Billy thought of
that rhyme about how the worms *play pinochle on your snout.*
Fucking worms. How about the worms *eat your asshole
inside-out.* For starters. Billy had been one super-sized organ
smorgasbord, and had suffered every delicious bite. Now a
whole fuckload of Triple Pines' good, upstanding citizens
were going to pay, pay, pay.

—ooo—

As day and night blended and passed, Triple Pines continued to mutate.

Over at the Ready-Set Dinette, a pink neon sign continued to blink the word EAT, just as it had before things
changed in Triple Pines.

Deputy Lee Beecher (the late) and RaeAnn (also the late)
came in for lunch as usual. The next day, Constable Dickey
(recently deceased) and the new deputy, James Trainor
(ditto), joined them.

Vanessa Billings became Billy Morrison's main squeeze,
and what with Vance and Donna's hangers-on, they had
enough to form a new kind of gang. In the next few days,
they would start breaking windows and setting fires.

Over at Callahan's, Craignotti continued to find fresh meat for the digging crew as the original members dropped out. Miguel Ayala had lasted three days before he claimed to have snagged a better job. Big Boyd Cooper stuck—he was a rationalist at heart, not predisposed to superstitious fears or anything else in the path of Getting the Job Done. Jacky Tynan had apparently taken sick.

Joe had packed his saddlebags and gunned his panhead straight out of town, without calling Doug, or anyone.

In the Gudgell household, every day, a pattern commenced. In the morning, Conroy Gudgell would horsewhip his treacherous wife's naked ass, and in the evening, Ellen Gudgell would murder her husband, again and again, over and over. The blood drenching the inside of their house was not ectoplasm. It continued to accrete, layer upon layer, as one day passed into another.

—ooo—

In the middle of the night, Doug felt askew on the inside, and made the mistake of taking his own temperature with a thermometer.

Eighty-seven point-five degrees.

"Yeah, you'll run a little cold," said Michelle, from behind him. "I'm sorry about that. It's sort of a downside. Or maybe you caught something. Do you feel sick?"

"No, I—" Doug faltered. "I just feel shagged. Weak."

"You're not a weak man."

"Stop it." He turned, confrontational. He did not want to do anything to alienate her. But. "This is serious. What if I start losing core heat? Four or five degrees is all it takes, then I'm as dead as a Healthy Choice entrée. What the hell is happening, Michelle? What haven't you told me?"

"I don't *know,*" she said. Her eyes brightened with tears.

"I'm not *sure*. I didn't come back with a goddamned manual. I'm afraid that if I go ahead and do the *next* thing, the thing I feel I'm supposed to do…that I'll lose you."

Panic cinched his heart. "What's the next thing?!"

"I was avoiding it. I was afraid to bring it up. Maybe I was enjoying this too much, what we have right now, in this isolated bubble of time."

He held her. She wanted to reject simple comfort, but succumbed. "Just…tell me. Say it, whatever it is. Then it's out in the world and we can deal with it."

"It's about Rochelle."

Doug nodded, having prepared for this one. "You miss her. I know. But we can't do anything about it. There'd be no way to explain it."

"I want her back." Michelle's head was down, the tears coursing freely now.

"I know, baby, I know…I miss her, too. I wanted you guys to move in with me. Both of you. From here we could move anywhere, so long as it's out of this deathtrap of a town. Neither of us likes it here very much. I figured, in the course of time—"

She slumped on the bed, hands worrying each other atop her bare legs. "It was my dream, through all those hours, days, that things had happened differently, and we had hooked up, and we all got to escape. It would be great if you were just a means to an end; you know—just another male guy-person, to manipulate. Great if I didn't care about you; great if I didn't actually love you."

"I had to explain your death to Rochelle. There's no going back from that one. Look at it this way: she's with your mother, and she seemed like a nice lady."

When her gaze came up to meet his, her eyes were livid. "You don't know anything," she said, the words constricted and bitter. "Sweet, kindly old Grandma Farrier? She's a fucking sadist who has probably shot pornos with Rochelle by now."

"What?!" Doug's jaw unhinged.

"She is one sick piece of shit, and her mission was always to get Rochelle away from me, into her clutches. I ran away from home as soon as I could. And when I had Rochelle, I swore that bitch would never get her claws on my daughter. And you just…handed her over."

"Now, wait a minute, Michelle…"

She overrode him. "No—it's not your fault. She always presented one face to the world. Her fake face. Her human masque. Inside the family with the doors closed, it was different. You saw the masque. You dealt with the masque. So did Rochelle. Until Grandma could actually strap the collar on, she had to play it sneaky. Her real face is from a monster who needed to be inside a grave decades ago. I should know—she broke me in with a heated glass dildo when I was nine."

"Holy shit. Michelle, why didn't you tell me this before?"

"Which 'before?' Before now? Or before I died? Doug, I died not knowing you were as good as you are. I thought I could never make love to anybody, ever again. I concentrated on moving from place to place to keep Rochelle off the radar."

Doug toweled his hands, which were awash in nervous perspiration, yet irritatingly cold. Almost insensate. He needed to assuage her terror, to fix the problem, however improbable; like Boyd Cooper, to Get the Job Done. "Okay. Fine. I'll just go get her back. We'll figure something out."

"I can't ask you to do that."

"Better yet, how about we *both* go get her? Seeing you ought to make Grandma's brain hit the floor."

"That's the problem, Doug. It's been the problem all along. *I can't leave here.* None of us can. If we do…if any of us goes outside of Triple Pines…"

"You don't mean 'us' as in you-and-me. You're talking about us as in the former occupants of Hollymount Cemetery, right?"

She nodded, more tears spilling. "I need you to fuck me. And I need you to love me. And I was hoping that you could love me enough so that I didn't have to force you to take my place in that hole in the ground, like all the rest of the goddamned losers and dim bulbs and fly-over people in Triple Pines. I want you to go to San Francisco, and get my daughter back. But if you stay here—if you go away and come back here—eventually I'll use you up anyway. I've been taking your heat, Doug, a degree at a time. And eventually you would die, and then resurrect, and then you would be stuck here too. An outsider, stuck here. And no matter what anyone's good intentions are, it would also happen to Rochelle. I can't kill my little girl. And I can't hurt you any more. It's killing me, but—what a joke—I can't die." She looked up, her face a raw, aching map of despair. "You see?"

Michelle had not been a local, either. But she had died here, and become a permanent resident in the Triple Pines boneyard. The population of the town was slowly shifting balance. The dead of Triple Pines were pushing out the living, seeking that stasis of small town stability where once again, everyone would be the same. What happened in Triple Pines had to stay in Triple Pines, and the Marlboro Reservoir was no boon to the community. It was going to service coastal cities; Doug knew this in his gut, now. In all ways, for all concerned, Triple Pines was the *perfect* place for this kind of thing to transpire, because the outside world would never notice, or never care.

With one grating exception. Which suggested one frightening solution.

Time to get out. Time to bail, now.

"Don't you see?" she said. "If you don't get out now, you'll never get out. Get out, Doug. Kiss me one last time and get out. Try to think of me fondly."

His heart smashed to pieces and burned to ashes, he kissed her. Her tears lingered on his lips, the utterly real *taste* of her. Without a word further, he made sure he had his wallet, got in his car, and drove. He could be in San Francisco in six hours, flat-out.

He could retrieve Rochelle, kidnap her if that was what was required. He could bring her back here to die, and be reunited with her mother. Then he could die, too. But at least he would be with them, in the end. Or he could put it behind him, and just keep on driving.

The further he got from Triple Pines, the warmer he felt.

–ooo–ooo–ooo–

WHAT SCARES YOU

Loneliness scares me. There, I've admitted it. Not being alone—that's something else entirely. If you can't enjoy your own company, why expect anyone else to? Isolation doesn't scare me. But the impingement of loneliness, which always leads to some form of despair, remains a scary thing.

This story probably isn't what you wanted to hear when you came in. You were in the market for a fine little fright; I know that—some little backsnap in the tail to make you smack your forehead and go *oh wow—never saw that coming.* A digestible kind of unease. A black midnight snack. But if I'm to be completely honest with you, I won't do that stunt; it's too much like being a party robot that flawlessly replicates the same trick every time you push the button or slap a coin into the slot. No.

Nor will I spiel off bullshit (or endure yours) until you "allow" me to fuck you. Before tonight, things might have gone differently, more like the long yawn you call seduction. Now, when I think of seduction, I think of what happened to me on the most basic level, and it still frightens me, because it forced me to stand alone. It infected me with a dread that never goes away. Being startled is not being scared. Being genuinely *afraid* is quite different. No wonder sane people choose the former, when it comes to safe risk.

When I think of what *you* call seduction, all I can see are parasites, eating each other to death.

Since you won't let me escape without talking, I'll instead tell you the story of Niall Otheringame, who succeeded in scaring me with the things he said. When I met him, I was flat on my back in a puddle of beer, watching an enormous boot swoop down to smash my face. I saw Clarity that night, too. No, don't roll your eyes—Clarity is a name; Niall's female half. But that's jumping ahead of the story.

About 40 mostly sleepless hours following my latest and final "discussion" (so-called) about "our relationship" (double wince) with the notably blonde and usually perceptive Giselle—you probably know *that* whole bitter drill, am I right?—I forced myself back into a nearly forgotten pattern and decided to visit a lounge called the Back 40, having just turned 40 myself. Numerical symmetry insisted. I pretended to ignore the sharky, trolling atmosphere of the place and lied to myself that I was just going for a drink or two, pretending my eyes were not laser-targeted for fresh females, pretending there was not a whole universe of new people to engage and bodies to newly unwrap.

I pretended I was a normal human, when in fact I was an alien from some planet of misanthropes, observing Earth mating culture and finding it lacking, sad, futile. I smiled at strangers, thinking of that oldie about the smell of desperation. I smiled once too often, and wound up on the floor facing the bootheel of a bald behemoth in a leather vest. I had smiled at the wrong blonde and now Ook the caveman was going to mulch my skull.

I should have taken that as a warning. A sign that I should not be in this place at this time. When such thoughts occur, it is usually too late for thinking beings to benefit from them, like the French notion of staircase wit—you know, *L'esprit de l'escalier*—thinking of the right rejoinder too late? A lot of people don't know that expression was coined by a guy named Denis Diderot, a free thinker and encyclopedist who advanced a very early version of the theory of natural selection in the mid-1700s. Never mind. The strong prevail. I was about to get my head crushed as proof.

Ook withdrew. I missed it. I was too busy shutting my eyes and reconsidering prayer. Bracing for impact and calculating hospital costs. Completely pathetic, am I right?

When I opened my eyes, I saw Ook talking to a man in a white topcoat. Ook was easily a foot and a half taller, but he wore a penitential expression akin to that of a chastised child. The gentleman in the topcoat smiled and spoke in a low, even voice. I could not hear what he said, but whatever it was, it humanized my assailant, who seemed mildly confused. I thought the man had Ook in some sort of nerve grab, squeezing his armpit hard enough to immobilize him, but no, that wasn't it.

The big man nodded in understanding and helped me up off the deck. "Sorry, dude," was all he said, and he melted back into the bustle of the Friday night bar biz. When I saw him half an hour later, he was sitting by himself and weeping.

Great, now I was obligated to a benefactor. Swell. I know that makes me an ingrate, but it was what I really, truly thought at the moment. But people rarely say what they're thinking, and that was kind of the lesson of the entire evening.

The man in the topcoat wore a tailored three piece suit. He had modest pattern baldness and a smile full of dentures. Paternal, with interestingly wrinkled hands. Now he was smiling at me. He introduced himself as Niall Otheringame and idly added that the rescue for which I complimented him was nothing, really.

Great, I've managed to attract an old fag, I thought. Swell. He sees a semen mouthwash followed by an asshole-widening. Outstanding.

"You were thinking about silverware," he said. "Just before. That's the first intriguing thought I've encountered all week. I'd like to hear more."

I'm afraid I made a ridiculous face. "Silver—?"

"Flatware," he said. "Knives, forks, spoons. You were trying to explain it to that young lady at the bar when her escort interceded. I fear he thought it was some sort of pickup line, you see?"

Oh, right. I once invented this perverse notion that people were largely the same, divisible into the three major kinds of eating utensils. It was an adequate rap to displace anything like genuine conversation. I was unenthusiastically explaining it to the cleavage of the now-vanished blonde lady, already knowing it was the same as talking modern art to a throw rug. For the benefit of Mr. Otheringame, who had done me a kindness, I reeled off the story.

At length. I should have just shut up.

"You know that expression about how someone 'was born with a silver spoon in their mouth?'" I began, feeling guilty for having refined my story to a speech. "Well, I'll tell you something: Everyone is born with a spoon in their mouth, and sometimes it's silver, and sometimes it's wood. Sometimes it's golden or platinum; imagine a black diamond spoon. But it doesn't mean the individual is spoonish per se. Some of them are born with spatulas in their mouths, or shovels. Or, considering their sloth and girth, ladles. Soft, plastic ladles, molded in uerythane so as not to harm, or impede the delivery of double shares. You know which people are spoonish, and which are soup-spoonish. Think about it."

"'Spoonid,'" said Niall Otheringame, with an indulgent smile.

"You are what you eat with. You know knive-ish people are aggro, direct, and all the adjectives—sharp, edgy, keen, pointed—all say the same thing. Handle with care. Forkish people try to have it both ways. They can say one thing and mean, or do, another. They have lots of utility. Politicians and actors enjoy forkishness. Sometimes they are knives or spoons masquerading as forks, or those multi-purpose tools that deploy from a Swiss Army knife.

"It is very important for knifely people to make love as though they are attacking one another. They strop themselves to sharpness on others. Fork-people service themselves while appearing to service others. And you already know about spooning.

"Look at a fork. Now look at a human hand. Add an opposable thumb—intelligence—and there you are. It is important to remember that you can take out a human eye with a knife, a fork, or a spoon. Or a chopstick, for that matter. The only operative differences are in degree of efficiency, level of sadism or pain, and available time. Spoons can kill, and frequently do. Do not underestimate the spoon. Spoons can clean up what knives or forks leave in their haste. Think of Dr. Frankenstein as a fork, his Monster as a knife, and Igor as a spoon, and you can figure out most human relationships.

"Life is a meal. Knives, forks and spoons are useless without the concept of consumption, and humans consume each other in order to amass what is called "a life." They chew each other up, spit out the bits they dislike, pick and choose, refine their appetites. They snack, gorge and starve. Bulemics and gourmands all use the same basic tools; it's all a matter of desires, objectives, and tastes.

"Roll the idea around on your palette. Knivish people, forkish people, spoonish people. Spoons secretly want to be knives. Forks pretend to be spoons. Everyone wants to be something else, and a lot of furious biological activity is devoted toward presenting a personality that may have

admirable aspects of all three, with no downside. In truth, there is no such person. But that doesn't stop them from trying to be silverware."

I took a long drink to signal my break. Niall Otheringame had paid polite attention. Around us, the patrons of Back 40 continued to swarm, but now it was as if we were inside our own hermetic bubble.

"Now that's amusing," he said. "You see? Much better than sitting in a bar, boring each other to death with chitchat. Better to say what is on your mind than erode your audience with business, politics, or religion."

"What people mean when they chat you up and say, 'what's your story?' and you tell them what you do to earn money."

"Exactly. I give not a tinker's damn what people do for money. There is no rational point to discussing politics—none. About religion I care even less. All that—" Niall Otheringame groped the air for an appropriate word "—*noise pollution* about some invisible sky-god."

"Bertrand Russell," I said.

He shrugged. "You see? I sensed you were a person I could talk to usefully. You would not waste time in yammer about family, friends, who you know. It all boils down to embarrassment, or worse, name-dropping. As if I could be impressed by that. So I ask you, here and now: Does that smooth story about silverware actually get you laid? Tell me what's *really* on your mind."

He'd had my character nailed from the start. He just let me prove it by flapping my lips. Maybe it was the liquor, but I told him what was on my mind. It was that perverse, flash impulse, the kind you always blame on drink. That's what alcohol is for.

"That woman by the jukebox, the one with the copper-colored hair? That's what's really on my mind."

She was also on the mind or within the cognizance of seventy per cent of the males in this zoo, and three other women I could see from my seat. I almost said, "I want to make love to her," but that was a lie, too. I wanted her bent over my sofa, spread wide, panting, begging. Indelicate, but closer to true.

"Tosh," said Niall Otheringame, with a snort. "Look where we are. Look at the behavior of these animals. Rampant ego, seeking to amortize self-abasement by rocking and rolling in each other's flesh. All propped up by cliches and fantasies, with booze to fuel dishonest passion. Besides, she's not for you."

"You're going to tell me she's really a guy, right?"

"No, she's real enough. You have but to meet her to fall for her. Can you imagine being that desirable? I can't. But watch how every time the door opens, her antennae go up, scoping the talent of the room. She won't go home with any of these failures, because she's not cruising. She's coming here for her self-image. If any of these guys got a photograph with her, they'd make up stories. They'd lie about how she was some past girlfriend. They'd invent a fake name for her. Whole delusional histories, fabricated by people who have no imagination to begin with. People ask if she's an actress, a model, a dancer. She has one of those long body-pillow things she hugs with her legs when she goes to sleep, alone. She actually feels comfortable that she has set standards for herself no human being could hope to meet. She cries a lot between binges and purges. She's fiery and attractive and ready to snap. She will not end well."

"How do you know all that?"

He made a dismissive gesture. "I just know. That's my curse."

This was already fun. "What about the guy in the mock turtleneck?" I said.

Niall Otheringame looked the target over. "Factless, hopeless, and useless. He's circling that woman at the bar like a fly trying to figure out a landing vector on a really choice turd. Look at her, ignoring him. They deserve each other so much they're practically grandparents already. Look closer at her: If you were to lean in and whisper the words *biological clock* in her ear, her blood pressure would blow the hair out of her scalp. Now look closer at him: Middle management, awaiting a full partnership. Pretty soon he won't have any time left to shop for an arm doily or life mate; every night he comes in here is like a pop quiz where one wrong answer means failure. The two of them will talk about not using lines while disdaining this bar for being a meat rack. They'll rattle on this way until they're sufficiently lubricated to attempt stupendously boring sex. She'll keep her eyes closed and teeth grit for most of it. He'll be lost once he's inside her. It'll be over relatively quick, like a car wreck, and then they'll lie to each other about how good it was, how long since they've felt that way…etcetera, etcetera…while all the time eyeing the nearest exit door. Each of them will lie to themselves about what just happened to them."

"You're making this up," I said.

"Am I?" He gave me an odd little tilt of the head. "By the way, I admire the way you flung in that tidbit about Red being a man, disguising it as both a joke and a question."

I think I blushed, just a teeny bit.

"Very sneaky," he said, signaling for a refill. "You were trying to goad me into reaffirming that I am not a homosexual myself, in order to bolster your acceptance of me. You see? People never *say what they're thinking.*"

I decided to ambush him with it. "You're not…are you?"

"More pan-sexual, if you'd like a mere word," he said, with the air of a prepared answer. "But let's consider some of our other candidates."

I did a quick scan-and sweep. "Boots," I said. "Long brown hair. Standing next to the booth by the restrooms."

Niall Otheringame scrutinized her for exactly five seconds. "She knows most men in the room want her and most women in the room hate her. It's that good length of leg, heft of bosom, the aqua eyes that doom all comers, and she is aware of her armament. She puts on makeup the way killers load shotguns. She tries to present a tough exoskeleton, but inside she's a terrified aesthete, so she marginalizes all contact, and tries to play the rowdy freebird by fucking bikers and car mechanics—anyone pitifully easy to control. It's child's play, literally. She's got great excuses for avoiding any real commitment, and can talk anything into a fight, hence, it's simple to shuck the tough guys and maintenance fucks she accumulates, because when it comes to real conflict, they're hopelessly outclassed. She runs through enough of them to amass a backlog of anecdotal drama galore, plenty to float her to the next diversion. People are fast food to her; interchangeable protein units that burn at variant rates, in assorted seductive colors, and she couldn't work up genuine despair even if she had a manual and a how-to video. That's the tragedy of her existence. She trolls one night per week. The rest, she sits at home considering methods of suicide suited to what she believes is her personality."

"So what you're saying is…'not for me?' too?"

He smiled, nodded. "Most of these creatures don't have the grace or honor to just kill themselves, which is what they should really do. Save our gene pool. As for imagination, well, decanting wine from crushed marbles would be easier. You're dealing with delusional beings who've talked themselves into mock-life. Listen to them right now—you'll intercept all sorts of prattle about lifestyles, spiritual delusions, and half-baked horseshit homilies usually shoplifted from

the pages of someone else's book. All kinds of reasons why they should live or dodgy justifications as to why the world at large owes them any damned thing; a menu of felicitous philosophies at lunch-special prices; discount dreams; bargain-rack, second-hand aspirations. Most were more honest when they were children: I want to be a firefighter; I want to go dinosaur hunting. Now that's all polluted, and we're looking at children, spouting childish nonsense from adult mouths, in adult bodies governed by childish intellects. Listen to them rationalize themselves long enough, and you'll start to hear a melody in the buzz of a mosquito."

Niall Otheringame held up a finger to emphasize his point. "I'm not trying to brag, or shock you, or redefine your boundaries, or anything like that. I'm just telling you what I know, and from your expression, you want me to keep talking. Guess that means *you're* not gay, right?"

I blushed, or blanched, or both, and it seemed to please him.

"Joke," he said.

"The guy with the corporate buzz cut," I pointed out.

"Violent," said Niall Otheringame. "The thinnest veneer of humanity. A yeller, a hitter. Beneath his lacquer of health and fitness he conceals a sadistic need to infect women with various diseases, as punishment for their being female. Chlamydia, yeast infections, urinary tract inflammation. He has this sensitive face he whips out for Phase One, but his real orgasm comes from seeing that glint of fear in the eyes of his victims when he whips out Phase Two."

"Jesus," I said. "This is getting a lot more complicated than *all women are crazy; all men are stupid.*"

"You want crazy? Check the guy-magnet in the corset and fishnets." Niall Otheringame tipped his recently-refilled glass to single out a dark siren with crystal-green eyes, definitely dressed to threaten as a primary culling filter. She had the rapt ear of no fewer than three male candidates and could assuredly pick and choose at any time.

"What am I not seeing?" I asked him.

"That the façade is all there is," said Niall Otheringame. "As far as relationships go, she behaves according to a very strict playbook that no one else has heard of, let alone read. The word *relationship* to her means *menu of assumptions*, which means *rules*, which she holds as immutable *law*. Any of these rules can be invisibly violated at any moment, to the eternal regret of the transgressor. Basically, her life is a howling void of nothingness. She wants someone to *complete* her, as the movie phrase goes. To fill the gap in her life. Unfortunately, in her case the gap is ninety-five percent of the life. You could pour your entire identity into hers and reap no reward save the privilege of being drowned second, after her, as she pulls you under with her. So…who's stupid, or crazy?"

"You mentioned relationships," I said. "I don't think that's what most of the people here are after. I mean, look at them."

Niall Otheringame smiled as though to spare me from the chagrin of having my thin attempt at foxing him exposed again. "No? You're still just seeing the surfaces, not the clockwork. Believe me when I say nearly everyone in here radiates the need, the craving for an architecture they mistakenly *call* a relationship. They muck through these clumsy couplings with an eye out for something better. They delude themselves they can meet their soul mate in a bar. Then, if luck prevails—they always depend on luck—the candidate must pass a previously inapplicable set of standards; what if you meet your soul mate but they don't fit the templates of position or power? What if one wants to breed and the other doesn't? If they're not the right race or the correct age, there are a hundred variables further down the ladder that all

handily disqualify the potential soul mate if one can't find a realistic excuse for saying no. So they all know they're going to flush and try again, but they delude themselves, and presume a mental faculty beyond their reach. They're born to wallow about, but won't admit it. I'll give them this: They're willing to keep on trying. Isn't that why you came in here in the first place?"

"Wow," I said. "Busted, I guess."

"Look at that bubbly, effervescent one, the woman just coming through the door," he said. "Attractive, yes?"

My tongue got thick in my mouth. "Yes indeed."

"You want to run as fast as you can in the opposite direction," Niall Otheringame said. "She got so preoccupied with the idea that men only wanted her for her sex that she actually stabbed herself in the vagina with a coring knife, the custom kind that costs nearly a hundred bucks at Sonoma Williams and is made from Japanese stainless steel? Out, damned G-spot! She wound up in the hospital and had to indulge a bit of plastic surgery. Now she has a shopping list of "special needs" she inflicts on anyone unlucky enough to get her clothes off. It's designed to drive lovers away, their horror proving their unworthiness and justifying her own self-mutilation. Her identity had localized to between her legs, and when she cut that up, she found that there was not a lot else to recommend her to the world at large, so it became self-prophecy fulfilled, in a sense."

"Now you're *definitely* making this up," I said.

"If you say so."

That was an alarm phrase; it meant *oops, I've succeeded in scaring you off.* The kind of thing you say as a verbal prybar to begin the process of working free and scooting out the door.

Niall Otheringame merely smiled again, as if he had just reached some sort of satisfactory decision or conclusion. He excused himself and headed for the restroom. I thought perhaps I should stop trying to read everything he did for deeper motive. He had me thoroughly swoggled.

Always remember that past a certain point, a smile is just teeth.

Not long after that, a woman came barside to introduce herself as Clarity. She had very long dark hair and violet eyes. She looked to be in her mid-thirties. Young enough to know; old enough to know better. Her hands had long pianist fingers and everything about her seemed precise. But she was the sort of beauty that defied pinpointing. You could focus on details but they were insufficient to paint the whole picture—that kind of latent mystery. The first thing she said to me was. "So, what do you make of Niall? According to him, each person in here has enough neuroses for six."

"I just knew somebody like that couldn't have come here stag," I said, a little too flippantly.

"He likes you," Clarity said. "He usually doesn't talk that long to anybody."

"He was frighteningly perceptive."

"He wants me to kiss you. How do you feel about that?"

Clarity had an inviting mouth. Above that, a saucy frankness to her gaze, as though we already shared a secret. The timing was impeccable. I was just about to blurt something about needing to make contact, to participate instead of just languidly observing.

"Is he watching us?" I said.

"What do you think?" Her mouth was already on approach, homing in.

And I thought, to hell with it, let's give ole Niall a show.

Her kiss was a powerful flood of resurgent memory, the kiss you fantasize when you're a teenager, loaded with portent and hot with hormonal flood. The kiss you crave before

the grown-up world scotches your dreams. The kiss you see as your hope for redemption once the world stomps on you. The kiss that ruins you for all other kissers.

Plus, something extra: an amorphous weight, a kind of sliding heaviness that caused my heart to take on gravity. It came from her and settled into me; that's the best way to describe it.

Clarity smiled again. Teeth. "That was very pleasant," she said, indicating no desire to continue. She collected herself as though her task was done. "By the way, that was really a corker, your story about the silverware."

Bang, adrenaline; a rush that screwed up my breathing.

As she made ready to excuse herself, her expression said, *you should see your face.*

Either: Women are crazy, and Clarity had done something crazy to me. Or men are stupid, and I was so stupid I did not twig.

They're the same, I thought. Niall Otheringame and Clarity are the same person. Niall ducks out and Clarity appears. I would kiss a woman who looked that good, but not a man. Somehow, Niall had slipped undercover, changed skins, and renewed his assault on me as a lady. It was the trick ending, the disposable scare, easily predictable. You probably guessed they were the masculine/feminine flipsides of the same coin. But I also think that Niall Otheringame read my psyche from the moment we were introduced, and somehow conformed Clarity to reflect my inmost desires. So I would kiss her back. The supernatural snap in the tail, story over, my, wasn't *that* fun?

The part Niall omitted was what he saw when he looked at me. What I saw when I looked at myself in the mirror, just a few moments ago.

Don't ask me about the crippled and terrified monsters in here. From where we stand I can see a man who murdered a woman and got away with it. Tonight he's using a little pick-me-up called D10, short for D4B toxin 10, discovered at Stanford, a quantum leap over roofers. It has bee venom among its constituents. It mildly intoxicates while amping the female reproductive urge. The morning after, she'll apologize instead of filing a lawsuit. If she survives.

That trio of women I noticed earlier? They're top-skim hookers who work the Plaza, having a day-off night-out. They'd rather be fucking each other, and they came here to mock the amateurs and destroy egos the way you'd toss back a cocktail.

I say all this, yet I know a little less than nothing about prostitute psychology, or metabolic chemistry. I know it the way I now know that stud over there has calf implants and a face full of botox. *That* one, the one being seduced by the woman who scratches herself to let the pheromones out. You can virtually smell her lubricating from here.

You think this is all risque patter; man-ramble as preamble. Then you'll say you don't see the relevance; you thought I was going to tell you a horror story.

You haven't been listening.

Loneliness?

What I was really thinking, before you stopped me at the door, was *don't even speak to me.* Don't risk it. I met some life-form to whom our inner selves are a naked, open book, and somehow the son of a bitch infected me with the same perception, and what I see makes me want to kill myself to stop the pain. But I can't even escape, not now. Especially not by just running out a door. Because I already know what you're going to say. Because I look at you and all I can think of is cutlery—knives, forks, spoons. Nevertheless, I linger.

Because you smile at me and you say, "How *interesting.*"

Afterword:

OPEN MOUTH, INSERT GUN

Really. Just kill yourself. I'm serious, says the voice. Robert Bloch once wrote about a time when self-termination didn't seem like such a raw idea.

Then he snubbed his smoke, abandoned his porch (and his middle-of-the-night misgivings about being a writer for 24 years "with nothing to show for it"), and, within a few weeks, began to write PSYCHO.

(I'm hoping you already know (1) who Robert Bloch was, (2) why his words remain important, and (3) why PSYCHO was a watershed. To paraphrase hardboiled writer *par excellence* James Crumley, if you don't know, there's no way I can explain it to you; if you do know, no explanation is necessary.)

Maybe I can twist this into a segue toward the real topic here—the writing of short stories, and what happens years after you've begun such endeavor.

Short fiction is like a mine in which many workers pick-and-shovel their way; some diligent, some slackers, some simply doing a job of journeyman work. The ore with which one fills the carts, so to speak, is sometimes just ore—it does the job. Other times, the ore goes out slightly refined beyond baseline standards—cleaner, more artful, or just inspired,

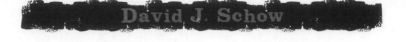

which is to say that it exceeds the job of filling a slot in a magazine or anthology, and is occasionally something that can induce actual pride in craftsmanship, despite the reality that most readers will perceive it solely as a package of words handily delivered per specs, i.e., just another load of ore.

After awhile in the short story mines, feeling the first prickles of literary blacklung in one's chest, the writer who is repeatedly solicited for this anthology or that magazine may begin to experience the odd sensation that he or she is merely being asked to repeat an old trick or venerable joke *one more time*, as if for a tireless child who is completely satisfied watching a worn-out cartoon over and over and over again.

We like THAT *story; do another one* JUST LIKE THAT.

"Elegant Pustules" is my FAVORITE *story of yours; why don't you write stories like* THAT *anymore?"*

Repetition is formulaic, and formula is the death of growth. Sometimes, writing-to-order is fun, and can yield *unanticipated* growth. Other times, revisiting certain themes can chart a different *kind* of growth. But most often, new short stories are requested by editors who expect a known quantity—brand name, pedigree, style, it all cooks down to one's reputation as a writer. Very rarely is a writer given free rein, since most short story outlets are defined by themology. There are exceptions, naturally—Steve Jones' DARK TERRORS books spring to mind, where the editorial edict is to produce stories that are well-written, unusual, striking, period. Yet the books themselves must conform to the general idea of a group of *horror* stories, because that's the quality signaled to the buyer by the title of the series.

Real writers will write what they have to write regardless of market, and sometimes a quality story that does not hew to a specific theme is *close enough* to that theme to merit inclusion in a themed anthology anyway. This is called "slipping by on the curve."

The short story is still the first, earliest, most basic, most challenging and best means of purveying fiction.

It can also be the most infuriating to write, in the midst of an avalanche of tripe by no-talents, the slow osmosis of the written word to internet venues and their attendant mutations, the decaying attention span of people who nonetheless declare themselves as "readers," and the nagging internal urge to write something *new.*

(And if you're one of those freestyle happy-go-lucky trend grazers with all the depth and passion of a new puppy, guess what? You're not extreme or intense or 100% pure adrenaline or cutting edge in your joyous celebration of the right-now. You, amigo or amiga, are a *hippie.*)

When one has had a fair amount of short fiction legitimately published, enough to stack up and judge, one descends to a whole new floor (thank you, Mr. Disch), where the deathtraps are different. Some, as Stephen Gallagher aptly put it, "get into the cloning business" and simply excrete the same story, over and over, with new names and settings. Others find that suddenly, they need all sorts of highfaluting *reasons* to write a new story, because frequently a story can be a long process of exploration and discovery, and therefore the trip needs to be justified. I think most readers can still tell the difference between a story that was grimly cranked out to meet a deadline or match a theme, and one that has an actual spark of life at its center. Format and formula are no match for fire.

And even a conflagrant talent has to face the next level of this particular hell: great short stories rarely get read, anymore, by anyone apart from a small coterie of true believers. All writers are emissaries of their faith, and they don't want to preach to the choir. Give me, instead, the sinners, the miscreants, the scum of the earth; the people who don't read

stories…but *had* to read *that* one, forced only by themselves. The ones who willingly read prose on pages instead of watching some TV show on their cellphone.

In larger terms, all writers want a bigger audience, if for no other reason (apart from the usual pecuniary ones) than to prove their point to naysayers, demonstrate literary values where doubters saw only pulp, or illuminate by any means necessary that which was formerly unseen. To stay alive. To prove to the world you're still kicking. To avoid fitting that gun barrel between your teeth.

To bring it all home, I discovered that the easier rationales for writing short fiction began to feel played out, leaving a distasteful *been there, done that* feeling experienced by nearly everyone who writes, then publishes, then re-publishes a body of short work—in my case, about a hundred stories in all. I grew to need a stronger motivator than just filling a slot with the proper weight of ore.

This led to variant degrees of experimentation within stories already on-deck—messing about with timeframes and POV, getting disruptive about structure, or just toying with some new notion that could re-energize the whole process. It wasn't exactly a slump, yet it felt like corporate downsizing, the kind that loses people their jobs. Inevitably the results ran the risk of (1) confusing readers, and (2) not looking like the expected "stories," uh-uh, no way. In other words, *not* market-smart.

Sometimes the exercise of writing is enough to keep one's skills in trim, and while that may be good cardio, it's nothing like genuine inspiration. Nascent or neophyte writers are in less danger of considering exactly what it is they're writing, because the dominant drive for beginners concerns seeing print and getting noticed. Once the work begins to pile up, though, most writers of conscience will take stock, step back, see what they have built, and judge whether it is worthy, or at least respectable. This isn't as stuffy or disillusioning as it probably sounds. You can't look behind you until you have a past, and general public memory currently seems to hit a stone wall around 1998. Just wait until 2020 or so, when the first generations of the 21st Century hit drinking age, and see for yourself how much of the previous century any of your friends bothers to remember.

Ancient history, they'll say.

Unfortunately, that crumbling papyrus contains most of my body of work—a paper mummy from a quaint, pre-digital age. Hence, another little Enoch on the back of my head, gnawing away on my brain and nagging me to do something fresh, already.

With a single exception, all the stories in HAVOC SWIMS JADED were transferred from electronic files, in various word-processing programs. That sentence would mean nothing to the pulpist who hacked his or her way through 10,000-word stories in a weekend for less than a penny per word in the 1950s, just as talk of second sheets and carbon copies will mystify most newer writers who have never worked on anything *but* a screen.

One would think short stories to be the perfect fiction medium for our attention-deficit culture...yet we're still hearing arguments from half a century ago, the paralogic of why anthologies and collections don't count as "real books." Nary a blip on the radar of contemporary fiction. Invisible, unnoticed, inconsequential. In the current literary climate, real books have girth and heft. Are novels.

I hadn't written a novel in 13 years. No kidding.

After my second novel, THE SHAFT (1990), there were a couple of hiccups and false starts, and one lumbering behemoth that staggered on for 350 pages before it fell over and died the

death it basically deserved, and after that, a void in real-book land. I guess THE OUTER LIMITS COMPANION is a conditional exception, being what publishing contracts call a "book-length work" and all, but it was (1) a rewrite, and (2) nonfiction.

Then came Pearl Harbor Day, 2000.

Surfing off one of the shittiest, most downright depressing years of my short life, I sat down to commit a story as soon as I woke up from the dream image that was its basic catalyst. And by January 7th, one month later, I had 50,000 words (about 3/4 the size of the book you're holding), and I thought: *Novel monster come back to beat Dave on widdle head; uh-oh.*

Several halting steps brought me to this stone on the path. The first couple were short stories that took a year each to write, followed by another that had percolated, in several forms, through several years. Long short stories. Then came Doug Winter and his anthology/novel MILLENNIUM (a.k.a. REVELATIONS), which explains the existence of "Dismantling Fortress Architecture," written in collaboration with Craig Spector.

And rewritten. And re-re-written. And re-re-re...until what emerged read very much like a severely compressed novel. Longform had been beckoning for quite awhile, but it seemed all at once, the spotlight had popped on and it was showtime.

MILLENNIUM was published in 1997, and I finished my new novel in 2001, which demonstrates my reflex time as

---

* And if you haven't read Fowler's FATHER GOOSE or MINUTES OF THE LAST MEETING, please go educate yourself. If you haven't *at least* seen I WAS A TEENAGE WEREWOLF and I MARRIED A MONSTER FROM OUTER SPACE— which were directed by his son, Gene Fowler, Jr.—now you have even *more* homework.

** Check out *www.wmspear.com.*

worse than that of an iguana on a cold rock. In the interim before completion, fearing the dreaded "mid-novel stall," I put it down on purpose, abandoning it to ferment, and began a whole different, other book. One hundred pages in, I socked *that* one away to ripen and resumed the novel, and sailed to the end. Then, in the middle of the second book, I began a third...and I think I've discovered a cheesy dodge around the usual writer's block about which everyone with an unfinished novel wails. I call it the Leapfrog Gambit.

Which explains why the second half of the contents of HAVOC SWIMS JADED took so long to get locked in. I'd lined up the first six stories out of habit, by sheer momentum, done deals. When it came to the remainder of the stories (I usually put thirteen into each collection), they were yet to be written, and I was tormenting myself with all the misgivings about short fiction listed earlier.

Plus, there were now *novels* to get out of the way. I finished the next new one on New Year's Day, January 2004...

...and not only was it was summarily rejected by the publishers of my rebirth novel, but my agents refused even to market it, on the basis that it was "too quirky and uncategorizable" (while adding the cold comfort that they absolutely *loved* the writing, though). That same week, a friend with a new studio deal had just delivered an eagerly-anticipated script into which he had poured heart and soul, only to have it slammed by the highest of higher-ups, who told him, quote, "we cannot put money into something this smart and metaphorical...it will not bring 14-year-old boys into theatres."

In an alternate universe, work that is quirky, uncategorizable, smart and metaphorical might be the basis for a pretty interesting career. In this universe, however, sales beat merit the way rock breaks scissors (with the fascinating codicil that

no matter how good your sales figures are, they're always held *against* you).

And it's back to the dead of night; gun-in-mouth time.

The *only* option is to write, write, and write some more—as effortless a task as Gene Fowler made it out to be when he said: "Writing is easy. All you do is stare at a blank sheet of paper until drops of blood form on your forehead." Don't want to write? There's always the alternative of the loaded firearm, the high ledge, or the vial of deadly pills. Write or die. That's how it should feel. *

And what if—gasp—you just up and die without your own prompting? Oh, shit, the dude with the scythe is knocking, and your novel won't be finished until the end of the year; have you at least left enough work behind for a decent post-mortem boxed set? When Anthony Burgess was diagnosed with a brain tumor and advised of his imminent demise in 1959, he embarked upon a fast-forward flurry of work designed to provide at least marginal support for those he was doomed to leave behind. By the end of 1962 he had published seven new novels (as well as two more under a pseudonym); one of those was A CLOCKWORK ORANGE. Then he fooled everyone by living for three more decades. The book that is probably his masterwork in prose, EARTHLY POWERS, was not produced until 1980.

Gigantic argument-by-example for not giving up, there.

(William Spear, maker of "the world's most wonderful enamels," whomped up a cloisonné pin featuring a typewriter keyboard and a skull with crossed quills, adapting a slogan from the modern-day credo of the iron horseman:

*** Of The Fiends, the LA band that did the classic "Die Bob Die" and two albums, GYNECOLOGY and WE'VE COME FOR YOUR BEER (with the stylin' CREATURE WITH THE ATOM BRAIN jacket). Bass player Sean Gwin also died 13 October 2005.

WRITE HARD, DIE FREE. That adequately encompasses the sentiment, too, while being a bit more forgiving.) **

As my illegitimate brother Lew Shiner said: "Eventually it became clear, even to me (that) I had to write not to become famous, not to become rich, and not to make up for a loveless childhood. I had to write for its own sake, for whatever satisfaction I could get from the act itself." In Lew's novel SAY GOODBYE, his protagonist Skip Shaw is equally blunt: "I used to be a tough guy about shit like this," says Skip, a musician. "You know, the whole *I'm just a yarn spinner* kind of crap, like writing songs isn't fundamentally different from making furniture. Except it is. It's more like what (painters) do, which makes you cut off your ear or jump off a bridge."

There's a feeling even worse than that repeat-the-trick thing I mentioned earlier: the sense that your good trick might be your *only* trick; to paraphrase Ramsey Campbell, many ordinary citizens too eagerly make the jump from *oh, so that's what you write* to *oh, so that's ALL you write*. Having done your trick, you are now just plain *done*. That sentiment is nothing new, but it's still a shock when you catch yourself sitting around in the middle of the night, actually thinking it. Because the glum reality is that if you attempt versatility and become chameleonic, what you wind up with in the eyes of a fickle audience is no discernable "identity," a.k.a. "marketing hook."

Another thing wistful retrospection causes is list-making. As in lists of stories, over the years. All tolled—amidst other diverse writing work intended to keep the corpus running and the lights on—I averaged between two and four short stories per year. That is, stories rendered decently enough that shoving them out into the world did not constitute an embarrassment. Two to four per year. If just *one* of those exhibited growth or a forward step for any particular year, I count that a win. One was enough. (Looking back, I find that

one of my most prolific, yet "worst" years was 1980—I cranked out *seven* stories in the 5000-7000 word range and never sold a single one of that cursed run. Because they all, um, kinda sucked.) I won the World Fantasy Award for my 17th published story. The magazines, anthologies and collections in which most of the stories appeared take up about 60 linear feet of shelf space in my home. The body of published short work, including novellas (but excluding the almost-novel-length ROCK BREAKS SCISSORS CUT, technically a "short novel") rounds off to about 460,000 words. Not quite half a million, charting nearly 25 years of work. Needless to say, I was paid more for my first screenplay (in 1989) than for all those stories combined, counting multiple reprints...so nobody, I mean no-body, can tell me writers do short stories for a living.

Salted between the stories were novels, film treatments and scripts, teleplays, stage plays (twice), work-for-hire tie-in books (about 17 of those), absolutely no poetry or songs, and a double-decker busload of nonfiction writing (interviews, articles, editorial gigs, essays and ephemera like book intros or liner notes). Not included in the tally are many books, scripts, and manuscripts that never went anywhere—my first "real" novel, a 100,000-word film book, assorted screenplays, and other abortions best left buried.

By now the stack of typed or printed pages is much taller than me. I hope some of it still casts a shadow when I'm no longer around. So there it is: writers write as a hedge against death. The very act itself is anti-entropy, anti-stasis, anti-death. Then again, there are fewer epitaphs more piercing than one voiced by the late Scott Morrow (1958-2005): "He was a brilliant genius. *Next.*" ***

—ooo—

This book is dedicated to Larry Brown, who died suddenly and unexpectedly in late November, 2004. I never got to meet him in person, but I remain a great admirer of his work. His trilogy of novels JOE, FATHER AND SON, and FAY, are essential for anybody who simply enjoys good writing. Odds are you've never heard of him or read him, which would be a damned shame.

I picked up Larry Brown's first book of short stories, FACING THE MUSIC, on a bookstore whim because it looked good. It was a strangely-sized Algonquin Press hardcover that virtually demanded to be taken off the shelf and examined. I did not know it at the time, but Brown was in the process of relinquishing his calling as a Texas firefighter to become a full-time writer, and damn if he didn't deliver. Along about this time (mid-1995), a fellow named Mike Baker approached me for a contribution to a book with the working title of THE ULTIMATE HORROR, and later, just HORRORS. The short list of picks—writers choosing stories by other writers—was depressingly predictable. Even sadder was the realization that out of twenty-odd stories chosen, only one or two was by a living writer, suggesting that the horror tale's glory days were far in the past, a closed book, as it were. I chose Larry Brown's "Old Frank and Jesus," from FACING THE MUSIC, because not only did it fulfill my criteria for a chilling story, but it was a work of contemporary fiction by a still-living writer. More pointedly, it was an opportunity to introduce a horror readership to something different and apart from the usual suspects and the same old flavors, and this was the sort of outside-the-box selection I knew Mike Baker would appreciate.

Mike died of lobar pneumonia on 7 January, 1997, and HORRORS fell into publishing limbo until it was resurrected by Martin H. Greenberg for DAW Books in 1999 under the

title MY FAVORITE HORROR STORY. Guess which story was omitted from the final table of contents, and guess why.

With a few flourishes, Mike's table of contents was replicated wholly from his original conception, except for "Old Frank and Jesus." Everybody hemmed and hawed and ultimately I was advised that nobody on the project had any idea of how to contact this Larry Brown guy, seeing as how he worked outside the usual pit stops of horror's pathetically small pond. Nobody knew how to contact this guy who, by 1999, had become pretty high-profile in the real world, had twice won the Southern Book Critics Circle Award, and was in the process of having his second collection, BIG BAD LOVE, made into a decent film. It did not occur to anyone to, say, pick up a phone or write a letter to Brown's editor at Simon & Schuster, and by the time I discovered no one had put forth any effort, it was too late to correct course even though I had anticipated such short-sightedness in 1995 and supplied contact information accordingly. The real ultimate horror is that it slipped through the cracks and wound up being no one's fault, even though anyone could stroll into the Barnes & Noble on New York's Upper West Side and find a whole *gang* of Larry Brown books, bam, right there on the shelf.

You still can.

Then, bam, Larry Brown dropped dead of a heart attack on the day before Thanksgiving, 2004, at age 53. I got an e-mail from Peter Farris (the youngest of John Farris' brood) bearing the news, and I thought, *that's my future.* That's what awaits all of us, no matter how invulnerable you think you may be right now. Be prepared. The unexpected can blindside you in horrible ways.

If I bite the hardpan tomorrow, at least this latest batch of stories has made it into this little safe house of ink and bound boards, and you might read it, having never seen or met me except through the work. That's one small hope that keeps many writers going, when things turn grim. Even if you detest *my* stuff, there's a possibility that one person *just might* see this and become curious enough to sample Larry Brown's work, and you know something? One is enough.

—ooo—

Pretty good, right? Steadfast, committed and fairly convincing. The writer is thinking: *Not only have I got them all fooled, but they'll probably quote some of the tripe I'm laying out on this buffet.*

Then, bam, just as I was writing that part above (December 2005), Rod Whitaker died at 74 of chronic pulmonary obstructive disease. My admiration for this chameleonic man is adequately contained in an essay titled "A.K.A. Trevanian," which you can read at length on my website (among other places), so I'll won't go into chapter and verse here, except to refer you to the recently-minted website *www.trevanian.com.*

Whitaker maintained so many literary personae that one is tempted to suspect a typical Trevanian trick in his stated demise and subsequent burial "in a private ceremony at an undisclosed location." Ironically, his agent noted that his enormous backlog of completed, unpublished work would be presented in due course, meaning that while Whitaker has gone down to meet the earth, Trevanian will be apparently alive and well for some time to come, without the benefit of a necrophiliac cadre of ghostwriters.

That might not be a bad way to go: slip out the back door, leave the work to speak, and everything else is nobody's business. Except then, I'd have no excuse at all for writing this Afterword.

I never got to meet Whitaker in person, either. Nor Tristan Egolf, another name I would not expect self-cloistered,

so-called "horror readers" to know. His scintillatingly weird third novel, KORNWOLF, was published posthumously. He committed suicide by "self-inflicted gunshot wound" at age 33, in May 2005.

So here we are, back to firearm time in the dead of night, where we started.

Glad to have you here with me, contemplating all this gorgeous, seductive killing hardware.

You *will* be that one reader, right?

—ooo—

"Front Matter" was written as a fake editorial in order to sneak it into the issue of HORROR GARAGE that otherwise featured themed stories. For it to really work, it would have to be placed at the head of a book (as here), or in place of the *real* editorial in a magazine...but you get the idea. The challenge was to tell a story by inference in the dress of non-fiction.

"The Absolute Last of the Ultra-Spooky, Super-Scary Hallowe'en Horror Nights" is another entry in my mini-series of Old Monsters, New Hijinks, proving I cannot stray from either for too long.

"Expanding Your Capabilities Using FRAME/SHIFT™ Mode" was rendered in two slightly variant versions for its respective US and UK publications; this is the longer version, but it has probably been subtly jacked around yet again by the writer, resulting in a *third* version probably indistinguishable from the first two.

I have always admired Jane Yolen's THE GIRL WHO LOVED THE WIND for the most obscure of reasons: It is a fable, and when you read it, it rings with the true tones of a classic, perhaps right out of the pages of the Brothers Grimm or Charles Perrault. Except that Jane's is a modern tale, written in 1970. Describe the basic story and nine out of ten people will say *yeah, I've heard that one,* as they flash back to some misremembered childhood. It *seems* as familiar as "Hansel & Gretel" or THE WIND IN THE WILLOWS, but it's not. To back-door the pool of common myth as deftly as Jane did requires considerable talent, and while I may not win the talent contest, I know that is definitely the feeling I was aiming for when I wrote "The Five Sisters: A Fable" in a single day (22 November 2001).

"Plot Twist" is one of those "experiments" I mentioned earlier.

I despise breast implants. I resent Botox. In my lexicon the word *collagen* is most often followed by the word *abuse.* Plastic muscles and artificial contours are for the emptiest of human vessels. I've never even dyed my hair, not even high-lights, not once, ever. Ruminations about one's writing career might smack of egomania, I think…then I spy an endless and ever-increasing parade of bad surgical augmentation, and wonder how anyone's vanity could ever get *that* colossal. It humbles me. There are a number of websites cataloguing egregious mistakes in "aesthetic enhancement" made by *big Hollywood celebrities you probably like,* and I urge you to seek them out, if only to expose yourself to the parlance of *bolt-ons, hard rounds, sag maps, capsular contracture, mandroids, trout pout, crepe-ing, micro-pigmentation, body dimorphism,* and *duck lips.* This unrest is probably part of the reason "Size Nothing" got written.

"The Thing Too Hideous to Describe" began life as two pages of notes entitled "Torches." Entombed in a file, it rose years later, gruesome…and then grew some more.

By contrast, "Wake-Up Call" is another one-day wonder, turning some turf that has also interested the likes of Franz Kafka, Orson Scott Card, Whitley Streiber and K.W. Jeter, among others. Imagine lamenting your obscure legacy, oh

woe, then dying, what a bummer…then hearing a little voice saying, "Congratulations—you've just completed Phase One of your actual work."

"Dismantling Fortress Architecture" was written in collaboration with Craig Spector for Doug Winter's "serial novel," MILLENNIUM, as previously mentioned. It was probably the last story I ever completed on my old IBM Automatic typewriter before the man who serviced it for ten years *died,* thereby shoving me off the cliff of word processing for good. I held out for another couple of years against e-mail, but most of the collaborative aspect was accomplished by 30-page faxes in the dead of night. How Craig Spector and I wound up in the same harness is simple—Doug only had ten slots available in MILLENNIUM, which was subdivided into one novelette for each decade of the 20th Century. I requested "the decade that nobody else wanted," which turned out to be the 1980s, and by then most of the other slots had been snatched up. It remains my sole fiction collaboration to date, so perhaps it retains some oddball curiosity value.

Not only is Scoop back in "Scoop Vs. Leadman," but he's back with classicist street cred: Writing in the ST. JAMES GUIDE TO HORROR, GHOST & GOTHIC WRITERS (St. James Press, 1998), Gary Westfahl singled out "Scoop Makes a Swirly" (from the collection BLACK LEATHER REQUIRED) as *"astonishing…(i)n summary, the story sounds like little more than an excuse for one gross-out after another; yet readers will find Scoop remarkably endearing in his stubborn determination to survive in the face of some of the worst indignities imaginable, and he oddly emerges as a truly heroic figure, a Ulysses for the 1990s."*

I would have thought Sisyphus, but you catch the drift.

"The Pyre and Others" reflects my continuing fascination with "lost works"—obscure books, missing paintings, forgotten films and such that become grail objects for the dedicated or obsessed—which become even more tempting when the writer invents them wholly (as Ramsey Campbell did the lost Karloff/Lugosi film *Tower of Fear* in his novel ANCIENT IMAGES, or Theodore Roszack's painstaking illumination of the entire career of director Max Kastle in FLICKER, to cite two marvelous examples among dozens). I also wanted to dabble in a story completely lacking formal dialogue, yet featuring people talking.

"What Happened With Margaret" is pretty self-explanatory, save that I should probably have added a big fat apology to Ambrose Bierce, at the end.

To prove that statistics can be slanted to favor any argument, I also just figured out that HAVOC SWIMS JADED marks my lucky 13th book, that is, a published book-shaped object with my actual name on the cover, not counting those aforementioned "book-length works" whose ripples were neither remunerative nor professional. This led to the perverse impulse to *count the damned books,* as well as see if I could remember them off the top of my head, in publication order. *Novels #1 and #5—never published; don't count. Do unfinished books count, and if so, where on a bibliography timeline should they be enumerated? Interim Collection #5—assembled, never happened, contents got redistributed. Two versions of THE OUTER LIMITS COMPANION only count as one (even though the revision consumed the time and labor of seven or eight books). If you stack four screenplays on top of each other, it looks like a manuscript, but is it a book?* (My answer is *no,* but I know a lot of people who've tried to get away with this one.)

Timewise, "Obsequy" and "What Scares You" are the two "newest" stories in this book, written during a period wherein "horror," especially in movies, has become increasingly braided up in a tangle with forensic torture shows whose

only real drawback is their complete lack of Scary Stuff; stories, books and movies that fail to scare, frighten, inspire dread, or unsettle.

Now, in another universe, to scare, frighten, or inspire dread might be the basis for a pretty interesting career, but I definitely have little interest in coaxing 14-year-olds into this theatre, although they're welcome, too. We'll let *anybody* in here.

Rest in peace? Never.

— DJS
February 2006

—OOO—OOO—OOO—

THE LIST OF DOZENS

For permissions, first buys, and editorial grace: Tom & Elizabeth Monteleone, Paula Guran, Lydia Marano & Arthur Byron Cover, the two Nancies—Kilpatrick & Holder, Christopher Golden, Darrell Schweitzer, Jeff Gelb & Del Howison & Jeff Gelb again & Michael Garrett, Darren McKeeman, Doug Winter, and most especially Stephen Jones, who can claim enablement of the largest portion of stories in this present volume.

If you look at my Afterwords of yesteryear, you'll find a lot of the following names recurrent. That's because their friendship is unflagging in all the best ways: Peter & Susan Straub, Douglas & Lynne Winter, Frank Darabont (who is, against all odds, one of the world's biggest Scoop fans), Mark & Rachel Ordesky, Gregory Nicotero & Howard Berger of KNB EFX Group, Lew Shiner, Douglas A. Venturelli, F. Paul & Mary Wilson, Bernie Wrightson, John, Mary Ann, & Peter Farris, Stefan Dziemianowicz, Richard Micheals, and of course Bill Schafer, Tim Holt & Gail Cross—my Subterranean stalwarts. Chad Savage and John Scoleri keep me alive on the internet, for which I really ought to mint some sort of medal. James O'Barr whomped together the only observance of THE CROW'S 10th anniversary that either of us ever experienced, so he gets special goodguy points.

The splendiferous (and now bicoastal) Kaz continues to infuse my household with his own special, manic energy, and for this I really should thank Linda Marotta, too.

Kerry Fitzmaurice demanded her own paragraph, so here it is, with love for my best Irish redhead, gambling queen, and Tab Jones devotee.

R.I.P. Team AIP: Me, Tom Weaver, Bob Burns, Frank Dietz, Vincent Di Fate, Woody Welch, and Kogar. We remain of stout heart, but the bean-counters didn't care.

The Creature Crew: Julie, Ricou, Ben, Lori, Gregg, Brett, and Rex; Sam Borowski, 42nd Street Pete, Mark Alfrey, Daniel Roebuck, Johnny Gilbert and all the other attendant fetishists, but most of all, Bob B., Tom W., and Frank D.

That selfsame Frank Dietz—The Deet—also provided the handsome *Havoc* illos, including a wholesale re-rendering of the jacket art in oils, and suggested the use of his own smartassed caricatures on the back flap. He does this sort of thing a lot, and you are urged to go check out his website at ***www.sketchythings.com***.

The cast and crew of **I, ROBOT**, including but not limited to Alex Proyas, Topher Dow, Wyck Godfrey, Will Smith ("if that really *is* his name"), Alan Tudyk, John "Oscar" Nelson, Marco Beltrami and the indomitable Kwesi Thompson.

The hardcore Ludovico Technique posse—Robert Meyer Burnett, Anthony Smedile & Dave Parker, and with much regret over Ludo's loss of

Ms. Julia Melnikov, who was mowed down by an idiot in an SUV at the end of September, 2004.

The cast and crew of CHRONICLES OF NARNIA: THE LION, THE WITCH & THE WARDROBE, including but not limited to Andrew Adamson, woof-man Howard Berger, and publicist Ernie Malik (whose very first such gig was on LEATHERFACE: TEXAS CHAINSAW MASSACRE III).

The unfailing kindness of Wellington's Fearsome Foursome: Richard Taylor, Tania Rodger, Peter Jackson & Fran Walsh—longtime friends, hosts, and co-conspirators—as well as the wily WETA Workshoppers who put up with me for six weeks in the New Zealand winter of 2004: Ben Wootten, Mary Connolly, Melanie Morris, Tracey Morgan, Tira Iraka O'Daly, Peter Lyon, Wayne Dawson, Kevin McTurk, Christian Pearce, Sourisak Chanpaseuth, David Meng, and everybody else in all departments, in particular ex-pats Bill Hunt and Gino Acevedo.

The cats at 3-Legged Cat: Mark Rance, Dana Kinonen, Francois Maurin and Andrew Sachs. One of these days we'll finesse that documentary; *you* know the one I mean.

Spotlight big moby thanks to Mick Garris, whom I've known longer than anyone else in Los Angeles, and with whom I finally got to work in-close on MASTERS OF HORROR (Mick's brainchild, entirely).

I'd also like to acknowledge certain insights brought about by the poetry of Jared Carter.

Special end-of-the-list thanks to the unsinkable Mehitobel J. Wilson, who proposed the title for this book, among other things that are none of your beezwax.

We persevere. Against creeps, betrayers, nitwits and obsessives who nonetheless provide us the joy of excising them from our lives. During certain snits the temptation to offer up their names or initials as indictment is massive, but they deserve their richly-won obscurity and the ones still breathing cannot kill themselves soon enough.

The rest of us, endure. See you next book!

— DJS